Skin Deep

Skin Deep

LIZ NUGENT

PENGUIN

IRELAND

PENGUIN IRELAND

UK | USA | Canada | Ireland | Australia
India | New Zealand | South Africa

Penguin Ireland is part of the Penguin Random House group of companies
whose addresses can be found at global.penguinrandomhouse.com.

First published 2018
001

Copyright © Liz Nugent, 2018

The moral right of the author has been asserted

Set in 13.5/16 pt Garamond MT Std
Typeset by Jouve (UK), Milton Keynes
Printed in Great Britain by Clays Ltd, St Ives plc

A CIP catalogue record for this book is available from the British Library

ISBN: 978–1–844–88393–6

For my dad, with very much love. Thank you for being the first person to take me to the library.

'Whatever beauty may be, it has for its basis order, and for its essence, unity. Beauty is only skin deep, but ugly goes clean to the bone.'

Dorothy Parker

I wondered when rigor mortis would set in, or if it already had.

Once I had cleared away the broken glass and washed the blood off the floor, I needed to get out. I inched my way past it, past *him*, and locked myself into the bathroom. I showered as quickly as I could. The cracked mirror above the sink reflected my bloodshot eyes and my puffy skin. I applied make-up with shaking hands and dried my hair. I emerged from the bathroom but could not avoid looking at the huge corpse slumped on the floor. I forced myself to be calm. I grabbed the first thing in the wardrobe that came to hand. My silk cashmere dress had worn thin with use, but it was the best thing I had. I needed to leave. I couldn't think straight with him lying there, a blood-soaked monster.

I negotiated my way down the narrow, cobbled streets to my favourite café on the promenade, stopping off to buy cigarettes. I bought a demitasse and drank it with trembling hands, watching the tourists absorbed by their phones and their maps, ignoring the beauty of the Mediterranean just across the road.

I had twenty-five euro in my bag, all I had left until my next maintenance payment. It wasn't enough to run away.

Something will happen, I told myself, *someone will be able to help*. I needed to be calm. To pretend. I was good at pretending. It was midday already, and the October sunlight was strong. Too bright for me. The world was too bright for me. I decided to walk the promenade. *I'm bound to meet somebody I know*, I

I

thought. *Someone will turn up and keep me company. I don't have to tell anybody. But a solution will reveal itself. It must.* For the first time in decades, my thoughts turned to God. I wished that I believed. I needed some divine intervention.

My eyes were drawn, as always, to the sea. Blue, gently lapping the pebbles on the shore. So unlike the sea I recalled from my childhood. As I walked, the image of the corpse seared my vision. I pulled some of my hair out to make it stop.

As I approached the Negresco, I added a swing to my hips, held my head up and walked with confidence until the pretence began to feel real. I recalled my father sitting me on his knee. 'You're my own special girl, Delia O'Flaherty,' he'd say, detangling my hair with the old tortoiseshell comb. Daddy was right. I am special. I entered the hotel.

In the bar, I positioned myself in a large armchair with a view of the corner entrance. I had not eaten a lot in the previous week. A tin of tuna and a baguette had lasted me three days, but I knew now that my money would have to be spent on escape. I was in the right place though. The Negresco was where my old moneyed friends liked to come occasionally for afternoon tea, though they liked to give out about the vulgarity of the tourists. Someone would surely be able to do an instant electronic transfer; it is so easy these days.

Sure enough, at about 4 p.m., my hands had steadied and while I was having my second coffee I spotted Harold and Rania Cross outside the entrance, dressed formally. I waved, but they did not appear to see me. Harold was carrying his cane and wearing his theatrical cape, so I knew they were headed for the opera. I waited for them to enter, but they stopped awkwardly and turned on their heels and walked away in a hurry as if they had forgotten something important.

I tried to remember when I had last seen them. It may have been at the British Consul's party four years earlier. I think I tried to persuade Rania to buy some of the handmade jewellery I'd brought with me, but she said ... no, maybe it wasn't Rania ... anyway, whoever it was said that my jewellery was tacky. It couldn't have been Rania, she wouldn't have said that. We were friends, for God's sake. I'd helped her through her depression back in the day. It wasn't Rania, was it? No matter. All water under the bridge now. Did she say the jewellery was tacky or that *I* was tacky, that woman who just couldn't have been Rania? So much has been lost in the fog recently.

The expensive coffee came with some nuts, olives and biscotti but they fell short of constituting a meal. Nobody else I knew had come through the door. There was a man reading the *New York Times* in an armchair on the other side of the bar. I had not been paying too much attention to him, but by 5.30 I was starving so I watched furtively as steak and frites were delivered to his table. The warm aroma made my stomach flip and contract. The waiter suggested he would be more comfortable in the restaurant, but he said he was waiting for someone. His dealer, as it turned out. When a scruffy young man arrived, steak man drained his beer, jumped out of his armchair and rushed outside with him. I did not know then that a quick transaction was taking place. He had taken his newspaper and I thought he was gone for good. The food was mostly untouched. I hovered for five full minutes watching it cool down before slipping into his chair and taking up the knife and fork he had just abandoned. I was about to take my first mouthful when –

'What the hell do you think you're doing?'

My face burned crimson. There was no way of explaining this. But I tried.

'Sorry,' I stammered, 'I'm an environmentalist. I hate to see food go to waste.'

It was the best I could come up with.

'That's the greatest piece of horseshit I ever heard in my life.' His voice was loud. American. Thank God there was nobody else within hearing distance.

He stood up and summoned the waiter with a wave of his hand. I feared I was about to be asked to leave, but instead:

'I need the same meal again, a cold Budweiser, and' – he glanced at me – 'what are you drinking, honey?'

The waiter looked at me with a hint of disgust on his face.

'I didn't know my wife was going to join me,' the American said.

The boy knew it was a lie. He had passed both of us several times. He must have known that we were not connected and that I had been trying to make my coffees last. Realizing his tip might be in jeopardy, he decided that the customer was always right. It gave me confidence. 'A glass of rosé,' I said, staring at him brazenly. We said nothing until he was out of earshot.

'Go ahead, eat up.'

I picked up the knife and fork and began to eat more delicately than my appetite demanded. He had clearly ordered a well-done steak. What a shame.

'So you want to tell me why I'm paying for your meal?'

'I am so sorry, you must think I'm awful, but honestly, this is not something I do . . . I just have –'

'A cash-flow problem?'

'No, it's because . . . I left my purse . . .'

He pointed at my clutch bag. 'Want to try again, honey?'

'I can't . . . I need . . . I am waiting for –'

'Hell, I don't give a damn. Want to go to a party?'

'May I finish my dinner first?'

4

He laughed the way that only a man with a large stomach can.

'You got balls, lady, I'll give you that.'

I cringed inwardly at the vulgarity, but smiled. 'It's Cordelia.'

'Sam.' He stuck out a giant hand and I put mine in his and shook it. He grinned.

'So, you're on holiday, or you live here? You're British, right?'

I wasn't going to correct him. 'I come here for the summer. London is too stifling. I hope to stay until the end of this month.'

'And how're you planning on getting by, if you don't mind me asking? I mean, you don't look like the kind of lady that should be going hungry. You got an accent like the goddamn Queen.'

'It's a temporary blip, that's all. I make jewellery at home during the winter and a friend sells it here during the summer. I'm waiting on a cheque. Really, it is just a short-term embarrassment.'

We chatted amiably as his meal arrived, as if there were no corpse in my flat and everything were normal. We did not ask each other any personal questions about partners or children. There was already an understanding that we were going to be private about our circumstances. He was well dressed and well groomed. He was not, however, remotely attractive. I would be able to ditch him later when the time was right. I needed his money first.

Two hours later, I was squeezed into a toilet cubicle with the American. The bald spot on the top of his head was smooth and tanned. White feathery hair surrounded it. A tonsure. His head snapped upwards and he sniffed and shouted 'Praise the Lord!' in the manner of an evangelist preacher. I was still a little nervous. 'Sshhhhh. Do you want to get caught?' I saw the irony of my question. Cocaine possession was the least of my crimes.

'Caught?' he said, grinning. We heard sniffing and laughter from the anteroom and I got his point.

He passed me the rolled-up banknote, and I bent towards the cistern and inhaled the thin line of tiny white crystals through my left nostril. He took the note back, to my disappointment. It was a fifty. I came up again, pinching my nose and checking the mirror over the toilet. My make-up was intact. A slick of cherry lipstick was all I needed. I smiled at Sam's reflection. He hugged me to him quickly with surprising strength.

'My God,' he drawled, 'we are way too old for this.' He pulled the door open and was gone. I waited a moment before following him out to rejoin the throng. But his words were ringing in my ears. I estimated his age to be somewhere between sixty and sixty-five, at the very least ten years older than me.

What age was the dead man? He must be thirty-three. He *was* thirty-three. He *had been* thirty-three. Wasn't that the same age that Jesus was crucified? Some of my school religion classes drifted back to me over the decades.

As I moved into the lounge area, I swiped a margarita from a passing tray, fumbling in my clutch for the cigarettes I needed badly. How could I use Sam? Might he help me? Or could I just lift his wallet? Where was the cloakroom here? There must be lots of wallets and handbags in there. I was about to light up, when a man in white-tie attire gestured that I should go outside to the terrace. I didn't know whether he was staff or the host. So hard to tell these days. But I obeyed with a gracious smile.

6

The door was pulled closed behind me by an unseen hand and I was made to feel . . . no, *I* felt – it was I that made me feel it – excluded.

It was quiet out there. The autumn air carried a chill now that kept most people indoors. In my embarrassment, I had left my lighter inside on one of the gold-swathed plinths. I was forced to approach the two thin Russian girls at the other end of the terrace, huddled together against the light breeze that rolled in from the Med in their tiny silk dresses, teetering on their vertiginous heels. One of them handed over a diamanté-studded lighter without looking at my face. The heft of it in my hand made me realize that it was not diamanté but actual diamonds. I began to chat, smiling at them indulgently. The girl snatched it back, throwing her eyes to heaven, as if I might have stolen it. Bitch.

As I moved away, I heard them laugh rudely and I knew, I just *knew*, that they were laughing at me. We had come up in the elevator with them earlier to this penthouse apartment. They were draped around an ancient actor I recognized but could not name. He has been in lots of things. I'm sure he has been Oscar nominated. I beamed at him, pretended to know who he was. I used to know these details.

I could probably have been an actress. It is not difficult to pretend to be somebody else. Isn't that what I've been doing for most of my life? Maybe I could still try it. In LA, beside the Pacific Ocean. My teeth and bone structure are very Hollywood. A lover told me that just last year. There were film producers at this party. *Sam will know*, I thought. Sam was the Director of Photography of the film whose launch we were celebrating, or so he said, but he didn't seem to know many people. He had not introduced me to anybody and only one man, good-looking, thirties, nodded in his direction. I could see him now through the window in conversation

7

with the same man, but Sam wasn't listening. I know coke addicts. The only thing he was interested in was the paper wrap tucked neatly into a slim silver case in his breast pocket. He was doing the maths in his head, calculating how soon he should do his next line. I bet if I asked now, he wouldn't remember my name. While I have done cocaine occasionally over the years to be social, it is not my habit. Tonight though, I needed cocaine. I needed anything I could get my hands on, anything to help me forget.

A sudden gush of noise behind me, and the door closed again. A waitress had appeared on the terrace. She carried a tray burdened with only two full glasses. I wanted both. She was disappointed to find anybody out here. I pretended I was waiting for someone and gave her my empty cocktail glass. She set the two drinks on a small white iron table beside a matching chair.

'Madame.'

'*Merci*,' I said, exhaling a plume of smoke deliberately away from her face. I waited for her to move away, but she stopped by the potted shrubbery to play with her phone. I hoped she wouldn't stay long. I sat down and turned to face the promenade and the Mediterranean.

Lights twinkled from the port on my left all the way to Cap d'Antibes on my right. In the bay, some party yachts bobbed merrily about in the water on the way to their various harbours, festooned with bright-glowing bulbs from mast to mast. I could vaguely hear the echo of laughter reaching out across the water. I lit another cigarette from the first before I extinguished it in the crystal ashtray. I wondered if I could wrap the ashtray and fit it into my bag. Just a little memento. The cocktail glass was too big.

I was distracted again by the high-toned tinkling reaching me from the bay. It used to be me who laughed on yachts in the Med. It used to be me who wore tiny dresses in London nightclubs. It used to be me who could flash a diamond bracelet and a Sobranie cigarette. It used to be me who was young and beautiful.

Now I was a middle-aged murderer. I quickly put the thought out of my head.

I stretched my legs out in front of me. They were tanned and still shapely. I reached into the bodice of my dress and pulled my breasts up into a higher position in their moulded cups. I heard a smothered cough behind me. The waitress was still there. She had witnessed the ungainly heaving of my bust into place. She looked back to the tiny screen lighting her small face. She was smoking now too. I was sure it was against her rules to be out here smoking, on her mobile phone, in the presence of party guests, so I no longer cared that she saw me drink the second cocktail meant for my phantom companion.

I turned to her and tapped on the table to attract her attention. *'Une autre, s'il vous plaît?'* I pointed towards my glass. She heaved a heavy sigh, stamped out her cigarette on the artificial grass and left the terrace with her silver tray under her arm. I watched her smouldering cigarette butt congeal the plastic emerald fronds into black floating commas in the air and waited.

I was trying to get my thoughts straight, away from the noise inside. When I arrived at this party, I had scanned the room for any sign of my old crowd, but this gang seemed younger, shinier and more confident than we had been in our day. I didn't know anyone. They were mostly American. Americans are hard to gauge. One can't tell if they are old money or new money and they mostly dress appallingly. Denim jeans and white sneakers for the men. Big hair and too much jewellery for the women. Last year, I dated a man from one of the Dakotas who forced us to walk half a mile along the beach to get a can of soda five cents cheaper than in the first beach club we'd hit. I dropped him when I found myself at the opera in the gods. The gods, for God's sake.

The waitress had not reappeared, my lighter was inside and both glasses were now empty. I stood up, but stumbled slightly. I'd had three cocktails and the glass of rosé earlier. I would have one more drink before I attempted to get money out of Sam. Just one more. I opened the door and the music slapped me in the face, some drum and bass arrangement at an ear-bleeding volume. I would not be able to bear this for long. I looked for a waiter, but they were now confined to the bar area and it appeared that I must queue for a drink. I had to shout my order at the barman, but before he had poured the drink, Sam was behind me, yelling in my ear, his hand on my shoulder.

'There you are! You want another bump, honey?' He patted his breast pocket.

I turned to see that one of the Russians was clinging on to his other arm.

'No, thank you.'

And now I was disappointed because I had assumed that Sam was interested in me, and even if I did not find him attractive, I resented the little Russian hooking her claws into him. They wandered off to powder their noses. I tried to make this drink last. I asked a pleasant-looking young girl which of the men in the corner was the film's producer. 'I am,' she said icily in pure New York and turned her back on me. So touchy.

Sam hadn't come back. Nobody had spoken to me, but I no longer minded. The trays were back in circulation. I had become immune to the sound level and gradually the techno music, if that is the term, was seeping into my bones. I glided sexily towards the dance floor and I lost myself there among the beautiful young people. I was remembering the days of Mayfair nightclubs. I closed my eyes and my arms reached for the sky. This was good. This was great.

I opened my eyes and a teenager beside me was laughing and pointing at me, yelling something in a language I didn't understand. More people were laughing now, and it was louder than the music. I looked down to where they were pointing. The whole seam of my dress had split from under my armpit to my hip. My expensive but old beige corsetry was on display, the overspill of flesh visible under my armpit. I laughed too. I didn't care enough to stop dancing.

At one stage later, I dimly recall Sam approaching, suggesting that we go back to my place. The Russian must have lost interest. 'We need to get you home, honey.'

I asked aloud why we couldn't go back to his room in the Negresco.

'And wake my wife?' he said, and it seemed right then like the funniest thing I had ever heard in my life. He offered to take me home, 'no strings', but I declined. I was happy, really happy.

Pain seared through my head as if the fluid protecting my brain from my skull had evaporated. I opened my eyes and saw daylight and a dirty parquet floor. The angle was all wrong. Somebody was prodding me. I realized I must have blacked out.

'*Madame.*' It was the smoking waitress from last night.

'*On doit partir, maintenant, s'il te plaît.*'

Te. All civility was dispensed with.

I fell upwards to a standing position, grabbing her shoulder to steady myself. She shrugged me away violently and handed me a barman's yellow canvas jacket.

'You must cover yourself,' she said in English. Her look of disgust alerted me to the gaping side of my dress. I stumbled towards the elevator and then out on to the street.

The sun was rising on my left, shimmering across the expanse of blue.

I made my way slowly down the promenade. I did not want to go home.

I walked unsteadily, the horror returning. Nobody had helped me. There was nothing to be done. I scoured the faces of everyone who passed, but they were mostly immigrants in construction clothing or nannies' uniforms, en route to the early shift. Only I was going home at this hour. Home, whatever that meant any more.

As I entered the flat, I could hear a low hum, and I could not ignore the smell.

It's too soon, I thought.

I had not expected it to happen so quickly, but then I had never been able to afford an air-conditioning unit. The flies had begun to swarm already, feasting on the corpse.

PART I

I

In our family, there were two sides, Mammy and the boys on one, and Daddy and me on the other. My brothers were loud and wild and rough. Brian was born two years after me, then Aidan a year later, and then five years after that, Conor. Conor was just two years old the last time I saw him, but he was already big for his age and could just about handle a bucket of turf. But Mammy looked after the boys and Daddy looked after me. I don't know why that was. It was just the way of it.

I liked the boys when we were left to our own devices, walking to school, playing on the strand or collecting crabs from the rock pools below the harbour. In those times, we shouted and jumped and sang together, and you wouldn't know to look at us that we were a divided family, but as soon as one or both of our parents appeared on the scene, we would immediately run to our champions, and Daddy claimed me. The boys were jealous, I told Daddy. 'Never mind the boys,' he'd say, 'you are the future of this island, you're the one that matters.'

We used to live beside the harbour until I was seven, but that all ended when Master 'Spots' McGrath made me stand outside the classroom for being violent. We were doing history, and Spots was teaching us about Helen of Troy and how her beauty had caused a war. I told Spots that Daddy had said I was the most beautiful girl alive. Fergal, Danny and Malachy and my brother Brian, who were the others in my school, all laughed at me and I threw the blackboard duster at them and told them all they should be on their knees to me because I was the queen of the island. Spots told me I shouldn't mind the silly old stories that my daddy told me and that queens knew how to behave themselves, so I bit him on the arm and he put me outside to calm down. Daddy was passing up from the harbour and found me outside the school door on the low wall, crying. Then there was a big fight in the village. I was pleased because I'd started a war too, so I was like Helen of Troy.

Almost everyone took Spots' side in our war, and nothing would do Daddy but he wanted us away off as far from them all as possible, so he built a house with his bare hands from the ruins of an abandoned cottage on the west side of the island. He wanted to go back to tradition, he said, and he thatched the roof and dug a well with the help of Tom the Crow. We had no electricity now and depended on batteries and oil lamps and a stove that was fed with dried driftwood and turf. The wind on this side of the island was so fierce that the first time Mammy put our clothes out on the line to dry, they blew away into the Atlantic. Mammy was furious, but Daddy said that she should stop complaining now because she was closer to America and that maybe America would get the use of our knickers and shirts.

It was wild and isolated on the western edge, and barren. The harbour side was fertile enough in the summer for grazing of goats and sheep, but nothing would grow out here. Daddy said we'd do better on our own without interfering busybodies who'd take the side of a sadist who'd put the island's only daughter out in the cold. Mammy argued that I would now have to walk further in the cold to get to the school and that he hadn't minded when Brian was put out three times in the previous term for messing. Daddy said maybe he'd take us out of the school altogether and teach us at home, and Mammy shut up after that.

Mammy had come to the island one summer when she was a young student, all the way from America. She had fallen in love with my father, who was an old bachelor of thirty-five.

In one of their arguments, he said Mammy wouldn't leave him alone till he married her. He said she had him persecuted. She said he'd never find anyone better than her, and he shouted back that maybe he didn't want anyone at all. She roared at him that he 'sure as shit wanted Delia', and that was true. Daddy wanted me.

I was the only one he wanted. I had always known it. The way he singled me out, took me out on the boat with him and Tom the Crow when Mam tried to say I was too small and it was too dangerous, the way he would take the food off my brothers' plates and land it on mine.

'I earned it,' he'd snarl at my mother, 'and I say who gets it.' And she would turn away from us and tend to the boys, and Daddy would smile at me and put his big rough paw on top of my head. 'Get that into you now, loveen, you'll need the fuel!'

Mammy tried everything she could to make Daddy love her, but he wouldn't even remark on the new hairdo, or the impractical high shoes that she couldn't walk in, or the short skirt that made her legs goose-pimpled, unless it was to say a harsh word. She got her love from the boys, who would nestle around her by the fire as she read them stories from the library books Spots McGrath had given her, while Daddy told me the island stories in my room. As he blew out the storm lamp each night, he'd whisper, 'Be who you want to be, my loveen.'

The boys shared another bedroom, and Mammy and Daddy had their own room too. I was the only one with a room of my own. When Conor was born, Mammy wanted to put him in with me, but Daddy said no, he could go in with the boys.

As I got older and too big to go on Daddy's shoulders, we'd walk the roads hand in hand, and once when I asked him if he'd marry me when I grew up, he said, 'Sure, I might join the queue,' and the two of us danced home that day, and if anyone had seen us they'd have got some laugh at a grown man dancing with a little girl, but I guess that was the good thing about living out west. Nobody would see us, bar some-one who'd made the special effort to cross the island.

The only ones who'd make the effort were Tom the Crow or Father Devlin. Tom shared the small trawler with Daddy and used to visit regularly with turf or groceries or deliveries from the mainland, and occasionally Father Devlin would come to bless the house, or before one of our first holy communions to make sure we knew the seriousness of the sacrament.

Father Devlin was always treated with suspicion by both my parents, but Daddy and Mammy both liked Tom the Crow and always gave him a great welcome. Tom was Dad-dy's best and only friend and they'd known each other all their lives. He'd been in school with Daddy but was a few years younger. Everyone called him Tom the Crow because he'd killed a crow with a catapult when he was seven years old. His old mam, Biddy Farrelly, had the bar and grocery in the village.

Daddy said Tom made him marry Mammy. The two men would be out at sea together for days on end, and sometimes they'd finish each other's sentences, they were that close. Mammy and Tom said they both had the patience of a saint to put up with Daddy. But Tom had stood by Daddy when everyone else had turned against him. He'd often stay for a bite to eat, and Mammy would take down the clear bottle from the top of the press and pour a dribble into each of their glasses and they'd knock it back and wheeze and cough afterwards, saying, 'God, that's powerful stuff.' Mammy and Daddy would be on good terms and nice to each other in front of him. Pretending.

Mammy said she was afraid Tom would have to leave the island to find a wife because there were no women his own age who weren't already married. Daddy said Tom would never leave the island because it was his home and leaving it would kill him. Tom said he didn't have the same fierce attachment to the island as Daddy and that maybe some day he would leave, when his mother passed away. Daddy laughed at that and said that Biddy Farrelly would never die and that she'd outlive us all. Daddy said that us children were the future of the island and that I would be its queen.

I used to listen to these conversations, often falling asleep in Daddy's lap. The next morning, I'd wake up in my bed, furious that I'd missed out on the end of the evening. The boys were always sent to bed, but Daddy said I could stay up because he wanted to show me off. Tom the Crow wouldn't be in the way of admiring me, but he always said a few soft words to keep Daddy happy.

Sometimes Daddy would be off fishing alone and Tom would call in to wait for his return. They worried about each other out on the seas, and since we'd moved out west, Daddy had insisted on taking the trawler out of the harbour on the lee side of the island and tying it up in a tiny inlet below our cottage. Tom had advised against it and worried that the boat was more vulnerable over there, but he gave in to Daddy in the end, to avoid a row. On those occasions when Daddy was out on his own and Tom would come to the house to wait, I'd be sent to bed along with the boys and I'd sit at the door and listen and hear the gales of laughter coming from

Mammy and Tom as they made inroads into the clear bottle. Mammy would complain to Tom about how Daddy doted on me. One night, I sat behind the door, wrapped in blankets, and heard a conversation between Tom and Mammy that I didn't like one bit.

'Oh my God, he follows her around all the time! He's obsessed with her.'

'Now, Loretta, is it not sweet that he pays so much attention to her?'

'I just want him to pay attention to them all. He ignores the boys. Why do you think that is?'

'Are you worried . . . like . . . do you think –'

'No . . . NO, nothing like that, he would never, it's just . . . it seems that sometimes . . . I don't know –'

'What? What is it? What has you so worried?'

'It sounds weird, Tom, but he puts her on a pedestal. As if everything depended on her happiness. I don't even know how to explain it. What was he like in school? Delia isn't doing that well. McGrath says she's slow on the uptake. Brian is streets ahead of her. Was Martin like her? When I met him, I thought he was the smartest man in the world.'

'He was fine . . . grand, but maybe . . .'

'What?'

'He's a few years older than me, like, but he didn't hang around with us much in them days. Spent a lot of time on his own, but you know, this island, it sends us all mad in the end.'

'In the beginning, he was so kind, and desperate to have children. When Delia was born, he was almost deranged with happiness, and he was so grateful to me. But then when Brian came along, he showed no interest and the same with Aidan. Since Conor was born, he can hardly bear to touch me –'

'Loretta, you shouldn't tell me these things. That's between you and Martin.'

'I want to go home, back to Minnesota, bring them all with me, but Martin won't even talk about it. I'm going stir-crazy. I was too young –'

'Loretta, don't be saying this –'

'Who else am I going to talk to, Tom? Martin's made so many enemies in the village that I'm on my own out here! You're the only goddamn person that comes to see us!'

I could hear tears in my mother's voice.

'I can't even get off the island for a few days because he says we can't afford it. It's just me and the kids here, day in, day out. My mom warned me and I didn't listen. She told me I was just like my deadbeat dad and that I was throwing away my career. I was too stubborn to write back to her after she refused to come to the wedding. She's never met her own grandchildren. It's all my fault, and now it's too late.'

'Why don't you invite her over?'

'And prove to her that she was right? That I'm living in poverty with four children and a husband who doesn't give a damn?'

'Loretta –'

'Tom, come on! You know it's true. The only thing he cares about is that girl. I'm jealous of my own goddamn daughter, can you believe it?'

'It's just a bad patch. Why don't you come into the village more? On your own, talk to Nora and Mary? They'd welcome you, I'm sure.'

At that point, my head dropped forward on to the door and made a noise. 'Hush,' said Mammy, and I heard the scrape of her chair. I soundlessly moved on to the bed with the blankets tangled around my legs. Mammy opened the door and stood for a moment. My eyes were shut and mouth slightly open, and I managed to keep my breathing low and even. She gently lifted the blankets and rearranged them on top of me. She kissed my forehead before she left. Traitor.

A few weeks later, on a June night, Tom came again to wait for Daddy as there was a storm forecast. Once again, I pressed my ear to the bedroom door.

'He won't let me leave the house unless I say where I'm going and when I'll be back. When I return, he insists on knowing who I talked to. If I get friendly with any of them, he says I'm betraying him. I can't stand it any more. I *am* going to write to my mother. I'm going to admit she was right and I'm going to beg her for the money to get me off this island and home with the kids.'

'What? Now, seriously, you can't go saying things like that, that's mental talk. I agree that things are going to have to change, but don't do anything for the time being. Let me talk to Martin. He's not a bad man.'

'Why do you always defend him, Tom? No matter what he says, or how he treats me, or the boys, you never say a word to him. I have no real friends here! Why should I stay? I'm taking the kids and I'm leaving.'

I was terrified. She sounded serious, as if, in the few weeks since their last conversation, she had made up her mind. Daddy said that America was a vast, ugly place jam-packed full of people, bigger than anyone could imagine, and that you'd get lost as soon as you set foot there and that we'd never find each other again if we went. Mammy said that was nonsense and Daddy couldn't possibly know because he'd never been there. It sounded to me like Mammy was intending to take us all away from Daddy.

The conversation had died down in the kitchen, and all I could hear was gentle muffled sobbing from Mam and Tom the Crow saying soft words of comfort. I put my eye up to the keyhole and he had his arms around her and she had her head on his shoulder. It didn't seem right. I'd never seen Mammy and Daddy holding each other like that. She turned her face to him and he tried to duck away, but she kissed him on the mouth and he hesitated before he kissed her back and then he did pull away sharply and wiped his mouth. I was shocked. I immediately crawled back into my bed, pulling the covers over my head. I heard the front door close quickly afterwards, but I knew now that my family was fractured for real. I heard Daddy coming in later and they did their usual growling at each other before they went to bed, as if nothing had happened.

Some days later, I found Mammy at the kitchen table, writing. I knew she was writing to her mother, and when she stuck the letter in an envelope, I deliberately spilled the kettle of boiling water over it. I've never seen Mammy so angry, and that made me even more furious with her. She didn't know that I'd seen her kissing Tom the Crow. She sent me to my room. I refused to go.

'Get into your room this second, you brat, or I'll take the wooden spoon to you!'

The wooden spoon was the instrument of punishment in our house. The older boys got regular doses, but I'd only got lashed once or twice, and never when Daddy was home. On those occasions, there was an understanding between my mother and me that I wouldn't tell him, because I'd always feared that the consequences for her would be bad. I loved my mother, though we didn't like each other. Well, I had loved her, until now.

'You won't lift a hand to me or I'll tell Daddy!'

'Tell him what?'

'About you kissing Tom the Crow!'

She dropped the wooden spoon where she stood, and looked wildly around her, but the boys were outside and there was only the two of us home.

'Does he have you spying on me now, is that it?' She whispered it, afraid that it was true. 'What else did you see, or hear?'

I knew I'd gone too far. I ran and wrapped my thin arms around her waist. 'Sorry, Mammy, I'm sorry! I won't tell him. I swear! But you can't take us to America. We'd get lost!'

She put her hand on the back of my head and held me close to her, and it was a long time since I'd felt her warmth, and I felt wet drops on my hair and could feel the shuddering of her body and I knew she was crying. I was scared. Mammy wasn't the crying type.

She turned away from me to the sodden mess on the kitchen table and began to clean it up. The ink on her pages was smeared and the words unreadable. It's only now that I wonder how hard it must have been for her to write that letter, a begging letter essentially, to a mother who had forsaken her for making what she saw as a bad decision. She lifted the clumps of paper and threw them on to the fire, where they smouldered before slowly burning into dark ash.

When the crying had subsided, she told me to sit down at the table and made us both a cup of coffee, strong and black for her, weak and milky for me.

'Delia, your daddy is not well, you know that, don't you?'

I was afraid. 'What's wrong with him? Is he going to die?'

She smiled to reassure me. 'It's hard to explain, he's not well in his mind. You know the way he has us living out here on our own and he doesn't talk to hardly anyone in the village? Well, that's not normal, honey. Most people get on with their neighbours. Most people love all their children in the same way with the same love. Your daddy is different –'

'You don't love *me* in the same way!' I accused her. I didn't like the way she was talking about Daddy.

'I do! Of course I do, but I have to pay more attention to the boys because Daddy ignores them.'

'He doesn't like boys.'

'But, honey, that's just not *normal*. You got to love your own kids! All of them, whether they're boys or girls, no matter if they're sick or well or anything, you got to love your own kids!'

'I don't want to go to America. I want to stay here with Daddy.'

She sighed heavily. 'That's the difference, you see? I wouldn't leave you behind, but he wouldn't care if he never saw the boys or me again. That's not *right*. Wouldn't you miss us?'

I thought about it. 'No,' I said. And before she had a chance to react, 'Why did you kiss Tom?'

She put her head in her hands and looked at the floor. 'Because I'm lonely, in a way that you are too young to understand.'

'What if I told Daddy?'

She moved her chair abruptly back from the table and stood up.

'Do what you want, but if I go to America, I'm taking you with me.'

Inishcrann translates from the Irish language as 'The Island of the Tree' — named after the beautiful oak tree that once stood proudly at the high point of our island. The tree had been a type of miracle, Daddy said, because no trees grew on these islands. The wind would not allow it and the salt in the freezing air killed any that were planted.

The tree disappeared sometime in the seventeenth century when the last chieftain hanged himself from its branches. His only daughter, the beautiful Dervaleen, in a fit of wild energy, cut down that mighty oak with her axe. They say it took her a week, and that ten men could not stop her. They say she never took pause for food, nor a sup of water, and neither did she lay down her head for those seven days. It was said that you would never think that she was capable of such rage, as if it were the tree that strangled her father out of malice.

And when the oak had been chopped into kindling, nothing would do her but to start digging out the roots of the tree, for fear it would rise again. The island men, who were all in love with Dervaleen, formed an army to dig out the tendrils of the oak, and it took them six months because the roots fingered out to every corner of the island. Drystone walls were toppled and a trench was dug through the front parlours of three cottages. Afterwards, they say, Dervaleen fell into a slumber that lasted fifty-seven days, one for each year of her father's life.

It caused trouble among the clans because, before we had lighthouses, the only way to distinguish our island from the others nearby was by the splendid oak. It had given us a magnificence that no other island could claim.

With ropes and harnesses, the island men and boys took the long granite stone that had lain at the entrance of our natural harbour since time began, and hauled it up to the top of the hill and stood it on its end.

Dervaleen never married any of the men who courted her. She would not settle to any life at all, but took to living wild, rarely eating or drinking. She made her bed in the lee of the long stone, and within a few years she was found dead of cold and hunger and was buried beside it.

Years later, a lighthouse was planned for the site, but the long stone could not be moved. The lighthouse went up ten yards from the stone, which is there now and known still as Dervaleen's Bed.

Daddy said we were of the same stock as Dervaleen, and descended from high kings. When he told me the story I could tell how much he admired Dervaleen O'Flaherty. 'Her act of loyalty changed the landscape,' he said. 'Imagine that. It was a fiercely courageous thing for a young girl to do.'

2

For the next few weeks, Mammy and I watched each other like hawks. If I went walking with Daddy, she was a nervous wreck on our return. I hid the pens and ink so that no letter could be written. Mammy accused Daddy of stealing them and trying to control her. When Tom the Crow called, I fought my exhaustion and closely watched the interaction between the three of them. Daddy didn't notice the tension that had crept in between Mammy and Tom.

'Now, Martin, 'tis time you put that oul' row to bed with the village. Come up to Biddy's tonight and we'll stand you a pint and I'll make sure you get a welcome,' said Tom.

'Indeed, and I will not.'

'Spots has forgotten all about it. It was near two years ago, and sure you are badly missed in the village, and Loretta too.' He nodded at Mammy.

Daddy put his hands on my shoulders. 'That man disrespected my daughter and everyone stood by and let him do it.'

'Oh my God, let it go! Look at her! She's fine,' said my mother, pointing and glaring at me meaningfully, willing me to speak up. I nestled further into my father's arms.

'I'd say Delia is well able to stand up for herself, isn't that right, girl?' Tom said to me. 'And she's a big lass now, almost too big to be sitting in her daddy's lap, isn't that right?'

I didn't like the way this was going. Mammy and Tom were trying to separate Daddy and me.

'Why don't the pair of you come up for a drink tonight?

Delia can take care of the boys. They'll not stir now, surely, it's after ten.' All the time, he kept nodding at me, and Mammy was trying to catch his eye.

Daddy looked at me. 'What do you think, loveen? Should I go up and forgive them?'

Mammy jumped up. 'Yes! Let's go to Biddy's! It's been too long. I miss them all.'

Daddy stopped her with a look. 'It's up to Delia. What do you say, *a stór*?'

Mammy begged me: 'We'll only be gone for an hour or two, honey. You'll be OK, won't you? The boys are asleep, you won't disturb them, will you?' She was torn between leaving them with me and desperately wanting a night away. Mammy caught me pinching Aidan and Conor one time, to make them cry. I wanted to see which of them would cry the loudest. She walloped me with the back of her hand. Next time I did it, I made sure there wasn't anyone to see me.

Our house was so remote that there was no chance of anyone coming to knock at the door on a bitter night. The worst that could happen was that the wind would wrench a straw bale from the roof, and the reality was that that would happen whether my parents were there or not. I nodded my permission. Daddy said he'd put me to bed first and tell me a story, and I could see my mother bristling with impatience.

'I'd say she's old enough to read her own stories, ha?' said Tom with a laugh even though it wasn't funny.

Daddy looked at him. 'Our stories don't be in books,' he said.

Daddy had a contempt for storybooks. They were written by 'outsiders', he said. I fell asleep while he told me the one about the Druid of Inishcrann – a warlock who turned ugly girls to stone.

*

29

There was a strange peace in the house the next morning, as if a raging storm had passed, and I saw my mother touch my father's hand in a way that was too intimate for my liking. He smiled at her and went back to mending the nets at the kitchen table. I sat on the floor, feeding the nets up to him. Spots McGrath had shaken my father's hand in Biddy's bar and they'd toasted each other, and Daddy was back in favour in the village.

Mammy of course ruined everything. 'Do you think, Martin, do you think it would be time for us to move back over to the harbour, so that you'd be among your own people? It's awfully lonely out here when you're at sea. And the wind here, I can grow nothing in our patch. What do you say?'

'No!' I shouted it. 'I want to stay here.'

Daddy looked at me and I could see he was trying to choose between Mammy and me. 'Maybe we could –'

I couldn't stand it. I was jealous. 'Mammy's only saying that so she can be near Tom the Crow, and kissing him again.'

My words had the effect of a lightning strike. The boys stopped what they were doing and stared at Mammy. I could see my father in side profile and I noted the side of his jaw tighten. Brian shouted at me, 'Mammy never kissed Tom the Crow! You're only a liar!'

'She did so. I saw them! And she's taking us all to live in America and leaving Daddy behind. She says he's sick in his mind.'

Brian breathed in heavily and I watched Daddy's chair scrape backwards along the flagstone floor as he rose to his feet, dropping the heavy nets on my lap.

'Don't mind her, she's confused. I don't know where she gets these ideas!' said Mammy in a hurry.

My father's voice shook. 'You kissed . . . Tom?' He broke down on the name of his best friend. Aidan ran into their room and shut the door. Brian grabbed Mammy's hand and glared at me.

'What if I did? When last did *you* kiss me?' My mother spat the words.

'Put on your coat and wait outside,' Daddy said to me, and his voice was ice-cold. Conor started to cry. Mammy scooped him up. I didn't move.

'Get outside!' Daddy shouted at me, and I grabbed my coat off the hook and went to the door. I tried to catch Mammy's eye as I opened it, but she was looking at Daddy over the top of Conor's head, defiance in her demeanour. I waited for a moment, but she never looked at me. 'Outside!' Daddy roared the word again and I slammed the door behind me.

With the wind roaring, I couldn't hear what was being said inside but I heard the crashing of furniture and the smashing of plates and I knew for sure that I wouldn't be going to America with Mammy. After what seemed like hours, Daddy came out and grabbed my hand and pulled me along the road.

'Where are we going?' I asked.

'Did he kiss her back? What happened after they kissed?'

I had made a mistake. I wanted our family to stay together more than anything in that moment. It was important now to make it all Tom's fault.

'He made her kiss him. It wasn't her fault, Daddy, she tried to stop him, but he had his hands all over her. He said he'd go to America with her. She told him to get out.'

'Did she? You wouldn't tell me a lie now, would you? Think very hard before you answer me, Delia.'

I shook my head vehemently. 'Tom the Crow grabbed her and kissed her mouth. I swear it.' Lies poured out of me, easily.

3

I was nine years old when I left the island in 1975, that day of the big argument. I knew there'd be trouble because of what I'd told Daddy, but nobody could have predicted what happened that night.

Daddy told me a secret. He said that he and I could live in peace only if Mammy took the boys to America with her, but that he and I had to play a trick on them first. He told me that we'd go on an adventure to the mainland. He said that we would pretend to run away together. Mammy, he said, would not stay on the island without us, so if we disappeared, before long she would take off to America with the boys, and Daddy and I could return to the island and live there happily ever after without them. When I asked how long we would hide, Daddy was sure that it would only take a few days. Daddy said we wouldn't have to share the food with them any more and that I could be in charge of the cottage. We could tell each other stories all day long, and I wouldn't have to go to school and could stay up as late as I wanted. Daddy said he would be the high king and I could be his queen. It was urgent, he said, and we must leave that very day.

I thought this was a fantastic game and I skipped all the way across the island to the harbour. I had only been to the village of Cregannagh on the mainland a handful of times and I was fiercely excited. When we got down to the ferry though, Daddy told me that I had to go on my own, and that he had some business to attend to and would follow on the next crossing. 'When you get to Cregannagh,' he said, 'just keep running away from the village. I'll catch up with you in a few hours.' I fretted at the thought of arriving alone on the mainland, but Daddy said that nobody would bother me if I kept going. 'Say nothing about running away,' he said. 'Tell anyone who asks that I'll be over on the next sailing in two hours.' He hugged me tightly as he said nice things to me, and then he said goodbye and smiled his most gentle happy smile. Then he waved until he was only a tiny speck in the distance.

I was found miles outside the village of Cregannagh that night, on the Ballina road. Daddy hadn't given me any other instructions but to run when I got off the ferry, and I had run as far as I could, and then slowed down to walking. He had said that he would catch up with me, but I wasn't sure how he would know which way I'd gone. The road went north and south out of the village. What if I had taken the wrong one? I continued along the same road, which carried few cars, and there were only occasional houses. Dogs barked. I was afraid to go too fast because the next ferry was only two hours later and I didn't want to be too far ahead of Daddy. It was much warmer here than it was on the island, and I knotted my woollen jumper around my waist and took off my boots to walk in my bare feet. The soles of my feet were as good as the boots, as I was used to not wearing shoes. As the bright summer day began to fade to dusk, I was parched and hungry and I sat down on a drystone wall to rest my aching legs. I made a bundle of my jumper and leaned over and rested my head upon it.

It must have been hours later when I woke to see two car headlights blazing at me through the pitch-darkness. I was cold and disorientated. And then the car's engine stalled and a man was looking down at me.

'What in the name of God are you doing out at this hour, child? Where do you live?'

I told him I was waiting for my daddy.

'And is he beyond in the pub in Cregannagh?'

'I don't know.'

'Where are you from, girl?'

I roused myself to say with pride, 'Inishcrann.'

'The island, is it? Well, get into the car and I'll take you to the village. We'll see if we can find your daddy.'

I told him I was Delia O'Flaherty and my father was Martin O'Flaherty and explained that my father would have taken the last ferry from the island, but the man did not understand what I'd been doing five miles outside the village and I couldn't explain it myself, without admitting that Daddy and me were running away.

He led me across the road to his big car. There was a lady in the front seat, smoking a cigarette. She began to fuss and took her coat off and wrapped me up in it on the back seat. I was alert now, and though excited to be in a car, I was scared. Where had Daddy gone? He and I were going to run away together, and yet he had not caught up with me. Perhaps he was still on the island? Or maybe he had taken the other road that led from the harbour.

In the village, I waited in the car while the man went into the bar across the road from the harbour wall. Under the sound of the water lapping at the sea wall, I could hear singing and chatter and pint glasses being placed on the bar, and I knew that Daddy would not be in there because he would have come looking for me.

When the man came back to the car, he shrugged his shoulders. His wife got out and I could hear them chatting and then they got back into the car.

'Now, love,' the lady said, 'you're not to worry, but Dr Miller here,' nodding at her husband, 'spoke to Owen the ferryman, and he said your daddy wasn't on the three o'clock ferry or on any of the later ones, and he hasn't been seen in the village, so the best thing for you now is to come home with us and we'll find your daddy tomorrow. It's after midnight and the first ferry won't go back to the island until ten in the morning. Our Clara is up in university in Dublin, but her room is all ready for her and she won't mind you having a go of her bed, ha?'

I burst into tears. I'd never spent a night away from my family before, never mind away from the island. But I knew I had no control over whatever was going to happen to me next. We drove on up to the top of the village to a great big house overlooking the sea, and I climbed the stairs and crawled into Clara's bed, ignoring Mrs Miller's pleas to have a wash first: 'God help us, when last did you have a bath? You're filthy from head to toe. Do they even have soap on the island, ha?'

Dr Miller told her to leave me. 'The child is worn out, she walked five miles, the poor craythur, leave her be. You can pretty her up in the morning.'

Later, I got out of bed and pulled the heavy curtains open, but I could only see tree shapes in the darkness. Fighting exhaustion, I listened to the strange noises in this cavernous house until all was quiet except the sound of the sea pounding the rocks below. I marvelled at the softness and comfort of the bed and the warmth of the room. I slept.

The next morning, Mrs Miller woke me and handed me a glass of milk. 'I've run a bath for you, love.' She led me to a large steamy bathroom. We didn't have a bath in our cottage, or a room for it. There was a pipe that ran cold water beside the outside toilet, and we'd wash our hands and faces before Mass. Every other Saturday night, my mother would boil kettles and half-fill a galvanized steel tub, and we would all take turns in it until the water ran mud brown. Whoever got to go first was always the cleanest. When Daddy was home, that was me.

In this bathroom, there was a tap each for hot and cold water and a large mirror on the back of the door, and a towel thicker than any fabric I'd touched before. Mrs Miller helped to scrub me with a yellow sponge and washed and rinsed my hair using a jug full of clean water. Afterwards, she gave me a big bag of clothes, shoes and boots. 'Clara won't be needing them again. You might as well get the use of them.' Out of the clothes I picked a pair of green tights and a full-length orange cotton smocked dress and red boots. 'Good lord, that's a party dress – over boots?' said Mrs Miller, but I grinned at her in the long mirror on the back of the door.

On the island, we had no mirror in the cottage. In school, there was an old speckled mirror above the washbasin beside the toilet, but I wasn't tall enough to see anything more than the top of my head and my eyes. Occasionally, if the wind died down, I could catch my murky reflection in a rock pool, but then a breeze would skitter across it and my image would close up like an accordion. Mammy used to have a hand mirror, but that got smashed in a fight a good while ago. Daddy had always said I was beautiful, but now I saw what he saw. Mammy was right to be jealous of me. I was prettier than Mammy, even though I looked a bit like her. My hair was long and silky like hers. Everyone else on the island had rough, coarse hair. And my skin was dark and clear too. Mammy had thin lines around her eyes and her mouth, but she said that some famous man once said she was elegant. Daddy mocked her for that. 'Elegant!' he said. 'There's no room for "elegant" on Inishcrann.'

I couldn't wait for Daddy to see me in my new finery. My hair was shining, and my skin was rosy pink from the heat and the scrubbing, and I looked like a fairy maid from one of his old stories of the island.

Downstairs, I sat at a big table and ate two bananas and two hunks of a fresh white loaf slathered in butter and jam. Dr Miller had gone down to the harbour to send word to the island that my daddy was to come and collect me, as they would not allow me to go back over by myself. I felt safe in this house. In another big room with sofas and cushions with flowers on them and overflowing ashtrays, Mrs Miller found beautiful dolls with which I could amuse myself in between running to the window to see all the people walking up and down, and cars and vans pulling up to the shop opposite, collecting and delivering newspapers and tinned goods and sides of beef. They had a television, but Mrs Miller said there were no programmes on until three o'clock. She let me turn it on and off though to watch it light up, and she showed me how I could turn a dial so that I could hear a fuzzy sound getting louder and quieter. I didn't tell her that I already knew about dials because we had a radio at home on the island.

I tried not to spill Mrs Miller's never-ending supply of glasses of milk on my dress, but after she left me to do a jigsaw with Mickey Mouse in it, the milk resting on the arm of the chair, I moved suddenly and knocked the glass over. I felt the dampness on my lap as it soaked into my new underpants, and saw the fabric darken on the seat around me. I was immobilized in shock, because I knew punishment was coming. It surely did.

Moments later, I heard the front door bang and I thought it must be Dr Miller with Daddy. He had been gone a long time. I ran out into the hall and looked behind Dr Miller to see if Daddy was hiding to surprise me, but he wasn't there.

'Where's Daddy?'

Dr Miller coughed and told me to go back into the sitting

room, and that he'd be in to me in a minute to explain things. Mrs Miller took a deep drag of her cigarette and then spotted the damp patch on my dress and was about to exclaim when the doctor half-pulled his wife into the kitchen. I knew something was wrong by the look on his face. I went to the bathroom for a towel and tried to mop up the wet mess on the armchair and on my dress, and then I sat waiting for ages.

The doctor came in with Mrs Miller, whose eyes were red-rimmed from tears. She picked me up and put me on her lap, but I scrambled away and stood with my back to the door.

'Oh, now, you poor girl. I have some bad news, I'm afraid. There was . . . an accident on the island last night –'

'Where's Daddy?'

'That's the thing, lovey, I'm afraid he . . . he died in an accident.'

I looked down at my lap, furious with myself. He wouldn't be dead if I hadn't spilled the milk.

'You had . . . have three brothers, yes?'

I stared at him.

'I'm so sorry, my dear, but none of them survived.'

'Mammy?'

He shook his head. 'They say a fire got out of control. A loose ember perhaps . . . A thatched roof these days and oil lamps, well, it doesn't make sense any more –'

Mrs Miller glared at him and cut him off. 'Look, lovey, I don't . . . they won't have felt anything. It happened last night apparently. They would have died in their sleep from the smoke. They wouldn't have been in any pain.'

'I want to go home.'

Dr Miller approached and kneeled on the floor in front of me. He put his two hands on my shoulders.

'Delia, there is no home. The house burned down. There's nothing left. They're still putting the fire out now.'

'Who says? How do you know?'

'Owen came over earlier with the news. The guards and the priest are waiting to go back with him to Inishcrann, but there's a storm brewing, and it's not safe to sail yet. We're waiting for it to clear up.'

I don't know why Mrs Miller started to cry. She still had her cigarettes and her house and her doctor and her Clara in university in Dublin.

Dr Miller went out again. He said he'd have to go over to the island in order to certify the deaths as soon as the wind died down. He wouldn't let me come with him. His wife sat with me and plied me with chocolate and different dolls. The chocolate was delicious, but I couldn't swallow it. Its sweetness clashed with the bitter taste in my mouth, and I spat it out on to a plate. At three o'clock, I asked if I could turn on the television and it fizzed to life, but there were just tiny men in suits talking to each other behind the glass, and I couldn't see what the fuss was about.

Within an hour, Father Devlin and Dr Miller had returned. The storm was rising and they couldn't get to the island. The forecast was not good.

Nobody on the island trusted Father Devlin. He came over to say Mass every week, weather permitting, and poked his nose in, wanting to know everyone's business and making insinuations about people. 'Tell him nothing' was the mantra repeated by the islanders, who nevertheless flocked to the tumble-down church every Sunday at midday, like the faithful Catholic devotees they were. All except my mother. 'Mumbo jumbo – a magic man in the sky is in charge?' she would say sarcastically. And Daddy would bless himself and say, 'God forgive me for marrying a heathen,' and Mammy would laugh at him, but not in a nice way.

Father Devlin said prayers over me now, while holding my

hand in his sweaty one, a Hail Mary and an Our Father, but he wanted to know why I'd left the island and where I was going when Dr Miller found me. He wanted to know why I thought my father would be joining me and why we hadn't arranged a place to meet. He asked me if I was running away, and if so, what was I running from? I stared at him, at the dark mole under his eye, and said repeatedly 'I don't know' until he became frustrated.

'I think she's a simpleton,' he said to Mrs Miller. The stain on my dress had dried, but the smell of sour milk was nauseating.

I clung to my father's last words to me, and played them over in my head. He had given me a five-pound note and told me to keep it safe. His eyes were glassy, but his grip on my shoulders was firm. 'There was never a girl as wonderful as you are. You are the queen of Inishcrann. Go now, I'll catch up with you.' And he pulled me towards him and buried his head in my shoulder and then shoved me roughly away. I had run to catch the ferry with the five-pound note in my pocket and the clothes I stood up in.

Now, he was gone, and Mammy and Conor and Aidan and Brian were all gone. I was old enough to know that dead meant that I would never see them again. A pain in my stomach came and rippled through the top of my head. Daddy said I could be anything I wanted, but all I wanted to be was Daddy's girl. How could I be that if I didn't have a daddy? Who was I if I wasn't Martin O'Flaherty's daughter?

4

It was three days before Dr Miller and Father Devlin and the guards could get to the island. I was desperate for news, but when it came, it was only confirmation of what I'd been told. Various people called to the house to offer their condolences and to get a look at the poor orphan girl. 'She's so pretty,' I'd hear them say, 'such a tragedy!' The pain in my belly was sorest at night when I was in bed on my own.

I tried to think what life would be like without my family, but I just wanted to go home to Inishcrann. Even if there was no home there, the islanders knew me, and knew that I was their queen, despite the fact that, as Daddy said, they wouldn't like to admit it.

I snuck out of the house the day after, and went down to the harbour and waited a short time for the ferry to arrive. Perhaps there had been a mistake and it was another cottage that had burned down. We weren't the only ones with a thatched roof. What if Mammy had done something to Daddy so that he couldn't come after me? I just had to see for myself that the house was gone, as they said. I hung back behind the wall until the cargo was loaded on to the boat by Owen. I went over and called to him. Owen looked at me. 'Go back to the doctor's house. I can't bring you home,' he said, and there was no warmth in his voice and no sympathy.

'Is it true, Owen? Are they all dead?'

'They are,' he said.

'I have money. Please take me home?' I held out the five-pound note to him.

He turned away and began to wind up the gangway. I attempted to jump on to it, but he caught me and threw me back on to the harbour wall. I landed on my bottom, shocked at his rough treatment. Owen was an islander. He stayed in Cregannagh a lot, but he was one of us.

'Why can't I come home?'

'There's nobody there for you now,' he said. He untied the ropes from their mooring posts and did not look at me.

I could feel hot tears begin to fall, and a plume of diesel fumes engulfed me as the ferry took off again. I turned to walk back up the hill, but an overwhelming anxiety swept up within me and I began to scream in terror. People stepped out of doorways, and I knew I was making the wrong kind of fuss but I couldn't help it. A neighbour of Mrs Miller's came and held me and rubbed my head and hushed me until my screams turned hoarse. She led me back to the Millers' house, stopping in the shop to buy me chocolate on the way. I had more chocolate in my room than I'd ever had in my life, but I could find no solace in it. 'Of course you miss your mammy, it's only natural, child.'

I missed them all. But I didn't need the others like I needed Daddy. I knew that if Daddy had survived, everything would be all right.

That night, I heard Mrs Miller saying to her daughter, Clara, on the telephone, 'They don't want her at the funerals. She has nowhere to go, the poor pet. She can stay here until something is sorted out. She must have relatives on the island who'll claim her. We'll just wait and see.'

I wondered why I wasn't wanted at the funerals. I had been to funerals on the island before. When someone died, everyone went. Even with the entire population we couldn't fill the church, so Mammy said it was important to show solidarity, though Daddy said she made a holy show of him by not knowing any of the prayers and refusing to learn. I knew that the people were put into coffins in the ground. I had seen Sean MacThomas's body laid out in his front parlour just last year, and his grown-up children crying over him. I remember it especially because we got lemonade that day. Why would someone not want me at the funerals of my parents and brothers? Daddy had one sister who'd died when he was a boy, and his own parents were older when they had him, and had died before I was born. And Mammy was from America. I wondered why none of the islanders had come over to see me, and why they weren't coming to take me home.

On the Friday of that week, Mrs Miller said I had to move into the boxroom, as their daughter Clara was coming home for the weekend. I had forgotten about Clara, even though I was wearing her old clothes and playing with her toys. I knew before I met her that I wouldn't like her. Her mother proudly said that she was going to be a doctor like her father. I was surprised. I didn't know that girls could be doctors. She turned out to be a grown-up lady with a woman shape, but I was relieved that she wasn't pretty like me. Her hair was dull and stringy, and big thick spectacles covered half her face.

The next day was the day of the funerals. Dr Miller and Clara were dressed in black in the hallway.

'Take me with you,' I begged him. I felt that if I didn't see my family go into the ground, I would never know for sure. What if Daddy was alive in the coffin? He had told me the old story of Timmy Mannion, whose broken coffin resurfaced after a savage winter storm. The skeleton was intact but there were scratch marks all along the inside of the lid. The custom now was that the corpse would be buried with a string attached to one finger that led to a bell on the outside of the coffin. The family would stay in the graveyard for a whole night before the grave was filled in. Daddy had no family to listen out for him in the graveyard.

Mrs Miller tried to reason with me. 'It's not a good idea, Delia, you're too young, even the islanders think so.' I ignored her and wrapped myself around Dr Miller. He prised me away, and left the house without saying anything to me. Clara shrugged her shoulders at her mother, turning her eyes to the ceiling, and followed him. Mrs Miller asked me to come and have breakfast in the kitchen and expected me to follow her trail of cigarette ash.

That night, when Clara and her dad came back, I expected they would have some messages for me from the island, but they were both quiet and not inclined to talk at all. When Dr Miller put me to bed that night in the boxroom, he asked me, 'Delia, you had friends on the island, didn't you?'

I didn't know what he meant. Everyone knew everyone; we were islanders together.

'I saw your house, what's left of it . . . Were you not lonely out there? Is that why you ran away? I tried to speak to some of your . . . the locals, you know, on Inishcrann, but I think maybe they don't like us from the mainland. It's an awful tragedy, what happened, but the most important thing now is that we make you as comfortable as possible and that you learn to trust us.'

I did trust Dr Miller. As the days drifted into weeks, and the shock and horror began to sink in, there were still no visits from the islanders. Without Daddy to remind them, they had forgotten that I was to be their queen. Dr Miller did not sugar-coat things for me the way his wife did. I told him there was nobody on the island who was a blood relative. He asked me about my mother's family, and I said she was from Minnesota. He took an atlas down from the shelf and showed me America, and that Minnesota was just one part of it and that it was more than twice the size of the whole of Ireland. He asked me if I knew the name of the town in Minnesota. But all I knew was that Mammy was half Cheyenne and that her daddy was dead and her mom didn't want to know us. I looked at the atlas. Daddy had been right all along. We definitely would have got lost there. I asked Dr Miller to show me Inishcrann and he laughed and said it was too small to show up in his atlas. He said that if they couldn't track down my mother's family, I would probably have to go and stay in an orphanage until some couple who wanted a beautiful girl like me could adopt me.

I didn't see why Dr Miller couldn't be my new daddy. I could tell that Mrs Miller wanted to keep me, but she was always trying to pet me and comfort me, and talked to me like I was Aidan's age. I was a lot older than she treated me. Dr Miller was kind, if a little gruff, and he was in charge. I would have to make him see that I was his favourite girl. When he came into the sitting room later that evening, I climbed into his lap and laced my arms around his neck, and I could feel the muscles in his shoulders harden and then he relaxed a little and accepted my embrace. I decided that this would be my new family.

There were visits from social workers and nurses and other strangers, all asking me questions that I wouldn't or couldn't answer, about my reasons for leaving the island, and where my mother came from. I said little at all to Mrs Miller, but when Dr Miller was in the house I followed him around and made myself as appealing as possible, smoothing his hair where it curled up at the back and kissing his face. I did not eat unless he sat at the table with us. At night I begged him to read me a story, and even though he read stories from old books in a bored voice, I knew he liked the attention I was giving him. I told him the story Daddy told me about the chieftain hanging from the old tree that the island was named for. He said he didn't think that was a nice story, and turned back to *Alice in Wonderland*.

It was to be my tenth birthday on the 1st of August, and I wondered what would happen to the special penknife that Daddy had ordered for me. The one I'd been using on the nets was almost worn down to its wooden handle. I had told Mrs Miller about my birthday and she said we must have a party. I'd never had a party before. On the island, if it was your birthday in school, Spots McGrath would give you a box of Smarties, or at home, you'd get a present and lemonade with your dinner.

On the day, some local girls my own age were brought to the Millers' house to play with me while their mothers clucked in the kitchen with Mrs Miller. There were no girls my age or any younger on the island, and I realized quickly that I was prettier than any of them in this village. They brought me presents – plastic bracelets and comics and sweets – and they fought over who was going to be my best friend. I accepted their gifts, like a queen. They sang me a birthday song and there was a cake with tiny candles on it. I didn't want to blow them out, but the girls said that I could make a wish come true if I did. I got a pain in my tummy having to wish only one wish. I wanted to live in this house, with shops close by, but on the island with Daddy and wearing my new clothes, but maybe Dr Miller could be there too. I had only one wish though, and I know people who are dead don't come back, so I wished that Dr Miller would adopt me.

Clara came back and forth at weekends, and I resented having to give up her bedroom for the small colourless boxroom which was used to store old tins of paint and a wooden stepladder. She tried to be nice to me, telling me the names of her old dolls, but I wouldn't talk to her and when she and her father tried to have a conversation, I wrapped my arms around his waist and put my head into the curve of his lower back. I hated it when I was sent to bed in the boxroom, which faced on to the street and from where I could hardly hear the sea. I often crept out of my room afterwards and sat at the top of the carpeted stairs to try and hear what they were saying, because I knew they would be talking about me. But the walls were thick, nothing like the thin wooden panels in our house on the island, and I could barely make out a word except for when the door opened or closed.

One night, I heard Clara say, 'I think it's unnatural, Dad, the way she clings on to you. You'll have to let the social workers take over, and soon.'

'For God's sake, Clara, the girl has suffered a huge emotional trauma! You're not going to go far as a doctor if you can't tell that much.'

'But, Dad, think about how it looks. You, and a strange child who is overly affectionate . . .'

I felt pleased with myself. People were fighting over me, just like home. I went back into Clara's room, threw her things off the bed and got into it, settling again to the sounds of the sea.

I woke up in the boxroom. Somebody had moved me in the middle of the night. I hoped it was Dr Miller. I went down to the kitchen to find Clara and Mrs Miller chatting quietly. They stopped abruptly when they heard me.

'There you are,' said Mrs Miller in her fake-cheery way. '*Somebody* must have been sleepwalking last night!' I ignored them and went into the sitting room to find Dr Miller in his pyjamas reading the newspaper. I tried to climb into his lap, but he pushed me gently away.

'Now, Delia, I think you're too old to be sitting on my lap, a big girl like you.' So, Clara's words had made an impression on him.

I sat beside him on the sofa and wrapped my arms around his neck. 'I love you, Daddy,' I said. He removed my arms and placed my hands firmly on my lap.

'Delia, I'm not your daddy. I can't be. You have to understand ... Angela and I' – he was talking about Mrs Miller – 'we're too old to be parents to a young girl like you. You need a family like the one you had. Don't you miss your little brothers? There's a social worker trying to track down your extended family in America.'

I was terrified. 'Can't I stay here? With you? I have five pounds. I can pay you?'

He turned away from me and shook his head sadly.

That night, I crept into Clara's room and, again, I got into her bed. Daddy had said that I could be whoever I wanted to be, but it wasn't working. Dr Miller didn't want me, because he had Clara, and she was his best girl. A sense of injustice overtook me that didn't allow sleep to touch it. The bedside light was on and I could see Clara's clothes hanging in the wardrobe, her records stacked neatly beside the chest of drawers. Her poster of the Bay City Rollers was pinned to the wall, her collection of old magazines and comics piled high under the window. I'd show her. I started by pulling the poster down off the wall and ripping it to shreds. Then I got a pair of nail scissors from the dressing table and scored it across the grooves of each record. I tore the magazines apart with my teeth and cut holes in the clothes in the wardrobe. I pulled everything out of the chest of drawers and threw the contents all over the room. I pulled buckles off shoes and cut necklaces in half, and I enjoyed it all until the door opened and Clara stood there, her mouth open in disbelief at the scene of devastation before her. I smiled sweetly at her.

She flew across the room at me and grabbed me by the hair. 'You little freak! You weirdo! Why would you do this? We've been nothing but kind to you. Freak!' She let me go and I walked calmly past her and went into the boxroom and closed the door behind me. I heard her shouting and sobbing, and I heard her parents trying to calm her in the corridor outside. They didn't come into my room or check that I was all right. And then I was too furious to sleep.

My mother's family in America could not be contacted. She had cut ties with them eleven years earlier when she refused to come home and married my father. She never did write that letter to her mother, it seems. It is likely also that no big effort was made to contact them, because they were not Catholics, and it was Father Devlin in those days, in that place, who decided such things.

Two months after the death of my family, I entered an orphanage for girls in Galway. I kicked the shins of Dr Miller and his wife as they tried to say goodbye. I couldn't believe their betrayal. Mrs Miller sobbed and held on to her husband as they left the building.

The clothes she had packed for me were confiscated and I was given a washed-out cotton smock, a woollen jumper and grey underwear. I don't know what happened to Clara Miller's clothes, because I never saw them again. My waist-length hair was cut to my neck. 'We don't want you getting lice,' said the hair-cutting nun, 'and you're still like a picture so you are, without it.'

I wondered for the millionth time why nobody from the island had come to take me home. The residents of Inishcrann had always been a family, despite the feuds and arguments that gave life to the place, but no one came. I heard the head nun say that a ten-year-old from an island known for its poverty and madness might be a hard sell to the childless couples of Ireland. The demand was all for babies, the younger the better.

There were girls and women of all ages there. Some had never known anything but the institution and had nowhere to go when they reached the age of sixteen, and so they stayed on as unpaid servants in exchange for their bed and board. The nuns who ran the orphanage were not all bad, but there were harsh rules imposed by the girls and women left in charge of us. I shared a dormitory with five other girls, of a similar age to me. One of them was deformed in her back and another was deaf and dumb. After lights out, we were not allowed to get out of bed, and consequently there was a lot of bed-wetting, punishable by beatings.

Some of the older girls would enlist us to help look after the babies, to clean up their sick and soak their disgusting nappies in buckets of bleach. Most of the nuns hated the babies as much as we did. My strongest memory of those months is the sound of children screaming and crying. Food was scarce, but as I was prettier than the rest they made a pet of me, and I made sure I didn't starve. One of the nuns gave me a doll, and I was the envy of every other child because nobody else had a doll. I was commended for the fact that I did not cry or complain. But as poor as our lives were behind those tall iron gates, the conditions were better than they'd been on the island. Much as I loved Inishcrann, in this place I was warmer and the meals, though meagre, were regular. I was no longer the queen of the island, but I would be queen of this orphanage.

We went to the primary school in the building adjoining ours, but apart from that we never went beyond the front gates. At recreation time during school, we were released into a stone yard, where we fell and cut our knees, or pulled the hair of younger girls and ran away from the older ones who would try to do the same to us. Prayers punctuated every day. We thanked the Lord for the rags on our backs, for the food on our plates and for the thin blankets that covered us at night, but I had already stopped believing. If Jesus could raise Lazarus from the dead, he could have stopped that fire from killing my family. Jesus only did miracles for people he met nearly two thousand years ago. He didn't care about those of us who lived on Inishcrann. I was in charge now. I told this to Sister Eileen, and she said it was a shame that a beautiful girl like me would mock the word of God. I thought it was God who was doing the mocking, but I knew better than to say it out loud. She assured me that I would be adopted, despite my age. 'The pretty ones always go first, and you're not illegitimate either, so you'll have a better chance,' she said. I didn't know what illegitimate meant, but I assumed that it meant damaged or deformed in some way. And at that time, it did.

After a few months, I was visited by a couple called Moira and Alan Walsh. They adopted me on the spot and I didn't object. I would have walked into the sunset with Attila the Hun to get away from the crying babies. As I left the forbidding Victorian building, I pressed my doll into the hands of the girl who was the next prettiest after me. Her eyes shone with gratitude.

Daddy told me there was a time long ago when no male child had been born on Inishcrann for ten years and every new girl baby was greeted with wailing and lamenting. One winter's day, an old widow woman called Kathleen Rags found a newborn baby boy at the foot of the long stone, Dervaleen's Bed. The baby was alive and squealing and nearly blue with the cold.

The baby should have been cause for great celebrations, but no woman on the island would claim him as her own. Kathleen Rags took him to the chieftain, and all the women of childbearing age were herded into the old barn that stood there before Biddy Farrelly's bar existed. The men waited outside while the old widow woman examined them. She eventually declared that three of them could be the mother of the baby but couldn't be sure which one, so they were each made to suckle the child to see if the child could draw milk. All three women leaked milk from their breasts though they hadn't a child between them, and the women protested that the child was a changeling and insisted that the old widow woman put the child to her own breast to see what happened. Sure enough, Kathleen Rags' breast began to engorge until a black stream of blood poured forth from it. Then the baby began to sing in a voice the like of which they had never heard before. The women were startled out of their wits and ran screaming out of the barn.

The men got involved then, but because it was a boy-child they were reluctant to blame the baby and instead had the three women and the widow stripped and beaten. The chieftain's wife, who had recently given birth to a girl of her own, was instructed to take the baby and feed it herself as an example to the islanders, but the strange baby's appetite was ferocious and left no milk. She protested that her baby girl would die without sustenance and begged her husband to take the foundling child away, but the chieftain and all the men were so enchanted by the little boy's singing that he ignored his own wife. The boy-child suckled until he drew blood from the woman's breast, and developed a thirst for that which couldn't be quenched either.

Even after the baby girl died and the chieftain's wife was being lowered into the grave, the chieftain would not yield up the foundling. Other nursing mothers were rounded up, and though they screamed and protested, the child was latched to their breasts until four of them too were emptied to the marrow of their bones. Still the baby sang and thrived, and his voice cast a spell on the men which made this sturdy boy seem more important than their sisters and wives and daughters.

It was Kathleen Rags herself who called the women together. At her great age, she had nothing to lose, she said, but they would all soon be dead if they did not cast out the evil that the boy had brought to the island. That night, she stole into the house of the woman that the boy was now devouring and took him away to her own cottage on the westernmost side of the island. There she threw the boy on to the sods of turf and flames and heard his last song. When he was naught but ashes and bones, she emerged from the cottage and returned to the village to find all the men gathered and weeping for the loss of their women. The spell was broken, but the remaining women took a long time to forgive.

Daddy said it was five full years before any baby was born, and the first birth thereafter produced twins, a boy and a girl. This was a sign of great good fortune and the island was finally at peace once more.

Never trust a foundling child, Daddy said.

5

I went to live in Westport, only about two hours' drive away from Cregannagh. The Walshes' house was smaller than the Millers' and stood on the Upper Quay, overlooking the bay. There were multiple cushions on every chair, sofa and bed, and I wondered what my mother might have done with such things. I had a bedroom of my own from where I could hear the ticking of the grandfather clock in the hallway below.

In the beginning, the spaces between the seconds seemed like hours and there was this yawning chasm of time stretching out before me, with nothing to fill it. No boys fighting and yelling, no Daddy to sing me to sleep and tell me the long-lost stories of Inishcrann, not even a mother to call me 'Daddy's girl' in her sarcastic drawl. Just Moira and Alan, who seemed so old compared to my mother. They wore matching cardigans in a house where the walls were so thin that even when they were whispering to each other about me, I could hear every word they said.

'She's as odd as two left feet.'

'Leave her be, she'll settle in. She's a great beauty though, don't you think?'

'Oh yah, bound to be a heartbreaker when she's a bit older. I hope she'll settle with us.'

'Sure, who else would have her?'

'The poor craythur, her family all burned up like that, how will she get over it?'

'We have to give her time, and breathing space. Don't be constantly asking her if she's all right.'

'But she never answers me.'

'She's an islander. They wouldn't tell you anything unless it was forced out of them. And stop trying to hug her. She doesn't like it.'

They introduced me to their friends as their niece who had come to live with them. I asked them why. Alan suggested it would be best if I told everyone that they were my aunt and uncle, as there might be a stigma attached to being an adopted child. 'Let's just say that I'm your father's cousin, all right? You can call us your aunt and uncle.'

'But why?' I asked.

Alan said, 'Because adopted children often come from parents who aren't married, and we wouldn't want *that* kind of shame attached to you.'

Moira interrupted him: '*Some* people might think like that, and it's unusual, you know, to not have a family to take you in, so let's just say that *we're* your family and then there won't be so many questions.' She beamed at me. My surname was changed officially from O'Flaherty to Walsh.

Uncle Alan was a small and pale man, so unlike my father that the thought of sitting on his lap or being his favourite girl made my stomach flip. Aunt Moira was stout, taller and fair. They were an ugly kind of couple and I was surprised that they seemed to like each other so much. I didn't think anyone would believe that I was related to them.

I tried siding with one, and then the other, but they made all of their decisions together. Initially, I favoured Aunt Moira over Uncle Alan and stopped talking when he entered the room, clinging to Aunt Moira when he approached me, but they mostly ignored my efforts to divide and conquer. Nothing could shake this couple, or their devotion to me. However, I didn't always get what I wanted and had to do chores to earn pocket money to buy the things I wanted.

Later, I realized that Aunt Moira didn't like the fact that Uncle Alan spent so much time in church, going to Mass daily. I began to ridicule him, repeating some of the things Mammy used to say about religion, but Aunt Moira came to his defence and docked my pocket money for being disrespectful. Eventually, I had to accept a life of boredom.

Aunt Moira liked to talk a lot. She told me she had been an only child and had inherited money from maiden aunts, so they were reasonably well off despite their ordinary lifestyle. At Mass, though, we sat midway down the church, which told its own story as to our status in the town. Uncle Alan insisted we say the rosary on our knees every night and go to confession once a week. Aunt Moira wasn't as obsessed about the prayers, but she said I was a blessing they should be thankful for. Aunt Moira had a gaggle of women friends who were loud and jovial. They came every Saturday afternoon with cakes and laughed for two hours and then went home. I got the impression that Uncle Alan didn't approve of them, but he was a quieter soul.

I went to the local school and tried to hide as much as possible. The school terrified me at first. In my school on the island, there had been five children in total and I was the only girl. In this school, there were equal numbers of girls and boys and the children were divided up by age. There were three different classrooms, each packed with twenty-five to thirty children. The noise was upsetting.

I never warmed to my new parents. In the eight years I was in their home, I never let them get close to me. They did every single thing they could to please me, and I repaid them with silence and a blank expression. I did not smile. They had me in and out to doctors of course, but I was stronger than all of them. At ten years of age, I knew I could be anyone I wanted. I just hadn't decided who that was yet.

Eventually, I got used to the school. Some of the other children thought being an orphan was cool because they'd read *The Secret Garden* and *The Little Princess*. When I read these books for myself, I realized that their parentless heroines came from wealthy, aristocratic backgrounds and that made me feel better. When the girls questioned me about my parents, I shook my head because there was nothing I could say. Nothing I wanted to admit. But the girls grew even more curious. As the shock of my loss receded though, I began to enjoy the notoriety. They wanted me to tell stories of how my aunt and uncle were cruel to me, but I wouldn't oblige.

Aunt Moira and Uncle Alan weren't cruel at all, just boring. They watched television all the time. The moving pictures made me feel dizzy at first, but I got used to it quickly. Uncle Alan was a postman, so he'd be up with the lark and gone by the time I went to school. We all went to bed at the same time. They gave me books to read, but often I just watched the sea from my bedroom window until the darkness hid it, comforted by its rush and surge and wane, rush and surge and wane.

Unremarkable years passed. Their real cousins visited at holiday times and I'd get a new dress and smile politely and help Aunt Moira make cakes. We got new carpets, and for Christmas one year I got an atlas. 'When you grow up, you can go wherever you want,' Aunt Moira said.

'I don't want to go anywhere,' I said, and they smiled at me, and each other, misunderstanding my meaning. My island wasn't in this book either.

I didn't need school friends, and I wasn't targeted by the bullies. I played the unwanted orphan well, feigning shyness and insecurity. I wouldn't let them in. Everyone wanted to befriend the orphan, but I remained aloof. I liked to see these girls fighting over who was going to sit beside me and who was going to walk home with me. They told me I was pretty. I enjoyed mirrors, looking at my clear dark skin and my shiny hair and my slim figure. I had enjoyed looking at myself that day in the orange dress, waiting for Daddy to come and admire me. Maybe I was still waiting.

Sometime after I turned fifteen, without ever meaning to, I began to attract the attention of boys and men. When we were twelve years old, boys and girls had been separated into different schools, as if we would be a danger to each other. But now lads of all ages sought me out. Remarks were passed, insults sometimes. One time, a man in the butcher's queue rubbed up against me in a way that I knew was deliberate. I, shocked and afraid to look at his face, stared at the fresh livers and chicken breasts behind the glass counter. A boy my own age in the cinema put his leg across mine, to the whoops of delight of his friends. Aunt Moira clattered him with her handbag. And then later, in an incident that terrified me, I was cornered by a group of schoolboys, younger than me, up a laneway, trying to pull up my skirt. I was rescued on that occasion, by an older boy who chased them all away and offered to walk me home. I knew him to see. He and his parents were always in the second row at Mass, which meant status or money, or both.

'No, thank you,' I said.

But the next day, that same boy was waiting for me after school: 'I'll see you home, keep you safe, sure, you're on my way.'

I protested, but 'It's no trouble,' he said.

He talked all the way home, about his mum and dad and his brother. He let slip that his house was in the town, so this trip was definitely not on his way home. He had been doing a line with a girl in the class above mine, Katie O'Malley, but he said they'd recently broken up though they were still friends. I knew who she was. The popular, pretty one in that class.

'You're from the island, right? I'm really sorry about your mam and dad and your brothers, but aren't you lucky you have relatives? Your uncle Alan is our postman. He's been at our door every other day for as long as I can remember.'

I said nothing. But he didn't try to touch me and when we got to my gate, he didn't ask for a kiss or a handshake or my phone number, or anything at all.

'Bye now,' he said. 'See you tomorrow!'

'Was that the Russell boy?' said Aunt Moira when I got inside the house.

I looked down at my feet.

She reached out and held my elbow. 'Well, don't get your hopes up about him,' she said, a frown creasing her face.

After a few days of walking home with him, I began to feel safe. He never tried to touch me or suggested going to the pictures, or anything like that, so I began to talk back.

'Do you like music?' he said. 'I'm going to be a musician, but my mam says I've to work in the hotel first.'

'I like music.' Aunt Moira and Uncle Alan had bought me a record player and loads of albums, so I was well versed in all of the current chart music.

'What are you going to do?' he said.

'When I leave school? I don't know. Go back to the island.' I said it dolefully, because that's how you'd expect an orphan to act.

'What? Go somewhere smaller than here? Are you mad?'

Perhaps I am.

'What would you do out there?'

I hadn't thought that far. But I wanted to go home. I didn't feel like I belonged anywhere else. I was a plant that had been uprooted and brought indoors. We lapsed back into an easy silence. He didn't mind that I didn't speak that much even though I spoke to him far more than to anyone else.

Two weeks after our first encounter, he asked if I wanted to go fishing with him. We cycled out to Mulranny, and he'd brought along his brother's rod for me to use, and he threaded the maggots on to the hook because he said he didn't want me to hurt myself, but I watched closely. It reminded me of the time on the island when I'd found a dead goat swarming with maggots. I'd loved watching their busy little bodies falling slowly in and around each other as they delved into the flesh. He said that most girls got silly and screamed when they saw maggots and that he was glad I was different from most girls.

I didn't have a best friend in school. Most of the girls in my class had paired off and there were just a few of us on the periphery: Barbara Anne, who still couldn't read and wore a bib at lunchtimes; and Eileen, who went to Mass every morning before school and to confession every afternoon on her way home. I kept myself apart. They had slumber parties in each other's houses and wore blue eyeliner and lip gloss when I'd see them down the town at weekends. They had boyfriends. But now, so did I.

A couple of weeks later, he asked if he could kiss me and I said yes. His lips pressed up against mine and they were surprisingly warm and soft. He had his eyes closed and I closed mine too. He put his arms around my shoulders and slid them down to my waist. I liked the feeling of it. The heat and the heft of him. I knew he liked me a lot because once, when I got a puncture in Newport, he walked my bike all the way home and sat me on his and steered us both.

The girls in my class renewed their interest in me, even more so when it was discovered that I was dating Harry Russell.

'I saw you with himself up the town on Saturday. What's going on there, then?'

'Does Katie O'Malley know about you two?'

'Did he drop the hand on you yet?'

Katie O'Malley had confronted me shortly after our first date and accused me of stealing her boyfriend. I tried to explain that he had broken up with her before going out with me, but she said it was a matter of days. 'Good luck to you,' she said bitterly. 'If he can dump me like that, he'll do the same to you.' It seems Harry had a reputation. He had dated lots of girls in the year above me, and maybe he was going to ditch me quickly too, but I felt his attention was sincere. After we'd been seeing each other for six months, everyone knew it was serious. I was the centre of attention again. Katie and her friends ignored me on the streets of Westport. Jealousy.

6

For my sixteenth birthday, Aunt Moira invited Harry to tea
and we ate at the dinner table instead of in front of the television. He said the dinner was delicious, and that next time
he'd bring fresh mackerel and cook them himself. I could see
Aunt Moira was charmed by him, and I noticed that she even
behaved a little giddily around him, laughing at everything
he said and flicking her spatula around like a magic wand.
He knew Uncle Alan because he delivered post to his house.
Unusually, Uncle Alan was in bad form that night. I could
tell that he did not like Harry, from the way he was being
overly polite and using bigger words than normal. I heard
him arguing with Aunt Moira in the kitchen when they were
washing up. I don't know what it was about, but I was embarrassed by it. Harry pretended not to hear.

I liked Harry well enough, and when his hands began to
wander further than I knew they should, I let them. I knew
all about sex, had seen it on the island when I was a child –
sheep, goats, and a pair of Dutch tourists once. I knew that
he'd probably want to be doing it soon. I'd heard from the
girls in my school that Katie had had sex with him when she
was going out with him. I was not nervous or excited about
sex. The groping made him happy and I didn't mind. 'Do
you like that?' he'd say as his hand searched below my waist-
line, and I'd smile, and he'd say, 'Oh God, you're such a tease,'
and become breathless.

One time I pushed his hand away. 'I don't want to be
another notch on your bedpost,' I told him.

He looked at me, deadly serious. 'You know everyone thinks I've done it? Well, I'm going to tell you a secret. I haven't. The nuns have you all terrified, thinking we're sex maniacs.'

Indeed, the nuns had told us never to be alone with boys and that they wouldn't respect girls who did any more than hold hands. They said that if we sat on a boy's knee, we had to make sure there was a telephone directory between you and him. We laughed at the nuns and at the idea of us carrying around telephone directories in our school bags in case you got lucky in the high field.

Aunt Moira used to cut my hair, but now she said it was time I went to the hairdresser in town, and in I went. I loved the whole experience and didn't read any of the magazines offered to me but just watched myself in all the mirrors, and watched everyone else looking at me. The resulting haircut was fashionable, after the newly married Princess Diana. There was talk of nothing else on the radio or even among Aunt Moira's friends. Her wedding dress and the ceremony were like something out of a storybook fairy tale. Aunt Moira and I were glued to the television the day of the royal wedding. I absorbed every minute of it and bought all the magazines afterwards. I remembered Daddy insisting that I was the queen of Inishcrann and it seemed silly now to compare myself to this family of enormous privilege and wealth, but I still dreamed of stately homes and royal carriages.

For someone who had grown up without it, I grew to love television. Aunt Moira and I used to watch some programmes together that we knew Uncle Alan wouldn't approve of, so when he went to his regular church meetings, we watched whatever we liked. *Dallas* was brilliant. I used to impersonate Sue Ellen's accent sometimes at breakfast time and Aunt

Moira would give me a warning look that told me I was going to give the game away to Uncle Alan.

That autumn, everyone in school was talking about *Brideshead Revisited*. When there were girls gathered to discuss the previous night's episode, I did Cordelia Flyte's accent and they hooted with laughter. I was a good mimic. But I liked those dramas about rich people who lived in great houses in the olden days, or the modern ones where they had telephones in their bedrooms.

I was used to talking now, so I began to join in a bit more at school. Everyone said that I'd snared the most fanciable boy in town. Harry was the star of the GAA football team and was tipped to be a county player in a year or two. He'd played the piano at things in the community hall and people always love people who can make music, even when they are ugly, but Harry was handsome as well.

I liked being the prize boy's girlfriend. I thought to myself that I should drop the whole orphan thing and become one of the cool girls in the class. That was who I wanted to be now. I began to take an interest in fashion and make-up. I *was* beautiful. I always had been. My eyes were ice blue. My skin was smooth and I'd never had the skirmishes with acne at puberty that my classmates had. My lips were full and symmetrical and my teeth were white and even. I bought eye shadow and lipstick and Wrangler jeans.

Gemma, who had a fight with her best friend over a borrowed skirt, declared that she was my best friend now. Gemma was the class's biggest expert on make-up and boys, and her mother let her go to the GAA disco, which was supposed to be over eighteens. She told me stories about drinking cider in the high field with lads and asked me what I got up to with Harry. I didn't tell her though, because he'd said those things were private and just between us. I began to go out with Gemma in the evenings and at weekends. Aunt Moira and Uncle Alan were so relieved that I was finally socializing that they never said a word about my late nights or the smell of alcohol on my breath. I had never given them any trouble, or anything to be proud of, for that matter. After six years in their house, they were still trying to be my parents, and sometimes I let them believe that I thought of them that way. They wanted me to be happy, so they let me do what I wanted. One night, I overheard them talking about Harry and me.

'I hope this isn't getting serious between them,' Uncle Alan said. 'His parents won't accept the postman's niece for their baby boy, and I don't trust that family. I never will. Not after what they did.'

Aunt Moira replied, 'Don't be worrying, they're only young. It will never last, and sure, she's never been invited to the house. That tells you everything. He's not serious about her. I just hope he lets her down gently.'

'If he hurts her, I'll break his face for him,' said Uncle Alan.

'Indeed, and you will not, you're overprotective of her. He has been good for her, and to her.'

'So far,' said Uncle Alan, sounding a sour note.

I knew I could prove them wrong. Harry's other girl-friends had been six- or eight-week flings. We were solid.

A year went by and Harry did not dump me. Harry did his Leaving Cert and began to work in his family business. His dreams of being a musician were put on hold, but he still played football every weekend and was 'one to watch on the field' according to the *Mayo News*. We did everything except sex – well, everything we knew about in those days. I told him I wasn't ready for sex and he agreed to wait until I was. Every couple of weeks, he'd check to see if I was ready, but I wasn't keen and pregnancy was the biggest fear a teenage girl had in those days. He would often try to get me to go to his house when his parents were out. His dad owned the Carrowbeg Manor Hotel and was an important man in the town and his mum was on lots of committees and their housekeeper only worked mornings, so the house was often empty. There was a grown-up brother too, Peter, who was living in London. He was some sort of genius apparently, according to Aunt Moira. Harry rarely mentioned him. I doubted if they had much in common. Harry worked in the hotel, in the bar or as night manager or whatever his dad asked. Sometimes he'd play the guitar and sing at wedding functions. He paid for all our trips to the Ideal Cinema, and to Westport House, and for the carnival when it came to town, and for trips to the Wimpy for chips. He never let me pay for anything.

Eventually Harry invited me to his house for dinner with the whole family at Christmas time. Everyone knew that this was a big deal. I'd been going out with him for a year and a half and never been across the door of his home. Uncle Alan raised his eyebrows to Aunt Moira at the news. Aunt Moira gave me money for another hairdo. They said little in front of me, but Harry was nervous about it. 'My old man is a bit of a snob. He'll want to know everything about you. My brother is home for Christmas. "The Pride of Westport" – that's what it said in the *Mayo News* after he got into Oxford. He'll be looking down his nose at Westport and comparing everything to London. Mind you, he probably won't talk to you at all. He barely talks to me.'

I was intrigued to see what Peter was like. In *Brideshead Revisited*, Charles and Sebastian had met at Oxford.

I was nervous too. I didn't like the sound of Harry's dad.

I dressed carefully that day and decided to play the sweet and demure girlfriend.

Harry's house was a big Georgian one with steps up to the front door and a large sitting room and dining room on either side. A staircase led down to a large kitchen with an Aga and there was a breakfast room behind it, and out in the back garden through the gloom of the December evening, I could see the glint of reflected glass from a row of greenhouses.

Harry's parents were welcoming.

'So, you're the girl who's been leading my boy astray!' said Mrs Russell, with a grin.

'Oh, I think Harry's always been a bit astray,' said his father, and although I think he meant it in an affectionate way, I could feel Harry bristling in the seat beside me. Mr Russell remarked on my accent.

'You're not local, are you?' he said.

I told them I'd moved to Westport when I was ten years old.

'From where?' asked his mother.

I'm not sure why, but I hesitated, and Harry spoke up.

'Mam, I told you before, Delia's from Inishcrann.'

'Oh, that's right,' she said, 'the postman's niece.' She didn't say it in a disparaging way. 'I was sorry to hear you lost your parents so young, dear, though I suppose at this stage you don't remember that much of them?'

She said it in a way that suggested I had been somehow careless with my family. And yet, maybe I had been.

It was that day that I decided I'd work on my accent to lose all trace of the island if I could. I was Harry's girlfriend now. I was cool.

Peter sat at the head of the table. He was quite like Harry, a scrawny version but quieter – more watchful, I suppose. He was twenty-four, which seemed impossibly old and sophisticated to me. He did not say much, but when he did, everyone listened. Even his father deferred to him. His accent was more refined than his family's, a little more clipped, like you'd hear on the BBC. He spoke quietly and earnestly about portfolios and derivatives, and he might as well have been talking about brain surgery for all I understood. Mr Russell looked at me sympathetically. 'Our Peter was in Oxford, did you know that, Delia? Studied economics. Brains to burn, you know. He's already working for a financial analyst in London. I think he's going to be a millionaire.'

Mrs Russell then said, 'We're proud of both our boys, aren't we?'

A millionaire! Peter didn't play it down either, like people normally did if they got a compliment. He corrected his father to say that he and his friend Daniel were actually setting up a company of their own. You could tell that Mr Russell was prouder of Peter than poor Harry.

'Ah yes,' I said, 'but Harry's going to play for Mayo.'

'That's right,' said Mrs Russell, and I could feel Harry squeeze my knee under the table. I stole a glance at Peter, who was not directly in my eyeline, and was a little startled to find that he was staring directly at me. He looked away quickly and we avoided looking at each other for the rest of the meal, but it had made me a bit uneasy, as if he had been passing judgement on me, and found me wanting. There was tension in the room. I wasn't sure if it was the rivalry between the brothers or their parents, but I liked it.

As we started our dessert, Mrs Russell asked me if I'd like some chambermaid work in Carrowbeg Manor on weekends.

'Thank you so much,' I said, 'but, well, I've got my Leaving Cert exams coming up in June. Maybe in the summer?'

Mr Russell spoke up, relieved, I think. 'Now, aren't you the smart girl, putting your studies first?'

Peter nodded and I felt it was good to have his approval.

'What are you going to do in college?' he said, the first words he spoke directly to me.

Harry began to speak for me: 'Delia's not going –' but I interrupted him. It seemed terribly urgent to say it.

'Medicine,' I said. Medicine was what the two really smart girls in my class were hoping to study. That, or law.

Aunt Moira's cousin, Theresa, had a shoe shop in Ballina and she had agreed to take me on after the summer, if I passed my exams. And I thought that would suit me because Ballina was closer to the island. There were college types and non-college types in my class, and I was always assumed to be in the latter group. My grades were slightly above average but I had no lofty ambitions for a career. Not until now.

Peter smiled with a hint of sarcasm. 'Really?' He didn't believe me.

Harry swivelled towards me. 'Medicine? You never said that before, I thought you were . . .' and I felt myself blush to my roots, and he saw and changed the subject quickly, but Peter continued to look at me; I could feel his gaze and his curiosity and felt a cold well in the pit of my stomach.

To divert attention from me, Harry leaped up and played the piano. He was good at it. I watched his fingers fly across the keys. His father sang a Billy Joel song and his mother joined in, but Peter picked up a newspaper. He was too good for singing songs, it seemed. I could sing a little and had done so sometimes with Harry, but I was too embarrassed to sing in front of the family. Later, when I said goodnight to everyone, I held on to Peter's handshake for a fraction longer than necessary, and tried to make him look at me. He did not appear to notice. Still, I had had a good night. I could sense friction.

Afterwards, walking me home, Harry said, 'You didn't need to say that about medicine, you know, to impress my parents? They already know I'm not college fodder either. I think they like you anyway, even my mother!'

'What do you mean? Of course I'm going to study medicine.'

'What? But you never mentioned –'

'I don't have to tell you every single thing that goes on in my head, do I?'

'No, but it's a big deal, you'd have to go away . . .'

I changed the subject.

'Your brother is quiet, isn't he?'

'Oh yeah, Peter's a snob. I'm jealous of his brains and he's jealous of my girlfriend.'

'What?'

'I saw him looking at you. He's never had a girlfriend that I know of. Too busy gambling other people's money or what- ever he does in London. He'll be back in the summer for two weeks to tell us what we're all doing wrong in the hotel.' I noted Harry's resentment for the first time.

'He seems . . . nice.'

'Nice? It's OK if you don't like him. I don't blame you. He's very . . . I don't know, superior?'

Superior appealed to me. I knew Peter thought I was beneath him. I didn't want him sneering at me.

When I got home that evening, Uncle Alan and Aunt Moira were waiting anxiously.

'How did it go, love?'

'Were they nice to you?'

'Did they turn their noses up at you?'

70

'Oh, Alan, of course they didn't! Why would they? Sit down and tell us all about it!'

'Their house is much bigger than this. And they have a housekeeper. And we had proper silver knives and forks and crystal glasses.'

Uncle Alan sighed deeply. 'Don't be getting notions,' he said.

But I was getting notions.

7

For the first time, I was thinking about my future. Did I want to go back to the island? The pull of home was strong. I hadn't been in so many years. Every time I suggested it, Aunt Moira and Uncle Alan looked stricken, like I was betraying them. I had sent letters in the early days to the boys in my class on the island, but they never wrote back. If I went home, what would I do there? But did I want to work in a shoe shop in Ballina? What if I did do medicine? Why shouldn't I? I remembered how proud Dr and Mrs Miller were of their daughter Clara, who was training to be a doctor. She'd probably be fully qualified by now. So there were already some women doctors. I thought I'd like to meet Clara sometime in the future and prove to her that I was just as good as her. I was taking all the right subjects for it anyway, just at the wrong level.

I decided I was going to be a doctor. I borrowed the higher-level books I needed from the library. I was good at science. I began to take my Leaving Cert studies much more seriously and cancelled many outings with Harry in order to revise at weekends. I made a concerted effort to get rid of my island accent. I had to remove the turf from my mouth. A doctor would never speak like I did. Aunt Moira and Uncle Alan were amused by this. Aunt Moira commented that I should take more breaks and go out a bit more, that too much studying could be bad for me and that they would still love me no matter what my results were, but Uncle Alan said I was right to keep my head down and that it was nice to have a scholar in the house as he had never had much time for schooling. Uncle Alan had left school at age fourteen. I think he regretted it, and it was unsaid, though obvious, that he felt he had married above his station. Photographs of Aunt Moira's merchant ancestors on the sideboard showed them dressed in some finery. Uncle Alan said his family could never have afforded a camera, though he had one photo of his father pushing a dustcart. Aunt Moira made sure that photo was displayed alongside her own family photos. She declared that her family loved Uncle Alan the moment they met him because they knew he'd be decent and kind to her. Uncle Alan always smiled wryly at this version and I got the impression that he may not have been as welcome as Aunt Moira liked to claim. It was Uncle Alan who had determined that I should stay on at school until the Leaving Cert, when a lot of girls left at age fifteen.

In February, I told him I wanted to go to college, and he was thrilled about that but the deadline for applications had just passed. I was told it was too late. I took to my room and did not eat. After four days, they were distraught and called upon Harry to reason with me. I refused to see him. They said I could repeat the year and try again, but I was adamant. They must find a way. I was going to study medicine that autumn.

Aunt Moira and Uncle Alan had a meeting at the school. My headmistress was surprised by my change of direction but reluctantly agreed that I would certainly be smart enough for university, though she thought aiming for medicine was far too ambitious. I would have to change from pass to honours in two subjects and she didn't think there'd be enough time to catch up. I swore I was able for it, and that I'd already been studying the relevant books. Uncle Alan said he'd pay for grinds to make sure I could catch up. The headmistress wrote letters to the Department of Education on my behalf to see if I would be allowed to make a late application. Finally, in April, we got a positive response. Aunt Moira asked me if I was sure I wanted to do this. I told her I was.

'I suppose that when you're a doctor, you won't be giving us the time of day. Sure, you'll probably never come back to this town.'

I said nothing, but I saw the sadness in her face. 'Harry would be sad to lose you. So would we.'

I was determined to go to Trinity in Dublin, though I applied for medicine in all the colleges that offered it.

Harry didn't understand my sudden enthusiasm for Dublin and college.

'You said you wanted to go back to the island,' he said. 'Why the sudden interest in medicine?'

'Wouldn't it be better than managing a shoe shop?' I decided to play the loving niece. 'Uncle Alan and Aunt Moira would be so proud. I owe them. They have been good to me. I'd be an important person in this town, or on the island, if I went back there.'

'Yeah, I suppose.' He was disappointed, I could tell.

'But wouldn't I? Really?'

'You'd be off in Dublin for years though. You might never come back. I'd miss you.'

I kissed him on the lips. 'I'd miss you too,' I lied.

The weeks leading up to and including the exams came and went in a delirious rush. I crammed right up until the last minute, up at dawn on the exam days, studying until midnight on the days in between. There was fire in my belly. Both Aunt Moira and Uncle Alan became concerned as I refused to stop for meals, survived on tea and toast while I worked, and banned Harry from visiting.

Gemma got annoyed too. 'You're getting fierce ideas

74

about yourself. First you manage to reel in Harry Russell, one of the richest lads in town, then you start talking all different and now you're going to be a feckin' doctor?' Gemma had always defined me by my relationship with Harry. Up to that point, I had been the poor little orphan girl to her. But what I now wanted had nothing to do with Harry, nothing at all. Gemma was hoping to get enough points to do an arts degree in University College Galway. She wanted to be a teacher and she had always been the smarter of the two of us and I think she liked it that way.

On the day of the last exam, when my whole class was going to celebrate in town, I went home and crawled into bed, exhausted, and stayed there for the whole weekend. I couldn't tell how I'd performed. I had taken in so much information in such a short space of time and then regurgitated it back out on to my exam booklets that I forgot everything I learned just as quickly, and if you'd asked me to draw an alimentary canal a week after my biology exam, I wouldn't have known where to start. Uncle Alan and Aunt Moira were relieved my ordeal was over, and Harry was pleased to have his girlfriend back. He and his mother persuaded his father to give me a summer job in the hotel.

Chambermaid work was fine once you got used to it. Changing sheets, making beds, cleaning bathrooms and scrubbing toilets were all bearable because I knew it was going to be temporary. I knew that I'd be off to Dublin soon and that I'd be the town's success story. I could write the headline myself in the *Mayo News*: 'Tragic orphan girl triumphs in exam success'. Harry and I saw a lot more of each other now. Often, he'd sneak up on me at work as I bent over to empty a bin or drain a sink and he'd grab me by the waist and throw me down on to the bed and we'd kiss and grope and play a little.

Peter came home on his holidays for two weeks shortly after my eighteenth birthday with ideas about getting a new machine for the hotel to run the bookings and invoicing, but his mother said they'd no room for it and nobody who'd know how to use it, and didn't they have a phone and a letterbox, and they'd already bought a photocopier the summer before at Peter's insistence and every time it broke down a fella had to come from Dublin to fix it. Peter and she clashed about what defined progress, Peter saying, 'Mark my words, computerization is the future. Every forward-thinking company in London knows it, and we have the space for it in the hotel. That storeroom behind reception is big enough.'

His father took his side as usual. Harry stayed out of it. 'Peter's the smart one, but he's always thinking of the future and never thinking of now,' Harry said. Peter's holiday was a working one in the hotel's high season.

That look we had exchanged over the dinner table at Christmas time was not forgotten by either of us. He watched me and I watched him, both of us ducking away from each other's eyes when caught, but always aware, circling each other. We rarely spoke, but I felt his eyes follow me down corridors and up the stairs. I wasn't sure how to interpret it. He finally had a girlfriend, by all accounts. Harry didn't believe she existed. 'Oh yeah,' he said, 'Peter's got a great imagination.' Peter never smiled at me, never deliberately engaged me in conversation, but he watched me. Maybe he thought I wasn't good enough to be in the family hotel; maybe he thought a girl with no background didn't belong with his brother. *I'll show him*, I said to myself, *when I'm a doctor, on the front page.*

The morning the results came out, all the girls were going to the school to get them, but I was rostered to be working in the hotel from 7 a.m. to 1 p.m. I told Aunt Moira and

Uncle Alan that I didn't mind, and we'd organized a celebration dinner at home that evening with Harry included. Aunt Moira would go up to the school and collect the results when it opened.

At about ten o'clock, I was coming back from the laundry room laden down with a stack of pillowcases, blankets and fresh towels when I heard Peter calling my name. I told him I'd no time to stop and chat, but he followed me into one of the bedrooms.

'I've news for you,' he said. 'Your Aunt Moira just rang . . . she wanted Harry to be the one to tell you . . . I can't find him –'

'What is it? Is she all right?' I was on high alert, his voice was grave and I knew something was wrong.

'Don't go getting yourself worked up, everyone's safe, it's not the end of the world, but –' His clipped accent irritated me.

'What is it?' I almost screamed at him.

'Your exam results. They were good, just not good enough for medicine. Moira thought you might be disappointed?'

I stood, waiting for the punchline, or for Harry to burst through the door and jump on me. It was just the kind of thing he'd do.

'Delia?'

'Yes?'

'Do you understand? You got mostly Cs, one B in biology, that's not bad at all, just . . . not good enough for medicine. Did you seriously put nothing else on the application form? I mean, you could definitely do an arts degree with those points.'

I slumped on to the bed, realizing finally that this was no joke. Peter sat on the bed beside me. He put his hand on my shoulder. 'Don't be like that. Didn't you have a little job lined up in Ballina? In the shoe shop, Harry said. And to be honest, it was a bit mad to try and cram for all As in five months.'

Harry must have told him.

'I could have told you it wouldn't work.' His tone was so condescending that I saw red. He had ignored me since he came home and now, when I had proven myself unworthy, he deigned to be sympathetic.

I reached out and slapped him as hard as I could. I'd made a fool out of myself, deluded myself, raised my hopes and expectations for no reason but to make him think well of me. My cheeks burned with humiliation.

The force of my blow threw him flat on the bed. He was stunned. 'What the –'

'It's all your fault!' I screamed at him. 'I'm nobody. I wanted to be important like you! You made me think it was possible.'

He sat up and I pushed him again forcefully, and at first I thought I might kill him but he put his arms up, first in a gesture of submission, but then reaching out and holding my face in his hands. I did not think. I put my mouth on his mouth and my first thought was that our lips fitted together perfectly. I should have stopped there, and I could feel his shock, and as my hands roamed his body I could feel his arousal. He kissed me back and a strange excitement took hold of me. Soon we were fumbling with each other's clothes and, at some stage, he broke away to lock the door. At some stage, he said, 'We shouldn't be doing this.' At some stage, I told him it was my first time, and he became more confident. At some stage, I said, 'Don't stop.' At some stage, we clung to each other and I cried out and he put his hand over my mouth to muffle the sound. And at some stage, he pulsed inside me, and it felt right.

*

Afterwards, we got dressed and he held me as I cried, but I didn't even know what I was crying about. I had just lost my virginity and Peter certainly wasn't going to respect me now. He thought I was just a cheap chambermaid. I was doomed to work in a shoe shop. I was never going to make the front page unless they were going to do a feature on the Most Deluded Girl in Town. I went into the bathroom and washed myself. I avoided looking at my face in the mirror.

Peter was hovering awkwardly near the door.

'What will we do?' he said.

'You're supposed to be the smart one, the one with all the answers.'

'So you never . . . with Harry?'

I shook my head.

He grinned then and punched the air.

'Stop,' I said. 'Was this to spite Harry?'

'*We* did this, together. But what will we do, I mean . . . about us?'

I looked at him properly now and this time he didn't look away. I realized I could play him.

'Nothing,' I said, 'this never happened.'

'OK, but, Harry, if he finds out . . .'

'Who is going to tell him? Not me.'

He looked at the ground then, and the bravado dripped away.

'It's stupid, I suppose. I mean, I'm living in London, and you . . .'

'I what?'

'You just . . . you wouldn't fit in.' There it was. I didn't belong in his world.

'Just as well I live here then, isn't it, and that you live there. After next week, we don't have to see each other again.'

'Yeah, but, like, do you fancy me?'

'No.'

'So you just had sex with a man you don't fancy?'

'No, I didn't, and if you ever say different, I'll call you a liar.'

'You must fancy me a bit?'

'I'm going out with your brother, or have you forgotten?'

'Yeah, but you didn't just have sex with him.'

'Aren't you supposed to have a girlfriend?'

'Sort of.'

'What do you mean?'

'Never mind.'

I stood, fully dressed, in front of him and kissed his cheek chastely. 'Forget this. It didn't happen. Now get out, and let me get on with the job your father pays me to do.'

He left the room, and I remade the bed again and hung the towels and straightened the curtains and polished the mirror. I continued working for the next few hours, rushing to make up the time I had lost. I thought how foolish I had been. I didn't even find him physically attractive, but there was something about him that had made me want to kiss him. Did it mean I cared less about Harry? Did I care about Harry? My head was full of turmoil. I decided not to think about Peter. But part of me felt powerful.

I wondered what I was going to say to Uncle Alan and Aunt Moira, who had scrimped to pay for extra grinds, who had boasted to all and sundry that I was going to be a doctor. Uncle Alan had made no secret of it on his postal rounds, he was that proud of me. The results for the entire class were posted on the school noticeboard. Everyone would know by now.

When I finished my shift, Harry caught me as I tried to leave the hotel unnoticed. Peter was standing behind him.

'Delia, I'm so . . . sorry! Peter just told me. Do you want to come with me for a walk, or a coffee?'

'I just want to go home.'

'Look, maybe it's for the best. I mean, I don't know what I'd do if you went to Dublin.' He folded me in his arms and tucked his chin over my head as if to protect me like a child. I felt the heat of his body and how substantial it felt compared to Peter's slimmer frame, and I was grateful for it. It was the way Daddy used to hug me. I felt safe. But I couldn't stem the feeling of excitement. Out of the corner of my eye, I saw Peter and he winked at me.

The mood at home was funereal. Uncle Alan and Aunt Moira tried to pretend that they weren't upset, but Uncle Alan, in particular, was shaken.

'And you didn't put anything else on the form? Why didn't you put some other course on the form?'

I choked on my words and couldn't answer him and he said, in his quiet way, 'I'll just go and put the kettle on. Everything will be grand.'

Harry arrived with a massive bouquet of flowers and a card at dinner time. The card said 'You'll always be an A to me'. I looked at the way his eyes sparkled more than Peter's. The way his hands were bigger but rougher than Peter's. I tried to put thoughts of Peter out of my head. I decided it hadn't happened. We ate a subdued meal. The ice cream cake that Aunt Moira had bought to celebrate my results was left in the freezer 'for another time'. She was more practical and feigned jollity.

'Well, look now, we just have to go back to Plan A. Theresa will be delighted with those results and, who knows, you could have a shoe shop empire yourself in a few years! And haven't you had enough of those old books? I bet you're secretly relieved. Sure, Dublin probably wouldn't suit you anyway, an island girl like you.'

It had been years since she'd referred to me as an island girl.

Gemma was more sympathetic than I'd expected. She rang that evening. 'Look,' she said, 'you're still going with the town's biggest ride. Everyone's jealous of that. And you know, I doubt a fella like that would stay faithful for the years you were in Dublin. It's better to stay in Mayo, where you can keep an eye on him.' She had been accepted into college in Galway but promised she'd be back every weekend. 'Who wants to be a doctor anyway? Surrounded by sick and dying people? Sure, that was a mental idea!'

My headmistress telephoned Aunt Moira and suggested that if I was determined, I could come back and repeat the final year and give myself time to do all of the study required. She diplomatically said that I should lower my sights though, that medicine was probably beyond my capability. I sat at the bottom of the stairs listening to the conversation, filling in the blanks for myself. I could not face going back to school for a whole year and feeling humiliated by all of the younger girls.

In the hotel, I got on with my work and ignored Peter as best I could, though still I'd catch him looking and when we passed each other on the staff corridor he would wink or blow a kiss in my direction if nobody was around. I felt a kind of nervous energy. Then, one day, in his second week, it did happen again. Sex. I didn't put up any protest at all. My curiosity had been piqued. He kissed me first, that second time, on the back stairs that led down to the laundry room. I could feel how nervous he was, how afraid that I would reject him. There was no reason for him to be on that stairwell. I guessed he was waiting for me. I was in control.

I kissed him back and he asked which room we could go to and I led the way, knowing it was wrong and yet excited by the secrecy and the danger of being caught. There was little conversation. He put his hands on mine and pushed them downwards. Without saying anything, he showed me how I might better satisfy him, using my hands, my mouth, my breasts. This time, Peter had a condom. He was certainly experienced, I realized. He told me I was beautiful and that he wanted me, things Harry never used to say, though I knew he felt them.

Afterwards, I felt the same mute excitement when Peter and I spotted each other, the same feelings of power and control when I let him brush his hand over my breast as I walked past him. Why had I done such a thing? Why had I initiated this sexual contact with someone I did not particularly care for, the brother of a boy that I was certain cared for me? There was something about Peter that Harry didn't have: he was sure of himself. Even though Harry was better-looking and had a greater success rate with girls, Peter had the confidence of the arrogant and I could not help finding it attractive.

One night, when Harry and I were going to the pictures, Peter tagged along, making faces at me behind Harry's back, being openly affectionate with me.

'You're a bit too close there,' said Harry to Peter in the back row of the Ideal Cinema on James Street, when he noticed Peter's leg touching mine.

Peter laughed. 'I don't think Delia minds?'

I squirmed and Harry forcefully pushed Peter's leg away and swapped seats with me.

When it came time for Peter to return to London, he wanted to know if I would keep in touch with him. He hinted that I might pay him a visit in London if he sent over the money.

'I thought you said I wouldn't fit in,' I said.

'You'd fit in with me. You can't be serious about Harry?'

I needed to keep him dangling, but right then, Harry interrupted us.

'You two look like you're planning a bank robbery,' he said, eyes wary.

'Your brother is boring the arse off me about how machines are going to take over the world,' I said, laughing.

Afterwards, Harry said, 'I don't like the way my brother looks at you. I'm glad he's going back to London.'

I nestled into Harry's chin so that he couldn't see my blushes. 'I only have eyes for you,' I said.

8

Harry's parents tolerated our relationship, but there was something in Uncle Alan and Aunt Moira's history with the Russells that went unexplained and it wasn't just the difference in status. The Russells had money and a big house and commanded more respect in the town, but I knew it was more than that. On the few occasions they would meet in the street, they behaved like strangers to each other.

I had asked Harry if his dad would give me a job as a receptionist in Carrowbeg Manor full-time, and I know he begged his dad to take me on, but the answer was no, with the excuse that he couldn't fire one of the current staff to give me a job. Harry was embarrassed to give me this news because he knew as well as I did that Claudine was leaving at the end of the summer and that Nicola had asked to go part-time. The Russells were never rude to me, but I knew they thought Harry could do better for himself. I think they were pleased that the hotel high season was ending and I was due to go to Ballina. Peter had gone back to London to his exciting job, and my life would begin a new chapter.

It was over an hour and a half on the bus from Westport to Ballina, so Theresa had said I could stay in a flat above the shop as a lodger and she would deduct my rent from my salary. I would go home to Westport every Saturday after work and return to the shop on Monday morning. Aunt Moira and Uncle Alan were pleased, I think, that I wasn't going to be too far away, and that I'd still be joining them for Sunday Mass every week. Harry was learning to drive his dad's car so that he could come to Ballina to visit at least once a week. After a summer of expectation and disappointment, I was feeling totally despondent. A shoe shop assistant. This was not who I wanted to be, and yet it seemed like the only option available to me. For the first time, I had no role to fulfil. Harry was behaving like I was moving to the moon.

I started work in Calvey's shoe shop on Tolan Street in Ballina on Monday the 19th of September 1983. Ballina was a traditional market town whereas Westport was planned, and though the Moy River was wider than the Carrowbeg, the town turned its back on the river and left it to the anglers, who enjoyed the peace. It was also just seven miles from Cregannagh village, where I had spent time in Dr Miller's house in the aftermath of my family's death, and from where the ferry left twice a day to Inishcrann. The proximity to my old home was hard to ignore, and yet I never ventured in that direction, not for the first few weeks anyway.

My bedroom above the shop was also a storeroom, stacked floor to ceiling with boxed out-of-season footwear, ready to take their place in the window come the spring. Beside the bedroom, there was a tiny kitchen containing a sink and an electric cooker, and a sliding door adjacent to that revealed a stained enamel bath and ancient toilet that was also in use by the shop's staff. Theresa was theoretically in charge as it was her shop. She was what we would call 'eccentric', and it was hard to see how she and Aunt Moira could be related. I think she was in her mid sixties, but she dressed as if she was a teenager like me, with legwarmers and ra-ra skirts. She was unmarried but loudly declared she had no time for boyfriends. I had met her several times over the years around Christmas when the extended family visited one another, but I had never taken much interest so didn't see how unusual she was until I went to work for her.

It was rumoured by Orla, the Saturday girl, that Theresa had been thrown out by the Sisters of Jesus and Mary in Crossmolina when still a novice. Aunt Moira had never mentioned it, but I was inclined to think it might be true. To model the shoes effectively, Theresa wore a different one on each foot in the shop every day. A stiletto on one foot and a hiking boot on the other was not unusual. Because she couldn't actually walk in these combinations, she sat beside the cash register, rather than behind it, in a chair on wheels, to attract the attention of her customers. When a sale was made, she would roll in behind the cash register to complete the transaction. The shop was decorated with her collection of dartboards. Any wall space that wasn't taken up with shelving or advertising had a couple of dartboards jammed into it. From her seat at the front, she would practise her game, flinging lethal arrows in various directions without any warning. In the first few days, I was terrified of losing an eye, but Frankie, who really ran the place, told me that she'd never so much as clipped anyone in twenty years.

The customers loved Theresa. She would ask everyone their troubles and they had no problem telling her, because she would then make firm promises to say novenas and to intercede with the Lord on all of their behalves. She handed out plastic holy medals to every child that came through the door. The only part of shoe selling she did was the modelling and the taking of cash. Frankie, a man in his forties, did the rest. He had been there with her almost since she opened. My teenage mind of course jumped to conclusions about Frankie and Theresa, but his buttoned-up manner soon put paid to those illusions. He was neat, quiet and polite, and only ever talked about shoes and selling them. He was responsible for the ordering from England and the stock rotation and shelving. I had replaced a woman who had given up the job because she got married and moved away. Apart from that, there was only Orla, who called in sick every other week. Clearly, she had a life elsewhere, but she didn't understand why I was stuck here. She was saving up to go to Canada, where her brother lived.

'What are you doing working here? You could at least work in one of the fashion shops in Castlebar, because you're good-looking, you know?'

I certainly thought about it, but jobs were impossible to come by unless you knew somebody. I hated every single thing about the shoe shop. The smell of shoe leather made me nauseous, and because I was new, Theresa started me off in the children's end of the shop. I hadn't handled small children since I'd been in the orphanage. I resented them on sight. I'm not sure why that was, but their noisy, demanding behaviour dredged up memories for me. I could not disguise my intense and irrational dislike of them. I did not like to touch their often-grubby feet for measuring purposes, and had to keep eye contact with their mothers to avoid looking into their faces. In the week of my training, Frankie noticed and reprimanded me. I pretended I didn't know what he was talking about, but when the door swung open with the chime of a bell and a child appeared, I would have to urgently go to the toilet and leave Frankie to deal with them.

The days of those first few weeks were long and boring. I wondered if I was sickening for home, for Westport, until I realized it was the sea that I missed. I could neither hear it nor see it from my upstairs flat.

Harry, his friend Marcus and Marcus's girlfriend, Triona, drove over to see me on the first Thursday night and we all went to the Savoy to see *ET* again, and afterwards we went to Cafollas. I didn't want to say anything in front of the others about how miserable I was, and entertained them with stories of Theresa's eccentricities. It turned out that her quirks were well known throughout the county, if not the province. 'I thought Moira would have told you about her?' But Aunt Moira and Uncle Alan never spoke badly of anyone.

At the end of September the evenings were still bright, and I thought about cycling out to Cregannagh one evening on a bicycle I could borrow from Theresa, but the shop work seemed to exhaust me and Cregannagh just seemed too far. One evening, I decided to head out towards the sea in the other direction. I cycled out of town across the Moy River, past St Muredach's Cathedral and along the Quay Road, from where I could see the SS *Creteboom*, the concrete husk of a ship that had been abandoned in the harbour since 1937, never used. Two miles later, I could feel the Atlantic air, and drank the sea into my bones. I was wiped out after that, so most evenings I read books in bed about posh people behaving badly and daydreamed about what my life could have been like as a doctor in Dublin or some other exotic part of the world. The effort of frying a chop and boiling some onions almost didn't seem worth it, and yet I was permanently hungry. For the sea, I thought.

It was only when the nausea became overwhelming in the middle of a busy Saturday at the end of the third week in October that I first realized it was not the smell of shoe leather that was making me sick, it was not the workload that had me exhausted, and I wasn't pining for the sea. I didn't need a doctor to confirm my suspicions. A quick calculation in my head was all I needed, and when the truth dawned on me, I was in a state of horror. I was nine weeks already. In school, the nuns had warned us that you could get pregnant the first time you had sex, but nuns told us all kinds of things that we suspected were not true. They told us that you could die of contraception, that unmarried girls who had sex would go to hell, that no man would marry a girl who wasn't a virgin. Where sex was concerned, the nuns had told us everything but the truth. Or so I had thought. But I was pregnant, after my first time.

There was nobody I could tell. Peter was back in London. I thought of writing to him, but what would be the point? I knew Harry was still a virgin. Aunt Moira and Uncle Alan would be appalled, and I would certainly lose my job if Theresa was to discover that her unmarried employee was pregnant.

I tried punching myself in the stomach. I bought a bottle of gin and boiled kettles. I sat in the bath, drinking gin until I passed out, only coming to when my head slipped below the water. The baby clung on to my insides like a parasite.

9

I was becoming desperate. The only idea I could think of to manage the situation was to sleep with Harry and then somehow pretend that the resulting baby was premature. I would still lose my job, but Harry would stand by me. Harry would marry me in a heartbeat. He would never suspect that he wasn't the father, and Peter would keep his mouth shut. I was sure of it. In my panic, I never thought of the long-term consequences of such a plan, but I knew that having a father for your baby had less dire consequences than not.

A week later, Frankie and Theresa noted my pallor and my exhaustion. Theresa said she'd been sold a pup. 'Moira told me you were a robust girl, that you'd be driven and energetic, but here you are all the time looking like you could be knocked over by a feather. What is wrong with you at all?'

I resisted her attempt to make me see her doctor, and tried to keep my nausea under control. The nylon smock coat that had been issued as the shop uniform belonged to my predecessor, who was considerably bigger than me, so thankfully it would cover the swelling I could begin to feel in my stomach.

When I went home on the bus to Westport that Halloween bank holiday weekend, Harry met me at the bus stop and I asked him if we could go for a cycle out the road. It was late already, nearly seven o'clock and duskening, but I got on his crossbar and we cycled out towards Murrisk. When we got to the tiny, broken-down, roofless abbey, I asked him to stop and follow me inside. I laid my coat down on the gravel.

'What are you doing?' he said.

'It's time. I'm ready.'

Time was running out for me, though there was no way I could tell him that. He was delighted that I was so keen. But he was clearly more religious than I had thought.

'Here? Jesus, Delia, we're in a *church*.'

'I know!' The sheer scandal of it excited me.

'You should have warned me, I'd have arranged something. There isn't even a roof on this place!'

'I feel it, Harry. It's now or never!'

He was nervous and I became impatient then. I just wanted to get this over and done with.

He fumbled with his belt as I took off my tights and I could feel his eyes on me. The rise in my belly was still slight and he had not seen me fully naked before, so I didn't care what he made of my body. I lay down on the coat and told him to lie on top of me.

'Can I not look at you first?' he said, rubbing himself.

I laughed. 'It's cold. I need you to warm me up.'

He climbed on top of me and it was awkward and uncomfortable and freezing cold and I could feel the damp seep through my coat. I took him in my hand as Peter had shown me, and then guided him inside me, but he softened immediately and withdrew.

'What's wrong?'

'I don't . . . I'm sorry . . . I just . . . it doesn't feel right. It's too cold. Look, you're shaking!'

I could feel his blushes.

I tried coaxing him, using my hands again, but he pushed me roughly away.

'What are you doing?' he said.

'I thought you'd like it.'

'Stop . . . just stop!' He stood up awkwardly and pulled his trousers up from his ankles.

'I thought you wanted to!' I was furious now. 'You've been at me for a year, pawing me every chance you get like a lecherous pervert, and now you're suddenly too shy?'

He spoke quietly. 'I wanted it to be special; I wanted it to be romantic, not like two pigs rutting in the mud. This is not how I imagined it.'

I was pulling my clothes back on and seething with anger. I walked out through the gate past him and towards town. He followed, scurrying after me, and then dashed back to get his bike. He cycled alongside me, apologizing all the way.

'I'm sorry! Look, you took me by surprise, that's all. I mean, I wasn't expecting it, like. I played a match today. I'm a bit wrecked, that's all. We can sort something out in the hotel next weekend, I promise.'

Slightly mollified, I allowed him to give me a lift back into town on his crossbar. When I dismounted the bike, he called after me, 'We won the match, by the way!' I didn't turn back. I told Aunt Moira and Uncle Alan I'd been splashed by a passing bus and went upstairs to shower and change into a jumper and a skirt that was getting a little too tight. Aunt Moira commented that it was nice to see that I was finally putting on a bit of weight, because I'd always been so thin. She said that hard work must have given me an appetite.

Having sex with Harry was now urgent. The next day, on the way home from Mass, I told Harry that he should come to Ballina and visit me in the flat above the shoe shop during the week. He knew full well what I was implying. Theresa had told me in no uncertain terms that I wasn't allowed to have 'gentlemen callers' to my flat, as if it were the 1950s.

'It would be fine if you had a sitting room up there, but

that bed is asking for trouble,' she had said on my first night. Aunt Moira had told her about Harry and they had met once at Aunt Moira's birthday tea. But after five o'clock every evening Theresa and Frankie went home, and I had the key to the front door.

On the next Wednesday evening, Harry arrived at seven o'clock as instructed and parked his father's car two streets away so as not to attract any attention to the shop. I hurried him along in the doorway, and nearly gagged at the intoxicating fumes of his aftershave. Any strong smell was making me nauseous these days. Harry was well prepared this time. He was clean-shaven and had had his hair cut. He had also brought a bunch of flowers and a picnic of sorts: four pint bottles of Guinness 'to relax us', he said, and six ham sandwiches.

'I was worried, you know, that I'd ruined things between us, I mean you know that I've wanted to, it's just that in that wet abbey, in the cold . . .' I let him gabble on nervously as I led him up the back stairs, around the stacks of shoeboxes that covered every available surface, including the cistern of the toilet. He laughed when he saw my room with its narrow bed. 'Well, it's not much better than the abbey, but it'll do surely.' He snapped open two bottles of Guinness with a bottle opener from his pocket and handed one to me. I gulped it down, ignoring the bitter taste, anxiety prickling the back of my neck. I was starving all the time, but the eating of sandwiches would delay matters.

'Are you not hungry?'

Rather than answer, I kissed him. He put his own uneaten sandwich aside and lay back on the bed. I lay on top of him, kissing earnestly, trying to make myself small and appealing in his bear-like arms. He unbuttoned my blouse and pulled it back from my shoulders. My Playtex bra was relatively new.

He stroked the line from my neck downwards and lifted my breasts free of the cups.

'Oh God, we're really going to do it,' he said.

'Yes,' I whispered, and kissed behind his ear.

There was a sudden frenzy then as he got naked and climbed on to the bed beside me. I took off my remaining clothes as best I could without his hands leaving my body. I let him take the lead this time. His breathing became shallower as he guided my hands downwards and I began to manipulate him. Within a few minutes, he stopped me and reached out of bed to lift a small package from the trousers he had dumped on the floor.

'What are you doing?'

'I went into Galway yesterday. There's a barber there I'd heard about.' He produced a slim, foil-wrapped condom. I had only seen one once before, in my second encounter with Peter.

'No,' I said, 'please don't use that.'

'What? Come on, we can't take any chances.' He was unrolling it as I spoke.

'It won't be the same.'

'The same as what?' he said, laughing.

'The nuns told us we could catch cancer from them.' They had said this, though nobody believed it.

'Sure that's only something they say, to scare girls and to force wives to have babies they don't want.'

I could not persuade Harry to dispense with the condom, and while our love-making was more gentle and considerate than I had experienced with Peter, all I felt was despair. As he exploded inside the condom, inside me, he buried his face into my hair.

'I love you, you know!' he said breathlessly.

I could not stop a tear trickling down the side of my face and he felt the wetness on his skin.

'Oh God, I didn't hurt you, did I?'

'No.'

What could I say?

He sat up and snapped the condom off, demonstrated to me how you could check to make sure it hadn't split. 'I had to have a bit of practice on my own, you know?' He was sheepish. 'The last thing we want is an accident, right?' He brushed the tears from my face and kissed it. 'I know it's emotional for women, to lose their virginity. I've heard that before.'

I wondered where he had heard this.

He held my head to his broad chest. 'You know that I want to marry you? In a few years, like. You know that, right? And what we've done . . . it doesn't change anything for me. Like, I know a lot of lads don't respect girls after . . . you know, but I love you more, if anything.' Harry had never told me he loved me before, but now there was a creeping desperation to his declaration.

'I love you too,' I said, and I supposed it to be true. I certainly liked him better than anyone else.

'You and me,' he said, 'we're for ever.' He circled his thumb and forefinger and mimed slipping a ring on my finger. 'For ever, yes?'

'Yes,' I said. I took courage from the fact that he did want to marry me. My future was secure. I had to make him sleep with me without a condom or fabricate some kind of 'accident', and soon.

He wolfed into the sandwiches then and I joined him. I let him have my second bottle of beer. Harry was in great form, talking about the future. He said that at some stage he would inherit the hotel and run it in his father's place. Peter had told him that he was never coming back to live in Westport. Peter was interested in financial analysis and bonds, and there was no call for his skills in Westport. I began to feel more confident. I would be a hotelier's wife, and Peter would only come back on occasional holidays with his wife. Their children and our children would be cousins, and nobody ever had to know the truth.

After midnight, I crept down the stairs with Harry. We kissed passionately in the narrow hallway and agreed that we'd do it again in his parents' house on Saturday, as they were going to a wedding in Castlebar. I would handle the condom next time, stick a pin in it and point out the leak.

As I opened the street door, the shop manager, Frankie, passed with another man and stopped short when he saw Harry exiting and me standing behind the door in my slip. Harry, a little merry, ran off in the opposite direction, and never noticed Frankie standing stock-still, staring at me. I slammed the door in his face. I convinced myself that Frankie would never tell. Sure, he was uptight and religious, but he wouldn't tell, would he? Someone like him?

At work the next morning, Frankie asked Theresa to keep the closed sign on the door of the shop. There was something he needed to discuss with her, about me, he said. He was bright red in the face. Theresa asked him if he was feeling well.

'I didn't want to be the one to tell you, but if I know, you can be sure that there'll be others –'

I tried to stop him. 'Please, Frankie, don't . . .'

Theresa sat up straighter in her chair. 'What in the name of heaven is going on?'

'She's been having a man visiting her. At night,' said Frankie, as if it were a regular occurrence.

'That's not true.'

'I saw him leaving last night. I wouldn't want a scandal.'

Theresa clutched her hands to her head. 'Oh Lord. It's what I was afraid of! What were you thinking?'

'My boyfriend visited yesterday evening –'

'She said goodbye to him in her underwear, at the street door. Anybody could have seen.' Frankie had turned out to be a treacherous little sneak.

Theresa blanched white and grabbed the crucifix at her neck. She stood up unsteadily, in one white plimsoll and one school brogue. It was the first and only time I heard her raise her voice. 'There will be no fornication under my roof! Do you have no regard for your position, for yourself? Defying God's wishes like a savage? This is a decent premises!'

'It is. Very respectable,' Frankie agreed earnestly.

'I'm sorry,' I said, beginning to cry, though at the back of my mind, part of me thought that this exposure was good for my story. It was Harry that Frankie had seen. When my pregnancy was discovered, nobody would suspect anyone else. All I had to do was keep the news of my pregnancy to myself until after my next encounter with Harry.

'Go to your room and pack your bags. I am going to St Muredach's. I'll have to talk to Father McDaid. Do not set foot downstairs until I return.' She changed into her good shoes and left the shop, slamming the glass door behind her.

'Why did you tell her?'

'It's my moral duty. Besides, I don't want you here. I've been working here nearly twenty years and I don't want some interloping relative taking over this place.'

I didn't see the point in telling him that I was not a relative at all.

'What were *you* doing last night, Frankie, out on the town, after midnight? Who was the man *you* were with?'

Frankie let his eyes glaze over. 'I have no idea what you are talking about. Go upstairs, like Theresa said.'

He knew exactly what I was talking about. By then, I had guessed that he was gay. Theresa and Aunt Moira talked fondly of Frankie's 'little ways' and his bow ties. They found his manner amusing but they didn't want to see it for what it was. No straight man in Mayo was as well groomed as Frankie.

I went upstairs and packed my suitcase. I would be on the next bus back to Westport. I wasn't going to miss this place. But I would have to face the music with Uncle Alan and Aunt Moira. I knew they would be disappointed initially, but everything would work out for the best. I put my hand on my stomach, as I felt it gurgling, and noted again the slight swell of my abdomen. I was nearly three months pregnant now. I thought about the baby for the first time. The thought of being responsible for a tiny human filled me with dread, but surely, once I'd had unprotected sex with Harry, every-thing would fall into place. After we got married, I'd probably move into his house, and no doubt the Russells' housekeeper and Mrs Russell would look after the baby too.

As I gathered my few things, I began to feel unwell. My head throbbed and my stomach lurched. My forehead was clammy and hot to touch.

Theresa returned with a one-way bus ticket for me. In my presence, she stripped the bed linen and doused the room in holy water. I stood in the corner of the room, trying to keep the nausea at bay.

'As a gesture of goodwill,' she said, 'I will leave you to explain to Alan and Moira why you have returned and I will not blacken your name in the town. I will even make sure that Frankie keeps his mouth shut. But may God have mercy on your soul and . . .' Her words drifted further and further away as I tried to remain upright.

I don't remember what happened next. I have a vague rec-ollection of Frankie carrying me down the stairs, and then I was lying on the back seat of a car, vomiting, while blood ran down my leg. Later, I knew I was in Castlebar hospital but I was too sick to care who found out what. A night passed. Theresa was sitting by my bed, sponging my forehead, and gradually I began to feel better. A doctor came and drew the curtains around my bed and stood behind Theresa. The news was not the news I'd hoped for.

'The baby is safe,' he said, embarrassed, as Theresa blessed herself and shook her head at me. The doctor continued: 'It's not uncommon, you know, to have a bleed towards the end of the first trimester, particularly when you have a urinary tract infection. Make sure to drink plenty of fluids to flush out the infection. Try to avoid any heavy lifting for a week or so and you will be right as rain.'

I wondered whatever had happened to confidentiality and the Hippocratic oath. It turned out that Theresa had not known I'd turned eighteen in August, and presented herself to the doctor as my guardian as they thought I was legally a minor. It was all a mess now. The timing of everything was wrong. Theresa knew, because of what the doctor had said, that I was three months pregnant. If that news got out, Harry would know that he was not the father. It was already going to be quite a challenge to persuade him that his baby was twelve weeks premature, and then only if we had unprotected sex that week. I must have been crazy to think I could fool everyone. But I had to try.

The next day, Theresa came to the hospital again. She had prepared a speech this time. 'Moira and Alan are coming to collect you this afternoon. They will be so ashamed. I was against this whole fostering business in the first place. I told them too. "You don't know what you're getting, you need to know the seed and breed of them, islanders are oddballs," I said, but then you came along with your pretty face and the two of them were enchanted. I could smell trouble though, when I heard you were turning down the job with me to become a doctor, and then I said nothing when that turned out to be some misguided fantasy. I should have guessed though, the rings under your eyes and the sluggishness. I should have spotted it. You are a disgrace to yourself and to my cousin, who was kind enough to take you in.'

Even in my weakened state, I wasn't going to be lectured by such a zealous old trout.

'If you must know, I am engaged to Harry and we are going to run Carrowbeg Manor together, when he inherits it.' That had been Harry's plan.

'Do you think so? We'll see about that. That is highly unlikely now, you stupid little fool. There are places for girls like you, and I am going to strongly suggest that Moira sends you to one of them until that poor unfortunate child is born. And then they can find it a home with good married parents. Your young man's family aren't going to want the shame either, and if I were you I wouldn't tell him, or them. Go away until the child is born and keep your mouth shut.'

It had never occurred to me that I could be sent away. Theresa left shortly afterwards and the doctor discharged me with a prescription for antibiotics. Theresa had finished packing my suitcase, and brought it with her to the hospital. I suppose I should be grateful that she paid the forty pounds that was owing to me and thanked me for my work. I sat in a corridor and waited. Theresa was wrong. Aunt Moira and Uncle Alan adored me. I could do no wrong in their eyes. No matter what happened, they would look after me.

Before long, Aunt Moira and Uncle Alan's ancient car rattled into the car park and a wave of relief and gratitude washed over me. I ran out to greet them, but instead of being welcomed into Aunt Moira's open arms, neither of them would look at me. Uncle Alan's eyes were red-rimmed.

'You've led us a merry dance,' he said. There was silence in the car most of the way home. They did not mention my pregnancy or Harry. I didn't say much either. I ate some buttered bread with tea and, exhausted from the exertions and the emotions of the day, I went to bed. Aunt Moira said they'd talk to me in the morning. They were obviously furious, but I knew they would get over it.

There was a sail-maker called Cormac. He lived in ancient times when there would have been at least a thousand people living on our island. Daddy said Cormac was a very popular fella, known for his entertaining gossip and wild stories about fairies pulling the hair out of his head, or a talking fish he'd caught.

Nobody minded Cormac's tales, because weren't they only stories that never harmed anyone? The winters were long and cruel and often the islanders would be bored and restless and looking for a diversion and Cormac could always be relied upon to tell a tale with a bit of colour to it. Cormac loved the attention and his stories began to grow rougher. When a sheep went missing, Cormac would say he'd seen who had taken it, and point the finger at some poor divil, who was taken away, tied up and stoned by the villagers, all the while protesting his innocence.

The islanders got great sport out of this because there was nothing they liked more than the excitement of pegging stones at bandits and robbers. And people probably knew the stories weren't true, but they didn't care until Cormac's finger pointed at them.

On the night of a full moon, the tide finally turned against him. Cormac was saying savage things about a woman who'd put a curse on her sick husband. Cormac said he'd seen her whispering the curse to the stars, and the islanders brought her down to the harbour and tied her to the sea wall when the tide was coming in. She would have drowned only that her husband rose from his sickbed and crawled on his hands and knees over the rough stones to beg for her mercy. The islanders relented when they saw the real love between the woman and her husband as they were reunited. They clung to each other, both half-dead.

The islanders began to regret their vengeful ways, but they needed one last spectacle. So they rounded on Cormac and marched him up to the cliff and forced him to walk off it on to the rocks and raging seas below. Daddy said there were no rough lies ever told on the island after that. 'A lie is a dangerous thing,' Daddy said.

10

The next day, a Sunday, I slept late, and opened the curtains to see Harry sitting on the wall outside. He waved and gave me a thumbs up. I raced downstairs and burst into the kitchen.

'You didn't tell Harry, did you? He's outside. What did you tell him?' I asked.

'We have to sort this out,' said Uncle Alan.

My heart dropped. I had wanted to be the one to tell Harry, and I had thought there would still be time to sleep with him and make him believe the baby was his.

'You told him! Does he know how pregnant I am?'

Uncle Alan and Aunt Moira exchanged a look and didn't reply. Uncle Alan went to the door and let him in.

Harry came down the hall and took my hand. 'There you are, thank God, are you OK? Did the doctor tell them it was a mistake? What kind of eejits are they in that hospital? It's ridiculous.'

'Come in, Harry, we have to talk to you.' Aunt Moira was gruff.

Harry squeezed my hand. 'Don't worry,' he whispered, 'it'll blow over. It's a storm in a teacup.'

When we got inside, Uncle Alan coldly informed us that Harry's parents were on their way.

'Ah Mr Walsh, there's no need to involve my parents . . .'

Uncle Alan ignored him and went into the kitchen and closed the door. Harry turned to me with what he thought were soothing whispered words.

'God, I don't know why they're making such a big deal. We'll look back at this and laugh one day. You're not pregnant. You couldn't be, it's all a stupid mistake!' He was so certain of my fidelity, and of my innocence.

Aunt Moira suggested that we go into the sitting room and wait for Harry's parents. It was freezing in there because it was a room rarely used except for when we had visitors. Harry attempted to embrace me, but Aunt Moira said sharply, 'Don't touch her.'

Harry was irritated. 'You're all scaremongering here. Why don't you ask Delia what she has to say for herself?'

'There is no point in continuing to lie about it, Harry,' said Aunt Moira.

Harry grabbed my hand. 'It was one time,' he said defiantly, and I could see how brave he was, 'just last week, and we were careful. I persuaded her,' he lied. 'There's no need to treat her like some kind of slut.'

'Then why is she three months pregnant?' asked Aunt Moira at the same time as the doorbell rang. She got up to answer it and I heard Uncle Alan coming out of the kitchen.

Harry looked at me. 'You're not . . .'

'I . . . I am,' I said, the first words I had been able to utter to him. He let go of my hand then and walked to the window and stood with his back to me. But I could see his face reflected in the dim winter morning light, and there was nothing there but confusion. He did not ask me anything, but his hands gripped the window ledge. I did not know what to say, so said nothing.

Harry's mum and dad entered the room. The air crackled with tension and hostility.

Mrs Russell was annoyed about being summoned. 'We're going to Mass at twelve, so I hope this isn't going to take long.'

Mr Russell knew, I think, that something serious had happened. 'Hush now, Elizabeth, let's find out what is going on. Harry?'

Harry stayed exactly where he was, facing the window. I felt absolutely wretched. I wanted to run away as far as I could and never see any of these people ever again, but Aunt Moira was standing between me and the door.

Aunt Moira offered to make tea, but nobody was in the mood for niceties. Uncle Alan cleared his throat then and glared at Mr Russell. 'It turns out that Delia is over three months pregnant.'

Harry's father whipped around at me. 'What? In the name of God, how could she be so stupid!'

Uncle Alan was immediately livid at him. 'Well, she didn't get pregnant on her own!'

'Harry!'

Everyone else was staring at Harry. Uncle Alan said, 'What have you to say, young man?'

He turned slowly to face us. 'I'm not the father.'

A kind of a mist washed over me then, and it seemed like I separated myself from my body and flew under the door and across the quay, out past Clew Bay, and maybe for a moment or two I was a seagull, wheeling around in the air, weightless, dependent on the elements as I glided between the islands and made for Inishcrann, but the noise brought me back. Uncle Alan had punched Harry. Mrs Russell was screaming and Aunt Moira was crying. Harry's Dad was shouting and holding Uncle Alan by the throat. Harry was slumped in the corner, nursing the side of his jaw, staring straight at me.

'Tell them,' he said, 'tell them it wasn't me.'

I had never seen his eyes as lifeless and cold. And now, everybody turned to look at me. 'It wasn't Harry,' I said.

Harry looked up and with a glimmer of desperation and shame asked, 'Were you raped? Is that it? Did some bastard attack you?'

It would have been so easy to say yes. Possibly everything could have been resolved. I was good at lying. Why couldn't I lie at this crucial moment? Probably because I didn't want to be the victim. Instead I shook my head. Aunt Moira let out a sob and buried her face in her hands. Harry stared at me and I knew that he was searching for the truth in my eyes. I knew that he was close to guessing it.

Mrs Russell stood up. 'How you bring up your own niece is no business of ours, Alan Walsh, but I will thank you to keep her away from my son in future.'

'She's not our niece. We adopted her.' Uncle Alan muttered the words.

'What?' Harry was so upset and confused. I had never told him the truth. He didn't even know my real surname.

'She's no relation at all. We took her in when she was ten years old after her family died in a fire. We did our best for her. We're as shocked as you are.'

Harry pushed back his forehead with the palm of his hand. 'You told me Alan was your father's cousin.'

I couldn't reply. There was no point in telling them it was what I'd been told to say.

'Who *is* the father of the baby, then?' asked Harry's mother.

All eyes turned to me again. I couldn't say the name. I simply couldn't say it.

'Peter!' Harry spat his brother's name in a growl, and I closed my eyes.

It was as if the air had been sucked out of the room, and again I was floating above and beyond the house while chaos reigned in the real world. I know that Harry left, followed by his mother, slamming both doors behind them. Moira also left the room, in convulsions of tears.

I was sent to my room while the arguing continued behind the sitting-room door, but instead I went up and collected the still-packed suitcase and then crept quietly down the stairs and out the front door.

Three hours later, I stepped off the bus and into the past. I hadn't been in Cregannagh village since the day I'd been shipped off to the orphanage in Galway. I looked up the street to where the Millers' house stood. I wondered if Clara was Dr Clara now, and the old envy crept into my bones again. My nerves were jangling, and I felt weak and tired. I composed myself, assured myself that I didn't need looking after. That I'd soon be meeting my kith, if not my kin. I walked down to the harbour wall.

11

Owen the ferryman did not recognize me as I boarded. I was the only passenger. It was not a good sign for the island. When I was a child, the ferry always carried at least two or three tourists along with the cargo necessary for island life. The rumour had always been that Mayo County Council was angling to get the less populated islands evacuated. They cost too much in subsidies to run, and they were largely lawless with no police presence and one doctor between four islands fifty miles apart from each other, and inaccessible for large parts of the winter. Councillors would show up from time to time with bribes to entice us to the mainland. I remembered the fuss on Inishcrann when threats were made that the primary school was unsustainable. As it was, the secondary students all went to the mainland at the age of twelve, only returning to the island for holidays. Most stayed away after they finished school. The island population was dying off. Any whiff of discord or scandal on the islands gave the council ammunition against us. On Inishcor, twenty years previously, a man had died of appendicitis because the sea was too rough and the ferry couldn't take him to the mainland for surgery. His death was the end for that island. The eighteen remaining inhabitants were forcibly evicted.

I wasn't sure that I wanted to be recognized. I pulled the hood of my anorak up to protect me from the biting wind. I could feel the temperature drop as the island came into sight, and I wasn't sure if I was imagining it, but as we approached I looked at the long stone at the crown of the hill where the mythical oak tree had been, and in that peculiar half-light, with the low sun shining on it, it seemed to grow branches. Daddy's old stories were always vivid in my mind.

We closed in on the quay. I saw a few figures on the wall, but they were all covered up in coats and anoraks, and I could not make out any face I knew. I took my suitcase and walked up the gangway, and as Owen took my hand he looked at my face for the first time, and immediately whitened. He dropped my hand as if it burned him, and I stumbled as I put my foot on to the quay, crashing the sharp edge of my suitcase against my shin. I looked back at him but he turned away. He recognized me. But why that reaction?

I walked along the narrow path leading past the small scatter of buildings, among which sat Biddy Farrelly's pub. I wondered if she was still alive. I recalled Tom the Crow saying he would never leave the island while his mother was alive. After ten minutes, I stashed my suitcase under the plastic lid of the old well where I used to hide schoolbooks to drive Spots McGrath wild. I struck out for the western side of the island along the path that I remembered as well as if it had been printed on my skin. I passed some English hikers on the way. They stopped, wanting to engage me in conversation. 'There's bugger all out there, love,' one of them said, indicating over his shoulder. I ignored them and walked on. The path was overgrown in places, and I chose a stick to beat back brambles where it narrowed. I dodged along walls and into fields, my homing instinct never wavering until I reached the end of the island. There, under a glowering sky as wide as beyond imagining, nestled among steel-grey rock and tufts of colour-drained reeds, stood the back wall of my house.

I ran now, as the path opened out, because there was nothing to impede me. Nothing grew here. It was stunningly beautiful in its barren way. No picture I'd seen in a book or on the television could match this. I filled up my soul with this view and felt hopeful and happy. As I got closer to the house, I stopped dead in my tracks. Half of it was missing. Of course, I knew about the fire, but I didn't think fire could destroy stone. I was not deluded, I had not come back to live in this house. I knew that it would be destroyed inside, but I'd thought the structure at least would be intact. With no timber to hold the place together, it had naturally collapsed upon itself. I picked my way through the broken doorway into what used to be our home and half of the dresser was still there, blackened, and a few springs from a mattress. There were pieces of fabric snagged on stones, and under the scorch marks I recognized the sunny yellow curtains my mother had made. I could see the colour vividly, though it was not there. There was nothing of my father or my brothers, nothing to say they had ever existed.

I had forgotten the depth of the cold. After half an hour in that most desolate of places, my bones were shaking and my teeth were chattering. It was early November.

I tramped back the way I had come. As I neared the harbour again, I thought about my plans, or lack of them. I was sure I'd get used to the cold again, but the life, the life here was lonely. The population of the island was less than seventy when I'd left eight years ago, surely less now, and in winter there were very few tourists.

I wondered if any of the children I had known at McGrath's school had come back to the island. Danny, Fergal and Malachy had been older than me and would have left the school in Cregannagh years before. But this was my natural community. I was old enough now to have lost my childlike notion of being their queen, but surely someone would take me in and teach me how to be something. The population was ageing so much that someone must want a strong, young girl, especially one that would give the island new life. I hoped Mary Scurvy would remember me. She could give me a job in her guest house in the summer, now that I had experience in the hotel, and maybe Tom the Crow would let me mend nets for him since I used to help Daddy with that, or if Biddy Farrelly was still alive, wouldn't she need someone to run the bar and grocery for her? Wasn't there an Italian woman who'd set up a pottery? Harry's mother had pointed out an article about her to me in the *Mayo News*. There was bound to be a role for me here.

I pushed open the door of the bar and walked in. I was, of course, a lot taller than the nine-year-old who had last entered these premises for a Sunday orange squash with my daddy, while he sipped his pint of stout, but it seemed so small to me now. The bar can't have been more than six feet from the door. The same four stools lined the bar and Duggan was sitting on one of them, the same as I recalled from eight years ago, his head hanging below his shoulders. The English hikers I had passed earlier sat on the bench seat at the only table. They looked up briefly mid-conversation but didn't interrupt their flow. 'I said to John, didn't I, John? I said it's the coldest place I've ever been in my life. Didn't I say that, John?'

John skulled his pint and ignored his wife.

'That's the best Guinness I've ever had. Another one, Nige?'

Nige nodded and checked his watch. 'What time did you say the ferry was?'

There was nobody behind the bar, and I waited because I remembered that even though the bell was there for service, Biddy Farrelly took an automatic dislike to anyone that used it, though she made an exception for tourists. She put great store in the virtue of patience. John got up and rang the bell, and by the sound of the shuffle from the room beyond, I knew Biddy Farrelly was still alive. She emerged then from the darkness, looking only slightly more wizened than I remembered. She did not look in my direction. I let John order his pints and sit down again, before I spoke to her.

'Biddy, it's me, Delia.' I smiled at her.

Her rheumy eyes opened a little wider momentarily. 'I know 'tis you. What do you want?'

I was taken aback by her lack of welcome. She had always been a stern woman, but kind too.

'I've come home,' I said, 'and I'll be looking for a place to li—' The words dried on my tongue as she turned her back to me and unnecessarily began to move bottles on the shelf behind her.

'I heard you have a suitcase with you. Well, you'll not be staying. You may leave the island this very day. You'll get no welcome here,' she said without turning around. I was astonished.

'What? But why?'

The English table had stopped talking and were agog.

'You may not have lit the flame, but you destroyed them all and nobody here will ever forget it.'

'What are you talking about?'

She spun around faster than her ancient bones should have allowed and spat words at me.

'Are you going to claim you were a child, that you didn't know what you were doing? There's innocent and there's guilty, and then there's malice. And there was always malice in you. Don't think we don't know it. We watched you from a baby. Now, get yourself out of my bar and down to the pier and wait for the four o'clock ferry.'

She slammed her hands down on the bar and tears came to my eyes.

'I don't understand? Biddy!'

She looked over to the English tourists. 'Get out!'

They meekly rose and left as obediently as children, John trying to force the pint down his gullet as he put his coat on. The door slammed behind them and swung open again like a carousel.

'Owen says she's back!' said the voice of Mary Scurvy before she saw me, and in the door behind her came Nora Duggan, the wife of the man passed out on the bar stool beside us. The two of them stared at me.

Mary spoke first. 'What are you doing back here, child?'

Nora said more gently, 'Hello, Delia. It's been a while. You're all grown up now, I see.'

I dug my fingers into the bar and ignored them. I addressed Biddy Farrelly. 'Why am I not welcome? This is my home.'

'After your father locked your mother and the boys into the house and set fire to it, he went outside and shot himself.'

I gasped in shock. 'What! . . . It was an *accident*, the fire was an accident!'

'Jesus, Biddy,' said Nora.

'Dr Miller told me they were all found dead in their beds, from the fumes, because of the thatch. He wouldn't have lied . . .' I held on to the bar as I felt the impact of her words roll over me like the waves I could hear beyond the loud buzzing in my head. I remembered the shotgun above the mantelpiece that we were not allowed to touch, though Daddy showed me how it worked when we'd go shooting rabbits.

'Stop!' said Mary Scurvy. 'She doesn't need to know any of this. Let her go back to the mainland and be done with us.'

Biddy Farrelly's mouth twisted in disgust. 'I'm only telling her so that she knows never to come back.'

Nora shook her head. 'Biddy, she was a child. She couldn't have known . . .'

Biddy Farrelly continued: 'My Tom told me. You poured poison in your father's ear about Loretta and my Tom. You told him they was up to no good. And my Tom would never have touched her –' She clamped her hand over her mouth.

'That's enough!' said Mary.

As I stood in Biddy Farrelly's bar, I felt the wash of the seawater outside in my body. Duggan stirred on his bar stool, and Mary lowered her voice so as not to wake him.

'I think it's best for everyone if you get on the ferry and never come back here. Enough lives have been destroyed. It's only the islanders that know the truth. The police were kept out of it. There was a storm that kept them away for three days. We were able to make it look like an accident. We don't need to give *them* another excuse to get us off the island.' *Them*. The authorities on the mainland who wanted to move everyone on shore.

'But I didn't know . . . I was a *child*. How could I know? And Mammy, and Tom . . . she was going to take us away, back to America –'

Biddy came out from behind the bar and pushed me roughly towards the door. I used the only weapon in my armoury.

'I'm pregnant,' I said. Everything went still for a moment. The women seemed dazzled by the statement.

'Are you?' said Mary, all the animosity vanished from her voice.

I did not have to answer as Nora pushed her hand to my belly. 'She is.'

'We need her,' said Mary.

I knew immediately what they meant. When I was a girl, a pregnant woman on the island was revered because her baby meant another student for the primary school, it meant an increase to the dwindling population. One woman whose drinking was believed to have caused her miscarriage was never forgiven, and eventually she drank herself to death. I remember her. I remember the celebrations when she announced her pregnancy. Nobody cared that the father was a tourist that we'd never see again. After the miscarriage, Daddy told me to turn away when she said hello on the road. I heard it was a week before they found her body. On this island, more so than the rest of the country, women were vessels. I would be valued here, I thought.

The three women eyed each other nervously, and for a moment nobody spoke at all.

Then Biddy said, 'It makes no difference. She can't stay.'

'But the boy –' said Mary, and Biddy slammed her fist on to the counter, startling us all. Nora glared Mary into silence.

'The father won't be with me,' I said. 'I'm here on my own. Just me and a baby. Isn't that what you need?' I pleaded with them. 'I have nowhere else to go.'

Biddy folded her arms. 'No.'

The other women looked at the floor. Biddy Farrelly still ruled the island.

I was reeling from the shock of the story about my father. I knew they wouldn't make up such a tale. I recalled what had happened leading up to the time I left the island. I had told my father that I'd seen Tom kissing Mammy. The truth was the other way around. It was unfair to blame me. And yet I knew well the ability of islanders to bear a grudge. Whatever they believed was set in stone and I would never be forgiven, not by that generation. I upended the table on which the tourists' glasses sat, and was satisfied as they smashed and splintered across the flagstone floor.

'Don't worry,' I said. 'I'm going.'

The women began to argue over the head of Duggan, who stirred and mumbled that he wanted another pint. I slammed the door and headed back to get my suitcase. As I passed the bar again on my way to the pier, I could see through the window that more islanders had gathered. I recognized the heads of Anthony and Breda, the parents of Malachy, and my old schoolmaster, Spots McGrath. They all stared as I passed, and not one gave a flicker of acknowledgement. No matter what happened back in Westport, I was going to be better off there than I was here.

As I approached the ferry, I could see a familiar figure standing beside Owen on the pier wall. Tom the Crow. I was sure he would understand.

'Tom!' I said. 'I've only just heard what happened the night of the fire. They're all blaming me –'

'Get on the ferry,' he said.

'Tom, come on, *you* can't seriously hold me responsible? I was nine years old. I had no notion –'

Tom pushed me roughly in the direction of the gangway and I stumbled, but Mary Scurvy had arrived behind me. 'Don't Tom, she's pregnant.'

I broke down. 'I'm sorry. I'm so sorry. I didn't want to go to America. I didn't want to be separated from Daddy.'

Tom did not look at me. 'You lied,' he said. 'Cast her off,' he called to Owen.

Owen unhooked the line from the mooring post and started the engine. The ferry wasn't supposed to leave for another hour, but my leaving of the island was clearly urgent to them. I sat in the hold, weeping, as Owen faced forward, never once looking back.

I could barely take in what I had learned. I remembered the rows between my parents, but I had never guessed the fire wasn't an accident. My father had murdered his whole family. All except me. Did he know what he was going to do when he sent me off on the ferry? It gave me some comfort to think that he chose to save me. He loved me the most.

12

When I returned to Westport late that night, neither Alan nor Moira asked where I'd been. Maybe they had hoped that I would solve their problem by running away. But now the problem was back under their roof and they would have to deal with it. From that time on, I never referred to them as my aunt and uncle. There was no further need for pretence. They must have noticed but they didn't comment on it.

It was left to the men, Alan Walsh and Declan Russell, two men in their sixth decade, to decide my fate while I sat passively the next morning, my mind churning with the facts I had learned on Inishcrann. My father had murdered my mother and my brothers and then shot himself. I recalled the excitement of his tempers and I knew in my heart that he was capable of it. These are the thoughts that were whizzing through my brain while people who were in no way related to me decided what was going to happen next.

Alan said to Mr Russell, 'Your family destroyed mine once before, but I'll not let it happen again – by God, I won't. You know what I'm talking about.'

Mr Russell tried to take control. 'You're talking nonsense as usual, Alan Walsh, and you need to let go of the past. It's all in your head. You have kept your distance from us for over thirty years, but then this' – he pointed at me – '*slattern* appeared. We weren't happy about it from the beginning. If we'd known she was a stray, we might not have welcomed her into our house, but we were led to believe that she was your *family*. Whatever you may think of us, we're not ones to hold a grudge —'

'You weren't the wronged party,' Alan growled at him.

I had no idea what they were talking about.

Mr Russell challenged Alan: 'Did I not see you punch my son in the jaw yesterday? I could have the guards up here if I wanted and you know it.'

Alan looked mutinous. 'I'm sorry. I punched the wrong son.'

Declan Russell pretended not to hear that. 'I'll have to ring Peter. For Christ's sake, keep this quiet until you decide what you're going to do with her.' He sat down heavily on the sofa, his legs spread wide. He was a man who was used to being in charge.

Alan was fuming, at me and at Harry's dad. He went to the drinks cupboard, which was rarely opened, and retrieved a bottle of whiskey, which I think had been there since the day I arrived. Alan was a teetotaller. He didn't offer a glass to Mr Russell but sat in the armchair and poured himself a large one. They both turned to stare at me, unsympathetic to my weeping.

'So were you playing the two brothers off each other? Are you mad or something?' Alan asked me.

I found my voice and addressed Harry's dad. 'It was in the summer, when I was working in your hotel, Mr Russell. Peter came to give me my Leaving Cert results and I was upset, and we —'

'Jesus Christ! I don't want any details. Was it only the one time?'

I looked to the floor.

Alan ran his hand through his thin grey hair.

Mr Russell spoke. 'Leave it be now, Alan. I'll talk to Peter. He'll tell the truth, one way or another. There's no point going on with this unless . . .' He turned to look at me. 'Were there others?'

'What . . . what do you mean?'

'Apparently, you slept with my two sons. What about their cousins, or their friends?'

'No!' I nearly shouted it, I was so horrified by the question.

'Well, you couldn't blame us for wondering.'

Mr Russell left and Alan told me to get out of his sight. I went to my room and lay on the bed, in fear for my future, listening to the sounds of Alan and Moira's distress downstairs. They were shouting, blaming each other. I had never heard either of them raise their voices before. Fighting over me. It shouldn't have been, but it was oddly exciting. Comforting, even. It reminded me of being a child again. On Inishcrann.

I was left alone in my room, and in the middle of the night I snuck quietly down the stairs to find some bread and cheese. I had not eaten properly in a few days and pregnancy made me hungry.

At the kitchen table I found Moira in her dressing gown, nursing a cup of tea. She didn't look at me and I ignored her as I found what I needed. When I had made a sandwich, I sat at the table opposite her. We could not avoid each other for ever.

'All we ever wanted was a baby, you know, but I couldn't have one, and so after years of disappointments we found you and adopted you. Do you have any idea how this makes me feel? How could you do it to us, child? How could you do it to yourself? And with the Russells, of all people!'

I was so sick of being judged and of their sanctimonious behaviour. Hypocritical too. They wanted a baby, and now I was having one. I could give it to them to raise. It was the obvious solution. I could guilt them into it.

'Alan told the Russells that I was adopted. I guess you never felt like I was yours. I know you'll want me to leave soon. Let me know when, so that I can begin to make plans.' I sounded braver than I felt.

'Plans? You must *know* what will happen to you now.' Her voice rose and wavered. 'Alan is heartbroken, as you might imagine. You might as well have kicked him in the head for the pain he's in. The Russells.'

'Why are you so . . . what is it about the Russells?'

She rose and retrieved the photograph of Alan's father from the mantelpiece. A shabby-looking man pushing a dustcart. She stabbed her finger at the picture. 'Alan's father was the Russells' gardener. They were the ones who took that photograph. There was a maid in their house at the time, a young girl, fifteen or sixteen. She was pregnant but nobody knew. She was found dead in a field after trying to give birth on her own. The baby died too. They fired Alan's father the next day, to give everyone the impression that he was the one who'd got her in the family way. The poor man never got a day's work after that. To his dying day, he said it was Declan Russell, Harry's dad, who got the girl pregnant. Declan was probably eighteen or nineteen at the time. Alan's father was a married man in his forties. Nobody could prove anything, but Alan's family was shamed afterwards.

'Alan was a young man at the time. His mother never came to terms with it all, but it seemed like she and Alan were the only ones in the town who believed his father. The Russells had lawyers from Galway threaten him to keep his mouth shut, saying he'd be sued. It was just one of those situations where nobody could prove anything, and the sacking of Alan's father was deliberate. He got the blame. He hadn't even known the girl's name until she was dead. His reputation was ruined. My family weren't snobs at all. They didn't care that Alan didn't have a university education or that his family didn't own a business, but they cared that he might be the son of a man who got that young girl pregnant. I fought them to marry him, but they never quite accepted him. Poor Alan.'

Layer upon layer of mistrust was rising to the surface all over again. Maybe Alan's father had got the girl pregnant. Maybe Mr Russell was completely innocent. People will lie about anything to get themselves out of trouble. I do.

'Alan didn't want you anywhere near the Russells, but I persuaded him to let the past be the past. He's angry with you now, and you can't blame him. You've lived in this house for eight years, and we did everything we could to make it your home and to make you part of our family, but always . . . always, there has been this . . . distance, like you don't want to get close. We kept telling ourselves that once you learned to trust us it would all come right, but you never wanted us as your family. Your attitude never changed. We felt it, but we accepted it, and loved you anyway. We still do, and when all this is settled we'll find our way again. But now we're tangled with the Russells in the worst way possible. What possessed you? The two brothers? Was it some kind of game?'

This is the point where I was supposed to break down and beg forgiveness and explain that I didn't know what I was doing and that I loved Moira and Alan with all my heart. Instead, I thought about Alan's pathetic family story and compared it to my own. His story was hardly a tragedy when you put it beside mine. I finished my sandwich in silence and went back to bed.

I got up early the next morning and slipped out of the house, as soon as I heard Alan go off on his postal round. I hadn't dared to ring the Russells' home, but I wanted to talk to Harry. I knew he loved me and I thought I might be able to talk him around, to convince him that we could still be a couple. I waited outside the hotel's side door for him to arrive. A few of my old pals greeted me on their way in. 'What are you doing back here? I thought you were off in Ballina? Couldn't keep away from Harry, eh?'

I nodded and smiled, relieved that word had not spread of my predicament and the scandal around it. I waited twenty minutes and then saw his father approach. Mr Russell grabbed me roughly by the arm and marched me into the hotel, past reception and into his office, smiling and waving hello at the girls as he went.

'Sit down,' he growled, as the door closed behind me.

I had never been in this office before. It was neat, a big mahogany desk with an old-fashioned lamp with a green glass shade perched on one corner, files of paperwork, a blotter and a container for pens and pencils and an inkwell.

'You don't want to have this baby, do you?'

I didn't see that I had any choice in the matter.

'It can be arranged. An abortion. I'd pay, of course, and it's expensive. You don't even have to pay me back. All over and done with, on one condition.'

He looked at me, waiting for me to ask what the condition was. I couldn't believe what he was suggesting. Two months previously, when I didn't know I was pregnant, nearly 70 per cent of the population had voted to keep abortion illegal in a referendum. I hadn't gone to the trouble of voting, even though I was old enough, because I never thought it was something that would affect me, but the anti-abortion campaign had been strong in Westport all summer long and there had been parades. Harry and I had marched together.

'Isn't that against the law?'

'Yes, in this country. But not in England. There is a clinic in Liverpool, like a hospital. All neat and clean. You could go over on the ferry, but you'd have to go this week.'

I thought of all the horrific stories I had heard about women dying in alleyways, having been dumped by abortionists. I thought about my own efforts with the gin and hot baths and my lack of guilt about it. Mr Russell clicked his fingers impatiently in front of my face.

'Or would you rather go to a mother and baby home, work like a dog in the convent laundry until they decide when to release you? Would you prefer that?'

'What did Peter say?'

'Never mind about Peter.' Obviously, Peter had admitted the truth. 'Never mind about Harry either. I don't want to hear my boys' names out of your mouth ever again. I am offering you a gift, an opportunity. You can start again, over there. In Liverpool.'

'What do you mean?'

'You go to Liverpool, have an abortion and never come back. That's the condition. I was given an address of a clinic that will do the procedure. Nobody will ever know. You just . . . disappear and send a nice letter back to your . . . to Alan and Moira, telling them that you're safe and that you've decided to make a new life for yourself. When the . . . baby would have been due, you can send them another letter, tell them you've had it adopted, and then you can do what you like, as long as you don't do it in Westport. Nobody will know, not my wife, my sons, your friends. It will be our secret, yours and mine.'

I eyeballed him. I was another of his dirty little secrets. He had used the services of an abortion clinic before. If I had had my doubts about Moira's story of him fathering the baby of the dead servant girl, I had no doubts now. None whatsoever. 'I suppose it's better than dying in a field giving birth.'

He reached across the table and struck me hard across the head. The shock was immediate.

'You can let me know your decision by tomorrow morning. Do not attempt to contact either of my sons. Now, get out.'

I stumbled out of the office, keeping my head down as the girls at reception called out teasingly, 'We'll tell Harry you were looking for him,' giggling among themselves. I mumbled a goodbye and made my way out of the front door.

The street was busy and I pulled the hood up on my anorak. I spied Harry across the road. He put his hand up in front of his face and turned away in a gesture that told me not to approach him. I had not intended to. Not yet. I had a decision to make.

When I got home, Moira wanted to know where I'd been. 'You can't keep running off. People will see you.' She insisted that I stay indoors until further notice. 'Anybody might guess at your situation if they looked closely enough,' she said, pointing at my belly. She had spent the morning on the phone to Theresa. They'd found a place for me in a home – a convent in Cork. I was to go the following weekend. 'Of course, you would have to work to earn your keep. And then, when the baby is born, it can be adopted . . .'

'Don't you want the baby?' I asked her.

'I'm fifty-six years old. It's too late for me to rear a baby. Anyway, the place you're going is fine. There will be lots of girls in your . . . situation, but I'd advise you to keep your distance. You'd only be a bad influence on each other . . .'

I stopped listening because I knew exactly what kind of place they were going to send me to and I knew I wasn't going there. I let her ramble on, let her think that I was in agreement, and then claimed exhaustion. 'I'm going upstairs to lie down,' I said.

She put her hand on my shoulder. 'We don't want to send you there, you know? But it's for the best. At least that way, you could get back to normal, get married one day, have a real family, not with Harry obviously or Peter, but you're a beautiful girl and there'll be some other lad . . .' She paused. 'There's been no word from the Russells. If Peter denied it, we'd have heard from them by now. I blame myself. Alan said we should keep a closer eye on you when you started going out with Harry, but I was so relieved that you were finally making friends. You were always by yourself before you met him. I don't know what to make of you.'

I trudged up the stairs and threw myself on the bed. Who did I want to be today? The girl who wasn't pregnant.

When Moira went to hang the washing on the line next morning, I rang Mr Russell in Carrowbeg Manor and agreed to his offer. He said he would arrange it for that Friday, two days away. He would drive me to Dublin himself, he said, 'to make sure you get on the ferry'. I dreaded a four-hour journey in a car with Harry's dad. The abortion would be easy in comparison.

'What will I do afterwards?'

'Do?' He sounded surprised. 'Get a cleaning job, or whatever a scrubber does.'

I ignored the insult. 'I'll need money, to get a flat, to keep me going until I find work.'

There was a long pause. 'You will have it. Be at the hotel at five on Friday morning. Don't be late.'

I resolved to steal every penny from Moira's purse before I left. I still had Theresa's pay-off of forty pounds. I would have to get a job straight away. I wasn't scared of the abortion. As far as I was concerned, it would be no worse than getting a rotten tooth removed. Uncomfortable, painful even, but it needed to be done. I had no religious hang-ups about it, despite my hypocritical marching for the anti-abortion campaign. It was just something everyone had taken part in. Even after years of weekly Mass, I never believed in a God that would take my father away and abandon me, and I certainly didn't believe in one that would let Daddy shoot himself.

I needed the abortion. Then, regardless of what Declan Russell said, I would come back and try to make things right with Harry. I still wanted to be the hotelier's wife. It would be harder now than ever before because Harry would have to fight his parents, particularly his father, but the love he had for me couldn't disappear overnight. I had hurt him, but he would get over that. Nobody knew but our close family circles, and that helped. We would move on, and in a few years it would all be forgotten.

Alan couldn't stay angry with me for long. He didn't know what Moira had told me about his family's relationship with the Russells, but within days his shame of me turned into fury towards them.

'Well, girl, you've got yourself into a pickle and no mistake, but I should have put a stop to it from the start. The Russells are bloody hypocrites, sitting up at the top of the church every Sunday, looking down their noses at the rest of us. Those boys persuaded you into it. I know what they're like. They're bad stock.'

'And me? Am I bad stock?'

'I'm sorry I said those things about you. You are part of this family and you always will be. We never found out much about your . . . parents, just that they were islanders and we heard they were . . . old-fashioned, traditional, you know? You never talk about them.'

'I don't need to. I remember them. You never knew them, so there'd be no point in talking to you about them.' I knew more now than I wanted to know. But I refused to think about that. It wasn't my fault.

On Thursday evening, I took two phone calls. Moira answered the first one. My old school friend, Gemma. Moira handed me the phone and gestured a finger to her lips.

'Hiya,' Gemma said. 'I heard you were back, are you not working in Ballina any more? Why didn't you ring me?'

'I thought you'd be in college,' I lied, knowing already that she was home on a break, because Moira had seen her down the town that morning. 'Oh, yeah, the job didn't work out, but' – I was conscious that Moira was standing at the kitchen door – 'I'm starting a new job in Cork at the weekend.'

There was a pause on the other end of the phone.

'Oh yeah, doing what? Will I call over to you?'

'No, we've visitors at the minute. I'll ring you tomorrow?'

'Is it true?'

Oh God.

'Is what true?'

'You're pregnant. Don't worry, I won't tell anyone.'

I attempted a laugh. 'No! Where in the name of God did you hear that?'

'My mum plays bridge with Elizabeth Russell's brother, Harry's uncle?'

'That's total nonsense!'

'So you're still going out with Harry then, and everything's fine?'

'Yeah, though I'll be in Cork for the next while.'

'Nine months, you mean?' She didn't believe me, but she had the maths wrong.

'What?'

'I'll call around tomorrow, around lunchtime, OK?'

'Sure.' I knew I wouldn't be there. I pretended that Moira was calling me away in order to shut down the conversation, and hung up.

Moira stepped out of the kitchen. 'Does she know?'

'Yes.'

I answered the phone the second time it rang.

'Delia?'

'Yes?' There was a slight crackle on the line. It was a second or two before I realized it was Peter, calling from London.

'I . . . I'm really sorry, OK? I'm sorry.'

'We were stupid.'

'We should have been . . . look, it's not the end of the world. Are they sending you to –'

I hung up. He didn't ring back.

That night, I quietly packed my bags. Alan always went to bed early because he was up at six for work, so I waited for Moira to go to bed and then opened the window wide so that the cold would keep me awake for a few hours. I couldn't risk using my alarm clock and rousing the house. At a quarter to five, I crept downstairs with my suitcase and extracted fifteen pounds from Moira's handbag. I went to Alan's coat in the hall and took the wallet out of his pocket. Another ten pounds. When I was returning the wallet, I heard a creak on the stairs behind me. I whirled around to be confronted by Alan in his pyjamas.

'Where are you going, girl?' He pointed to the suitcase. 'Running away? My ten pounds isn't going to get you far.' He shuffled into the kitchen. 'I'll put the kettle on.'

I heard him turn on the tap and run the water for a moment. I picked up the case and walked out of the front door, pulling it softly behind me. Once outside, I began to run, though it must have been the pregnancy that made me nauseous, and I had to stop after a few minutes to catch my breath. I looked behind me and through the darkness, I could see a shape about a hundred yards behind me and I knew it was Alan and I thought that running would not be good for his chest. But I kept going, fast and determined. When I got to the hotel there was no sign of Mr Russell, but then I heard an engine idling and saw his car in the laneway beside the hotel. He waved at me furiously, and I ran over and opened the passenger door.

'You didn't think we'd meet on the street, did you?' he said by way of greeting. He barely waited for me to close the door before he rolled the car out on to the street. We turned the corner before Alan appeared in the middle of the road in front of us, a look of anger and confusion on his face. He hammered on the bonnet, his coat flying open to reveal the paisley pyjamas.

'Get out of my way!' Mr Russell shouted.

'Where are you taking her?' Alan roared back. He came around the side of the car and yanked the passenger door open. 'Where are you going, with him?'

'I'm taking care of your problem, Alan.' Mr Russell hissed the words.

'Get out of the car.' Alan pulled me out and grabbed my suitcase and took me by the arm.

'You stupid bastard!' bellowed Mr Russell. A door opened on the other side of the street and the pharmacist stuck his head out to see what was causing the commotion.

Alan pushed me in front of him and we walked up the silent street towards home. Mr Russell threw the car into reverse and went back up the lane.

'Where was he taking you?'

Alan was incandescent with rage. I was furious too that my plan had been thwarted.

'He was taking me to Dublin. I was to take the ferry to Liverpool to have an abortion.'

He turned back in the direction of the town and I walked home. Everything was already bad enough without having to witness a public street brawl between Alan and Declan Russell.

I'm not sure what happened, but Alan came back within half an hour. He didn't go to work that day. I think he was guarding me, to make sure I didn't get out of the house, to keep me away from Mr Russell.

He grilled me on the abortion plan. He was horrified. 'Holy God, he is the worst, most evil man walking. That's a little baby you have in there. And he wanted to kill it? The hypocrite! Pillar of the community, my eye!' He began to tell me the story of the servant girl and Declan, and his own father. Moira told him I already knew.

'You see?' he said. 'He doesn't care about you, or that child inside you.' He looked to Moira.

She had been quiet since she'd found out where I'd been planning to go. I thought it was because of the money I'd taken, and since returned, but now she said, 'Alan, maybe it wouldn't be the worst idea in the world. At least, then, it would be over.'

Alan was stunned. He raised his voice. 'Over? Over? You're talking about a baby's life! It's murder.'

'I don't see it like that,' she said quietly.

'Neither do I.' I was grateful to have an ally. 'I don't want a baby, and I don't want to go to the mother and baby home either. I want it gone. It's not a baby. It's just a . . . a thing in me, making me sick and tired, I don't want it!'

'Then you should have kept your legs shut. May God forgive you, the pair of you. You are carrying a child, albeit a bastard child –'

'Alan, for goodness' sake, people don't think like that any more. I will not have that child ever referred to as a bastard again.'

'The way you're talking, you don't want it to be a child. You want it killed. I cannot believe I have lived with such a godless wife for all these years!'

'Just because we weren't blessed to have our own child, we shouldn't be forcing Delia to –'

'Forcing? It's natural. It's what God intended. We taught her the birds and the bees. She has to live with the consequences of her actions.'

'Even if they destroy her life? Nobody in this town will touch her if we can't manage this effectively –'

Moira and Alan were shouting at each other. A sudden thrill ran up my spine. The doorbell rang in the middle of this argument. I'd forgotten Gemma was coming, because I hadn't planned to be there. Moira and Alan took their argument into the kitchen while Gemma came up to my room. Gemma wasted no time.

'Are you giving it up for adoption?'

'I am *not* pregnant!'

She grabbed at my jumper and pulled it up and I clenched my stomach inwards. She wouldn't be able to tell for sure.

'I don't mean to be mean, but your stomach used to be flatter, so if you're not pregnant, you've put a few pounds on.'

'I was so miserable in Ballina that I was eating like a horse. I'll lose it all soon.'

'Then why is Harry going around with a face like a slapped arse? I saw him up the town this morning and he practically ran away to avoid talking to me.'

'He doesn't want me to take the job in Cork, that's all.'

'Oh yeah?'

The sound of raised voices rumbled through my bedroom floor. Gemma rolled off the bed and put her ear to the door.

'What are they fighting about? They never fight.'

'Moira doesn't want me to take the job in Cork either.'

'Right.' She was still dubious. If Moira won the argument, I could be un-pregnant within the next week, so I was keeping up with the lie.

Alan went to the parish priest, Father Cummins, who made contact with a monsignor. The next day I was brought before another two old men and treated as the defendant. They called me a Jezebel among other things. I quite liked the name. It sounded exotic. Alan had told Father Cummins about the planned abortion and Mr Russell's role in it. The monsignor didn't even look at me. He asked if the Russells could be summoned to the parochial house. Father Cummins went out to make a call to the hotel. The monsignor broke the silence by discussing events in the parish until Declan Russell and his wife showed up. Father Cummins suggested I wait outside, but Alan insisted I stay put to tell the story of Declan Russell's plans for me in my own words. I lied that I had been forced into going along with it, that I had been bullied. I made it sound like all the Russell men had taken advantage of me.

The abortion plan was obviously all news to Mrs Russell and she was horrified to discover what her husband had been up to. Alan was determined to blacken the name of the Russell boys. He insisted that the Russells would have to make things right.

A new plan had formed in my head.

'Harry will have to marry her, and that's all there is to it,' said Uncle Alan.

Mr Russell objected, but the priests had already decided he was the devil and weren't going to listen to him.

'But Peter is the father,' I said. 'Shouldn't a baby be with its mother and father?'

They all looked at me for a moment. Mr Russell lost his temper. 'You must be joking! That boy is doing well in London, he's the pride of this family –'

Monsignor Kilcannon interrupted. 'Declan Russell! You have disgraced your family in the eyes of this church. The idea that you might have procured an abortion and murdered an innocent child to protect your pride is enough to have you excommunicated from the Catholic Church. The girl is right. She must marry the father of the baby, and quickly.'

'What?' said Mrs Russell. 'Excommunicated!'

The prospect of public humiliation was too great for her to bear. Within ten minutes, it was decided that I would go to London and marry Peter Russell as soon as possible. I would become a respectable married woman and live in London with my respectable husband. We would not come home on visits. The baby and I would be out of the way.

Moira and Alan did not speak to each other for my final week in Westport. The unified couple were finally divided. Moira was livid that I was to be willingly married off to a man I hardly knew. 'What about Harry?' she said.

'He'll get over it.'

Alan was thrilled with the outcome. It was all about Alan's revenge on the Russells for the loss of his father's good name. A scandal from a previous generation had to be paid for. By me, by Peter, by Harry and by our baby. But everyone paid in the end.

At that time, I thought about having a husband who was going to be a millionaire, and Oxford University and *Brideshead Revisited* and London nightclubs and *Top of the Pops*. I wasn't welcome on Inishcrann; I wasn't wanted in Westport. But I could be someone else in London.

Harry

I loved her from the first day I spoke to her, when I saw her being teased by a group of third-year lads from school. I'd seen her around and she was so beautiful that it was hard not to stare, but I think she was used to men staring at her and didn't notice. I'd heard she was an orphan and that made me want to wrap my arms around her and never let go. Within six months, I already knew I was going to marry her, even though we were so young. I knew my parents would probably object, because Delia's uncle was a postman, and they would want me to marry one of their friends' children, their friends from the golf club or the tennis club. But when Mum and Dad eventually agreed that she could come to dinner, she charmed them like she charmed me.

In my future, I saw Delia and I running Carrowbeg Manor together, working side by side until our own children could take over. I guess the first sign that something was changing was when she declared she was going to study medicine that first night in our house when she met Peter. God knows, she was no fool, and she almost always got what she wanted, but she wasn't book smart. We were alike in that way. But then she started studying like a lunatic. I should have guessed it was all about Peter.

I could have forgiven her, if they had just given me time, and if it had all been kept secret. But from the moment we found out it was Peter's baby, I had to get some space away from everyone. Nobody told me what was going to happen. Mum said it was Delia's idea. She's just saying that so that I'll hate Delia. But I'm not stupid. I know now that Delia wanted to sleep with me so that she could persuade me the baby was mine. She wanted to be with me. I simply don't believe it was Delia's choice to marry my brother. My mother is lying to protect me, to make me hate Delia.

I think Dad was right to arrange an abortion for her if that's what she wanted. Then nobody need ever have known and, given time, we could have got back together. If her uncle hadn't interfered, and then the religious old bastards, everything would be OK now. Well, maybe not OK, but better than her marrying my fucking brother.

So many things could have happened. So many things could have been kept quiet. Delia and I could have had a future if everything hadn't been so rushed.

When I close my eyes, I see Delia in bed with my brother. They did it in one of the hotel rooms. Dad told me when he was drunk. I didn't need to know that. I bet Peter forced her. Why would she sleep with him when she hardly knew him, when she wouldn't sleep with me?

They should never have forced her into this marriage. It's like something you hear about happening in India or the 1950s.

The whole town is laughing at me and I can't stand it. Such juicy gossip could never be kept quiet in a place like this. Dad is sleeping in Peter's old room now. Mum is the only one who goes to Mass. I can barely look at either of them. I haven't gone to training since, knowing that the lads are talking about me, feeling sorry for me.

I close my eyes and I think of her over there in London, lonely and afraid, probably bullied by my brother. She misses me, I'm sure of it. Mum says that I am not to expect a letter from her, but she will write to me, I know it. I'm writing to her every week.

My brother and I were never the best of friends, but even Mum doesn't believe it when she says we'll all get over this. None of us will. Ever.

13

Seven days after the aborted abortion attempt, I flew on a plane for the first time, to London with Alan and Declan Russell. Moira and Mrs Russell were too distraught to come with us. We went straight from the airport in a taxi to a registry office where I met Peter. We exchanged a few sentences. He seemed embarrassed and apologetic and utterly delighted. A registrar married us under a portrait of the Queen in a civil ceremony that took no more than ten minutes. I wore a bottle-green tweed skirt and a brown corduroy jacket and some plastic leather-look zip-up boots that were scuffed at the toes. Peter was wearing a suit with a shiny tie. He had a carnation in his lapel and pinned one to my jacket. I stared at him. Everything about him was so angular and he was such a serious type of man, he looked all the time as if he was solving equations in his head, and perhaps he was. At the end of the brief ceremony, the registrar smiled and said, 'You may kiss the bride,' and Peter kissed my cheek and I heard Declan Russell behind us muttering, 'Jesus Christ.'

Afterwards, we went to a restaurant and had an awkward meal where nobody spoke much. Alan insisted on paying for it, as father of the bride, despite the fact that Mr Russell ordered the most expensive bottle of wine on the menu and drank most of it himself. After dinner, Declan went to a hotel nearby, and Alan went to a distant cousin's house somewhere on the outskirts of London. They were both flying home the next morning. I can't imagine there was much conversation between them on the journey. Peter and I were left alone together. I took his hand as we left the restaurant and he looked at mine with surprise.

I went on the Tube with Peter, stunned by the crowds of people and their varying shades, getting on and off, masses of them through endless low-ceilinged corridors, up escalators, pouring forth like a river. I had been to Galway, and to Dublin, and of course I'd seen London on television, but I was taken aback by the sheer volume of people everywhere, and I didn't know any of them. We got off the Tube after twenty minutes and emerged at Walthamstow station. From there, we walked about two hundred yards to a street packed tightly with terraced houses and cars parked on either side. We stopped at a doorway, and while Peter was searching for his keys a man emerged from the doorway to the right of his.

'All right?' he said to Peter, who grunted in response.

'Who was that?' I asked.

'No idea, one of the guys who live downstairs.'

I couldn't understand how you could live in the same building with someone and not know their name.

Peter's doorway led on to a narrow, steep staircase. I had never been in a flat before, and I roamed the three rooms several times, aghast at the limitation of space. All of the houses on this street were split into two flats. Two front doors, instead of one. No garden, no sea pounding in the distance. Even in my childhood cottage, it had felt to me like we owned the ocean and the sky around us. Here, I could only glimpse the sky by craning my neck upwards. The view was of other houses closing in opposite or other back yards and kitchens from the rear. I felt immediately confined by the walls around me.

'I thought you were rich?' I said.

Peter laughed nervously. 'Is that why you married me?'

I said nothing, but I couldn't stop bitter tears from falling.

Peter saw my disappointment and tried to reassure me. 'I know it doesn't look like much, but business is good, very good. I'm only living here because I've been saving up and I'm buying my own place soon, *our* own place.'

We stood at the door of the bedroom. It was a bachelor pad. A poster on the wall showed strange staircases that appeared to go up and down.

'It's an Escher,' said Peter.

I had no idea what he was talking about. Another poster I recognized as the periodic table from my school days. The books on the floor appeared to be scientific volumes, or biographies of business moguls. Over dinner, Peter had showed us all his digital watch, which had a calculator on it. Even Alan had been impressed. Now, looking at evidence of his interest in science, I was emboldened to ask him, 'What *is* your job?'

'My friend Daniel and I opened a brokerage. I study the markets and invest other people's money in stocks and various ventures,' he said.

I admitted I didn't know what stocks and ventures were. He started to explain, but I didn't understand any of it. 'It's like a different language,' I said, and Peter declared that computers did in fact use a different language. I think he thought that I should be impressed, but I was staring at the double bed, realizing that we would sleep together in it every night. Peter kissed me then on the lips.

'I never dreamed that . . . My beautiful wife. Look, I know it's a crazy way for it all to happen, but I think I, well, I think we *can* get on together, have a family, make a life here. I feel like the luckiest man in the world, right now. I think we're going to be all right. Harry won't stay angry for the rest of his life. One day he'll forgive us and we'll be able to visit home, if we could be bothered. Westport is such a backwater. One day it might catch up with the rest of the world.' He pulled me towards him and put his hand on my belly. 'Our baby!' he whispered, and his eyes shone with happiness.

I felt like screaming.

'I'll look after you,' he said. 'I promise.'

I was married to a man I barely knew in a tiny flat in a strange country and pregnant with a baby I didn't want. Millionaire? What a fraud. That night, we slept in the same bed, but I kept my back to him. His arm crept around to cradle my stomach, but he did not pressure me. Sex was within my power, and I intended to hold on to it. I was furious. I had been duped. Pride of Mayo? Hardly. I kept my thoughts to myself.

Peter planned to introduce me to his friends. London didn't care about sex before marriage, he said. He thought it best that we pretend that I had been a long-term girlfriend from home, and that we had chosen to get married for the sake of our baby. It reminded me of the time that Alan and Moira said we should pretend that I was their niece. Peter said he wanted his friends to think well of me and that there was no reason to mention Harry. I wondered if they would think well of *him*, if they had known the truth.

I didn't sleep well that night. I was not used to sharing a bed. I woke early to find Peter gazing at me. 'My beautiful bride,' he whispered, and kissed me on the mouth. I did not kiss him back, but rose quickly and went to the bathroom to shower and dress.

When I emerged later, he handed me a cup of strong coffee and told me he would take me shopping. We went back underground again and swapped trains until we came out at Brent Cross and walked to a large shopping centre. Peter took me to C&A and Marks & Spencer's and Dorothy Perkins and told me I could buy anything I wanted. At first, I was cautious, asking his opinion on that dress or this cardigan, but he insisted that I get what I wanted. I was a bigger size around the waist than I had been before, and it annoyed me that I had to go up a size in skirts and trousers. I had never really been interested in fashion, but maybe that was because there were three ladies' shops you could buy from in Westport, and sometimes, if it was my birthday, Moira would take me on the bus to Galway, into Gaywear for a new coat or to Clarks for a new pair of shoes. We were always on a budget. This time, Peter showed me his credit card. He told me I would have one too. He left me alone in the lingerie department in John Lewis, and there my spirits lifted as I examined the lace and satin and chose everything I wanted. When he wasn't watching me, I indulged myself without embarrassment. I realized that this was a life I wanted to lead. The big house could come later. My mood improved.

Afterwards, on the street, both of us laden with bags, I kissed him, caught him by surprise, and he grinned broadly. His whole face softened and he puffed up his chest. 'You're worth every penny,' he said, and put his arm around my shoulder. We then travelled out to the suburbs again and stopped to look at an estate agent's window. 'What about something like that? We'll need at least three bedrooms to start with,' he said, pointing to a photo of a small red-brick Victorian semi-detached house with a driveway and a large cherry blossom tree in the front garden. I wondered who he thought would sleep in the third bedroom. 'Well, visitors!' he said. 'And maybe we'll give this one a little brother or sister some day.' He pointed at my stomach. I didn't dare to respond to that. I looked at the asking price and laughed. Peter wasn't laughing though. 'Let's enquire, will we?' he said, and led the way through the glass door.

The estate agent looked me up and down, and particularly at the cracked toes of my plastic boots. I wished I had changed into some of my new purchases, which included three pairs of real leather shoes. Peter made an appointment for us to view the house in Finchley the next day.

'We could be in our new house for Christmas,' he said. It was beginning to sink in that I was here to stay. My stomach fluttered with nerves. Or perhaps it was the baby.

That evening we went out to dinner *again*, to a small bistro a short walk from the flat. 'I can't cook,' admitted Peter, 'and you should have a week off. This should be our honeymoon.' I had never been to proper restaurants before, unless you count the chippers and cafés of Ballina and Westport.

We drank some wine with our meal. He asked me lots of questions that evening. About my birth family and my adopted family. He knew from his father that I was no blood relation to Moira and Alan. The wine loosened my tongue a little, and I told him that I was an indirect descendant of an island chieftain, that my ancestors were noblemen, that my father was a hard-working fisherman, honoured and respected by the entire community. I related the story of how my family died tragically in a fire. I did not tell him that my father had murdered my mother and brothers and shot himself. It seemed unreal to me. I had only learned this information two weeks previously and so much else had happened that I didn't know how to process it.

'But that story, about you being found outside Cregannagh village the night of the fire back on the island, what were you doing there?'

'I don't remember.'

'But you must have taken the ferry over by yourself? Where were you going, and why?'

'Daddy was going to catch the later ferry. I don't know why.'

'But you must remember?'

I couldn't think about that now. I snapped at Peter. 'Stop asking me questions about that. For God's sake, don't you think that might be insensitive?'

My voice was raised loud enough that a drunk diner from another table leaned over to Peter and said, 'New to the mainland, is she? You want to make sure she doesn't have a bomb in her bag, mate.' He was smiling, being chummy. The previous year, an IRA bomb had killed eleven members of the Household Cavalry and seven of their horses.

Peter bristled and turned red. 'Piss off, *mate*, and mind your own business.'

'All right, keep your hair on, I was only having a laugh, wasn't I?' said the man, behaving now like he was the injured party.

Peter was furious. We finished up our meal quickly and in silence. He paid the bill and led me out of the restaurant, passing the other diner, who was now very drunk, and even louder, to the mortification of the man he was dining with.

'Sorry, man, I didn't mean nothing by it, I quite like the Irish really . . .' He began to stand up and I could see that he was considerably taller and broader than Peter.

Peter was ready to square up to him, but I pulled at his sleeve and said sweetly to the man, 'No offence taken, enjoy your dinner, but check under your car in the morning, all right, mate?' I waited for the look of confusion on his face before we exited.

'It's not a great time to be Irish in London,' Peter said.

'Nobody would know *you're* Irish,' I said. Having lived there for five years, he already sounded posh English, and confident in that way that British people can. Back home, when you heard that accent on the television or radio, it added a certain weight to what they said. Authoritative and knowledgeable.

'I'm terribly sorry about . . . it was tactless of me, I should have thought.'

I stopped him. 'It's quite all right, let's not mention it again.' I mimicked his clipped tones perfectly, and he looked at me, amazed.

'You don't have to change your accent –'

'Oh, but I think I do.'

He laughed.

'You told me once that I wouldn't fit in, in London. I'm going to prove you wrong.'

He thought it was a joke that I might tire of, but I had changed my accent once before, from bog island to West-port, to impress his family. He just hadn't been around enough to notice that.

He smiled then at his brand-new wife, but at the end of our marriage, Peter would shout at me, 'Who are you? I don't know who you are. You don't even sound like you!'

At that time, though, he was in love with me. I did not have sex with him that night, and though he did not ask me, it was clear what he wanted. The next day we were both tired, but we got up and went to our house-viewing appointment. The house was small but twice the size of the flat, at the bottom of a long leafy avenue. It was empty of furniture. I could not visualize anyone living in it. While Peter went around with a measuring tape, talking about where the sun would hit the bedroom in the morning, I went into the small back garden. It was a yard. Tall trees on one side protected the house's privacy from the next-door neighbour, and a high fence on the other side was doing its best to block out noise from the adjacent street. I could see a patch of sky between the fence and the trees. I closed my eyes and tried my best, but I could not remember exactly how the ocean sounded. Only three days away from it, and already I was lost. I felt Peter put his arms around my shoulders. 'Did you see the stove? Come in and take a look.'

'There isn't enough sky,' I said.

The estate agent standing at the back door laughed indulgently. 'Perhaps madam would prefer a penthouse apartment? We have one in Crouch End.' He wasn't being cheeky. He was deferential to me. The new accent and the new clothes had slipped on like a skin. This Delia commanded respect.

'No, we need a house, with a garden. We're having a baby,' said Peter.

'Oh, how exciting. Congratulations!' The man shook Peter's hand, and when he took mine I noticed him looking at my other hand. It was a moment before I realized that he was looking for my wedding ring. At the civil ceremony, we hadn't needed one.

When we left the house, and walked back towards the Tube station, Peter insisted we go along the high street first. He stopped at a jeweller's shop, and there he bought me a sapphire and diamond engagement ring and a solid gold wedding band. 'Now,' he said, 'it's official', as if the certificate on the kitchen table in Walthamstow wasn't validation enough. He paid a small fortune, and I thought that perhaps this life might not be so bad. We just needed a proper house with space, and sky. That evening, I allowed our marriage to be consummated. Sex was never as exciting again as it was that first time, so I used it, granting it and withholding it according to my mood. I learned slowly how I could be satisfied, but the physical sensation was only ever fleeting. I never understood why people make such an enormous fuss about it. That night, Peter held me tight and looked into my eyes. I stared right back at him.

'We'll make this work, won't we?' He rubbed my rising belly.

The nausea and physical exhaustion of the first three months of pregnancy had now passed and I was feeling relatively normal again, but during the following week Peter made an antenatal appointment for me, which I attended alone. The obstetrician was kind, and told me that my baby and I were in perfect health.

'There is no chance of a miscarriage then?' I asked.

He looked at me strangely. 'No, nothing to worry about at this stage.'

I was glad that Peter was back at work, as he had barely left my side at the weekend. He left me plenty of cash and showed me bus and Tube routes. He would buy a car soon, he said, so that we could go on family outings. He would even teach me how to drive.

I spent my first weeks as a tourist, taking bus tours and river tours, seeing St Paul's Cathedral, Buckingham Palace, museums and art galleries I had read about in schoolbooks. Central London was magnificent. I walked along the Thames, branching off into Covent Garden or Westminster, marvelling at the scale, the grandeur and the architecture. Each evening, I had something to discuss with Peter, something to ask or tell him about what I had seen. He had been a student in Oxford, or as he used to say, pompously, '*up at Oxford*', and had only worked in the City for the last two years. My knowledge of central London was soon better than his. The *A–Z* was my bible. The Tube map was his.

But every Friday I left the house early with Peter and travelled as far as King's Cross with him. There, I changed levels and platforms, and caught a train to Southend-on-Sea or to

Margate, and walked their piers and sat on the rocks, drinking the sea into my brain, topping up for the week. On my only visit to Canvey Island, I felt utterly cheated that it was not an island at all. Peter laughed at my outrage when I told him. 'Come on, Delia, Oxford Circus isn't a circus either!'

The English Channel could not possibly compete with the wild Atlantic.

The goats on Inishcrann had been there for as long as anyone could remember, Daddy said. They were distinguishable from all others by their unusual green eyes. They'd be used for milk and meat, but their real value was in their skins. In ancient times, the island women would make gloves of their skin that were then sold to noblemen and their ladies across Ireland and beyond. It was the Quilty family that had the running of the goats.

From time to time, a goat farmer from the mainland would come over with one of his own nanny-goats for breeding purposes, but our billies were choosy about who they mated with. The foreign nanny-goat wouldn't always take the fancy of our billy. The farmer would pay good money for the attempt, and if it was unsuccessful would be spoiling for a fight afterwards, feeling cheated.

When the mating was successful, the nanny was kept on Inishcrann until the first kid was born, and that kid would be kept with the Quilty herd. The nannies gave birth to one or two kids at a time, and it was tough luck if the nanny only had one kid. But a goat born of the Quilty herd was a money-spinner all by itself.

One year, our best billy-goat went missing. The whole of Inishcrann went searching every cave and crevice to look for that goat, and the Quiltys put up a reward because this lad was fierce valuable and could put out ten kids a year. But the goat was not found and it was thought that maybe a gust had blown him off a cliff, though it had never happened to a goat before, only children.

It was many months later when news reached Inishcrann that a farmer in the parish of Kilmane had been attacked and eaten by his own billy-goat. It was the talk of the nation, because goats were never flesh-eating creatures, but of course the islanders were always the last to hear of any news at all. That goat had the townland terrorized, and an army of men and boys were unable to catch him or kill him or get within an acre of him.

The Quiltys, known for their expertise in the way of goats, were requested by the local chieftain to come over and see if they could capture and slaughter this beast with a taste for human flesh. They were offered good money to kill him.

The Quiltys were a big family in those days, and fourteen of them undertook the expedition to Kilmane to catch that wildest of wild goats. No sooner had they crossed the border into the Cankilly demesne, than the billy-goat appeared to them on the top of a hill. The Quiltys knew immediately by the cut of him that he was their own, and he came to them when called, as docile as the lambs he had grown up with, and they could see the gladness in his green eyes. Further enquiries proved that the eaten farmer was one of those disappointed that his own nanny hadn't been covered by Inishcrann's best billy.

The farmer's widow was whipped by the Quilty men until she admitted that her husband had rowed across to the island in the dead of night four months earlier and stolen the Quiltys' prize possession. A fight broke out between the Quilty clan and the local boyos with sticks and knives, but the billy-goat fought on the Quiltys' side and they sailed home victorious.

That same billy-goat lived another thirty years and fathered many kids, and when he died the Quiltys, out of respect, did not have him skinned, but buried him instead in their family grave at the south of the island.

Daddy said that billy knew where he belonged and that being away from home sent him out of his mind. Daddy said people should know where they belonged too, lest they become savage and deranged.

'Everything has its place,' Daddy used to say, 'and everyone, too.'

14

In those first weeks, I took on my newest name. My husband learned that my real name was not Walsh, the name of my adoptive parents, but O'Flaherty. Now I was to be a Russell. Delia Russell sounded like a woman of significance, and when I received my own credit card with that name on it, I felt like my new identity was confirmed. Peter set about educating me, and I was an enthusiastic student for the first time since my ill-fated Leaving Cert studies. There were to be linen napkins with the place settings at dinner time. I was no longer going to lick my knife. I was to say 'Peter and I' and not 'me and Peter'. I resented Alan and Moira for not having taught me these things.

Peter told me his friends were shocked when he had told them he was married. He arranged for me to come and meet them after work one evening for Christmas drinks in a wine bar near his office. 'Maybe pretend you're twenty-one?' he said. Of course. We were excellent at pretending. There were seven or eight colleagues and their wives or girlfriends, all in their twenties and early thirties.

'No wonder you kept her a secret,' said Daniel, Peter's partner and co-owner of Russell Wilkes, 'she's bloody gorgeous. You're a dark horse.'

'Why, thank you,' I said, smiling sweetly.

'You don't sound Irish at all,' said Hannah, Daniel's wife.

Peter gave me a sideways wink.

Daniel laughed at her. 'You're Scottish, darling, you're hardly one to talk.'

Hannah had bleached blonde hair, bright red lipstick and dark eye make-up. She looked like a rock star in her leopard-skin printed shawl and high heels. I had seen that look on magazine covers, but nobody in Westport ever dressed like that. To look at her, one would think she'd be cockney, but her accent was refined. I noticed after some time that all upper-class Scottish people had distinctly English accents. I thought that I could fit in quite well. We drank champagne for the first time that night, and these new friends toasted the bride and groom. Peter made a speech about how I had always been the love of his life. I gazed warmly into his eyes and played along.

I loved the taste of champagne, the subtle fizz on my tongue and the dry coating it left on the back of my throat. An older woman, called Vanessa, said it wasn't healthy to drink too much while pregnant. Peter agreed. He had bought a book on pregnancy and read it constantly, leaving it on the bed, in the kitchen, on the sofa, hoping, I think, that I might pick it up. I thought Vanessa was Peter's secretary. I had heard him mention her before. In any case, she was a busy-body who had no right to opinions on my body, but during the next round of drinks somebody bought me an orange juice. I accepted it politely but did not drink it.

'Oh my,' said Vanessa, noting my disdain, 'I didn't mean to offend you, darling, but it's not good for the little one.' She reached out to touch my bump, but I recoiled from her touch and ignored her patronizing tone.

'So do you work for Daniel and Peter too?'

'Well, not exactly, I'm an investor,' she said, laughing.

I looked to Peter, but he and Sam and Daniel were smoking cigars at the far end of the bar.

'What do you do?' she asked. 'How did you meet Peter?'

'Oh, our families have known each other for years. I'm

afraid I haven't quite joined the workforce yet. I've only finished university.'

'I see, you must have good genes, you still look like a child!
What did you study?'

'English and philosophy at Trinity,' I said, because that's
what I'd heard Katie O'Malley was doing.

'Well, darling, my advice to you is, as soon as that baby is
born, get yourself a nanny and get a job. Women need to be
in the workforce these days, you know. We have a lot to offer.
It's no good being dependent on a man any more. Find
something that you're interested in and work at it. And if
being a stay-at-home mum floats your boat, that's fine. Just
make sure you have your own bank account. Motherhood is
a job too.'

'Actually, I plan to work in publishing.' There had been a
documentary on television the previous evening about
publishing.

'Well, that's simply marvellous. Brains as well as beauty?
You have the complete package.' She called over to Peter,
'You never told me she was clever as well. I'm impressed.'

Peter looked at me, and nodded. 'Oh yes, she's a smart one
all right.'

I was the one who was impressed. All of these women
were well groomed, with perfect hair and painted nails. The
men wore sharp suits and good shoes.

Afterwards, at home, Peter said, 'Why did you tell Vanessa
you went to Trinity?'

'Well, I have three years to account for, since I'm supposed to be twenty-one.'

He was embarrassed. 'Right. Good thinking. I'll get you
the English texts so that you can swot up on your Joyce and
Shakespeare. Nobody's ever going to ask you about philosophy, and even if they do, all you need to say is that you're a

devotee of Nietzsche. They'll be so shocked, that will shut them up.'

We laughed, and it felt comfortable for the first time. Like we were actually on the same team in a game.

'Who the hell is Nee— who?'

'He famously said God is dead. I happen to agree.'

'I don't believe in God.' It felt daring to say it.

'Really? I have a most unusual wife! Can we please not go to Mass every Sunday then? I only went last week because I thought you wanted to. I've only been into a church for weddings and funerals since I left Westport six years ago. Don't tell my mother.'

'We're terrible sinners,' I said, grinning.

'You're an absolute Jezebel,' he said, and we fell to kissing, more passionately than we had before. That exotic name again. I felt a genuine warmth for him, but then he ruined it.

'What about Harry?'

'What?' I had seen letters in Harry's handwriting hidden at the bottom of the bin. Peter needn't have worried.

'You haven't mentioned Harry. It's as if he never existed. I honestly thought you would hate being dragged to London, that breaking up with Harry would be upsetting for you, particularly under the circumstances.'

'What is the point of being upset about Harry? I can't change anything now.'

'But you were going out with him for over two years. You must have . . . have cared for him. Do you miss him?'

I thought about it for a split second too long. I didn't want an argument. 'Why would I think about him? I am pregnant with your baby and my future is with you.'

My answer seemed to puzzle Peter, but in a positive way.

'And one day, you might love me?'

What is this 'love' that everybody is so obsessed by? There

have been people I enjoyed spending time with, people who made me laugh sometimes, people who have taken care of me, fed and clothed me, but am I expected to reward them with declarations of love at every turn? I don't know what it is. The only person I ever had strong feelings for was my father. I loved him. But if Daddy felt the same way about me, why did he shoot himself? I don't think love is useful.

I smiled at Peter, and he kissed me again.

Christmas came and I had to go shopping for proper maternity clothes. On my first spree I had bought clothes one size bigger, but now nothing fitted across my chest either. I was nearly halfway through the pregnancy, but although I felt relatively healthy, the baby hurt me sometimes with its kicking and pressing down on my bladder. My breasts had almost doubled in size and there was no hiding the bump any more. People stood to let me sit down on the Tube or the bus. I hated that kind of attention and spurned their courtesy, relishing their embarrassment when they thought I was merely overweight.

Peter sent home extravagant Christmas gifts to his parents, and a tweed jacket to Harry, a jacket that I knew Harry would never have worn, even if nothing had happened between them, or us. Peter bought Christmas cards and stamps and gave me a list of his friends and colleagues. I patiently wrote 'with best wishes from Peter and Delia Russell' on each card, but I didn't send any to Westport and did not spend any time worrying about how Moira and Alan would be spending Christmas. We had Christmas lunch in the Strand Palace Hotel. Peter said that next year, the three of us would go to the Dorchester. It took me a moment to realize who the third person was. Peter had got a good bonus and said that we really should look at buying a house soon, as I would shortly be in my nesting period. Every time he mentioned the pregnancy, I gave him the silent treatment.

'I know you're scared,' he said, 'but you'll feel differently when the baby is born.'

15

In the new year, we began in earnest to look for a new home. Peter found one in East Finchley, not too far from the first one we had viewed. It had a large back garden but the house was probably the same size as Alan and Moira's, not nearly as big or grand as Peter's family home. I did not hide my disappointment.

'When exactly are you going to be a millionaire?' I said.

'Not yet. We're only getting going. This house will do to start. You can't compare London prices to Westport. This is one of the most expensive cities in the world to live in.'

'Well then, let's move!'

Peter laughed. 'Where to?'

'Home, not Westport, I understand that we can't go back there, but Sligo, or Connemara, or even Donegal, somewhere on the west coast.'

'Delia, be realistic. I'm a stockbroker with my own up-and-coming firm. London is where it's at. There is nothing to compare it with in Ireland. I'm never going home. *We're* never going home. You are going to get used to it, I promise. Once the baby is born, you'll make friends with other young mums.'

I started to walk out of the room, but he put out his arm to stop me. 'I still get the feeling that you are just visiting sometimes, but you're my wife and this is your home.'

'I can't . . . I, I miss the sea.'

'We can go on holidays. We can go for weekends to Brighton or Eastbourne, or wherever you like.'

Peter was trying to keep me happy, but he was also incredibly busy. He worked a lot of weekends and I spent a lot of time on my own. There was no point in me trying to get a job in my late stage of pregnancy. He had encouraged me to join antenatal groups and bridge clubs and cooking classes, but I preferred to spend my time on trains to the coast every chance I got. I kept these trips to myself.

Eventually, I found another house, detached, on a third of an acre in Ealing. Peter was reluctant. 'It's way out of our league. Maybe in ten years' time, but we can't afford this now.'

I forced him to come and look at it with me. The two reception rooms were spacious, the garden was beautiful. This is where I wanted to live.

'It's beautiful, of course it is, but we can't . . .'

I sulked for a week. I took the train to Brighton and checked into a hotel for a night. I knew Peter would be going out of his mind with worry. He was so relieved when I returned that he immediately capitulated. 'Fine, you'll get your house, but we'll have to cut back on everything else. You got used to that credit card too quickly. No more shopping.'

Moving house took up time, the bedrooms needed to be decorated, furniture needed to be sourced. Peter sent away for catalogues, but I couldn't decide, so I hired an interior designer, Isabelle, recommended by Daniel's wife, Hannah. Peter hit the roof. 'What are you doing? I told you, we don't have the money for this, Delia! We have a baby coming and that's not going to be cheap either.'

'I can't un-hire her. What would Hannah say?' I knew that Peter was the brains behind Russell Wilkes. Daniel Wilkes came from old money, and was Eton-educated. His name opened doors in the City, but it was Peter's powers of persuasion and ambition that kept them going. I don't think Daniel even worked full-time. He was more of a figurehead for the firm, but Peter still had to keep on the right side of him, so he understood why I couldn't renege on the deal I had made with Hannah's friend.

The designer, Isabelle, made all of the decisions for us. I liked her immediately. She dressed in bright clothes and wore long dangly earrings. After our first meeting, she produced a bottle of champagne from her bag to seal the deal. Peter left her and me to work out the finer details of what would go into each room. She could see that I didn't particularly care for a pastel-coloured baby's room, so she went ahead and had it painted olive green with recessed bookshelves. Peter ordered a cot, but I closed the door on the room and ignored it.

Isabelle had extremely good taste and was not remotely judgemental. She had had two abortions and felt no guilt whatsoever. She was a self-confessed party girl, and I learned quickly never to phone her before twelve o'clock. Over the course of eight weeks, we became friendly. She and I and Hannah went to each other's homes and on nights out together. Isabelle had grown up in a large country house, but now she lived in a tiny flat in Mayfair and declared herself a born-again virgin.

Isabelle told me that Hannah was jealous of me. Hannah had always been the centre of attention until I came along, but now, everyone in their circle of friends was talking about me. That cheered me. I could tell that Peter did not quite approve of my friendship with Hannah and Isabelle. It was annoying because he had encouraged me to get to know people. He thought they were a bad influence with their afternoon drinking and smoking, but as the pregnancy progressed, I began to withdraw more from their company anyway.

I hated the way my body was changing, hated the swollen ankles, the constant weeing, the acid reflux and the sore breasts. My hair was thinning and my legs seemed to twitch all night and keep me awake. I suffered from excruciating pelvic pain from time to time. The doctor insisted all of this was normal. Peter did his best to keep me comfortable. He ran a bath for me every evening and bought a tape of whale music which was supposed to soothe me. I became more bad-tempered as time went on. I gave up on housework and lay on the sofa in the afternoon, watching black and white films, often sneaking a little brandy from our drinks cupboard. I hadn't read any of the baby books that Peter had bought.

I remembered babies. In the orphanage, their crying had kept me awake at night. And at home, on the island, if one of my brothers had begun to cry in the night, my father used to get up in a rage and put the cot outside the back door. 'You never cried, Delia,' he'd say to me, 'you were as quiet as a little mouse with slippers on.' Mammy would get up and bring the cot back inside and spend the night in the chair beside the fire, trying to calm the squalling brat.

I began to think about my mother for the first time in years. She had gone through four pregnancies. I didn't remember her being pregnant with Brian or Aidan, but I remembered her swollen with Conor. I remembered my father on his knees, praying to her belly for another daughter. Mammy was so upset when Conor was born. Daddy was out at sea that day. Nora delivered him. She said, 'He's a healthy boy!' and Mammy said, 'Martin's going to be so mad with me.'

Hannah had two children, and a nanny. Peter warned me that we couldn't afford a nanny. I said nothing. He tried to divert me by talking about names for our child, but I was in no mood to discuss such a thing. I insisted that Peter sleep in the spare room until the baby was born, now that we had a spare room.

My overnight bag was packed by Peter from the seventh-month mark and placed in the hallway ready to go. I spent my days lying on the sofa, eating peeled carrots and feeling bloated and uncomfortable in between trips to the toilet as the baby made a playground of my womb and bounced on my bladder. Every day, Peter gave me five different phone numbers and the schedule for his day in case I needed to reach him urgently. His daily meetings out of the office had increased; he said he was on the verge of 'something big'. He probably explained it to me, but I had perfected my listening face many years previously and knew well how to appear attentive while wondering how soon after the baby was born I could take a trip to the coast again. The journeys in recent weeks had become too exhausting and too inconvenient, and I longed to feel the sea air on my face.

The day before my child's premature birth on the 5th of May 1984, I tried cocaine for the first time. That morning, I had phoned Hannah.

'Darling!' she said. 'It's been bloody ages since we've seen you. I don't suppose you've popped that sprog yet, have you? I remember what it's like. Are you miserable? Shall I call over? I'll ring Isabelle, and see if she'll get out of bed for lunch.'

I was thirty-seven weeks pregnant, I looked awful, but I was bored and bloated and restless and I hadn't been out of the house in weeks.

Isabelle and Hannah arrived together, laden with oven pizzas and wine. The wine wasn't going to do any harm at this stage and I had a ready supply of Rennies to keep the acid in my stomach at bay. Hannah said Daniel and she were going to the Caribbean on holidays soon. The children would stay home with the nanny. She showed me the holiday brochure. I looked at the exotic photos of sea and sand and palm trees and felt a stab of jealousy. Isabelle noticed my look and laughed at me.

'Oh, Delia, you are so funny. I hope you're not judging Hannah for leaving the children behind? Are you going to be a typical Irish mother?'

I protested, 'Not at all, I wish we had the money for holidays like that.'

They exchanged a look and I realized that it was not the done thing to talk about money in that way.

The girls changed the subject and started talking about baby names.

'What about Toby?'

'Or Elliot?'

When Peter had raised the question of names, I had rolled my eyes, but now I played along.

'What about Aisling, or Siobhán?' I spelled the names out.

They hooted. 'If you're going to live here, you're going to want a name that people can pronounce! Why put the poor child at a disadvantage?' Hannah said.

Isabelle poured the last of the wine into our glasses. 'What about Charlie?' she said, nudging Hannah meaningfully.

'Do you have some?' said Hannah.

'What are you talking about?' I was bewildered.

'Charlie, coke, cocaine,' said Isabelle, producing a tiny white envelope from her handbag. She showed me the snow-white powder, like the talcum Peter had bought to pack in the hospital overnight bag. I thought she was joking for a minute, and Isabelle laughed at my shock. 'Delia, you're pregnant, so probably not a good idea for you, but you don't mind if we . . . ?'

We had been warned about drugs at school, and even in Westport you'd know the few who were rumoured to be dope smokers, but cocaine was a terrifying drug that I had heard made people jump out of windows and run in front of speeding cars. Isabelle got a bit huffy.

'Look, we can go to the pub down the road if it's such a big deal?'

'No, no, it's fine. I, I haven't . . . I've never seen it before.'

'What is the name of your little town again?'

'Westport.'

'Was it very boring?'

'I suppose it was.' I felt defensive. 'But it is beautiful.'

I watched them chop out lines of powder with the edge of a credit card. 'Does Daniel mind you doing this?'

'Mind? Where do you think Isabelle got it? Just one of Daniel's many little sidelines, if you'll excuse the pun. Peter's a good boy though.'

'Oh, Hannah,' interrupted Isabelle, 'now we know why Peter has been so straight-laced. He's been saving himself for his new bride! Honestly, we thought he was gay.'

'What do you mean?'

'Well, look in the mirror, darling! There's no one in our set that can match you for youth and beauty, even in your current condition. Peter kept his cards close to his chest. We didn't even know you existed until you were married. How long were you dating? Were you childhood sweethearts?'

I deflected the question by nodding at the lines on the table. 'Would it really be bad for the baby?'

Hannah was pleased to change the subject away from my youth and beauty. 'My God, depending on who you listen to, everything is bad for the baby!'

'May I try it?'

Isabelle was doubtful, but Hannah told her not to be such a spoilsport. I felt like taking a risk. After all, my husband gambled with people's fortunes every day. Why shouldn't I take a chance with the baby? Maybe this could be the solution. Hannah showed me how to close one nostril and inhale with the other. I didn't feel anything for a few moments, and then I heard a sudden rushing in my ears, and a soothing heat crept through my body. I put my hand on my belly; it felt like the alien thing inside me was a person, illegally occupying *me*. I stood up and walked about the room, trying to walk delicately like a dancer instead of the lumbering elephant I had felt like ten minutes previously. I was exhilarated and powerful. The girls started to hum some pop song and I swayed to their music. I said aloud, 'Hurry up, baby, I'm totally fed up with you!' Hannah and Isabelle went to the hi-fi and rifled through our record collection, pouring scorn on Peter's taste until they found the Madonna album he'd bought me for Christmas. We all danced for a while, then Isabelle chopped out another three fat lines of white crystals. I still felt brilliant and didn't need to indulge, but I wanted very much to be a member of this exciting little gang. How cool and fun and free we were. I didn't even feel the discomfort this time as I bent at the knees to the low table and sniffed up the powder.

As I sat down again, I felt a leakage.

'What's that? You've spilled your wine, Delia. Wait! Oh shit, your waters are breaking!' said Hannah, as I felt a warm gush pass through my pants.

'Not the sofa!' cried Isabelle, who had commissioned it from a Chinese man in Camden Town.

I watched the stain spread out underneath my lap, and was reminded of the glass of milk I spilled on my dress when I was waiting for Daddy to collect me from the doctor's house in Cregannagh. I felt a split second of panic, but then, happiness. Finally, this creature would be on the outside of me, and I would be independent again. There was no pain. Not then.

An ambulance was called, though I could have taken a taxi, but Isabelle said I was crazy to take any chances. 'It's a baby, for God's sake, Delia. Get a grip. You have to act normally when they come.'

By the time the ambulance arrived, all evidence of the cocaine had been hidden. I was still scattered in my thinking. Isabelle had rung Peter and told him to meet me at the hospital.

The ambulance men took in the scene swiftly: three giddy women surrounded by empty wine bottles. 'Have you been drinking, love?' one said, but before I could answer, Hannah imperiously interrupted, 'How dare you? What is your name?' He and I ignored her.

'I still have three weeks to go, is it too early?' I said.

The other man looked at me and I realized the stupidity of my question.

'Maybe the baby won't survive?' I said hopefully. 'Maybe it will die. Could that happen?'

I could feel the room freezing, as if I had spoken the unthinkable. Unthinkable to them, but all the time since I'd discovered my pregnancy I had wanted this baby to die. The London adventure was all very well, but I wasn't sure if I wanted to stay here, in this vast city, with Peter, miles from the ocean.

As the effects of the cocaine wore off, my mood darkened and all of these thoughts whooshed through me in the later hours as wave after wave of agony washed over me, chasing the earlier swarms of energy away. In the labour ward, I even forgot my cut-glass accent. Doctors came and went and con-firmed that I was dilating quickly, that the baby's head was engaged. One chirpy Pakistani nurse told me, 'Don't worry, Mrs Russell. At your age, delivery should be straightforward.' Here, they knew my real age. Other women in the labour ward with heaving bellies and anxious partners cried out in pain and fear. Hours and hours passed. Day turned to night turned to dawn. I contained my fear, scared that screaming might somehow help this baby to survive, this baby I did not want. Peter came and held my hand, but I told him I did not want him there. The constant poking and prodding and examinations by medics seemed so much more intimate than our sex life, and I deeply resented the fact that it was Peter who had inflicted all of this upon me, poisoning me with the parasite that I was finally about to expel from my body.

The contractions sped up and I was wheeled into the delivery room, biting down on a rag the midwife had given me to stop me biting my tongue. The baby arrived quickly and I felt no more than a lurching and stretching in my pel-vis as it emerged, slippery with my own juices. The nurses whisked it away immediately into the next room and I didn't hear it cry. I was still hopeful.

'Just got to clear his little airways, dearie, and make sure he's all right.'

'It's a boy?'

'Yes, didn't you look?'

I hadn't. Within minutes, another doctor came in and laid this small squealing creature on my chest. He was alive.

'Just for a few minutes, then we'll have to pop him into an incubator, Mrs Russell. Shall I call your husband?' The doc-tor did not wait for my answer and Peter was by my side within seconds, eyes shining.

'Oh my God! We have a little boy!'

I looked down at the tiny scrunched-up face, feathery dark hair, his button nose and the little rosebud lips that caught the light with their spill of drool.

Peter kissed my face and the baby's face and said in a tone of wonderment, 'Look what we made, Delia! A perfect little boy. This is what's important.'

The child we had made was nestled into my shoulder. I waited for that moment of joy, of bonding, of pride. And waited.

16

The baby was taken away and put into a small plastic box, and I was told that I could visit him in the room with all of the other boxed babies as soon as I felt strong enough. Peter went to ring his mother from the phone box. I was given tea and toast, the most delicious meal I ever ate, before or since. They say it's a hormone thing.

The baby was small, five pounds in weight, so the doctors decided that it should stay in the incubator for a while, but we were both discharged after three days. The nurses tried to persuade me to breastfeed, but I point blank refused. The child had already used up so much of my energy. I needed my body to return to normal. Peter had borrowed Daniel's car to collect us from the hospital. He made a big fuss and had filled the car with flowers. 'My beautiful wife and my beautiful boy,' he said, eyes gleaming.

When we got to the house, I saw that Peter had set up the cradle on the sofa beside me. He gently laid the baby into it, and the child didn't stir.

'Put him in his room,' I said, and Peter looked at me curiously.

'We can't keep calling him "him".'

I stared at the baby, who began to squirm under my gaze. 'I think we should take the baby back to the hospital and put it up for adoption.'

He was totally stunned. 'It?' he said. 'You're talking about our son.'

'I don't want him. I don't want . . .'

'What?'

'I don't want the baby.'

He was pale, exhausted from working late and running back and forth to the hospital. 'Is it because of the money?'

'What money?'

'Is it because you can't have a nanny?'

I didn't know how to explain it to him, but the reality was that I didn't want a child.

'No, it's not that, it's . . . I never wanted this baby. I'm too young for all this. I should be out living my life. Please, let's take it back to the hospital, please.'

Peter stared at me. 'Was this your plan all along? Get to London, marry me and ditch the baby?'

'I don't know. I didn't have a plan. I didn't think ahead. I thought London would be fun, exciting, you know? I'll be a terrible mother.'

'I know,' he said, 'that you wouldn't have married me if you weren't pregnant, but we have something here, something real between *us*, don't we? I mean, you could have stayed in Mayo and given the baby up for adoption. You came here for me because you felt something.' His tone was authoritative. He was trying to convince us both.

'I don't want the baby.'

Peter held my face tenderly in his hands. 'You are scared and you have baby blues. I read about it in the book. It's actually quite normal to feel like this. Don't worry. Those feelings will pass.' He kissed my mouth. 'I'll never get tired of your beautiful face, Delia. It might have seemed like a mistake in the beginning, but our baby is not a mistake, not now. I'll get you a nanny. God knows how we're going to afford it, but I'll do anything, Delia, anything for –'

We were interrupted by our ringing doorbell. He clapped his hand to his forehead. 'Shit, it's probably my mother.'

'You invited your mother?' I was incredulous.

'She wants to see our . . . son. Please pretend that everything is OK. Be normal!' His desperation was pathetic.

I braced myself for the arrival of Elizabeth Russell. I anticipated hostility, but when she walked in, she surprised me.

'Congratulations, Delia, you poor thing! You must have got such a fright with him coming early like that. How *is* my grandson?'

I replied in my new accent, taking her by surprise. 'Well, see for yourself, there he is.'

'You sound so different, Delia. You've picked up the accent quickly.' She whooped when she peered into the bassinet. 'May I hold him?' She pushed him up in the air for a few seconds and then cuddled him close. 'Oh Lord, he is the most perfect thing ever. Peter, he is just like you! I can't see you in him at all, Delia. Sorry! Is that insensitive? I mean that it's like going back in time. He's the image of you, Peter.'

Far from being insulted, I was relieved that she could see nothing of me in this baby. It made me feel a little less responsible for him. 'Yes,' I said, 'he's like his daddy.'

'And what are you going to call your little boy?'

'Harry,' I said, and it was a spiteful thing to say, but that's how I react sometimes when I'm trapped.

Peter glared at me. 'We haven't decided yet, Mum. Delia is joking.'

Elizabeth looked appalled. 'I don't think that's an appropriate joke, Delia. I don't think we should ever joke about Harry.'

I felt a little surge of inner triumph. 'I'm sorry, I know. I'm . . . tired.'

Elizabeth brightened. 'Of course you are. Get yourself into bed. Peter will show me around the house and we'll watch the baby. Go and rest, dear. I'll make up some bottles for you.'

I happily went to bed for the afternoon. When I woke hours later, Elizabeth was hovering at the bedroom door with a cup of tea for me. I roused myself and accepted the tea. She sat on the end of my bed. 'You don't mind, do you? I think we should have a chat, woman to woman. I've sent Peter off to get groceries. There is nothing to eat in this house!'

She was much kinder than I expected, considering I had broken one son's heart and stolen the other one. 'Look,' she said, 'you are the mother of my grandson and I want to be in his life and I also want to keep in better contact with Peter. He has distanced himself from us all over the last few years. Sometimes I think he'd prefer to deny his Westport roots, but you, well, no matter what's gone before, you will keep him grounded, won't you? Remind him where he came from?'

I nodded.

'How are you feeling?' she said. 'Overwhelmed?'

I nodded again. 'Yes, the whole thing, the pregnancy, marriage, London – and the baby coming early was quite a shock.'

'I've had two boys, as you know, and let me tell you, it's always a shock, no matter when they arrive.' Her fingers fluttered to a crimson patch at her throat. 'I wanted to . . . to apologize to you. My husband should never have tried to force you into an abortion. It was so . . . wrong. I think he realizes that now – well, at least I hope he does. We don't talk about it.' She was speaking quickly, nervously. I hated her sanctimoniousness. She wasn't the one who was going to be left to rear this baby.

'I wanted the abortion too. I didn't want a baby. I still don't.'

She stood up and blessed herself, and I could see that she had simply decided to ignore what I'd said.

'You are too young to understand. We needn't talk about that any more. What is important now is that you and Peter settle down and raise that child together. Give him the mother and father that you didn't get to have for long. I'm sure Moira and Alan were good in their way, but this little boy will have two parents of his own.'

I began to weep.

She leaned over and hugged me. 'Of course, you will be missing your mother at a time like this. What were they like, your parents?'

Nobody had asked me that, not ever. I began to think of them and I wanted to speak, but choked on the words. I thought of the fact that my father had burned his wife alive, and all of his sons too. It was something I had not allowed myself to think about. Had I made him do that? A sob escaped. Elizabeth leaned forward and enveloped me in her arms, and the tears came then, wracking my body.

'It must be hard for you. Peter told me that you find the idea of motherhood difficult, but you know, lovey, postnatal depression is a real medical condition. In my day we had no idea why we felt so awful, but it's quite normal to feel rage and despair. You'll find it disappears gradually, and when you look into that little boy's eyes and see how much he needs you, a maternal instinct kicks in.'

My crying subsided. Could it be true?

'Are you sure?'

'Yes, Delia, it's hormones. That's all it is.'

I had heard so much about hormones over the previous week. I wished they would go away and take the baby with them.

'How is Harry?'

She let go of me then. 'Harry is . . . well, I won't say he's fine, because he's not. He went to bed after I told him about the baby a few days ago, and he hadn't got out of it when I left home this morning, but . . . in time, he'll get over you.'

'Poor Harry.'

'It was wrong, what you did. You know that? But you will be a faithful wife to Peter because you have learned from your mistakes, right? Peter is as infatuated by you as my Harry was. You cast a spell on my boys, but now you have Peter, for keeps. He's a good soul, but different, you know? He's serious and committed to whatever he does, and that includes you and your son.'

I decided that maybe I should make an effort with the baby. Peter had been so horrified by my suggestion of giving him up. And Elizabeth was insisting that I would fall in love with my son and, in a week or two, I wouldn't be able to imagine life without him. Now that I was getting a nanny, maybe it wouldn't be too difficult.

We called the baby James. It was Peter's choice. His maternal grandfather's name, though the grandfather was known as Jimmy. Peter insisted that here he would only be called James. Elizabeth was delighted. I didn't care.

Elizabeth stayed for a week and did nearly all of the feeding and changing. At first, she was delicate about it, trying not to get in my way or to take over, but I was happy to let her, and then I saw her concern grow.

'Delia, you really should pick up the baby and hold him close to you. You need to bond with him properly.'

'He'll be fine,' I said, 'we'll have a nanny next week.'

Our nanny was a fifty-something Italian woman called Chiara. Peter thought she'd be too old, but we got a bargain because she came cheaply and was also prepared to cook and clean. She was self-contained, gave no personal information and asked no personal information, but she was a stickler for routine. In the early days, I asked her if she'd ever been married or if she had children of her own and she simply ignored my question and asked if she should add mustard to the shopping list. I took that as my cue to respect her privacy. I did the night feeds and the first one in the morning, and she took James for the rest of the day.

During those night feeds, I looked in the baby's face, winded him over my shoulder, cuddled him a little before laying him down again. He cried as soon as the bottle was removed, and my cuddles made no difference. Peter said he had colic. I remember when my little brother Conor had colic and he cried solidly for a week. Daddy moved out and slept on the boat to get away from the screaming. He wouldn't let me come with him. I remember watching Mammy and Conor crying together, and now I understood her exhaustion and misery.

Chiara ate her meals in the kitchen, alone. She made one weekly telephone call home, and maybe once or twice a month she got letters from Italy. She took Sundays off. I have no idea where she went or what she did. I peeked into her room from time to time and it was stacked with Italian romantic novels, with garish 1950s covers. Occasionally, I would invite her to watch television with us, but she refused. Peter thought she was odd, but she came from the same agency that Hannah used, and James loved her immediately.

Hannah laughed when she saw Chiara. 'Everyone else gets a young Irish nanny, you know. You lot have so *many* children. Looking after them must be second nature. Are you going to have ten children, Delia? Are rubber johnnies really illegal there? How hilarious!'

There was always something patronizing about Hannah. She once quite baldly announced that all Irish people were peasants, in the context of some conversation about some ancestor of hers who had been a duke of Ormond. 'Even Peter and you, darling, sorry to say it.'

I knew the poverty I had come from, and even though Hannah did not, she had a way of not letting me forget it. Isabelle was a lot less class-conscious. 'Oh, bugger off, Hannah. Who cares about your bloody ancestors? You could bore for England!'

Moira and Alan and Elizabeth visited for the christening about three months after the baby was born. Moira and Alan were still together then, just about. We kept it to family – well, Peter's mother and my 'parents'. Peter wanted to invite his friends, but I knew that I'd be judged by Moira and Alan's ordinariness and that Alan would lick his knife or that Moira's tights would be darned.

Alan took the christening seriously. Elizabeth had brought over the christening robe her boys had worn as babies – a long silk gown, which James threw up on before we got to the church. Peter had hastily made contact with our Catholic parish priest. Alan was disgusted that Peter and I were no longer regular Mass-goers. 'This heathen country!' he declared. Peter held my hand and gazed into my eyes as the ceremony concluded. He had never stopped gazing at me.

I hadn't told Alan and Moira much about our house move, so when we did the tour I think they were stunned to see how plush and modern our house's interior was.

'Lord save us,' said Moira, 'they've a phone in the bedroom. It's like *Dallas*!' She was uncomfortable with Chiara and kept trying to help her in the kitchen.

'Leave it,' I said, 'it's her job. We pay her.'

'Well!' she said. 'Servants!' But she thanked Chiara every time she entered or left the room.

Elizabeth had grown up with servants and I could see she

found Moira's uneasiness irritating. She acted cordially to Chiara, but casually reminded everyone that it was Peter's hard work that had paid for her and the house.

I had asked Chiara to prepare something simple after the christening, so we had cucumber and salmon sandwiches and tea back in the house. 'Have you no ham?' said Alan.

Elizabeth produced a bottle of sherry she'd bought in the duty-free, and I was grateful for that little slip from reality it gave me. The heat was stifling that mid-August Saturday in our luxurious velvet-swathed living room, even with the French windows open, and we soon made the decision to decamp to the garden. I insisted on bringing the sherry and a few glasses. Alan disapproved of the drinking. His attitude towards me was suspicious. I think he would have preferred to see some sign of gratitude from me towards him, and even though he thought he had 'saved' me by marrying me off to Peter, I was spoiled in his eyes. Moira was more forgiving. She confided that Alan had become more pious since I'd left Westport. He felt that he had to atone for my sins in some way. The cracks in their relationship were obvious. I could see the doubt in Moira's eyes. Alan had become distant with her, telling her that he would pray for her holy soul.

On that day, at least, the baby got plenty of attention as he was handed around between Elizabeth and Moira and Alan. They vied over which of them got to change his stinking nappy. I sipped the sherry, wishing for oblivion.

Alan

I couldn't believe my luck when Moira Gillen agreed to marry me, despite the opposition of her family. She loved me then and I knew it and thanked God every night for the love of that woman. But we were not blessed with children and that upset Moira greatly. I felt bad too, but Moira was inconsolable and we were too old for a baby by the time we put in our adoption application. It would have to be an older child, they said.

When I first saw Delia, I thought she was an angel from heaven. I never saw a child as beautiful before or since. We heard the tragic story about her parents dying in a fire on Inishcrann, and we prayed about it for a few weeks. I was the one who was keen. That girl needed a family. Moira was hoping for a younger child, but she agreed that taking Delia was the right thing to do. We were a bit worried, because of the reputation the island had for insanity and inbreeding, but the girl looked perfect. Inishcrann is the poorest of all the islands and I can't imagine she had an easy life growing up there, but Delia never spoke much about home, or anything else.

For ages, we thought she was shy, and we tried to get her involved in clubs with other girls her age, but she wouldn't go. Eventually, with the help of God, we accepted that we had a quiet child and we were determined to do right by her.

The Russells destroyed my family once before and ruined our good name and I suppose they have done it again with Delia. But now I believe that God made us barren in order that we could save that girl from the flames of hell. If she had had that abortion, her soul would have been damned for ever.

I don't understand why Moira can't see that. She has stood by my side for all these years, but she wanted Delia to have an abortion and I don't understand it. I went to Father Matthew so many times about this, but Moira refused to go to confession. Father Matthew even came to the house, but she wouldn't talk to him. I married a godless woman and I don't know how I didn't see that for the last thirty-five years.

Recently, I've been thinking back to the accusations made about my father by the Russells when I was a boy. What if my father did get that girl pregnant? What if all of what's happening now is the final punishment that I must suffer for the sins of my father? He must have been guilty.

I had to leave Moira. I couldn't reconcile continuing to live with her and being true to my faith. Father Matthew said I was being rash and that I should 'work' on my marriage, but how could I live with a heathen under the eye of God? The last three times I tried to speak to Father Matthew, he said he was too busy. He avoids my eye at Mass and cuts my confession short every week. I have always found solace in my faith, but if the church turns its back on me, what do I have?

17

I worked hard to get my figure back. But having a baby gave me headaches I'd never had before. Two or three times a week, I would have to lie down for the afternoon. Doctors sent me for CAT scans but nothing ever showed up. I knew it was James that caused them.

Peter worked hard to pay for the nanny and the mortgage and the baby, as he constantly reminded me when he'd come home late and exhausted. He was never too exhausted to check in on the baby. I went on the pill shortly after James was born. Peter thought it was wise 'until we're in a more stable financial position'. I was never going to have another child. I had already decided that before James was born.

I read the parenting books finally and followed all of the instructions to the letter. But within three months of his birth, I gave up on forming an attachment to my son. He would never settle in my arms, and cried until I handed him over to Peter or Chiara. It was obvious that he did not like me and did not trust me. Peter insisted that I must keep trying, but the screaming and crying and frustration were too much for me. The smell of baby sick and stinking nappies was revolting. I remembered the days on the island when Mammy would lock me in my room in case I harmed Conor and Aidan. Brian, though younger, was bigger than me by the age of seven, and could stand up for himself. Daddy would come home and beat Mammy for locking me up. 'What was I supposed to do?' she would scream at him. 'Let her kill them?' and I would cry and hold on to Daddy's leg.

In Chiara's presence, I would lie to Peter about having taken James for a walk, or report on his first smile or his first tooth. These were all things Chiara had done, or told me about. She never contradicted me, but kept her eyes averted. She was the perfect nanny. When James cried, Chiara took him away to another room or into the garden.

I spent my days on the train, heading to Eastbourne or Brighton, stopping for an occasional drink in a wine bar with a view of the sea. Peter and I were OK for a while, though he constantly warned me about my credit card spending, but we managed and I tolerated him and the child reasonably well.

Hannah and Isabelle and I went out to nightclubs and parties together. Sometimes Daniel would come with us and provide the party powder, but Peter was always too tired. He didn't like me going out so often, but I think he grew to accept it because I always came home to him, and even though I could have cheated many times, none of the men particularly interested me. I loved the attention and the flirting and I loved the champagne. Hannah or Daniel usually paid for everything. *The Jewel in the Crown* was on television at the time and their set of friends were like characters from the show. I did my utmost to fit in. I thought I was doing so successfully.

One December weekend, Daniel and Hannah invited us to Cornwall, where Hannah's uncle was having a Christmas house party. 'Children are banned,' she said, 'you'll have to park the tyke somewhere else.' Isabelle was going too.

I was keen, but Peter didn't want to ask Chiara to forgo her Sunday off, and offered to stay home to look after James. 'It will be good for me to spend time with him on my own. Sometimes I worry that he barely knows who I am. Would you mind going without me?'

I shook my head vigorously.

'I have some work to do on Saturday,' he said, 'but on Sunday it will be just baby James and me. And besides, it won't cost us anything.' He didn't mind being left alone with James at all. By then, James was seven months old and sleeping through the night.

I was thrilled at the thought of getting as far away as Cornwall without Peter or the baby. Hannah had mentioned that the house overlooked cliffs. I hadn't been to Cornwall before. I was sure the sea would be wilder there than any of the places I had been to on my day trips.

Hannah gave me an etiquette lecture a few days before we left.

'Don't wear a white blouse with a black skirt or you'll be mistaken for a servant, like you were at Kate and Malcolm's last week.'

'What?'

'Oh, darling, we all had such a laugh. Nobody wanted to tell you, but I suppose dress codes were never a big deal in that boring little town from whence you hail.'

My face burned with shame. Her instructions were mostly unnecessary. I had learned quickly from Peter, but Hannah always liked to put me in my place.

'At dinner, your napkin is the one on the left, and your glass is on the right. The larger glasses are for red wine, the smaller for white. Don't make eye contact with the staff. Don't thank them, not more than once anyway. Otherwise, people will get the impression that you were once staff.' She looked at me as if she knew. My faux pas had obviously been noticed. I was furious with myself for missing the mark so widely. Expressing gratitude was something that Moira had always taught me. I hadn't realized I was still doing it. 'Oh, and the plumbing there is terrible, so be prepared to fill the cistern with a bucket. There may not be hot water in the bathrooms, so you might need to bring plenty of perfume.'

Hannah's Uncle Jory's house was like something from the magazines in the Harley Street waiting rooms. High gates with stone lions on pillars led on to a long tree-lined avenue which swept up a rolling hill to a Georgian mansion. I could hear the waves crashing below and was immediately drawn to the sea. Behind the house, sheer cliffs dropped down to the water, though a hundred yards to the left there were stone steps cut out of the rock. I scrambled out of Isabelle's retro Morris Minor and ran down a few steps in the darkness. It was beautifully wild down here, much more akin to what I remembered on the island. Daniel called me from the cliff top – 'Come back up, it's perishing, and pitch-dark!' – and I reluctantly tramped back up the steps. 'Bloody nutter,' he muttered.

An adjacent field had horses grazing in it. 'Do you ride?' said Hannah. 'I forgot to ask, but if you want to, I can get you kitted out.' I remembered my days riding bareback on Inishcrann ponies along the strand behind the harbour. I wouldn't know what to do with saddles or bridles. In my childhood, we clung fast to the horse's mane and hoped for the best. I made an excuse about a sore back.

'Oh,' said Daniel, 'I have the cure for that,' and he showed us a small green leather pouch. 'I have some James in here.'

James was their new name for 'charlie' since I went into labour after doing it for the first time. They all found it hilarious.

Daniel nudged me. 'I always knew Delia was one of us.'

I wasn't one of them. They knew it, and I knew it. Hannah never let me forget it. But we all played along.

As it happened, none of us saw the horses again until the day we left. A Christmas tree taller than our house dominated the entrance hall, and huge fireplaces were blazing in every room and the smell of wood smoke pervaded the house. We spent most of the weekend getting trashed on champagne and cocaine. The house was packed with people of all generations, all with the same plummy accent, the one I had perfected. Uncle Jory – 'Call me Daddy, sweetie' – a baronet of some kind, took a shine to me, and the fact that he was three times my age didn't bother him at all. He followed me about the vast house and I was thankful that I was sharing a bedroom with Isabelle, who found the whole situation hilarious.

'The gamey old pervert!' she said. 'But honestly, Delia, all the men here are asking about you. You'll have to put a bag over your head if you want them to leave you alone. Hannah is furious. She used to be the star of Jory's parties.' There was always some man nearby ready to fill my glass or light my cigarette. I was certainly the focus of a lot of male attention and I could easily have cheated on Peter if I wanted. But it was not attention that I craved. It was freedom. I wanted to be free of husband and child and obligations.

Everyone who came and went over the weekend was on the same buzz, but even I was shocked at some of the behaviour of the so-called upper classes. There were food fights at the long dinner table on the first night, and I felt genuinely sorry for the servants who got caught in the crossfire. So much for etiquette. Men and women, and men and men, disappeared into broom cupboards and emerged dishevelled and half dressed. One matronly woman lifted her dress and flashed her large pale bottom during a disco on the first night. Nothing like this ever happened in Westport. The Russells had always tried so hard to be refined. But here were people who had always had money and status and therefore had nothing to prove.

On the Saturday, I stayed sober for the early part of the day despite offers of port with breakfast and marijuana after lunch. I managed to get away from everyone in the afternoon. I chose the warmest fur coat I could find in the cloakroom and someone's greasy old deerstalker hat and made my way through back kitchens and sculleries to a back door, apologizing to the white-bloused girls as I passed them, ignoring the look of surprise on their faces. I must have appeared strange, but I wasn't thinking about that. I was in a rush to get outside.

There was almost total cloud-cover and the sun must have been low in the sky, but daylight was streaking through in parts, casting beams on the grey seas. I clambered down the man-made steps and walked out on to the rocks, as the sea surged below me. I hadn't worn fur before, but there were sheep fleeces on our beds when we were children that we often wore as shawls, and I felt like a child again, watching the waves crashing and receding, the surf bubbling, the foam glistening on stone. It was wilder here than it was on the east coast of England, and for a little while I looked out on to the horizon as the wind whipped around my head and recalled waiting for Daddy's boat to appear on the sea-line. The wind grew stronger, however, and the hat lifted from my head and disappeared into a rock pool, twenty feet away. I began to climb over rocks to reach it when I heard a voice.

'I shouldn't bother if I were you. It wasn't terribly flattering, that hat.'

I turned. A man was standing in the shelter of the cliff behind me. I hadn't noticed him.

'It wasn't my hat. I . . . I borrowed it . . .' But the wind took my words away and he moved forward, looking at me curiously. He was older, tall and beaky, and despite his overcoat and gloves I could tell that he was a thin man. His hair was grey at the temples and thin on top. I was annoyed that I was not alone. I wondered if he had been watching me, or if he had followed me from the house.

'Oh Christ, you weren't going to jump, were you? Ruin the weekend for everyone?' He saw the surprise on my face and began to laugh. 'I was joking!'

'No, I wanted to get the hat back.' I watched it bobbing on the surface until it disappeared in a rough swirl of foam and descended to the deep. It was gone. I climbed back over the rocks. The man extended his arm to help me, or to touch me, I couldn't be sure, but he looked so frail that I could have pulled him down, so I allowed him to think he was assisting me as I threw my weight forward on to the ledge at the bottom of the steps.

'I didn't expect consideration from such a pretty girl,' he said.

Inwardly, I groaned at the thought of having to avoid the grabby hands of yet another man.

'Your hair is frightful by the way. I should run a comb through it before rejoining the company if I were you.' He was leaning back against the rock and held a long stick in his hand. I noticed a bundle of something at his feet, and when I looked closer I saw that it was the remains of a bird. 'A baby seagull,' he said by way of explanation, 'probably whipped into the cliff by the wind. There are always some that are weaker than others.' Half of its skull was missing and a few feathers clung to the blades of its wings. A purple mess of entrails oozed out of its belly. 'A recent casualty, I imagine.' He prodded it gently, flipping it over, staring intently at the small carcass.

'Oh,' I said, surprised that anyone could be absorbed with such a thing.

'I think it is exquisite,' he said, 'but everyone thinks I'm an oddball, even my wife.'

I grew less wary. If he had intended to seduce me, he would not have mentioned his wife. I smiled at him. 'I think your wife might be right.' I looked down at the bird. I tried to see the beauty in it, but all I saw was decay.

'Did you come down here to get away from the insufferableness of one of Jory's interminable parties? I'm trying to decide if I am totally bored or totally boring. What do you think, young lady?'

'I think you are probably a bit of both.'

'You cheeky pup! Run along then, back to the beautiful people.' There was a note of amusement in his voice.

'Thank you,' I said.

'For what?'

'Helping me up on to the ledge.'

'Oh God,' he said, 'just what the world needs, another pretty liar.'

I climbed the steps, and it wasn't until I got to the top that I looked back, expecting him to be following me. He was not there.

As I entered the cloakroom to replace the fur coat, I caught Daniel and another man in a compromising position, but not one of a sexual nature. Daniel was counting out a large wad of cash, and a flamboyantly dressed man was dabbing some white powder from a small clear plastic bag on to his gums. Daniel was dealing in a bigger way than I'd previously thought.

'Fuck off,' said the man, glaring.

'Don't worry, it's only Delia,' said Daniel, throwing his arm around me. 'Would you like a toot?' And I took the tiny silver spoon offered and whooshed myself back up into a kind of euphoria.

Hannah soon joined us in the cloakroom. She eyed Daniel's arm around my shoulder. 'Well, isn't this cosy?' she said.

I left them to go look for some champagne, promising to return with a bottle, but I don't recall if I did.

The party ended early on the Sunday morning when the house's ancient plumbing could no longer cope with the sewage expelled by thirty guests. Everyone and everything was beginning to smell. Uncle Jory wasn't in the least apologetic. 'Oh, do stay, we'll get the local boys in to dig a latrine!' He was still drunk and hadn't been to bed since the night before. Neither had Hannah or Daniel.

Isabelle told me that some of the local staff had already deserted their posts, outraged by the guests' behaviour and their treatment of them. 'I don't think he'll find anyone to dig a latrine,' she muttered.

Hannah declared in a loud voice, 'I'm sure Delia wouldn't mind rolling up her sleeves. She's Irish, you know!'

I was tired and irritable and had had enough of Hannah's barbs. I turned on her. 'What *are* you talking about, Hannah? For God's sake, spit it out!'

There was quite a gathering in the breakfast room at this time, with maybe ten or fifteen others hovering around in various stages of hangover. They sat up straighter now, alert to what might be unfolding drama.

'Well, Delia, none of us know where you come from, do we? You told us you went to school in Kylemore Abbey in Connemara, but Belinda Sheridan went there and she has never heard of you. You never talk about your family. One would almost think you had something to hide. And that accent, darling, it really slips when you're drunk. You sound like a peasant. Perhaps you'd be more at home in the kitchens, or scrubbing out the toilets.'

A short silence descended upon the room before Isabelle interrupted it. 'Shut up, Hannah. Don't be such a bitch.'

I could feel all the blood rush to my face as Isabelle took

me by the arm and pulled me out of the room. As I left, I noticed the tall man who had been down by the cliffs, lounging by the door. He put out his hand to me. I don't know what he meant by the gesture, but I kept my head down and ignored it.

'Much too pretty,' he said, dismissively.

Isabelle drove me back to London. 'Daniel and Hannah can make their own way back. Sod them.' She waited until my tears subsided. 'Look, Hannah is jealous. Most of us don't give a damn where you're from or who you are. You are a mystery to me, but I like it that way. Your past and your background is nobody else's business. Please don't judge all English people on the basis of bloody Hannah.'

I smiled at her. 'She's Scottish.'

'With that accent?' Isabelle said. And then we started to laugh.

'Thank you, Isabelle,' I said.

'I do have to kiss up to her though, you know – she gets me all my clients. I must continue to be her friend, and so must you, for the sake of Russell Wilkes.'

'What? How can I even talk to her again? She deliberately humiliated me!'

'That was mild. I've seen much worse from Hannah in my time. If she decides to really turn on you, she could persuade Daniel to ditch Peter. Everyone knows that Peter is the brains of the company, but Daniel opens doors that Peter would not otherwise have access to.'

I *am* a peasant. By their standards, that's what I am. And by any standards, I suppose. I grew up on an impoverished island in a stone-wall cottage with a thatched roof and no running water. How could I have come from that to this? And how could I ever belong?

18

I grew fond of Peter. He was endearingly earnest about everything, and although I still would not have called it love, I
enjoyed his company. I might have loved him if the child
wasn't in the way. James loved Chiara and reached for her
when he wanted attention. I guess he knew he wouldn't get it
from me. But he got it from his father. Peter noticed the distance between James and me and tried his best to forge a
bond between us. I made an effort and took over the bedtime routine from Peter, but James cried and screamed for
his daddy, so the experiment was short-lived. My husband
bought me many books on parenting. I would crack the
spines and put the books beside the bath so it looked like I
was reading them, but I pointed out that James simply didn't
like me. And the evidence of James's attachment to Chiara
and aversion to me was obvious, though Peter never knew
how much time Chiara actually spent with him.

As James grew and moved on to solids, cut teeth, began to
crawl, to stand, to toddle, Peter celebrated each of these
milestones as if they were acts of genius. Since all babies
grow up, I couldn't see any reason to make a fuss. Peter
showed concern for my ongoing headaches. I went to crack-
pots and healers and neurologists and acupuncturists, but
nobody could find the cause. 'It's James!' I wailed to Peter
one day.

'Don't be ridiculous, darling. Look at him,' Peter said,
'he's beautiful!'

I looked at my child, and while I could see that he was a

handsome little boy, I felt only resentment and hostility. I was supremely bored and drank a lot of wine and ate a lot of breath mints. Chiara did the domestic chores that I couldn't summon any interest in. She even brought me tea in bed after I'd had a late night at Annabel's. She was quite pathetic.

Chiara did, however, get me interested in cooking. In the beginning, she would prepare the food and I would present it to Peter as my own work when he came home, but I was interested enough to watch and to learn from her. Peter didn't notice much about food, only whether it was there or not, but I learned from going to London dinner parties that you couldn't serve up scrambled eggs on cream crackers, which used to be a Friday night treat at Alan and Moira's in Westport. At one dinner party, I heard Hannah and Daniel sniggering at pineapple and cheese on cocktail sticks. I tasted mushroom vol-au-vents, quiches, avocado, devilled kidneys and pâté de foie gras and I liked them all. I used to watch Keith Floyd on the television, cooking fish. I liked his style. Isabelle watched her weight all the time and Hannah only ate salads in public. I could eat whatever I wanted and retain my slim figure. I bought cookery books and learned gourmet recipes from Robert Carrier. Chiara was relieved, I think, that she no longer had to cook and mind the child at the same time. I banned James from the kitchen. It was impossible to do anything while he was there.

Peter encouraged me to read books about history and science. He suggested that I could take A levels at a senior college and study medicine, and for a while it seemed like a good idea. I started doing night classes in A level physics, chemistry and biology, but even though some of the coursework was familiar to me, I was paralysed by fear of failing again. The students often went for a drink together after class. The men, including one of the tutors, flocked around me, offered me help with my studies, walked me to the Tube station, ignored my wedding ring, tried to kiss me. I knew that if I told Peter, that would be my way out. It was. He was outraged. He suggested that I try to study the books on my own, but physics in particular was a different language to me. I had not studied it in school. He was exasperated when I gave up.

'I'll get a job,' I said. 'I don't want you thinking I'm useless.'

He kissed me. 'That would really help.'

I thought I might be able to work as Isabelle's assistant and was a little taken aback when she balked at my suggestion. 'Oh, Delia, this isn't a hobby for me. I'm not Hannah. It's my living and if I were ever in a position to take somebody on, it would have to be a person who was as enthusiastic and committed as I am, not someone who is simply bored.' She softened the blow. 'Look, a friend of mine has the franchise for a cosmetics company. They're always looking for pretty faces to flog make-up at department stores. I'll put in a word for you.'

At the interview, I thought it was going badly at first. 'A perfect face,' said Joyce, the interviewer, 'but you don't even need make-up. I don't think you're the right person to sell it.'

I was about to thank her for her time when she said, 'You're a perfume girl. Natural beauty sells perfume. And you can sell to men.'

I got a part-time job selling Ocean aftershave at a counter on the ground floor of Debenhams. It smelled nothing like the ocean. There was no training involved, apart from smiling and spraying, and telling the gormless fools how this particular scent suited them. I did well at that counter, and Peter was happy that we had another income, small as it was.

*

James was four years old when we went on our first holiday. Everyone else in our circle went on foreign holidays all the time. Back in Westport, two girls in my class had gone to Spain for a week and we were all insanely jealous. They'd come back looking like Americans, with teeth shining whiter out of tanned faces.

We went without James. I thought I could try hard with Peter on a week away, that maybe I could try to fall in love with him without the pressures of work or the needs of our son getting in the way. Peter thought it was a crazy idea because James had just started prep school. But Isabelle's friend's villa was only available for the second week in September and she had offered it to me at a knock-down rate. Peter thought our sudden absence would disturb James. I had arranged for Elizabeth to fly over to take care of the boy for the week, which I thought meant that we would be saving money on Chiara, but Chiara didn't want to take a holiday and Peter said we couldn't not pay her just because we were going away. I was able to counter Peter's argument by pointing out that James would have Chiara *and* his doting granny. Then Peter balked at the cost of the flights. Peter was always making a fuss about money. We were only going to Nice. Daniel and Hannah took off to the Seychelles and Mauritius regularly, but Peter insisted they weren't going on company money. Hannah's mother was minted, apparently. I suspected that Daniel might be making a tidy profit from his drug dealing, but I wasn't about to tell Peter that. I pleaded with him, impressing upon him the fact that he needed a holiday. He did. He was always working and even Daniel helped me to persuade him to take a break. At the time, I thought Peter's reluctance was because he couldn't trust Daniel to run Russell Wilkes in his absence. He made every excuse under the sun to stay, but it was Elizabeth who finally convinced him. 'You are going to work yourself to death, and then you'll be no good to wife or child,' she said.

Peter agreed but insisted on giving the phone number of the villa to all of his clients and taking a stack of files with him.

I had seen it on television and in magazines and other people's photographs, but the reality of the blue Mediterranean was breath-taking. The azure in Côte d'Azur is richer and softer than any blue I have seen. The one-bed villa was on a hill above Villefranche, and several flights of vertiginous steps led down to the beach. Even Peter was taken by the beauty. The cloudless skies and bobbing yachts and sun-kissed people and the simplicity of bread, olives and cheese and cheap wine all worked their charms.

On our first day at the beach, Peter dived into the sea and swam out, beckoning me to join him. He was shocked to discover that I couldn't swim. 'How is that possible, when you grew up on an island, and you, of all people, are so infatuated by the sea?'

I was the daughter of a fisherman, and on the islands fishermen deliberately never learned to swim. 'Drowning is a horrible death if you fight it,' Daddy always said. '"Tis always better to let go.' I tried to explain it to Peter, but he insisted that swimming was an enjoyable leisure activity and not just about survival, and set about teaching me how to do it. The water was almost lukewarm at this time of year and, despite my fears, I learned quickly in a matter of hours. When we emerged from the gentle waves, a small gathering of locals cheered and whistled, and I felt prouder than if I'd graduated as a doctor or an astronaut, and heart-achingly grateful to Peter for releasing this ability of mine.

It was a shock to me that I had always had this power in

my body, that this knowledge was always within me, that I could float on top of the water or I could plough my way through it, like the tiller of any boat, turning my head from side to side.

The next day, I learned to swim underwater and opened my eyes to a world below where voices and things and people were irrelevant. I had always loved the sea, the shift and the surge and the swell of it, but this experience of immersion, of being part of it, was extraordinary. The fact that Peter had showed it to me made me feel genuine warmth towards him. Those few days were the happiest of our short marriage. I hoped it was the same for Peter, and though he was distracted by business phone calls from London, we drank wine, made love every night and spent as much time as possible in the water. The frequent latherings of suntan lotion we applied to each other became a sexy ritual, and I told him I loved him, and I may even have meant it. 'I think you might be a mermaid,' whispered Peter one night, and I kissed the words right out of his mouth. If only we could have stayed there in that perfect bubble for ever. I was happy. We talked a lot. He admitted that he was stressed about work because he was waiting for the outcome of a deal. He was under a lot of pressure, he said. He tried to talk to me about James again, but I changed the subject every time so he gave up.

On our last evening in the local cheap restaurant where we'd been most days, he eyed the hovering manager and said, 'Doesn't it bother you?'

'What?'

'The way men look at you. I'm not being jealous, it's that it's creepy sometimes. That guy doesn't even care that you're clearly with your husband.'

The restaurant manager he was talking about made no

secret of what he thought of me. When I'd emerged from the sea on the first day, I'd heard a long slow whistle and I'd looked up and seen the glint of this man's gold tooth as he watched me, eyes ablaze with lust. When he turned out to be the same man that later welcomed me into the restaurant, he did not let an opportunity go by to touch me, shaking my hand – '*Cette belle fille!*' – taking my elbow, unnecessarily placing the napkin on my knee. It didn't bother me in the slightest.

'It happens in London too, all the time. I'm used to it. They're harmless.'

'I suppose I can't blame them. I remember the first time I saw you, at my parents' dining table . . .'

We hadn't ever talked much about Westport.

'When I was with Harry.'

He looked mildly irritated, as if he were imagining an errant fly buzzing beside him.

'Yes, but I'm not talking about that. I'm talking about the first time I *saw* you. I spent the whole of dinner trying not to look at you.'

'You stared at me!'

'Did I? I thought I was doing a good job of hiding my feelings.'

'You stared at me as if I wasn't good enough to be at your table!'

'That's what my "falling in love" face looks like.'

We laughed, and although we did not talk about Harry, some element of awkwardness that had always been between us vanished that night.

When Peter paid the bill, the gold-toothed manager took my hand and kissed it. '*Enchanté, mademoiselle,*' he said.

Peter, loosened by wine, corrected him – 'It's Madame, actually' – and offered his own hand to be kissed.

Raoul, according to his name badge, was offended and scurried back towards the kitchen. We giggled all the way up the steps to our villa, stopping for long kisses on the way. I had not had a single headache for the whole duration of our holiday. I knew all along that James had some secret way of causing me pain.

When Daddy's great-grand-uncle, Malachy O'Flaherty, was seven years old, he went out with his uncle on a fishing boat and a hook got caught in his thumb, piercing the nail. It was the days before proper doctors came to the island, so the butcher was called from the mainland to remove the top of Malachy's thumb. But Malachy, as terrified as a small boy had every right to be, went into hiding before the butcher arrived, and refused to come out. The butcher stayed two nights on the island before sailing back, never having amputated the thumb. When Malachy eventually reappeared, he swore blind that the hook digging into the flesh of his thumb did not pain him in the slightest and that he would happily live with it. He was dosed with whiskey, and pliers were used to remove the part of the hook that was visible, but as he grew it broke through the skin again.

Live with it he did, and that thumbnail never grew past a child's size and the hook remained embedded within it. He became known as the man who wouldn't shake your hand, unless a deal went sour. Daddy said that Malachy's bride, his great-grand-aunt Noeleen, often bore the scars of the hooked thumb, because a man and his wife would always be in the way of touching each other and accidents happened between them. It was said that Noeleen had a wandering eye and needed to be kept in check.

When Malachy was thirty-five years old, he and one of his brothers were lost at sea after being offshore for four days. Parts of the boat were washed up on the western shore of Inishcrann, but the sea never surrendered the bodies of the men and no amount of prayers or lamenting by one of the wives made a difference. In those times, fishermen were often lost and the islanders soon accepted they were gone for ever. Noeleen, however, was still a girl of twenty when her husband drowned. She was not for lamenting, but for remarrying straight away, to a man from the mainland who had rethatched Malachy's roof the previous spring. Less than nine months after her first husband's drowning, she had a baby girl and insisted that Malachy was the child's father. In the beginning, the family of three were shunned and regarded with suspicion, but gradually people forgot about her haste and went back to buying her bread and letting her new husband thatch their cottages.

It was eighteen years later, on the occasion of Noeleen's daughter's wedding, that a feast was organized in the parish hall. During the meal, Noeleen began to choke on her mackerel and no amount of slapping her on the back or reaching into her throat could remove the suspect bone. She died there, splayed over the wedding table, but with her last breath, out of her mouth popped a small blackened fingernail impaled by a hook.

Daddy always said that the sea had its own justice, and that it had its own way of taking revenge on island traitors. The sea allowed Malachy to set the record straight. The new bride was not his daughter and Noeleen had betrayed him and the island. Daddy said it was a wife's duty to be ever faithful to her husband.

19

It was soon after we got back to London that things began to change. Just when we found each other, everything started to go wrong. Peter was working later and later and seemed permanently exhausted. Sometimes when I would ring the office, his secretary would admit that she didn't know where he was, that nobody knew. When I later questioned him, he'd react as if I was accusing him of having an affair. That thought had never crossed my mind. Several times he suggested that we could do without Chiara, now that James was older. I insisted that we keep her but he lowered the credit limit on my card and for the first time began to look at the statements that he kept in a filing cabinet.

'What were you doing in Brighton last month?' 'How could a dress cost that much?' 'You spent how much on wine?' The questions were relentless and I eventually guessed that he thought I was the one having an affair. I ordered an itemized phone bill and showed him there were no strange phone calls listed except for Chiara's weekly calls to Italy. But he ripped it up and threw it in the bin.

'I trust you,' he said, but he was annoyed.

And then two weeks later, Peter came home late, ashen-faced. I hauled myself up in bed and put down my book. He didn't come and kiss me straight away like he normally did.

'Is there something wrong?' I asked.

Without answering, he disappeared into James's room and didn't come out for another ten minutes. I heard him go downstairs to the dining room and I recognized the hinge squeak as he opened the antique drinks cabinet. 'Where's the brandy?' he called out.

I got out of bed and threw my robe around me. Chiara came out of her room and looked at me as I passed. I told her everything was fine and flew downstairs.

'I don't know. We must have drunk it,' I lied, knowing that Isabelle and I had finished off the bottle two days previously.

'Fuck,' he said, and he kicked the cabinet door shut. He was mild in his use of language usually; I knew it was something serious.

'What is it? Is it your parents . . . or Harry?' I asked, sitting down beside him at the table.

He put his head down so that I couldn't see his eyes, but his shoulders began to shake and tears splashed on to the rug at his feet. I felt a flicker of something. Impatience? Annoyance? Was my husband actually crying? A grown man? Harry had never cried, not even when I broke his heart.

'For God's sake, Peter, what the hell is wrong?'

He wiped his nose on his napkin. It was disgusting. All those little points of etiquette I had learned, and for what?

'It's the business. We're going under.'

'Under what?'

'We were on the verge of something, but it went wrong. We staked everything on one deal and it didn't work. It's as simple as not putting all your eggs in one basket, but we were sure and eventually it all fell apart. We're being forced to shut down.'

'Russell Wilkes? What does this mean?'

What did it mean for me?

'It's really, really bad. Not just for us. Dad put a load of money into this, their life savings. He had such faith in me. He mortgaged the hotel.'

'But we have the house?'

'We're going to have to sell, Delia. It's gone. It's all gone. I've been meeting with banks and lenders, but everyone's nervous since Black Monday and it's all happened suddenly. I honestly thought we'd be OK. We both took bonuses last May. That's how we got James into that prep school with Daniel's kids. But I think once people started looking at the bigger picture ... our project required long-term investment, and they couldn't hang on.'

'You gambled everything?'

'I guess I got seduced by the lifestyle that we couldn't afford. I'm not blaming you. I got sucked in too, trying to keep up with the Joneses, but the bills were mounting up. We couldn't get any more credit. We had to take the risk.'

'Well, what are you going to do?'

'Thanks for the sympathy.' His self-pity was pathetic.

'Hang on! I'm not the one who lost every—'

'I was hoping for loyalty, for support.' The chair scraped over our solid oak floor and Peter slammed the door on his way out.

Later, when I was in bed, Peter crept in and lay behind me, spooning. 'I'll figure something out,' he said quietly, and kissed the back of my head. I pretended to be asleep.

The next day he went to work.

'Why are you going in?' I asked.

'We have to clear the building. The bailiffs are coming for the furniture.'

'Already? Isn't that very quick?'

He put his hands up to stop me questioning him any further.

Hannah rang as soon as he'd left the house. 'What the hell happened at Russell Wilkes, Delia? Daniel has gone on a total bender since last night. Has Peter said anything?'

'I . . . I don't know. I think there's some trouble at work.' I wondered what Daniel had told her, and if it matched what Peter had told me.

'I'm coming over. I'll ring Isabelle.'

Hannah knew less than I did, but she knew that Russell Wilkes was sinking. 'Oh God, Daniel has lost the run of himself completely. Too much coke. I mean, most of us can take it or leave it. Maybe he was caught doing a line by a client and word has travelled?'

That did not seem unlikely. Hannah and I were bonding slightly more now, as the wives of failing businessmen. But I felt I had the upper hand. I smugly pointed out that Daniel was rarely ever in the office and that Peter had always done the lion's share of the work, that it couldn't be Peter's fault. I could see that Isabelle was getting ready to referee a row between us, but Hannah was surprisingly calm and didn't seem to be particularly perturbed.

'It would all be fine if Mummy wasn't being such a bitch. She has the money to bail Daniel out and save the company, but she is simply refusing to. Daniel actually begged her on the phone yesterday. Really humiliated himself. We haven't got a pot to piss in now, but I know Mummy. She's not going to let us starve. She owns half of Aberdeenshire.'

'But what about us? Peter and me?'

'You can hardly expect *us* to help you, darling. It's not as if Peter is family. But don't worry,' she said, patronizingly, 'as you say, your Peter is such a clever chap, he'll think of something. It is a terrible shame, but it can't be helped, can it?' She popped the cork on the bottle of wine.

Isabelle lit her cigarette and said, 'Well, all good things must come to an end.'

By the time Chiara collected James from school, I had gone to bed for the afternoon. It was partly the wine, but I was more rattled by the fact that if Peter didn't have an income, we wouldn't be able to afford Chiara, and I would be stuck with my son. I had sent off for some prospectuses for boarding schools the previous week. If Peter wasn't working, he could mind James. I was sure I could get more hours in Debenhams.

It took a week or two before I gleaned the full story. Far from being a paragon of virtue, Peter had had his hands in the till. It wasn't Daniel's coke dealing or lack of interest in the business that had been the ruination of Russell Wilkes. It was Peter's embezzlement. The financial situation was far worse than he had led me to believe. He had risked clients' money by investing in deals without their permission. Daniel didn't even know yet the full extent of the losses. Peter didn't have the courage to tell him. But he feared that he could be prosecuted.

'But why, Peter, why would you do such a thing?' I asked.

He did not blame me directly. He loved me too much for that. But he looked right at me as he said, '*We* wanted a proper house and a good school for our child, but I couldn't afford it yet, and the bank wouldn't lend me as much as I needed, so I thought I could temporarily borrow from certain accounts. I was sure I'd be able to pay it back, but then the furnishings were so expensive, and Chiara's wages, James's school fees and the credit card bills mounted up, and I got a bit more desperate and risked more money. I've been fobbing off clients and shuffling money around for the last four years. And then, before we went on holiday, these aviation leasing company shares came up. I talked to a guy I shouldn't have talked to.'

'Insider dealing?'

'Yes, but he was so sure that a merger was happening, so I moved everything into that stock. I trusted him.'

'Are the police coming?' I asked.

'Not yet. I hope Daniel will be able to get the money together to cover the losses.'

'Peter, you *stole* other people's money.'

He was collapsed in anguish on the sofa. 'I'm so, so sorry.'

'You'll have to ring your father.'

'Jesus.'

Within a matter of months, we lost our home, credit cards, furniture and friends. We lost Chiara. She was distraught. But not as much as I was to lose her. She was the one who took James shopping, bought his clothes and noticed when his little shoes were getting too tight. Chiara adored James, and I think she was secretly pleased that he preferred her. Even after years of living in our home, she was intensely private and had no friends or social life that we were aware of. James was her world, and even though she didn't technically work for us in the evenings or on Sundays, she was always happy and eager to babysit if we were going out.

'Do you think Chiara is too attached to James?' Peter had asked one evening, as the child sat patiently outside her bedroom door, waiting for her to come out.

'It's good for both of them,' I said. I could tell Peter wasn't entirely satisfied with the answer. But I kissed his brow and he leaned into me.

What would I do without her? I hadn't given much thought to what might become of her. We had had an alliance of sorts, but we had never become friends. Peter had to give her a month's notice and she spent most of the month hollow-eyed or weeping. Peter thought Chiara was unstable. 'It's as well she's going,' he said. 'She acts as if James is her child. It's completely inappropriate.'

As close as she had been to James before, over that last

month they clung to each other. It was pitiable. In her final week, Chiara came to me and said, 'What about James? Who will be his mother?'

I knew exactly what she meant and I think the question gave me more sleepless nights than it gave Chiara. When she left, she was sobbing, and although we had explained to James that she was going away for a little holiday, he knew that it was more than that. He kicked and screamed and pulled everything off the dining-room table. I sent him up to his room and locked the door and turned up the radio.

Peter stayed out of jail, as Hannah's mother was eventually persuaded to cough up to keep Daniel and Peter from being sued or arrested. Daniel had countersigned all of Peter's transactions, so legally he was equally culpable. Word spread around the City though, and Peter and Daniel's names were synonymous with dirty dealing and they could never work in finance again. Hannah rang once thereafter and called my husband and me every name under the sun.

I knew deep down that Hannah and Isabelle had adopted me like children do with a stray dog. They had been friends with each other for years. They would soon tire of me and move on to their next little pet. They were old money, and Peter would always be 'trade' to them. Hannah and Daniel came from aristocracy, and Isabelle's father had owned a stately home somewhere in Norfolk. Her interior-decorating job earned enough money to maintain the old place and keep her in a tiny flat. She had always been generous and welcoming to me, but now she no longer returned my calls and the nightclub invitations stopped.

Peter did everything he could to pay off the people he had defrauded, but it wasn't enough. In the end, the Russells had to put Carrowbeg Manor and their beautiful home in Westport on the market and downsize to a smaller house, and were no doubt forced to move back a few pews at Sunday Mass, if they were still accepted there. Elizabeth told me tearfully in one of her weekly phone calls, 'That's what you do for your son. You will do anything you can to protect him.'

Peter's father, Declan, took another view. He arrived in London a week after Peter told him the catastrophic news, and out of Peter's earshot told me, 'This family was doing fine until you walked into it. You're a fucking hex.'

20

Peter laughed at the idea that we could live on my Debenhams' salary if I went full-time. 'Did you ever look at the
price of rent in this city, Delia? Do you even know how much
our mortgage repayments were?' Peter, despite his track
record, had a better earning capacity than me because of his
degree and experience, he said, but he would have to move
into a different area of work. His choices were limited and he
would have to start at the bottom, so, he insisted, I would
have to do the childminding myself. James was taken out of
the expensive prep school and installed in the local primary
near our new home. By the end of November 1988, we were
renting a three-room ground-floor flat in Cricklewood with
a shared bathroom, below a man with a spider's web tattooed
across his face. Peter told me I should drop the accent now.
Cricklewood was an Irish ghetto. I thought that was all the
more reason to keep it.

I had not told Moira anything, until I wrote to tell them
our new address. I knew from her previous letters that she
and Alan were living separately now, and that it was all
because of me. Her letters had been infrequent. I knew she
begrudged me the high lifestyle I'd been leading. This time,
she replied promptly, asking if I knew what was going on,
and why Carrowbeg Manor was up for sale. Westport was
rife, she said, with gossip about Declan Russell and his sudden drink problem. 'And Harry's no better,' she said, 'father
and son rolling around the streets at all times of the day and
night, making a disgrace of themselves.'

I feigned ignorance and suggested that Declan was approaching retirement age and wanted a break. But Moira was shrewd in her reply: 'Why is he selling in such a hurry then? And why wouldn't he pass it on to Harry?'

Debenhams would not work around my son's school schedule and I could no longer afford the weekly Tube ticket that took me into Zone 1, so I was forced to give up my job. We lived hand to mouth on social welfare, trying to eke the money out over the two weeks between giros. We had no luxuries now, but we had food on the table, a solid roof over our heads and central heating. Peter kept apologizing to me. I couldn't tell him that I had lived in far worse conditions than this, and I was happier then. We talked about selling our clothes. I had a few designer pieces and he had some Savile Row suits, but thankfully Peter insisted that we could still look the part if we wanted.

Because we had to cut back on all expenditure, I had to cook every meal on the cheap, with the most basic of ingredients. Chips and frozen burgers from Tesco instead of fresh produce at Waitrose. The tiny, badly ventilated flat smelled of cooking oil and sour milk. Now that he was unemployed, Peter pulled his weight in the parenting department and I was more than happy to hand James over. When Peter was out of the house on his endless job hunt, and James was home from school, I left him to amuse himself and ignored his constant demands for attention. He wailed for Chiara. When was she coming back? He went from being a fairly placid child to a child with freakish temper tantrums. I stuffed cotton wool into my ears and went to bed and left him in the kitchen cum sitting room cum dining room with the knives and the hot taps. My headaches returned with a vengeance. I was clearly allergic to my son. Peter would no longer listen to these complaints. 'Stop it, Delia, that's ridiculous!'

Despite everything, Peter never stopped loving me, though I made it difficult for him, and I never warmed to our child. My fleeting love for Peter disappeared too. I turned my back to him in bed. There were no more trips to the coast. Just constant drudgery – washing, ironing, cooking, cleaning, feeding – interrupted sleep and cramped conditions.

On Christmas Day, we ate tinned ham and had pineapple chunks for dessert and watched *Chitty Chitty Bang Bang* on the small television that sat on top of the fridge. Peter had made a mechanical toy for James by hand. It was a clever piece, a robotic puppet of sorts. But he had nothing for me. 'Sorry, my love, but Santa Claus is more important to him, don't you think?'

I had nothing for either of them, except jealousy. Why should James get a gift before me?

Peter, more aware now of my estrangement from my son, nagged me about how I was neglecting him, how I never looked at him. We rowed about this constantly. James was a chatterer and would tell Peter exactly what happened during the day when he wasn't home. Two days previously, Peter had given me money to take James to see Santa Claus at a shopping centre while he went for a job interview. I couldn't stand the thought of being in a shopping centre full of things I could not afford, surrounded by my own and other people's overexcited children. I had used the money to put James into a crèche while I went to a wine bar. Now Peter was asking James about Santa Claus. James said he hadn't seen him. I told Peter our child was a liar, but I could see that Peter believed him over me. I left, slamming the door behind me, leaving them both in tears. I walked down to the high street and found an open pub. I sat at the bar and drank whatever I could get with the few pounds I had in my purse, and enjoyed being the centre of attention again, as drunken locals, mostly old Irishmen, tried to make my acquaintance. I slipped back to my old accent, and before long they were buying me drinks and arguing over who was going to walk me home. In the end, I slipped out a side door when an actual fight broke out and chairs went flying.

When I got home, Peter was waiting up. 'I can't believe you walked out, tonight of all nights,' he said.

I wasn't ready for Round Two. But I was drunk enough to tell the truth. 'I don't like him,' I said.

Peter blamed himself. 'I should never have agreed to hiring Chiara. You and James never got a chance to bond. And I never noticed.'

I let Peter believe what he wanted to believe. He put his hand out to touch my face. 'We'll fix this, together. We are a family and we must start to act like one.' Peter thought he could fix everything. Poor Peter.

Some weeks later, I got a postal order for five hundred pounds from Moira. She told me what she had learned from Elizabeth. Elizabeth's version of events was that Peter's business partner had embezzled money and the company had gone bust, leaving the extended Russell family in financial jeopardy. I don't know what Moira must have sold to get the money, but it coincided with Peter finally getting a job as a photocopy machine salesman for IBM, so I didn't feel the need to tell him about the postal order. At first, he had resisted taking such a menial job. He had sought out his other old Oxford friends, but maybe they had never seen him as one of them either. Hannah had declared that we were both peasants. I had always thought that Peter was a cut above me, but now we were just another two Irish immigrants among thousands in London trying to scratch a living.

Once he started the job, his mood improved. He was technically minded and was genuinely interested in the machines he was selling and their capabilities. His salary didn't stretch to that much more than the dole, but his working meant that I was stuck with James when he wasn't at school. I could take no joy from cooking either, now that we couldn't afford the food I had learned to cook from Robert Carrier's books.

I had to be more careful with James, but there was one secret that James and I did not tell Peter. Even his young mind grasped that he had too much to lose by betraying it. We were co-conspirators, my son and I.

One day, waiting at the school gates, I was surprised to meet Chiara. She asked me if she could see James, if she could take him to the park. I knew Peter would not approve, but then James emerged from the scrum of children and his face lit up with happiness when he saw her. It would have been cruel to deny them each other's company, so I swore them both to secrecy. And we made an arrangement. Chiara was now caring for an elderly man in his home in Hampstead. She had two afternoons off a week, so on Tuesdays and Thursdays she would collect James from school and drop him back to the house before Peter was due home from work at 6.30. She even fed him sometimes. It was an agreement that suited all of us, and when James came home, excited by his afternoons with Chiara, I gave him stern reminders about how, if he told Daddy, the afternoons would be stopped. Sometimes he forgot and blabbed things about going to the zoo with Chiara or some such, but a sharp look or a pinch from me would shut him up and he would agree with me that he was just pretending. Peter was concerned. 'I was hoping that after six months, he'd forget about her, but he still talks about her all the time.'

His behaviour was better though when he was seeing her. I comforted Peter by telling him I was proud of our loyal and imaginative child.

So, for two days a week, once I had dropped James at school, I was free for the day. I used Moira's money wisely and eked it out for nearly a year. I took the train to Folkestone or to Dover and walked the cliffs or the piers and had a long lunch in a grand hotel somewhere overlooking the sea. When the weather was better, I brought my swimming togs and went for a dip, though the English Channel could not compete with the Mediterranean in the autumn for colour or temperature. I bought myself time and freedom. I assume Chiara thought I was having an affair, and in a way I was. A secret affair with myself.

Often, I thought about not coming back. Looking back, it would have been better for everyone if I had just disappeared one day with Moira's money, but I did not think that far ahead. All I worried about was how I would get to the sea when the money ran out. I think there must have been some bond between James and Peter and me. It is strange, I suppose, that I never thought of them as family. I never thought of Moira and Alan as family either, but giving birth to James should have changed that. I have been described as heartless so many times over the years, but if I was truly heartless I would have walked away from that child, and from Peter. I stayed until James was almost seven years old. And I didn't leave. I was banished. What happened was an accident, though everyone holds me responsible.

Peter's technological skills were recognized. He moved from selling photocopiers to fixing them, and then into their design department, and then to designing computers for the same company. He was a quick learner and within two years his earnings had increased substantially. He had been honest with IBM about what had happened at Russell Wilkes and they told him that they would never put him in a finance position, but he was happy about that because he enjoyed the mechanical design work. They had him doing a diploma in electronic engineering, at night. He would come home talking about microchips and circuit boards and it made little sense to me, but he was genuinely enthusiastic about it, more so than he ever had been in the company that he co-founded. This time there was less responsibility and almost no risk.

I got a part-time job on reception in a hair salon in Golders Green two mornings every week and all day Saturdays. We rented a bigger flat nearby. This one had two bedrooms like the last flat, but the kitchen and sitting room were two separate rooms and we could finally eat our dinner at the kitchen table rather than with our plates in our laps. We had our own bathroom.

I should have been happier, but more than ever I felt the pull of the sea, and in the few hours when I did manage to sleep I dreamed of swimming and searching for something on the ocean floor, though I never knew what it was. As frustrating as those dreams were, it was worse to wake up to find Peter gazing at me and James pulling at him, demanding his breakfast. The money from Moira had run out. I had to survive on what Peter gave me and my own salon earnings. My secret day trips and daytime wine-tippling were no longer possible. While Chiara took James, I stayed home and watched Oprah Winfrey and *Neighbours* on the television. My salon job was merely respite from the stifling domesticity of home. I was still using my upper-crust accent, and while the manager thought it might bring class to the place, the other girls there distrusted me. They assumed that someone like me was working there as a hobby. I didn't care. I wasn't there to make friends.

The best part about the hair salon was the magazines. Glossy ones filled with pages of impossibly expensive clothing and glamorous models and photos of society parties.

One day in March, I came across a photograph of Hannah and Daniel at the Tynedale Hunt Ball in Welton Hall. Hannah's hair was fashionably highlighted, considerably toned down from her peroxide days. Her trademark scarlet lipstick was intact and her slinky full-length gown showed off her curves. Clearly, she had not faded from society. Daniel, bekilted in the photo, was caught holding a handkerchief to his nose. Their lives hadn't changed at all. I felt a surge of jealousy course through me. Hannah didn't deserve any of this.

I wasn't jealous of her. I didn't want money necessarily, I wanted to live a life in the fresh air with an open sky and the sound of waves to soothe me to sleep. I wanted isolation. That night, I begged Peter again to move somewhere else, anywhere closer to the sea. He shook his head in sorrow.

'I can't, Delia, you know I can't. IBM has taken me on and trained me up. I'm doing well there. It would be crazy to leave now. Computers are the future and we'll be in on the ground floor. This is a real chance, darling. We can make it again. Make it big.'

'That's what you said last time,' I said, making no attempt to keep the bitterness from my voice. He reached for me, but I turned away. Peter was a relatively calm person, but he was a hard worker and emotionally strong. He never lost his temper, but this time he was annoyed.

'For Christ's sake, Delia, I have taken all the responsibility for this family. I've done everything for you, and you never acknowledge that!'

'I share your bed.'

'What? Are you saying you only have sex with me because I earn the money? Are you actually saying that?'

I had to backtrack. 'No, it's not like that. I'm sorry.' I allowed him to hug me.

'Anyway, we haven't had sex in months, you know?' He kissed me on the mouth.

I felt nothing and let my mouth go slack.

'What is it, Delia? You know I'm not a magician. I can't fix everything overnight, but things are getting better, aren't they?'

'I suppose.'

'I think maybe if we had another baby, we could start over. A little brother or sister for James. You missed that bonding time with James because of Chiara, but it's not too late to find that mothering instinct within you. What do you think?'

I thought so many things, but mostly I thought about the fact that my husband knew me so little. How could he possibly think that *another* child would improve things?

'No.' I said it loud and firmly.

'At least think about it?'

'NO!' I roared the word in his face.

We had another major row that night. I slapped him and bit him and told him I felt like a prisoner. I said it was bad enough having one brat, without the thought of having another.

That night he slept on the sofa and I was glad.

The next day he got up and made James's lunch and prepared to take him to school. I stayed in bed. Before he left, he came and stood at our bedroom door.

'OK,' he said, 'we won't have another baby. Please don't leave me.'

I did not respond.

After he left, I dressed in my best clothes. I hadn't had occasion to wear my Vivienne Westwood jacket for some time, but today I was on a mission. I took the Tube to Chelsea, stopping off to buy a copy of the *Sun*, and walked through the park to Carberry Gardens, to a house I had visited so many times before – for cocktails before we hit Annabel's, for birthday parties, for afternoon wine and cocaine. I noticed that my boots were clogged with mud. I didn't care. Hannah opened the door, and a sly smile appeared on her face. 'Well, look what the cat dragged in!'

'May I come in?'

She opened the door wide and stood back to let me enter. This time, I didn't bother to wipe my feet to protect the cream woollen carpets, and she was about to scold me, to remind me, but I put my hand up. 'I haven't got all day, Hannah. Put the kettle on? Or open a bottle of wine? Let's keep this as civilized as possible. I assume the children are at school?'

She was taken aback and said nothing as she followed me into the kitchen. She didn't open a bottle of wine or put the kettle on, but stood with her arms folded and her back to the kitchen table. 'What is this all about? How dare you come swanning in here as if you own the place?'

I decided not to pussyfoot around the situation.

'It's simple. You and I both know that Daniel used to supply half the City boys with cocaine. I have names, dates and places.' This was a lie. 'You were right about one thing, Hannah. I am a nobody. And that means I have nothing to lose.' I threw the paper on to the table. 'All I have to do is make one phone call to the editor.'

I wish I'd had a camera to take a photograph of her face. It was, as they say, a picture.

'I get it,' she said. 'He's the embezzler and you're the blackmailer. What a team. Daniel almost lost everything because of Peter. He's landscape gardening now, trying to scratch a living because of your husband.' She raised her voice to a shrill scream. 'We haven't got any money!'

I gestured to my surroundings. The plush furnishings, the

expensive paintings on the walls, the state-of-the-art designer kitchen. 'Really, Hannah? I thought Mummy owned half of Aberdeenshire?'

For the first time, I saw Hannah tearful. I felt a surge of power. 'Yes, but that's her money. She's helping us out until Daniel can get established, that's all.'

'Well, I'm sure she can help me out too. Don't worry, I'm not looking for a fortune. Just a monthly payment, into my post-office account. Two hundred pounds a month. You can tell her you had to give the nanny a raise.'

A look of relief swept over her, and I knew that she'd thought I was going to ask for thousands. I am not greedy though. I only wanted to fund my private affair.

'We don't have a bloody nanny any more. Why do you think I look like this?' She was bare-faced and her hair showed an inch of dark roots. Her jeans bore a stain that had dried in and crusted. Cornflakes, perhaps.

'I don't care. It's not a lot of money to you, or *Mummy*. I'm sure you can manage it. For now though, I'd like to have whatever is in your purse, please.' I was thoroughly enjoying myself.

'Delia, for God's sake, you think I won't report you to the police as soon as you leave?'

I picked up the handbag that was hanging over the back of the chair.

'I know you won't. Remember, I have nothing to lose. You have all this.' I waved my hand around. There was forty-five pounds and some change in her purse. I took it all. She didn't try to stop me. I left a piece of paper with my post-office account details on the kitchen table. 'Next week, please. Two hundred pounds. I'm taking this as a sign of your good faith. Have a nice day.'

'I always knew I was dealing with a fucking peasant. I was

right all along,' she screamed at me as I walked into the hall, dragging my muddy boots through her thick-pile carpet. I slammed the front door and tasted victory, power and freedom.

I caught the train to Brighton and walked the pier, reviving myself in the salt air. Then I sat in a newly opened wine bar and had a long boozy lunch. A group of businessmen invited me into their company, but I shunned them as I flicked through the glossy magazines I'd bought. I had another two glasses of wine on the train back. I bought a bottle from the off-licence on my way home. Normally, I was a solid drinker: it took a lot to get me drunk. But that day, I drank a lot.

When I got to the flat, Chiara and James were waiting outside in the cold. I joined them on the doorstep. I hugged her, thanking her profusely. But she shrugged me off.

'You are drunk. You should not be caring for a child.'

'I agree completely,' I said.

'We went to cinema to see the Teenage Turtles, so he has not had his dinner. He won a gold star for his drawing today. He is exceptional boy.' She kissed James and walked away. He waved at her, grinning and blowing kisses, until she disappeared around a corner.

I let us into the flat. James was excited, no doubt full of fizzy drinks and sweets that Chiara had fed him. He wanted me to look at his prize-winning scribble, but I was trying to fit the corkscrew into the bottle and ignored him. I poured myself another glass and turned on the television in the sitting room so that he could watch cartoons. I set about preparing dinner.

My memory grows fuzzy at this point. I was too tired and drunk to make much effort. I remember chopping potatoes clumsily and putting the pot of oil on to the electric ring to heat up. I went into the bedroom with my replenished glass and turned on the radio. Then I remember the sound of Peter shouting and pulling at me, and not being able to see anything. I remember something falling across my face and shoulder. I remember that I couldn't breathe. I remember being outside in the open air, facing the sky, and being able to breathe again. I remember him screaming James's name. I remember looking at the faces of neighbours who were crying and praying. I remember the sound of sirens. The strange thing is that I don't remember physical pain, not that day. I remember being in the ambulance, and I remember another stretcher containing a mass of hot burning meat being pushed in alongside me. It was days before I realized that was James.

Chiara

I thought I would have had my own child. It is normal for woman.

I had been working in the family restaurant, in Rimini, good restaurant, top class, later take care of my mother and my father until they die, both demented in their last years.

My brother won a bursary at the Milan University, where he never came back. He stay there now, a retired professor of psychology. We live different lives. I do not know him, even with the letters and phone calls. He never got married as well. I think that, if I was a boy too, my parents would make me study more hard.

But the only thing they want from me is grandchildren. Neighbours and cousins have children, but I am busy for so many years, working all day long, taking care of my parents, keeping them company.

I had boyfriends but they are not always kind. When I fell in love, it was with a man who is married. He swear he will leave his wife. It never happen. Time went by. Twenty-two years after the beginning of my love story, I still was spinster with no children. My lover choose a younger woman.

I could no bear the betrayal. I go to his wife and I tell her everything. I hope he come back to me, but he went spend a week with the new young girl before accepted back with wife and children.

Now I was the bitch, the family-wrecker, someone to avoid. The mayor, a friend of my lover, raise the restaurant rent. My loyal customers eat somewhere else.

When my father died after some years, I sell the restaurant, to go travelling around. I hoped for romance, an encounter on a faraway beach, just like in the novels I reading.

I have been in pensiones, guest houses and B&Bs all over Europe. But nobody fell in love with me.

In two years I run out of money, but in London my English was good enough to sign up to a childminding agency, looking for a job as a live-in nanny. The woman who interview me said I am too old for that job. I had fifty years.

'You need energy for the kids,' she said, but I insisted: I have been fit for the job. As I was older, I was cheaper too. That's why the Russells choose me.

I immediately like Peter. Delia seem just fine, but that woman no want her own child. I no understand why. James was the perfect boy. They had everything: a big house, good clothes, good furnitures. And the loveliest boy. Since when he was just a little baby she did no care of him. It was me to feed him, change his diapers, to watch him in the eyes. Peter say that Delia would get used to the boy: it was just a matter of time. Meanwhile I was get used to the boy, even if he wasn't mine.

She kept doing nothing at home. As soon as she lost her big belly, she go out party until late. I no understand her husband allow her doing that. He was so in love with her. It was him to get the money home, but she was the boss in the house. He allow her to do whatever she wanted to. He try keep her happy. I realized that I should say nothing about Delia. I would be fired.

She was no cruel to me, but she prefer me and her child not exist. Sometimes, when she bored, she allow me to have lunch with her. Then she had been asking about my family, but she had no interest in me answering, switching the radio on. In the beginning, it was me doing the cooking, like in my family restaurant at home. I am very good cook. Then she start watching me and she start cook. Just because she was bored, I think.

The boy was my reason of life. For four years and half, it has been like James was my own child. We loved each other. Peter work a lot. When he back home he tried to spend time with his son, but it was usually bedtime. They rarely did something together, like a family. During weekends, Delia have been saying that the boy had exhausted her, and that it was right for him to spend time with his father. Then it was Peter to go out with him, to the park or for a milkshake.

I will never forget James's first day of school. That little man, in all his buttoned-up uniform. Peter went to work early as usual. I had given for granted that Delia would have brought James to the school of St David's. James had been nervous the night before, after I had spent weeks trying to reassure him that everything would have been fine, with new classmates and friends. He calmed down, falling asleep while I was reading him a story. In the morning, I prepare the breakfast and I dressed him up, waiting for Delia to appear. I knocked her door. 'Could you not bring him?' she yelled, without even opening the door, without even getting out of the bed. I was glad. I worry about how she have managed the stress, how she react if James start crying. That day James was nothing less than a brave boy: the only sign of nervous, his hug to me on the classroom door, longer than usual. Delia did not even ask me how had it gone, back home. At least she went to take him from school, only to leave him to me and go back to watch the TV beyond a close door.

Then I had from Delia the notice of dismissal. She was as upset as me; I was struck by her distress, until I realize that what it was upsetting her was she had James from now on her own. The last week in the house I feel anxious for what could have happened to the boy. Only God knew how he would have been without me, and who would take care of him.

I could not help thinking of James, after I had to leave. I went to the St David's: chatting with the other nannies, I came to know that the Russells must relocate to Cricklewood; James now was going to a state school. I do not care that he was in a worse school, now: I worry about his life at home.

I found an opportunity as nurse to an old war veteran, but my new home was close to the new James's school. Sometimes, hiding,

I have gone there to watch him playing in the courtyard. I want to talk to him. Sometimes I waited for the moment Delia went to take him. She always was the last of the parents. I could see how sad and upset he was when she arrived. She no even take his hand, walking ahead of him as he was a dog. I could not bear it.

Delia was happy of my proposal to have James with me for two afternoons in a week. I did not care of no pay. I just wanted to spend some time with him. Our secret. The last day I spend with him, James was happy. He had some friends at school, now, and he had made a drawing for me. I still have it. We went to the cinema, with me stare at his little face, lit by screen. I wish I could run away with him. I wanted him to be my child.

When I brought him back to Delia, she was completely drunk. She fall against the gate. We had to wait for her opening the door for half an hour. I should no have give him back to her.

Peter is right. I should have told him Delia was a bad wife and a bad mother.

Yesterday, I see a boy in park and he look like James much. I go talk to him and he smile, happy boy like James. I take his hand and we go walk. Then lady is scream at me. Police come and now I warn must not talk to children.

21

James survived. I was informed that my son's scarring and physical deformity as a result of the fire were extensive. He faced a lifetime of surgeries and skin grafts. It might have been better if he had died. For all of us. We would have been able to move on.

When I became fully conscious and aware of my sur-roundings, a hospital counsellor came to see me. She told me that I mustn't blame myself for what happened to my son. She said the important thing for me to do was to support him through what was going to be a very long and complex recuperation process. I looked at her and wondered who was going to support me through my recovery.

I endured the daily agonizing undressing and redressing of my face, neck and right shoulder with lanolin cream, gauze and bandages. Surgery was not an option for me. The poly-ester curtain in our bedroom had fallen in flames on to my head and welded to my skin. The flesh was red raw, and exposure to the air was excruciating. My eyelid drooped on one side, and the right corner of my mouth turned down-wards. Muscles in my neck and shoulder had contracted, and I needed daily physiotherapy to stretch those muscles out again so that I could hold my head up. The painkillers barely took the edge off. A nurse offered me a mirror in those early days, but I declined. While I knew the damage was bad, I did not have to see it.

As it happened, I did not see James after that first day in the hospital because the truth came out about everything while I was heavily sedated. Apparently, Chiara had seen the fire on the television news and rushed to the hospital to visit James. She was inconsolable and blamed herself. She told Peter everything – that I had never cared for James when she had lived with us and that she had continued to see him twice weekly for the last two years with my consent. She told him I was drunk when I got home that day. Peter was furious with her for keeping all of this from him. He banned her from ever seeing James again and stopped her from coming to the hospital, but not before she had found me in my ward and laid vicious blows on to my bandaged head. I have a vague recollection of her being escorted from the hospital by burly security guards, and I heard her screams echoing down the corridor as all the other patients and visitors in my ward shouted abuse at her.

That afternoon of the fire, Daniel had rung Peter at work, demanding to know what I was doing, blackmailing his wife. Peter didn't know what he was talking about. He thought it must have been some kind of joke and promised to talk to me, but our home was on fire when he got there. He rescued his wife first and then went back into the flames to find his son. The other occupants of the building had not been in at the time. Peter's hands were burned and he suffered from smoke inhalation, but he only spent one night in hospital. The last time I spoke to him, he told me that the biggest regret of his life was rescuing me first. He told me I deserved to be ugly. 'What is wrong with you?' he asked, tears in his eyes.

'I'm sorry, it was an accident.'

'You never cared about him. You haven't even asked to see him. Your own son.'

I did not have the energy for histrionics, and I wasn't even shocked by what Peter said next. 'We can't go on. I'm divorcing you. I'll be looking for sole custody of James, though I don't imagine you'll put up a fight about that. You're on your own, Delia. You'll be better off that way.'

'I'm sorry.'

'I don't believe you. Do yourself a favour and don't get involved with anyone again. You'll only end up hurting them, and yourself in the end.'

He turned and walked away.

My way of coping was not to think about it at all. I had my own scars to deal with. The right-hand side of my face was badly damaged, and it would have been worse apparently if Peter hadn't rescued me so quickly. That was the end of my perfect beauty, my marriage, my home and my London life. I was exposed. Once the prettiness had been seared from my face, everyone could see the warped and ugly truth.

Peter's mother, Elizabeth, sat by my bed one afternoon and warned me in tones of pure steel that if I ever tried to talk to her sons or my son again, she would kill me herself. Declan Russell came and stood at the end of my bed for ten minutes one day. He said nothing, just looked at me with pure hatred in his eyes. Eventually he spat into what was left of my face. Moira did not come. Isabelle did not come, though I didn't expect her to. If Hannah had told her about my visit, she must have guessed that she might be my next target. None of the girls from the salon came. No surprise there.

As the rumours of what had happened began to spread throughout the hospital, I found that the curtains were pulled around my bed by other patients and staff. Their attempts to isolate me didn't bother me at all. Word of my drunkenness and my boy's horrific injuries had got out. James had been transferred to Great Ormond Street. My bed was beside a window overlooking rooftops and car parks and factories, but I pretended that it was the sea out there.

When the doctor removed the dressing for the final time, and I saw myself in the mirror, I could not speak. It was not me in the mirror. I heard him saying that the scarring would fade over time, but that the skin would always be somewhat puckered and warped on that side. He mentioned a surgeon in Edinburgh who specialized in cosmetic grafting, but said that surgery was prohibitively expensive and not available on the NHS. He said there was nothing more he could do for me, that the weeping sores would dry up over the coming weeks and that I should continue to see a counsellor and try to get used to my new appearance. All the time he spoke to me, he addressed the 'good' side of my face, ashamed, I think, of his failure to make anything of the bad side.

On the day of my discharge from hospital seven weeks after the fire, I received the salvaged contents of a wardrobe in a large suitcase and a letter from Peter's solicitor via a courier, saying that from now on all communication was to be fielded through her, Anna Fox. Peter would begin divorce proceedings immediately but would honour his legal obligations to me so I should let her know where I was residing. She strongly advised that under no circumstances should I try to make contact with him or my son again if I wanted maintenance payments to continue, that legal proceedings could be brought against me for child neglect and reckless endangerment if I defied the advice. The letter contained a cheque for eight hundred pounds 'for a fresh start'.

I was twenty-five years old, single, friendless, homeless, orphaned, childless, mutilated and, according to the hospital counsellors who had come to see me, an alcoholic. But I was free. My beauty had always mattered to other people. I didn't think it meant a great deal to me. Not then.

The day I left the hospital in May 1991, I cashed Peter's cheque and went to Heathrow Airport. I purchased some toiletries and ordered a glass of wine at the bar. I sat with it in front of me and resisted the urge to take a single sip. I was never going to drink alcohol again. Shop assistants and wait staff who approached me, smiling, looked away quickly when they saw the bad side, unable to disguise their dismay. My hair was cut in a fashionable short bob, not long enough to hide behind. Young men ignored me, and two of them made joking comments about the Elephant Man within my ear-shot. I was not bothered by them, not at that point. I left the bar and bought a wide-brimmed sun hat.

PART II

22

When I flew into Nice on the 19th of May 1991, my one plan was to go back to Villefranche and to get into the sea, but it was only on the flight that I read the fat folder of medical notes the nurses had given me. There were dire warnings about exposure to sunlight because my skin had been so damaged, and further alarms about swimming in pools and in the sea. I would be prone to infections, it said, and should be extremely careful about hygiene and disinfectant. The damage to my neck and shoulder had already healed fairly well, and I had the full range of movement back. My face, though, was a mess. I soon realized that things that had been so easy before were now difficult. My face had been my passport, my access to everywhere. When I was beautiful, people went out of their way to help me. Now that I was damaged, they either avoided me, stared at me or pretended not to see me at all. Also within the folder were leaflets about alcoholism and contact numbers for AA meetings in London. No good to me here, and besides, I was not an alcoholic. I had been bored.

Looking for a place to live was not difficult. I spoke with my cultivated English accent. It had become normal to me by then. It was no longer an accent that I had to affect. My schoolgirl French was not good enough to make myself understood, but thankfully this was a tourist town and most people who wanted to do business spoke fluent English. After a few days of staying in a hostel-style hotel, I rented a flat in the old town of Nice, several streets back from the seafront.

The elderly Russian landlady, Madame Marzikova, wanted cash up front. She recognized something in me, perhaps my neediness, and we sealed the deal over a glass of lemonade (for me) and three glasses of *rouge* (for her) on her tiny balcony. Her English was not good, but the alcohol eased her understanding. She pointed to my scars. 'Fire,' I said, and pointed to the box of matches beside her ashtray. She refilled her glass and blessed herself, and I watched her gulp at the glass and felt proud that I was strong enough to resist it.

I decided on a new identity. I had been Delia O'Flaherty and Delia Walsh. My passport said Delia Russell, but I wanted to leave her behind. I decided on Cordelia. It was close enough to Delia and sounded more aristocratic. I remembered Cordelia in *Brideshead Revisited*. I was now a single girl called Cordelia Russell whose Home Counties family had fallen on hard times. I had an arts degree from Bristol University and had got caught up in a fire at a nightclub in Soho (there had been one just a few weeks before my own inferno). I was down here to bide my time until the scarring healed and to improve my French. That was the story I decided upon, but nobody cared enough to ask.

The flat consisted of two small rooms, one containing a single bed, a wardrobe and a fridge, the other a sofa, coffee table, an oven and grill, and a sink. The landlady boasted about the fact there was a telephone. But who would I ring?

It did not get any direct light, but in the late afternoon a narrow sunbeam crossed the floor of the bedroom and disappeared halfway up the wall. The wide, old-fashioned brass bed stood beside an exterior window. It looked straight into the kitchen of a restaurant in the alley opposite. Several mouse-traps were set in corners, and I quickly got used to evacuating and resetting them. I remembered the sea-rats from my island days and how they would gnaw through the straw in our roof.

A week after I moved in, coming out of our shared bath-room, I met Sally from Scunthorpe. She was a barmaid who lived on the top floor. She was the first person to hear my story.

'I heard about that fire,' she said. 'I think you're brave, coming here on your own.' She'd only been in Nice a few months. 'I can't wait to get out of this dive,' she said, refer-ring to the house. She warned me that Madame Marzikova could knock on our doors at any time of the day or night, roaring drunk, that she did nothing to maintain the building and that if anything in my flat was broken, I should fix it myself.

I was living on my own for the first time, and I took delight in making a home for myself in my shabby little space. There were handles missing from the wardrobe door, and the soli-tary window was not sealed. One shutter was broken. I was handy though. When I was living with Peter, I had played the part of the trophy wife and left all the manual tasks to him or a hired man, so he never knew that I could fix nets and sand rust from the hull of a boat and card wool at the age of ten. Even Alan had taught me how to change a fuse and to fix leather satchels and mend shoes to get an extra year out of them. Sally had some tools and borrowed others from the bar where she worked, so I was able to fix up the flat well. The air-conditioning unit did not work, so I moved my bed in front of the fridge at night and opened its door. Electricity was included in the rental price. Finally, I had my own private space.

I asked Sally about getting a job and she said she'd ask around, but bluntly told me that bar work was out of the question with my face the way it was, and that if I didn't speak French I wouldn't get a waitressing job in restaurants either. 'I'm surprised at a posh bird like you looking for a 'waitressing job,' she said, but told me she'd keep her ear to the ground for anything suitable.

I traipsed the streets anyway and offered to wash up in restaurants, clean bars, chambermaid in hotels. The answer was always no, as my interviewers tried not to look at my face. After sunset, I walked the Promenade des Anglais and paddled in the Mediterranean, grateful to be close to the sea again but itching to get into it. Every day, I practised my French from some Linguaphone tapes and a Walkman that Sally lent me. I bought the local newspaper and watched French television and immersed myself in the language.

Sally was right about Madame Marzikova. Some nights, I let her in when she hammered on the door, looking for company, and in she swept, clutching a bottle of wine. It was good to have somebody to feel superior to, and I could practise my French on her. The drunker she was, the more confident I became, less afraid of making mistakes.

Sometimes, when she woke me and I didn't answer the door, she would sulk with me for days, hinting that she might need the room back. It never happened.

After six weeks of job hunting, I was feeling despondent. I decided to take the bus to Villefranche. I covered up from the intense heat of the day, wearing my wide-brimmed hat and high-factor lotion, but I was still conscious of the vivid red welts on my face, which had barely begun to die down. I realized I would just have to get used to it, and so would everybody else. People still winced and some turned away when they saw me, but at least one side of my face was still normal. I tried to convince myself that it could be worse.

I walked down towards the beach, packed today with tourists. It was mid July, and the heat was intense. As I walked past the restaurant on the cliff side of the road, I heard a long slow whistle, and turned slightly to see the gold-toothed

manager. He waved his arm. 'Bonjour, Mademoiselle, welcome back!' He had recognized my body, my walk, or perhaps
the distinctive sundress I'd worn on that blissful holiday
three years previously.

I watched his face fall as I walked towards him. A glance
towards his name badge reminded me of his name. 'Raoul!
How lovely to see you again.'

He looked at my hairline, at my left ear, at my left shoulder, concentrating on my good side. 'Madame,' he said
courteously, all of the lascivious flirtation gone, 'you have
returned to holiday, with your husband?'

'No,' I said, laughing, 'he is soon to be my ex-husband,
and I am looking for a job.' I turned the bad side of my face
away and offered my hand for him to shake. He took it, but
when I said nothing more and looked expectantly at him, the
penny dropped.

'Here? You want a job, here?'

'Yes, anywhere.'

'To serve?' I could see him trying to equate the beautiful
rich young girl with the disfigured wannabe waitress.

'Yes.'

'We have nothing, I am sorry.'

I squeezed his hand. 'Please? Anything? In the kitchen?'

His eyes took in my entire body from my toes up to my neck.

'I think you are not strong enough for the kitchen.' He
had been assessing my body for its strength, unlike before.

I flexed my biceps. Keeping my damaged side in shadow,
I smiled gratefully. I placed his hand on my tightened upper
arm. 'Please?' I could still flirt. I still had the body, even if I
didn't have the face.

'What is your name?'

'Cordelia Russell.' I said it without any hesitance. Delia
had died in the fire.

'Come back on Tuesday, Cordelia. Seven in morning. Hard work.' He spoke as if to a stroppy teenager.

I wanted to know how much I would be paid, and he said that after Tuesday he would decide.

He pointed to my face. 'What is . . .' He struggled to find the words in English.

'A fire,' I said, 'an accident.'

'*Tant pis*,' he said. His tooth glinted in the sunlight.

I went home and bought myself some flowers on the way. I ran up the stairs, passing Sally on the way out.

'Congratulations, Cordelia!' she said. 'Can't imagine you getting your hands dirty, though!'

The others who worked in the restaurant were mostly students from southern Europe. They were all younger than me. I was the only Irish person there, or the only English person there, depending on how one looked at it. They were fun, free, happy-go-lucky. Their kindness to me was touching. I knew they felt sorry for me, and the words they constantly used to describe me were 'brave' and 'courageous'. But they all had their own obligations to partners or parents and children.

Sometimes, I would climb the rock-hewn steps up to the house in which Peter and I had stayed, half expecting that I might see Isabelle, since it was her friends who owned it, but there were only ever strangers, mostly the same British family, and later, as the season wound down, occasional couples, like Peter and I had once been.

The work in the restaurant was tough. At the height of the season, the restaurant was busy all day and dirty dishes stacked up quickly. My hands, once soft and manicured, soon became as rough and raw as my face. Thankfully, my work station was outside in a lean-to behind the restaurant in the shadow of steep rock, so I was spared the heat of the kitchen, the intensity of the sun, and worked mostly alone. I would also slice endless baguettes and prepare salads. Customers did not see me unless there were still some stragglers at closing time, when the staff gathered for a collegial bottle of wine and shared cigarettes. I began to smoke regularly then. It was a way to fit in. There was nobody to tell me that it was bad for the child. There was no child. I could pretend there never had been. This was a new opportunity. I decided that Cordelia Russell was not going to be washing dishes for long.

23

Hidden away in the restaurant, I did not get the opportunity to meet too many men, but Raoul, who also lived in Nice, would drive me home in the evenings in his Ferrari, of which he was incredibly proud. Top-end sports cars were everywhere on the Riviera. The rich and famous lived here, and ostentatious displays of wealth were common. Raoul was a generation older than me, perhaps in his early forties. It didn't take me long to notice that he whistled at all the pretty ladies who passed his restaurant. I hadn't been that special. He was, I discovered, not just the manager but the owner. He worked hard when he was there and rarely took a day off. He had several business interests in Nice and Marseilles, and when the restaurant closed at the end of October he would tend to those, he said.

I learned not to enquire too closely about Raoul's businesses because he would become cagey and monosyllabic when I tried, but those night-time journeys on the winding coastal road were surprisingly companionable and I would catch him looking at me from time to time. My good side faced him in the car. He chatted easily enough when he could fool himself that he had a beautiful young woman next to him. Sometimes, to emphasize a point, he would put his hand on my thigh. I let him. I needed the job. But his hand never moved upwards, and I realized after a short time that his way with women was always like this. I watched him through the small window of the restaurant from my outdoor wash-up area. He flirted with every woman, touching their arms, their shoulders. He was a tactile person. There were some good-looking young waitresses on staff and he behaved with them in the same way. He was married, he told me, to his first love at the age of sixteen. Arabelle, he said, was the only woman in his life.

It is my failing that I saw this as a challenge. As damaged as I was, as kind as he was to give me a job in the first place, I set out to seduce him.

There was also a mercenary reason for my seduction. At the end of October, the restaurant would close for the winter until Easter and I needed money. The maintenance that Peter paid covered my rent and basic food, but there was no money for extras. I still had some items of designer clothing from the old days that had been untouched by the fire, kept wrapped for special occasions, but I wondered what and when those occasions would be. I needed to feel glamorous, to feel like I mattered.

As the season wound down, I became friendlier to Raoul, more respectful and courteous, and I knew he was flattered. On the drives back to Nice, I might mention how he was still in such good shape, or what a good people manager he was. Little compliments dropped casually into the conversation, and occasionally a peck on his cheek as I got out of the car.

One evening, I suggested he should come up to my flat for a coffee before he went home. He was reluctant, and claimed to be tired, but it did not take much to persuade him, just a tip of my head on his shoulder and my hand on his knee.

When we got upstairs into the flat, I poured him a glass of wine from a bottle I had bought specifically for this night, then nipped into the bedroom and let my hair down, discarded my work dress and threw a silk kimono-style gown over my slip, tying the belt loosely around my hips. He pretended not to notice as I sat myself to his right so that he would not have to look at the bad side of my face. We smoked and chatted for a while in French and English about the restaurant and the other staff members, the recent tax increases and the different types of tourists that patronized the restaurant. He wondered how I could afford an apartment on my own. Most of his workers, he said, stayed in youth hostels, rented houses together or commuted long distances. I admitted that I was in receipt of payments from my ex-husband, but that they didn't stretch very far. He had never enquired about my personal life or the fire, but he was emboldened now to ask. I decided to change my rehearsed story. It seemed the best way to garner sympathy and to tug on his heart strings while shyly looking at him from the beautiful side of my face. I explained, halting sometimes for emotional effect, that my husband had been violent, and had set fire to our house. As I expected, Raoul's arm slipped around my shaking shoulders.

'Is he in prison? He is rich man, yes? Why you no stay in London?'

I could tell some of the truth now: that my husband had been caught embezzling money from his company, but that his powerful friends had kept him out of prison for his assault on me. I said honestly that I was an orphan with no family and no other means of income. I feigned upset and began to weep quietly. Raoul drew me closer, as I knew he would, and I nestled into his shoulder and turned my lips to his neck.

He jumped backwards as if startled, and inhaled deeply, with his hands up. I reached out and tugged him towards me by his belt, but he stood firm and put his hand up before my face. In French, he said, 'Do not mistake my sympathy for anything else. I came here because I felt sorry for you. I have told you often that, for me, there is only my wife.' He saw my confusion as I turned the bad side of my face away. 'It is not because of that,' he lied, gesturing towards my face. Of course it was.

It was a great shock to me. After he left, I spent a long time looking in the mirror. I had spent my whole life under the gaze of men. Their marriages had never stopped them pursuing me before. Despite the damage, up until now I still had confidence. I stared in the mirror, and whereas previously I had been mentally able to block out the ugly side of my own image, now I saw what Raoul saw. The scars were permanent, though significantly improved since I'd left the hospital. I felt ugly for the first time in my life. Who would ever want to kiss this face again?

I never went back to the restaurant. I stayed indoors for months, wallowing in my shame. I ate little, smoked a lot, but resisted the urge to drink. At night, I would slip out and paddle in the sea, stopping in the late supermarket for bread and tinned food. I contemplated a life in which nobody would fight over me, because nobody would care enough. I missed my father so much in those days and longed to be back in his strong arms. He had loved the fact that I was beautiful, but he had also loved everything else about me. He would not have been put off by my disfigurement. It would have been, it should have been, just him and me on the west side of Inishcrann, away from everyone. Daddy and me.

Autumn turned to winter, and the weeks of being cooped up while my money was stretched thinner took their toll. I didn't want to die, but I didn't want to face the world either. Sally had gone back to university in Leeds.

On Christmas night, Madame Marzikova invited me to her flat and, having nothing better to do, I went. She tried to insist that I drink with her, but I refused.

'You are an alcoholic, Cordelia?'

I laughed at her. 'I don't drink,' I said. 'You are the drunk one!'

'The difference,' she said, 'is that I know what I am.'

She was wrong. It had been nine months since I'd had a drink and I'd given up all by myself, without need for support groups or prayers or AA meetings. And besides, Peter's maintenance payments wouldn't even stretch to the occasional bottle of wine on top of the rent, so I couldn't afford to drink. I was saving up for a consultant's appointment.

She changed the subject, pointing to my face. 'It is better, your face,' she said, slurring her words, 'I can see how beautiful you were,' and she cupped the good, left side of my face in her gnarled old hand. 'But the rest of us live our lives with the faces we are born with. You will get used to this too.'

In the new year, I had my appointment with an eminent English-speaking skin specialist, not available on the French health service. Dr Giraud told me nothing new. The scarring was permanent, though it would fade in time. There were experts who could work wonders, but they were prohibitively expensive and must be paid for privately. There was no guarantee that such an investment would be successful. Dr Giraud was sympathetic but unimpressed by me and didn't show any interest in the details of the nightclub fire or my financial plight, how I'd just been divorced by my embezzling husband. He charged me the full fee and barely met my eye when I shook hands to say goodbye.

I wondered what I could possibly do to make enough money to pay for the operation I needed so badly.

In desperation, I telephoned Raoul, begging him for news of any work he might know of. He said there was nothing, but I think I was on his conscience, because a few days later he rang to say I should go and meet his nephew Christian, in a shop a few streets away from my flat. It gave me comfort to think that Raoul had not forgotten me.

Christian was younger than me, maybe twenty-two, but

boyish. He was nothing special to look at. His face was thin and his shoulders sloped but his eyes were warm. He ran a gift shop that sold Niçoise souvenirs, rugs, ceramics, soaps, candles and tablecloths to tourists. It was not a shop that would ever make a lot of money, so my thoughts of stealing the takings were immediately redundant. He gestured towards things in the shop. My French was pretty good by now, after six months of total immersion, but within minutes it became clear why I was doing all the talking. Christian had a noticeable lisp. He spoke when he absolutely had to. Customers laughed at him sometimes, and I wondered if Raoul had put us together deliberately, thinking that we might be good for each other with my disfigurement and his speech impediment. Damaged goods selling fancy goods.

My job was to unpack the products and to go from the shop to the lock-up with a trolley cart to replenish stock whenever required. I could also serve and gift-wrap for customers, but I was not to handle bank lodgements. The pay was not much better than it had been in Raoul's restaurant, but the work was easier. In February, there was little or no business but we were open all day. Christian would disappear for hours at a time without explanation. He had several visitors who came to the shop regularly, older men in leather jackets. Often, Raoul was among them.

Initially, I would be sent to the lock-up during these visits, but as time went on I was allowed to stay. Some of the men spoke in a language I did not understand. They did not notice me. Packages and cash changed hands, and I understood quickly that the shop was a front for something else. I kept my head down, my face averted, and did not ask questions. I assumed it was drugs. I was surprised that Raoul was involved in such an enterprise. He had seemed so dedicated to his restaurant, but then I recalled his Ferrari. His pride and joy, parked beside the restaurant for all to admire. He had let tourists sit inside it and take photos of each other. I thought it was just a restaurant gimmick, but for Raoul it was the ultimate status symbol. So, there was money running through this place. I just had to bide my time. Watch and learn. It might take a while to gain their trust, but I reckoned this was no small-time enterprise, not with so many people involved.

Christian and I eased into a comfortable non-verbal friendship. He did not appear to have a wife or children. Sometimes I made him sandwiches at home and brought them in. He was surprised and grateful. Sometimes he would open a bottle of wine at the end of the day, and I would sip from a can of Coke in companionable silence. He took a pack of cards from the shelf one day and we began to teach each other the card games from our childhood, and then he showed me poker. We played for cigarettes. We were both good bluffers, as it turned out, and were evenly matched.

I had grown my hair long and managed to wear it forward over the bad side of my face, but I couldn't glue my hair into place, so inevitably the scarring was visible. By September 1992, eighteen months after the fire, my face was as healed as it was ever going to be. From a distance you would not notice anything wrong, but anybody within ten feet would see the rippled skin and the turned-down mouth, my right eyelid hooded more than my left. My smile, which had been my greatest asset, was uneven. It was hideous to me, though Christian insisted it was not so bad.

Christian began to speak a little more to me. I learned that his friends were Corsican. He said that they were just using his warehouse, a different place from the lock-up, as temporary storage from time to time, and that it supplemented his income. I did not ask any questions, and I think he knew by my silence that I did not believe him. 'You think it's drugs, don't you?' he said, confirming my suspicions. Christian was not smart.

I watched the money and the drugs from behind my hair as they passed from hand to hand, stuffed into envelopes or well-sealed parcels.

'I trust you, Cordelia,' said Christian one day, as he leaned over and kissed the corner of my mouth. The ugly side. He withdrew quickly, embarrassed, and his inexperience with women became obvious. In the old days I would have slapped him away, but now I wondered how my lifestyle might improve if I were a gangster's moll. His self-esteem must be pretty low if I was the person he chose to kiss. Christian started to buy me gifts: ostentatious jewellery, designer watches, oversized bunches of flowers. He gave me a pay rise, took me to dinner. I knew I could use him.

In the new year we finally slept together and then, inevitably, he began to spill the beans. The Corsicans were bringing in drugs from Morocco to Marseilles. From there, they were delivered to Christian's warehouse somewhere outside Nice, hermetically sealed within stacks of rugs or ceramics or whatever other tat we were selling. Business was never conducted at the warehouse because the gendarmes would periodically check storage units with sniffer dogs and some of the Corsicans' distributors at the port of Marseilles were on an Interpol watch list. Christian's little shop had become the business hub, but in reality Christian worked for Raoul, who laundered the money through the restaurant in Ville-franche. It all made good business sense and my respect for Raoul increased, but Raoul was wary of me. He felt sorry for me but he did not trust me.

He did not like the fact that Christian and I were close. He warned me not to hurt Christian, said that he was a good boy. 'You are the one who puts him at risk,' I said, and I could see he was furious to realize that I knew exactly what was going on in his businesses. In public I taunted Raoul, being overly affectionate towards Christian, playing up our new romance. In private I kept Christian at a certain remove. He wanted me to come live with him and I was tempted. His flat was bigger than mine. You could see the sea from his bedroom. But I liked being on my own. I even liked Madame Marzikova. I secured my privacy by claiming to be religious. Indeed, I did spend a lot of time going in and out of the magnificent churches that were dotted all over the city, not to pray, but for peace and privacy, and because I could wear a mantilla and feel like everybody else with an unblemished face.

In the shop one day, Raoul sent Christian on an errand while the Corsicans counted cash in the back room. He beckoned me to come join him on the bench outside. 'Cordelia. He is just a boy. Do not use him for entertainment.'

I laid my head on Raoul's shoulder and put my hand on his knee. 'You have nothing to worry about. I am totally devoted to your nephew,' I lied.

He flinched away from my touch. 'Don't play games. You have been warned.' He jerked his thumb towards the back room.

The Corsicans were dangerous and ruthless. Christian had told me stories of former accomplices who had had their throats cut, and occasionally I would see two of the men who came to the shop around the town, these middle-aged men, accompanied by impossibly young girls. Prostitutes, I assumed. Certainly underage. When I remarked on this to Christian, he agreed that it was terrible how they treated people, but Raoul needed these men and we had to keep on their right side. When they were around, I kept my mouth shut and my head down.

24

One night in September 1993, over a year after Christian and I had started a relationship, I came home from work to find Harry standing outside my building. It was a Wednesday, my half-day in the shop. It had been ten years since I'd seen him, but he was immediately recognizable, even though he was flabby around the middle and his face was bloated. The familiar broad grin appeared when he saw me. 'Delia!'

Nobody in France knew me by that name. The last time I had seen him, he had refused to talk to me, and that was before I had married his brother.

'Harry, what are you doing here?'

'My God, where did you get that accent?'

I said nothing.

He moved forward to embrace me and I could smell alcohol on his breath. 'Jesus, you are still beautiful, you really are. The scarring isn't half as —'

'Harry —'

'Do you know how many hoops I had to jump through to find you? I tracked you —'

'Harry, let's go and get a coffee, OK?'

'Sure. Can I leave my bag in your place?' He was carrying a rucksack.

'Wait here.' I took his rucksack and opened the door and went inside.

What was he doing here? He couldn't have come here just to see me, could he? Or had something happened to Peter? Or James? I no sooner asked myself the question than I realized I didn't want to know about them. Outside again, I led the way to the promenade. Harry kept up a light chat all the way, as if we were old friends. I suppose we were old friends.

'God, it's beautiful here! So warm compared to home. One of Mum's friends from the golf club has an apartment somewhere round here I think, or maybe it's in Cannes, I can't remember. Look at the colour of the sea!'

We went down the steps to one of the beach clubs. I ordered an espresso. Harry ordered a glass of rosé. 'When in Rome!' he said. He stared out at the sea. Facing him now, I could see his eyes were glassy – from drink or exhaustion, I couldn't be sure.

'Harry, why have you come here?'

'Jesus, are you going to keep up that accent? Can you not talk in your normal voice? You were only in London for what, seven years?'

'It is the way I talk. I can't help it.'

'You must be fluent in French now too?'

'*Oui.*'

He looked at me. 'You are still a stunner, you know?'

'So you said.'

'Am I boring you? Do you have anything you want to ask me? About Moira or Alan? About your husband or your son?'

I lit a cigarette. 'No.'

'Well, I'm going to tell you anyway. Moira is fine, still living in the house. Her eyesight is bad though. Alan . . . well, Alan is a lost soul. After they split up – you know they split up, right? Nobody could believe it. He lives in a cottage way outside the town. He built an enormous crucifix and stuck it on top and calls it his church. He's just a sad old lad now. Lives like a hermit. Talks to no one.'

'I'm sorry to hear that.'

'Are you? Really? Moira says you hardly ever write to her. That's pretty bad manners, Delia, you know? They brought you up. You owe them some loyalty. It costs nothing but the price of a stamp to stay in touch.'

His eyes were dancing and his mood was a little manic. When the waiter came around again, he ordered a bottle of wine and two glasses, despite my protestations. I did not touch my glass of wine.

'Harry, I don't need to hear any of this.'

'Yes, you do, you do. You need to hear everything. Your son lives with my mum, did you know that?'

I got up to leave, but he grabbed me and held me sharply by the wrist. 'Sit the fuck down and listen to me. We're only scratching the surface.' People at other tables looked over. I smiled to reassure them. I did not want a scene.

'Let's go back to my flat,' I said. 'If I have to hear all this, let's do it in private.'

His grin returned.

On the way, I picked up some bread and cheese, and Harry bought wine.

In the flat, I persuaded him to have a coffee and to eat something. He looked around.

'Is this all you can afford? I thought my brother was supporting you financially.'

'He "maintains" me. I work to earn my living.'

'Oh yeah, what do you do?'

I shook my head, unprepared to tell him anything.

'Why don't you trust me, Delia? What did I ever do to you? Did I cheat on you, lie to you, marry your brother, burn his house down, abandon my child?'

'I did not abandon my child!'

'But you never fought to keep him. From what I hear, you never gave a shit about him. Is that true?'

'Harry, stop! Why are you here? It's been ten years. Why now?'

'Because I've gotten to know your son. I have to admit, in the beginning it was hard to look at him. He was so badly disfigured in the fire, and you got away so lightly.'

'No, I didn't!' I pulled my hair back so that Harry could see the full extent of my wounds.

'For Christ's sake, that's nothing! You'd barely notice it. You can still walk the streets without people staring. You can live a completely normal life. Your son is only just out of hospital for the fifth time. Peter couldn't work and take care of him at the same time, so James is home, living in West-port with my mum and dad. It's a miserable existence for him. Living with a grandfather who can barely look at him. Mum tries her best. He started school a few weeks ago in the town. Nobody wanted to sit beside him. Can you imagine what that's like? He's nine years old. Did you know he lost most of the fingers on one hand?'

I started to hum inside my head to block out this noise. I opened the window to the street. I opened the bottle of wine. Maybe if Harry drank more, he would pass out and I could have him removed.

'Oh, Delia, did you ever care about any of us? Moira and Alan? Peter or me? Do you carry on as if we never existed? Here's some truth for you, OK? You think you're so bloody clever, but you're not. You thought you were going to end up living the high life, but look at this place.'

I refilled his glass.

'Why won't you drink with me? You needn't pretend you're so pure. You got what you wanted, Delia. You wanted to abort him, didn't you? I know it was my dad's idea, but you were prepared to go along with it. He told me.' He took an extra glass from the shelf, filled it and pushed it towards me.

'Drink it. You never wanted that child. I used to believe it was because you wanted *my* child, and not Peter's. I was sure that you would write to me from London, to explain, to apologize. I was so sure he had forced himself on you. So sure.'

His eyes filled with tears. I had never seen him cry before.

'You would have preferred it if I'd been raped?'

'Yes.' He whispered it.

'I think you should leave now.'

'I'm not going anywhere.' His eyes drifted away again. He could not focus on one subject at a time. 'Your son is a good boy, you know? He lives in constant pain. More and more operations. Peter plans to move back to Westport next year. He's going to open a factory. Computers or something like that. He comes back every other weekend to see James.'

'Are you and Peter . . . are you . . . ?'

'What do you think, Delia? How could I ever look up to that bastard ever again? He was my brother.'

'It wasn't his fault –'

'Don't say that, don't tell me that!' He reached across the table and lifted the right side of my lip so that it matched the good side.

'That's better. That's how I remember you.'

I pushed his hand away. 'Have you come all the way to France to tell me that my son is miserable? Is that why you came? How did you find me anyway?'

'I sort of broke into Peter's house the day before yesterday. Mum has a key. It was easy. I found a file containing your bank account details and your address. I came because I wanted to know if you ever cared about me, but I already have my answer. It's been what, nearly two hours now? And you haven't asked a single question about me.'

He drained his glass and then reached for the one I hadn't

touched. He slurped from it and leaned back in the chair, his hands behind his head.

'How are you, Harry?'

'Well, let's see. The hotel is long gone, along with my future. I guess I can't blame you for that, though Dad does. I'd never have guessed in a million years that Peter would turn out to be an embezzler, but I suppose a man who can cheat on his own brother is capable of anything.' There was so much bitterness in his voice.

'I never went to college, because I was expected to take over the hotel and learn on the job, so I'm qualified for nothing. I give piano lessons from time to time. I got some bar work in a few of the pubs, but none of those jobs worked out. I'm on the dole. That's it, that's my life.' His words were slurred now.

'Don't you have a girlfriend, Harry? Didn't you want to get married, have children?'

'Yes. With you. I still do.'

'Harry —'

'I've been out with every girl in Westport who'd have me. None of them are you, Delia. None of them can hold a candle to you.'

I looked at this man who I'd been going to voluntarily marry at one stage and felt nothing but disgust. He lurched forward in his chair and tried to hug me.

'No, Harry, stop. Get off me!'

'Come on, Delia. You know we were meant to be. We can forget everyone else. I've come all this way to be with you. We can live here, just the two of us, as if nothing ever happened.'

His mouth was on mine, his grip tight around my waist.

The buzzer of my flat sounded. Harry was momentarily disorientated, long enough for me to escape his clutches and press the access button. I opened the door. I knew it was Christian.

'Who's coming?' said Harry.

'My boyfriend.'

His mouth hung open, as if it had never occurred to him that I might have a relationship with anybody else. Had he assumed that after the fire I had hidden myself away, done penance, lived like a nun? I was furious.

Christian took one look at the scene. 'Who is this?' he demanded in French. Before I could answer, Harry took a swing at Christian and missed, landing on the floor on one knee. Christian grabbed him roughly by the neck. Christian was six inches shorter than Harry, but he had the advantage of being sober. 'Who is he?'

I spoke rapid French. 'My ex-husband. Get rid of him, please. I'll explain later. Don't hurt him, he's not worth it.' I threw the rucksack and Christian caught it in his other hand.

As he started to drag Harry out the door, Harry started to scream all the foul words he could think of at me, words that needed no translation.

Later, I heard that Christian, who believed that my ex-husband was the one responsible for my facial deformity, enlisted the help of the Corsicans. They gave Harry a severe beating and dumped him at the airport. I don't know if they broke bones or stabbed him, but he must have got on a plane. Christian wanted me to be grateful. It made him feel like a man, but in my eyes he became pathetic. He did not have the courage to take on Harry alone.

A month later, I received a letter from Ireland, unsigned. But I knew the handwriting. Inside, in a giant loose scrawl, was written FUCK YOU. That was the end of Ireland and me, or so I thought.

Peter ·

My brother was six years younger than me, so we weren't exactly close growing up. We didn't look alike, nor did we have anything in common, but up until 1983 we got along fine. He was only out of school a year or two, but he was broader than me, active in the GAA Club, better-looking, and he could sing and play the piano. I was interested in science and studying. I was weedy. A girl once called me a chinless wonder. I never had many girlfriends. I should have been jealous of Harry, but until that Christmas I thought of him as my slightly annoying but amusing kid brother and nothing more.

Having had my head turned by living in the UK for a few years, I found my home town small and provincial; I had little patience for small-minded politics and local gossip. I was a snob about Westport. It all seemed so insignificant when compared to London with its splendour and size. I came home at Christmas time and occasionally during the summer, out of duty, to oblige my parents and help out in high season at Carrowbeg Manor. Harry had been seeing Delia for over a year before I met her.

I was shocked when I saw her. Nobody in Westport looked like this. She was beautiful from head to toe and her eyes were startlingly blue. There was something rough and simple and exotic about her, but also something magical. I caught her eye that night, and the way she looked at me, it was like she knew every single thing about me. I'm a person who deals with numbers and facts, but this quality she had was so weird and unnerving. I tried to hide how much she fascinated me that first night, but afterwards I asked Mum about her.

'Not you as well,' she said. 'Your brother is completely smitten.

He'd walk over hot coals for her.' I denied any interest in her, but mum shook her head. 'Just as well you live in London.'

Back in London after Christmas, I thought about her often. She was going to be a doctor. I guessed that she wouldn't stay in Westport after she qualified. Harry was going to lose her. A girl like that belonged in a big city.

When summer came around, I looked forward to going home just to see her, to be around her. It would never have occurred to me to try and seduce her, but that day in the hotel room when I went to deliver her results, she was so angry. She attacked me and then we kissed. The kiss was mutual, and so was what followed.

I didn't see why I should say no to the marriage. It was my baby she was carrying, and I loved her. I was sorry for Harry, but she chose me. I thought Harry would move on, meet somebody else. We lived in separate countries, so it's not as if he had to be confronted with us every day.

She came to London and turned my life upside down. I was so proud when my friends met her and slapped me on the back like I'd won an enormous prize. I thought I had. She made friends and we went out to bars and restaurants. She absorbed London life like a chameleon, immediately adopting the accent and attitude of her new friends. I thought it odd, but I was encouraged by how much of an effort she was making to fit in. I thought she was doing it for me.

I hid the letters that came to our home addressed to her in Harry's writing. I didn't read them, because I guessed what they would say, but they never stopped coming, even after James was born. I told Chiara to get rid of them too.

I never stopped trying to make Delia happy. I gave her everything she asked for, but I couldn't move to the seaside and she always resented that. I encouraged her to study for A levels and I couldn't understand why she wouldn't stick with it – after all, she was so disappointed at not getting into medicine. But I realize now that Delia was never academically smart. She was clever and lived on her wits. Clever enough to fool me. I began to question her partying and her drinking but then she would withdraw from me, so I learned to let her do as she pleased. She was faithful to me. Dad said she'd cheat on me the first chance she got, but he was wrong. Daniel told me she had no interest in other men when they went out. I convinced myself that she must feel something for me because, God knows, I had some stiff competition in London, and she did not stray. The passion of our first wild sexual encounter was never repeated, and I always thought that sex was something she saw as a function of marriage. I never forced her, but I felt she was never fully present. On that holiday in France, I got a glimpse of the excited young girl she should have been, glistening with seawater and, maybe, truly happy.

I could handle her emotional disconnection from me, because she returned my affection and did not run away, but I can't get my head around why she couldn't love our son. An innocent baby. I'd heard about baby blues, but with Delia they never went away. I don't think she ever thought about the consequences of her pregnancy or about the responsibility of raising a child. But she was only eighteen when she had James. Maybe she just wasn't ready to become a mum yet. She never adapted to motherhood and I don't think she tried.

Chiara took over and Delia let her, and I turned a blind eye because James was safe and cared for, and because I was so damn busy trying to keep our heads above water. We were living on credit.

I knew it was wrong and I knew it was foolish, but I really believed that one good deal would solve our problems. I talked to the wrong people and took a ridiculous risk and I lost everything. That was bad enough, but all the money Dad had invested went too. I bankrupted all of us. I was worried sick about everything, but I was most worried that Delia would leave me. When she didn't walk away, I convinced myself that she did love me, even though our sex life died then. She complained a little, but she was surprisingly stoic when we had to move to a tiny damp flat with no garden. In the beginning she hated it, and became more distant, but then we both got jobs and James settled into his new school and I thought things were improving.

She almost killed him. In some ways, she might as well have. Poor James has endured so much pain and isolation. I divorced her and she went without a backward glance. She has never once written to enquire about her son. Apparently she doesn't care if he is alive or dead. She almost certainly doesn't care about me, beyond how I support her financially.

I never knew her. I married a stranger.

It hurts that I've had to send my boy back to Westport to my parents while I try to make a living here and learn as much as I can about computer design. The long-term goal is to move back home and raise my son there. I think Westport will absorb a boy with James's difficulties more easily. Without a mother, he needs family and community around him and I'm simply not enough on my own. Mum has been fantastic, despite all the trouble I have caused the family. I chat to James every week on the phone and get home as often as I can to see him.

Harry keeps his distance when I'm home, but I'm surprised to hear from Mum that he's taken such an interest in James. I'm not sure now if that's a good thing or not. Mum said Harry disappeared for a few days last week and then turned up completely battered and bruised and wouldn't speak about where he'd been. I'd like to make amends with my brother, but I fear that it is too late. Perhaps things can be different when I move home for good.

25

Towards the end of 1993, shortly after Harry's visit, I moved into Christian's flat. He wanted to keep me safe, he said. It was substantially bigger than mine, one whole floor of a building whose bedroom overlooked the sea. I was able to drink in the sea with my morning coffee. Christian proposed marriage. I claimed that as a Catholic who had already been divorced in defiance of the Church's laws, I could not countenance ever marrying again. Raoul, at least, was relieved.

Now that the scars had healed over, I risked sea swimming again. I still wore high-factor sun protection, even at night. I could not risk those wounds reopening.

Some wounds, however, would not stay closed. A month after Harry's visit, just before I moved in with Christian, I received a letter from Moira.

> I met Harry Russell in the street today. He is not in good shape. He told me in confidence that he went to visit you. What kind of people are you associating with, Delia? This will not end well for you. If you lie down with dogs, you will wake up with fleas.
>
> I can never forgive you or condone the way you treated your own child, but I would like to know that you are all right, so please let me know, one way or another. I tried to be a mother to you, even if you didn't see it like that. You know where I am.

I binned such letters. I saw no point in keeping up contact

with Moira or hearing the local gossip from Westport. I was never going to see any of them again. Why should I care? She wrote once every six months for about three years before she gave up, or perhaps she died. I never knew.

Christian fell in love with me, and I played my new role well. When the Corsicans came over to the apartment, I would fix them drinks, smoke their cigarettes, let them pat me on the bottom, smile when they made comments about my face, join in with their crude jokes. But I could not love Christian back, and it drove him insane. Like Peter, he did everything possible to win my love, but he got my company and he should have been satisfied with that. He paid for everything: the rent, my clothing and our bills. I worked in the shop only when I wanted to. In the beginning, he didn't mind at all.

Peter's maintenance payments continued, increasing periodically in line with inflation. The terms and conditions stated that they would cease if I remarried. I had no intention of ever giving up that measure of independence that Peter had given me. I saved up the maintenance payments for the operation that was going to fix my face. I had watched and waited and followed the money of the drug deals, but the risk was too high. If I was caught taking any, they would have no hesitation in killing me, so instead I saved my secret money.

In November 1994, a new drug distributor from Antibes started doing business with the Corsicans. There were some fights. People further down the food chain got stabbed and tortured. Christian's and Raoul's interests were curtailed heavily and it looked like their little empire was shrinking. Christian said they were lucky now to have any part of the pie. Raoul was worried about the restaurant. It did well in high season and paid for itself, but he worried the tax authorities might become suspicious if his income dropped in half. How would he explain it? He was forced to sell his beloved Ferrari. I hadn't thought that any of this would directly affect me, but years previously I had told Raoul about my maintenance payments from Peter and one day Christian confronted me with the fact of this secret money.

'It is mine,' I said.

'But you make no contribution to this home.'

I turned the bad side of my face towards him and told him honestly that I was saving to have an operation that would fix the scarring.

'But you don't need this operation! I love you already.'

I lost my temper with him. 'I'm not doing it for you! Do you think I care what you think?'

'We need that money – we will lose this apartment. You want to be on the streets? We need it.'

'It is mine.'

'How can you be so selfish? I have done everything for you and all you care about is yourself. I love you!'

I shouldn't have done it, but I felt threatened. I imitated his lisp and parroted back what he had said to me. '*I love you!*' It was the only time I had ever said the words. It was cruel of me and I knew it.

That was the first time he hit me. A red punch across the good side of my face. I remembered my father hitting my mother in the same way, and the way my brothers would scatter. Mammy would glare at me as if to say, *Look what your precious father has done,* and I would ignore her. When Christian hit me, I felt exhilarated. I know that I should have left him then, but part of me felt that I earned that punch. It was long overdue.

I stayed at home until the bruise on my face had disappeared, and for months afterwards Christian tried to make it up to me, crying and apologizing. In January, Raoul came to see me and informed me coldly that I must hand over my bank card and its pin number to Christian. Christian cleared out the almost thousand pounds I had managed to save in the year I had been living with him. It was rent he owed, he said, and then: 'Your name on the card is Delia, not Cordelia?'

'So what?' I said. 'It's the same name, just a different version.'

Christian shrugged. He had always accepted the story that I was an English girl, down on my luck, victim of a violent, drunken, embezzling husband. But he was suspicious.

A few nights later, I came home from my walk along the promenade to find Christian holding my passport. My Irish passport, which he had found in a bag of summer clothes I kept at the bottom of the wardrobe. He had torn the place apart looking for it.

'You are Irish. Why have you never told me this?'

'It doesn't matter what the passport says,' I said brazenly. 'I might have been born there, but I grew up in England.'

He began to quiz me about my parentage, my upbringing, and when I stumbled over facts and the names of schools, the towns I had lived in, he grew livid.

He hit me again that night, not as hard as the first time, but he was furious that I was keeping secrets from him.

'It doesn't matter!' I screamed at him. 'None of it matters!'

'This husband you had. You always say his name was Peter, but the man who came to the house, his passport said Henry Russell. Which is your husband? Tell me!'

I slammed the bedroom door on him.

'I tell you everything!' he roared. This might have been true, but I didn't often listen to him. Once you've heard the sob story of living in the slums of Paris with his single mother

263

and two brothers, you tend to switch off. He had no idea what real poverty was.

The drama of our relationship – the flare-ups, the tears and recriminations – was energizing. Christian pointed this out one day. 'You are like a robot! The only time you come alive is when we fight. Is that what you want? Is that what you like?' and he grabbed me by the hair. I learned to fight back and I learned to fight dirty. Christian often carried bruises too. Sometimes, if I felt bored, I would provoke the argument, by belittling him in some way. He had a short fuse, but after that first time he learned not to target my face, not until the very end.

By autumn 1998, Christian and I were still together, but just barely. He loved me without liking me, and I could scarcely tolerate him. He was, by then, a 'businessman', with a new shop near the Cours Saleya from where he sold carpets ostensibly but mostly stolen goods: electronics, phone cards, knock-off designer goods, or whatever came through from Paris or Marseilles. It was a step down from the drug dealing and not at all as lucrative. His criminality was even more petty. I did not like his new associates, who had replaced the Corsicans. Christian complained that I thought myself too good for them. He was right. When Daddy had told me I was special, I am sure he hadn't imagined this grubby life for me. Christian and his friends and his whole shady world were beneath me, and I told him so. Still, when his new friends were around, I stayed in the shadows and ignored their cat-calls and their lewd suggestions that Christian might 'share' me. I sat in the apartment in the evenings, watching the sea through the narrow gap between the buildings opposite, watching it turn from the purest turquoise to the darkest ink, while Christian stayed out, playing poker and drinking beer.

My role as the gangster's moll had seemed exciting when we had first got together, but those old films never showed the violence or the tension, just the nightclubs, the jazz, the cocktails and the cash. Christian adored me, I knew it, but not enough to keep his fists to himself when I threw insults his way. I stopped provoking him, but the attacks still came.

In ancient times, MacDermod the weaver was famous throughout the length and breadth of the country for the fine garments he could produce from even the roughest wool. But MacDermod had a scold for a wife. She was possessed of the longest red hair that swung down to her ankles, and it was her pride and joy. She would sit outside her cottage on a stool, combing it through with hard fish bones, to be admired by the passing islanders. But she was lazy, it was said, and if her children ran wild and hungry like stray dogs, and brought trouble to the harbour, where they'd be hopping boats and pegging stones at fishermen, she would blame her husband and roar at him in the street, bringing shame upon the man.

MacDermod could not help but love her, despite all her nagging, but the neighbours got fed up of it and one day they held her down and hacked her hair off with knives. Then they ordered MacDermod to weave a sheet from her hair that would sit on the harbour wall, as a warning to all the wives. Daddy always said that the red fronds that covered the wall were the woven hair of MacDermod's wife, but I was old enough to know it was seaweed.

MacDermod and his wife and children rarely ventured outside their cottage after that day, except to collect necessary items for their household. They spoke little, and kept their heads down when at the market.

The wife's hair grew back faster than anyone had imagined possible. When one year had passed, her flame-coloured mane reached her knees and she began to look up again, to hold her head straight and look the world in the eye. But the islanders did not like her arrogance and it was said that the nagging had begun once more, that children passing could hear it through the thick walls of the cottage.

266

One day, MacDermod's wife was caught in the act of badgering her husband, complaining that he hadn't built the fire hot enough for her to bake bread. This time, her neighbours were merciless. They dragged her down to the harbour wall and hacked her hair off again, but this time they forced her to eat it until she choked. To death.

Daddy used to tell me this story while I was curled on his lap, but he'd be staring at Mammy while he told it. Daddy said if a man couldn't keep his woman in order, his neighbours would have to do it for him.

26

In an effort to create some distance between Christian and me, I got a job in a high-end gift shop, La Belle Époque, on the Quai des États-Unis. I made some friends: Élise, a Swiss girl, who had engaged me in conversation at the dentist's one time; and Marielle, who worked with me in the gift shop. I still brushed my hair forward on the right-hand side, still ashamed of the imperfection.

At home the fights were constant. I no longer even remembered why they started, though money was always a problem. I dutifully handed over my maintenance payment every month, resenting every centime. It did not even cover my half of the rent. Though Christian could be cruel and violent, he was not particularly mean. If he had had a good week, he would give me money to spend, but it had now been a long time since he had had a good week. I could not have survived on my own. If I hadn't needed Christian financially, I would have left him. I had written to Peter's lawyer in London, requesting a change of account, so that I could regain control of my own money. The reply asked for my reasons for the change. The maintenance of this account cost her client a considerable amount in fees, and she saw no reason to change the status quo. The letter included a breakdown of medical expenses incurred by our son. Harry was right about the years he had spent in hospital, but I couldn't think about that. I was stuck.

One day I was rearranging the window display in La Belle Époque when I noticed a man watching me, staring at me intently. It had been quite a while since I'd had that kind of attention. After a minute or two, he entered the shop and joined a middle-aged woman looking at the glassware, but he kept turning his head towards me.

'Look, Marjorie, that girl, how do we know her?' He was upper-crust British. He assumed I was French and would not understand him. I turned sideways, pulled my hair forward.

'I've never seen her before in my life. What are you on about?'

'I *know* her.'

I approached him, smiling. 'May I help you?' My accent matched his.

'Ah! I have it! We have met before, I think? You were the pretty liar.'

I had no idea what he was talking about.

'In Cornwall?' he said. 'Jory Lattimer's place.'

I remembered him then, the tall man poking at the innards of a seagull on the edge of a cliff.

'Freddie Baird.' He put out his hand. 'I don't think we were properly introduced that weekend.'

'Cordelia Russell.'

'Cordelia, eh? And do you love your father the most?'

'What?' I was rooted to the spot by the randomness and accuracy of his question.

'*Lear. King Lear?* Not an English scholar, then?'

I was completely thrown. I had never read or seen *King Lear*, despite Peter's efforts to educate me. Before I could gather my thoughts, his wife joined us and Freddie introduced us.

'Well, what a small world,' she said, 'and how do you know the Lattimers? So sad about Jory, wasn't it?'

'Oh, I didn't know him at all. I was only at that party because friends of his invited me. What happened to him?'

269

Freddie smirked and Marjorie poked him in the ribs. 'Don't, Freddie, it's no laughing matter. The man is dead.'

'Remember that bloody great stag's head over the arch in the hallway? It fell off the wall, clocked him on the head and killed him outright. Only fair, I think.'

He hooted with laughter. Marjorie tried to smother her amusement, and I laughed at the thought of that drunken oaf being taken down by a stag he'd probably shot himself.

'What happened to your face?' said Freddie, and I realized that my hair had swung back when I laughed. My hand flew up to the scarring.

'Don't,' he said, 'it makes you much more interesting.'

'Freddie! Don't be so rude. I'm so sorry, my dear. My husband has a morbid fascination with wounds and scars.'

'But it's perfect! I should like to paint you,' he said. And of course, that used to be flattering to hear, but no longer.

'Paint me? Like this?'

'Oh, Freddie, leave the poor girl alone!'

Marjorie's attention was taken by some ornate gilt-framed mirrors, and she wandered off to look at them.

'Would you be so kind as to visit my villa?' Freddie asked. 'I will pay you and you may bring an escort if you fear my intentions. It is just your face I would like to paint.' He gestured towards my right cheek and I knew he meant the damage. He seemed a little desperate, making this request. Afraid that I would refuse.

He was older than me, twice my age at least, and he looked at me as if I were a curiosity rather than a woman. Marjorie left, saying she would see him later for dinner. Freddie invited me to go for coffee with him. Marielle told me I could take half an hour.

I felt relaxed with him, and it was immediately clear that he had no romantic intentions. Over coffee, Freddie told me he had come down to the Riviera to paint. He was an industrial engineer and a frustrated artist, he said, and all of the best painters found the light here conducive to good work. He explained he had spent the morning painting a bruised nectarine, and had wondered how it would look if it were scorched.

'Is it painful?' he said, waving loosely towards my head.

'Not at all. It's been over seven years since the fire.' I began to tell him about the nightclub fire. I told him that I lived with my boyfriend in Nice. He asked where I was from and I told him Hampstead and I think he believed me, but he did not press me. He told me Marjorie thought his painting was a frivolous exercise and that he was too old to take up such a hobby, but he was bored and restless and he had always wanted to paint. He had rented a place for a month, he said, but had not been inspired to paint much at all and would shortly return to London. He gave me his card with a scribbled address beside the printed London one in Regent's Park, and he drew a small map on the back with a thin-nibbed Montblanc. He asked me to call the next afternoon or the one after. He was staying in Vence, a hilltop village an hour's bus ride from Nice. I had been there with Christian once or twice in his car, and it seemed quaint and pretty and quiet. Christian had done business there with a local and we did not have time to look around.

Two days later, I feigned illness and Christian went to work, complaining that I'd better get sick pay.

I took the bus. I sat, as always, on the sea side of the vehicle and watched the coastline all the way until it disappeared as we headed up the mountain road. I found the house easily, using the meticulous miniature map on the back of the card. Crossing a narrow bridge over a steep ravine, I followed a signpost to Gattières and found a pale villa on my left. Freddie was leaning over the balcony upstairs, peering down.

'I hoped you'd come. Let me see your face!'

I doffed my hat, revealing the imperfection that so fascinated him.

'Perfect!' he exclaimed. 'Come up!'

I ascended some steps on the outside of the building to join him. He was excited and less needy than before, when I had been the one with the gift of my impairment to bestow. Now it was his, and he knew it.

'You came alone,' he said, surprise in his tone.

'I decided to trust you.'

'Brave, and yet foolish, but you are young enough to be my daughter and I have no intention of touching you, so you are perfectly safe. I should tell you that my wife flew back to London this morning.'

I knew I was safe. I looked around from the roof terrace. 'Where is the sea?'

'Oh, beyond that hill. I know, I should have a place with a sea view, but I'm here for the light.'

'I don't like it when I can't see the sea,' I said aloud, and instantly regretted it. I knew this peculiarity about me was best left unsaid. It drove Christian insane. I had pulled our bed from the wall to the floor-length windows and refused to close the curtains at night because I needed to know the sea would be there when I opened my eyes. Christian would complain that he couldn't sleep and often went to the sofa in the salon as soon as dawn broke, noisily cursing and kicking furniture on his way out of the bedroom.

'And why is that?' asked Freddie.

I could not explain it, even to myself, but went with the notion that used to charm Peter. 'I think I might be a mermaid,' I said with a coy smile.

Freddie frowned. 'I see.'

He drew me that morning and took several photographs as I held the rotting nectarine beside my chin out on the terrace. He chatted about his life in London, his wife, his work – 'I guess you could say I'm semi-retired,' he said, 'I only go into the office once a week or so' – his travels all over the world, his wayward daughter 'Audrey, she's twenty-five, not that much younger than you.' I didn't see the point in telling him I was thirty-three.

'What were you doing at that dreadful party in Cornwall?' he asked.

'Partying,' I said simply.

'Didn't some ghastly girl make a fuss about you? What was that about?'

I claimed not to remember. When I lowered the shoulder of my wrap, he noticed the bruise there, inflicted by Christian.

'How did that happen?'

'A shoebox fell from the top of my wardrobe,' I said.

It was a futile lie. If one looked closely enough, and he did, you could see the imprint of Christian's fingers.

'Perfect!' he said, taking up his pencil again, and made no further enquiries. He was only interested in the injuries. He did not appear to care what caused them.

After an hour or two, I was stiff from not moving. Freddie invited me to come and take a look at his graphite drawings. I was shocked by what I saw. I wondered if this was how the world saw me. Like a half-rotten nectarine, one side smooth and glowing, the other sick with decay.

'You don't like it?'

I shook my head. 'Sorry, it's good, it's just that I look so . . .'

'I've made it worse than it is. This is what interests me, you see. The pretty models with their perfect teeth and their smooth complexions bore me to death. You hold so much in your face. The damage goes deep, does it not?'

I was startled by this sudden intimacy and shied away from personal details.

'You are an amateur, aren't you? I mean, you aren't going to exhibit this anywhere?'

'Good Lord, no! I would be laughed out of the academy with my scribblings.'

I looked at the picture again. Damage was the word he had used. So close to damned.

Afterwards, we drove to the next village and he bought lunch in La Colombe d'Or, a restaurant and hotel I had heard about but had never been able to afford. He drank a carafe of wine and I sipped a lemonade. He walked me to the bus and shook hands formally.

'I thought you weren't going to touch me,' I said, looking up at him from under my eyelashes, my pretty side facing him.

'Young lady, you are either trouble or you are *in* trouble. I can tell. Please stay safe and call me in London if you need anything. You have my card.'

'I am neither!' I protested. But he didn't laugh or smile.

He gave me an envelope stuffed full of francs and I tried to refuse it, knowing he would insist. 'For your time,' he said.

'When are you leaving?'

'Tomorrow,' he said, and the bus pulled up and I boarded and waved as he raised his hand in salute.

I wrote to him several weeks later. I didn't ask for anything, just said it had been a pleasure to meet him and I wished him well with his painting. A courteous, non-flirtatious letter with my address at the gift shop in the top-left corner. I could have told Christian about my encounter with Freddie Baird, but I knew he would be suspicious, or would interfere in some way. Something about that morning with Freddie felt innocent. Neither of us had an agenda. Not then.

A week later, I received a card from England with a line written on it: 'I should have taken you to the Matisse chapel. Go visit. Freddie.' I had no idea what he meant. I was curious enough to ask Élise, who worked as a guide in the Matisse Museum in Nice. She rattled through the legend of Matisse, the chapel and the nun.

It seemed that when recuperating from an illness while living in Vence in 1941, Henri Matisse recruited a night nurse, Monique Bourgeois. He was in his seventies; she was twenty-one. When she left his employment, he asked her to return, to pose for him – he liked how she was a straight-talker and unafraid to offer her opinions of his work. She was amazed that he would want to paint her as she was no beauty, but she agreed.

In 1946, to his dismay, she entered the Dominican convent in Vence to become a nun. He visited her, and when he saw that the nuns were using a disused garage with a leaking roof for their chapel, he undertook to build a new chapel for them.

With the help of Monique – now Sister Jacques-Marie – he dedicated six years of his waning life to building a chapel for the Dominican sisters, designing everything from the building to the candlesticks to the priest's vestments. So determined was he to finish the project that he painted from his wheelchair and from his bed.

Élise showed me photographs of him at work, a paint-brush strapped to a bamboo stick as he sat up in his bed, painting holy figures on the high walls beside him. When Monique told him that she believed he was inspired by God, he said, 'Yes, but that god is me.'

That weekend, I made an appointment to see the chapel. I

took the bus back to Vence. The Chapelle du Rosaire was situated a mere hundred yards from Freddie's rented villa, now boarded up and empty. The blank exterior walls of the chapel could easily be missed by a passer-by who didn't know what to look for, but once inside, the building startled me. Living on the Riviera, I was not unaware of the number of artists and painters who had lived and worked here, but I did not move in arty circles and had little education in the subject. I might recognize a Caravaggio or a Renoir if I saw one, but this chapel was unlike any I had seen before.

A hawk-eyed nun watched me closely as I wandered around, but was thankfully disinclined to conversation. On the island, and in Westport, churches had been cold, austere places furnished in dark wood and suffering but, in the afternoon sunlight, this was a blaze of warmth. Heat seeped through the stained-glass windows and cast the white walls in a hue of rose pink. The holy figures painted on the walls were so simple and childlike, and even the Stations of the Cross, usually portrayed as a trail of torture, looked more like an instruction manual to build a crucifix. The God or Jesus figure (I couldn't tell which) was blank-faced, swathed in monk-like robes and carrying a Bible.

The tall drawing of Madonna and child stood out, as if the child, standing, grew from her hands and was about to take flight, surrounded by cartoonish floral shapes. It comforted me, the thought that a mother is *supposed* to launch her child. And yet you could see the bond between them and I shuddered, and then I put the thought out of my mind because my son would now be fourteen years old. I could not think of him. But I could not help thinking of my mother. She had wanted to take us home to America, to her mother. For the first time, I thought about the fact that she didn't just leave the island without us. She could have gone home any time. My father would not have followed her. He did not love her. But then, he did not follow me either. Instead, he killed her and my brothers and himself. Was that really my fault? Did he love me? Did my mother? The feelings of confusion overwhelmed me, and I sat in one of the simple pews to gather my thoughts. I decided to put them all out of my mind. I had to live in the present.

I wrote to Freddie that night when Christian was out on one of his nocturnal prowls. 'I went back to Vence and found the chapel. How beautiful!' I did not have the technical vocabulary to appraise it in any meaningful way. I was afraid that my simplistic reaction might give away something about me, and when he didn't reply I began to think that I had disappointed him. I didn't know *King Lear.* It was obvious I knew nothing of art. He had expected more.

27

That winter, business was bad. Despite all of his nefarious dealings, Christian never seemed to make much of a profit. It was tied up, he used to say, in a business investment that would make him rich. I had heard this before, and maybe he was investing returns in bigger and bigger deals. I had a feeling that it wouldn't end well. I remembered what had happened to Peter and his investments. Christian's rages became more dangerous as his gambling problem became more serious. At the end of January, the manager of the gift shop told me that my services would not be required again until May. Marielle had seniority and would be kept on. I did not want to tell Christian. We lived from week to week, and half of my income went towards the bills, though Christian still paid the lion's share.

We rarely went out together any more. We no longer played cards together, though he played, with others, for money. It seems I had escaped a gambling husband only to end up with a gambling boyfriend. I couldn't remember the last time he had paid me a compliment or bought me a gift, and yet in the beginning of our relationship he would have done anything for me. I asked around for other jobs but there was nothing, nothing legal. Élise said an assistant was required in a modern art gallery but that I would need to prove my knowledge of art and that the owner was difficult. She also hinted heavily that I mixed with the wrong people and that my associations would work against me. She meant Christian.

I convinced her I could pass muster in an interview, and

she prepped me as much as she could. I dressed carefully in my best clothes and turned up to be interviewed by Monsieur Arnaud, a vicious old bastard who knew immediately that my degree in fine art from Bristol University was a fiction. I gabbled about Matisse, about the nun and the convent in Vence, but I did not convince. He quizzed me about the names of the known art collectors on the Côte d'Azur.

'Sweetheart,' he said, 'please don't insult my intelligence, you know nothing. Your Matisse story is well rehearsed, but my dog knows that story better than you. Even if you could be the *face* of my gallery' – he pointed at the right-hand side of my face – 'I need someone who has heard of contemporary artists and can tell the difference between a César and an Arman. Your short skirt will only get you so far. The Russian oligarchs are here of course, but you are too old for them. From what I hear, you are the wrong side of nubile for their tastes.'

My humiliation was complete. My face flushed.

'Oh no,' he said, 'you are not going to cry, are you? I can't bear crying women.'

For the whole of February, I continued to hide my unemployment from Christian. I left the apartment every day at the regular time, and went job hunting. Tourists were thin on the ground at this time of year and nobody was hiring. My French was perfect, and my English accent was crystal. I thought I could get a job showing houses for an estate agent, but they all wanted to know who I knew, who my contacts were among the ex-pat British community, so I made up names that did not check out and did not tell them that I was Irish. I don't know if they knew I was a fraud but they knew that I must have fallen from grace, if I ever had it. The job in the gift shop had been a favour. I knew I'd been lucky to last as long as I did there. I lowered my sights, but unfortunately

Carrefour was fully staffed. When the rent was due in early March, the game was up.

Most of the time, when you anticipate somebody's bad reaction to bad news, it is rarely as awful in reality, but this time it was worse.

'What are we supposed to do? You think I am going to pay for you to swan around, eating my food, sharing my bed, acting like a princess? I took you in when nobody would even look at you, as a favour to my uncle. I gave you a job, and a home . . . and you repay me with what? You are a fucking ice queen and I've had enough.'

He upended my handbag and took my last francs out of my purse. He threw the coins at me. 'Why can't you even cry like a normal woman?' He grabbed me and held me close to his body. I should have put my arms around him, said some soothing words, for self-preservation at least, but I slapped him and then let my body go limp, expecting the blows to rain on me. To my surprise he released me, and I slumped on to the sofa. There were tears in his eyes. 'You make me crazy, you know? But I will teach you. You will learn the hard way.' He left the apartment then, and I was confused. His rage was white hot, but he had not struck me. Maybe this was progress in our relationship? I composed myself, made a pot of coffee and watched the sea.

A few hours later, Christian's friend Louis let himself into our flat without ringing the doorbell. I did not like him. I knew only that he was senior to Christian in the pecking order of their pathetic little gangster world. I had always avoided him.

'What are you doing here? Who let you in?' I asked nervously.

Louis smiled and dangled a key from his forefinger. His gold necklace flashed in the fading sunlight. 'What kind of welcome is this for one of Christian's best friends? I am here for you, *chérie*,' and he reached out and pulled me roughly towards him. The smell of bad breath and body odour was sickening. I struggled away and backed up until the sink was behind me.

'Stop! What do you think you're doing? Don't you dare touch me! I will tell Christian. He will kill you.'

Louis waved his finger in my face. 'No, *chérie*, I don't think so' – he spoke in a sing-song voice – 'you must behave yourself. You must be nice to me now. Get to your knees so that I don't have to look at that face.' He roughly pulled my hair so it covered my scar. He grabbed me around the throat and began to push me downwards to my knees, as he unbuckled his belt.

I was choking and trying with both hands to release his grip, but as I slid downwards I quickly grabbed a pair of scissors that was on the draining board behind me and plunged it into his thigh, which was as high as I could reach. He screamed and roared and kicked me in the stomach, catching my left hip too, and ran from the room, blood streaming down his leg.

'You fucking whore!' he screamed, as he half fell down the stairs towards the front door.

A number of doors off the stairwell opened, and Madame Tissot shouted up at me, 'What is it this time? You are nothing but trouble! I am complaining to the *propriétaire* again! This used to be a respectable building until you moved in.'

I shut the door on her angry tirade with my elbow. I was trembling from head to foot. I could hardly stand up, I had been so winded by the kick. I crawled to the icebox for ice to numb the pain, and in it I found a bottle of Russian vodka that I hadn't known was there. I rang Christian but he did not answer. I almost felt sorry for Louis. Christian would tear him limb from limb when he caught up with him. Christian loved me. His problem was that I did not love him. I took the vodka bottle out and poured a glass. I needed something for the shock. But vodka wasn't it. Pouring the glass down the drain, I decided to make some strong coffee. I lit a cigarette and looked into the flame as I struck the match.

I sipped and waited for Christian's return, ready to fall into his arms, but when he arrived, he was in the foulest of moods. 'What the hell did you do to Louis?' he demanded. I was bewildered.

'He was going to rape me! He had a key. He tried to force me –'

'I know, I gave him the key. I told you I would teach you a lesson. You were supposed to do whatever he wanted. Don't you understand anything? I owe him thousands, you were a holding payment, are you stupid?'

'You . . . you *sold* me? To that animal?'

'What else are you good for?'

I grabbed the vodka bottle by the neck and swung it towards him, but I was still shaky after what had happened with Louis, and missed. This time, Christian showed no mercy. Instinctively I held my elbows over my face, but he punched and kicked and stamped on me until I passed out.

I woke later in the Saint-Roch hospital, in a crowded ward, with Christian stroking the smooth side of my face. Christian, who only ever wanted me to love him back. Everything hurt, but it was a distant kind of hurt, as if a cloud were protecting me from the real teeth of the pain. Blessed morphine. I slipped in and out of consciousness and sometimes, when I woke, I thought I was in London, after the fire, and was surprised to hear people speaking French around me, and further surprised that I could understand them. My left arm was in a plaster cast, my fingers splinted. When I moved my head painfully to look down, all the parts of my body that weren't swathed in bandages were swollen, red and scraped, blood close to the surface of my skin.

'Baby, what has happened to you? Who did this?' Christian was speaking more loudly than usual. A nurse hovered nearby, and I remembered through the fog that Christian had done this, and I knew immediately that though he may have been genuinely contrite, my job was to play along. His face was creased with sorrow as he leaned in and whispered, 'Darling, I am so, so sorry, I was angry. It was just business – I should have told you he was coming.'

I remembered Louis then, and the snap of his belt as he pushed me to my knees. I opened my mouth to speak, but my tongue was parched. Christian passed me a paper cup of water. 'He's after me now. I'm going to have to go on the run, but I'll come back for you in a week. We've been evicted from the flat. I couldn't save any of your stuff – they threw it away. Sorry, my darling, but I'll sort it out.' He kissed me gently on the forehead, and my ribs hurt as I tried to incline my body away from him. He cupped my face in his large rough hand. 'I'll be back for you, *chérie*, just give me a week.'

I had nothing, nothing but pain and a violent boyfriend who didn't think that selling me to a business associate to settle a debt was anything to apologize for. *I should have told you*, he'd said, as if it were just a tiny oversight. Even through the morphine-induced mist, I knew this was beyond wrong.

Our neighbour, Madame Tissot, visited a few days later. She told me she did not want to get involved in our domestic rows but I was better off without Christian. She said the flat was being rented out to new tenants at the end of the week. She, at least, had grabbed some of my things before they were dumped. A handbag, a hairbrush and, most importantly, my passport. I was tearfully grateful. She wished me well.

As time went on, the morphine dosage decreased and the pain bit hard as physiotherapy began. The nurses were no fools; they knew who was responsible for my injuries. A surgeon spoke to me about my face and I told him the old nightclub-fire story. They offered to call my family, but I didn't have any – none that wanted to hear from me, at any rate. They told me I must report Christian to the gendarmes and that a home-less refuge would take me in, but those places were like prisons, with curfews and fights among women who identified them-selves as victims. They were no place for me.

I told them that Christian's version was correct: a stranger had broken into my flat and attacked me. A policewoman came to take my statement. I told her the same story, and watched her face harden towards my lies. All of my posses-sions were gone, except the contents of my handbag. Christian had, of course, taken my ATM card. I waited for him to come back.

A week passed, and I could walk slowly with the help of one crutch. My legs were miraculously not broken, but I could not do simple tasks like buttoning my shirt or comb-ing my hair. They would not discharge me until I could walk unaided and, until Christian returned, there was nowhere for me to go. Élise came to visit. She had heard through the grapevine what had happened. 'He's a pig. You cannot go back to him and that life!' She did not understand that I had no choice.

Christian did not return. Three weeks after my emergency admittance to the hospital, I was deemed fit for independent living. I could walk, slowly, but my badly fractured fingers were still swollen with infection. They prescribed further antibiotics. On my last evening in the hospital, I was in deep despair. I had telephoned Élise and begged her to let me stay on her sofa, just for a few days, but she did not want to help me. Élise was the kind of friend who would be happy to meet for a coffee on a Friday afternoon, but she had never invited me to her home and one evening, when I had been with Christian and his friends outside a bar in the Port, she had spotted me and walked on, pretending not to hear me calling her name.

'I'd love to help, you know I would, but my sister is coming from Lyons today, and I have no room.' She had never mentioned a sister before.

No matter what happened on the island, Happy MacDaniels would smile and laugh his way through it. He was the most amenable and easily pleased man. The mainlanders might take him for a simpleton, but back in the days of the chieftains it was known he was a shrewd and fearless worker.

Happy had a small abattoir out the back of his cottage, and he'd slit the throats of the lambs and the goats and grin his head off as they thrashed and twitched their way out of life, the blood draining into the buckets below them. It was a savage kind of work, and even the hardy island men were wary of the way a lamb might fix its eye on you as you sharpened your knife. Happy MacDaniels never let it bother him.

There came a day when a storm reared up so violent around the island that everyone stayed indoors for four days as children were whipped into the air and dragged over cliffs and dashed on the rocks below. Twelve fishermen were lost at sea that week. The island went into deep mourning, and, as was the way of those times, ate naught but grass or thistles until the burials had taken place of the seven bodies that could be recovered.

Happy MacDaniels's glee could not be contained, however, and his laughter proved too much to take for the islanders. When the last corpse was interred in the graveyard, the islanders turned on Happy and threw him in on top of the remains of a child who had been decapitated by a loose slate. Then they hurled mud in after him with such ferocity that it swallowed him faster than he could climb out of it.

And all the time he was giggling, until a clod of earth smothered his last smile.

Daddy took me around that graveyard when I was a small girl. We lay on the ground and Daddy said, 'Listen!'

We put our ears to the sodden earth, and I swear I heard a chuckle rising up through the clay.

'There you are,' Daddy said, 'being agreeable does not suit everyone. People who go through life smiling miss out on the dignity of sorrow.'

28

I sat in the armchair beside my bed with my handbag and other belongings in a plastic bag: the bloodstained dress, my underwear, a toothbrush and facecloth provided by the hospital. I wore a shapeless smock dress that some other patient, probably dead, had left behind. The doctor came and signed my discharge papers. I rang the bank from a free payphone in the hall. They told me my account was empty. Every centime had been withdrawn, the day after the last deposit from Peter two weeks previously.

A social worker came and gave me the name and address of a homeless shelter. I had never felt so low and so awful. I thought that was the lowest point of my life, but there have been so many, it is hard to know. In a zipped pocket of my handbag, I looked for Freddie's card. I asked the social worker if I might make an overseas call. Reluctantly she agreed, and I was brought to the nurses' station to make my phone call.

'Hello?' A woman, upper class. Marjorie.

'Hello, could I speak to Freddie, please . . . I mean, Mr Baird?'

'Who is this, please?'

'It's Cordelia, from Nice.'

'Oh, Cordelia.' There was a slight pause. 'Yes, right, hold on.'

I could hear a muffled conversation, as if her hand was over the receiver, and then:

'Cordelia, what can I do for you?' It was Freddie.

A nurse standing beside me tapped her watch. She was doing me a favour.

'Freddie, I'm in trouble, I'm sorry –'

'Where are you?'

'Still in Nice, but I'm in hospital, just getting out, but I have nowhere to go.'

'Why? What happened? Are you all right?'

'No, yes, I have no money, I was . . . attacked by a str—'

He didn't wait to hear the lie on the tip of my tongue. He knew.

'Go to the airport,' he said. 'I'll book you on a flight home.'

'I can't,' I said, 'I can't go home. There is nobody . . .'

The nurse glared at me again and tapped the phone with her biro.

'Freddie, I'm not allowed to stay on the phone much longer.'

There was another muffled conversation between Freddie and Marjorie.

'Marjorie says you are to go to the Negresco Hotel. You know it? We will book a room for you. I'll telephone you there later.'

'Thank you. Thank you so much.'

I hung up and walked in a daze from the hospital down to the Promenade des Anglais, then made my way along the seafront to the Negresco Hotel. It was a hotel I had never dared enter before, notoriously expensive and upmarket. The doorman looked me up and down but held the door open. I went through to reception, where a concierge immediately stepped out from behind a desk. I thought he was going to hustle me towards the exit.

'Miss Russell? We have been expecting you. This way, please.' He took me to the elevator and held me loosely by the elbow, courteously I thought, as if he knew I might faint.

He punched a number on the wall, and I felt a small lurch and then heard the hum of the machinery as we ascended. 'Is there anything we can get for you?' He looked down at my handbag and the opaque hospital plastic bag that contained my worldly goods. I shook my head. 'Mr Baird has told us to give you anything you require. Do you need a doctor, medication?'

The hospital had given me boxes of tablets and lists of instructions. It was everything else that I needed. 'No, thank you.'

I wasn't in a fit mental state to take in the opulence of the room, but I gravitated naturally towards the window and the view of the sea right across the road. The concierge told me about lights and switches and minibars, but I was grateful when he left and closed the door behind him. I put the *Do Not Disturb* sign on the outside of the door and climbed into bed. Hours later I was awoken by a telephone on the bedside table.

'Hello?'

'Cordelia, I am glad you have settled in.' Freddie.

'Freddie . . . I . . .' My voice broke.

'Now, look here, there is nothing to be upset about. You are perfectly safe. Marjorie and I are flying into Nice tomorrow, as it happens. We decided to buy a place down there so we were coming anyway, to finalize the sale. You stay put and we'll see you tomorrow. They have room service, you know. Order anything you like.'

'But I don't have . . . I won't be able to pay you back.'

'Nonsense. You already have. See you tomorrow.'

I had no idea what he meant, but I was in no position to argue with his act of charity. That evening, I ordered a lobster salad and some chicken soup and the food was delivered to my room and revealed from a silver dome as if the delivery girl had conjured it out of thin air. I had to ask her to cut everything into bite-sized pieces. After she left, I opened the minibar and looked inside. How tempting it was, as I peered at the small bottles of gin, vodka, whisky. I could have drunk them all. But I made the choice not to. I am not an alcoholic. I selected a cold can of Orangina and a bottle of water.

At night-time, I left the hotel, walked across the road and descended the steps on to the beach. I kicked off my shoes and walked into the sea up to my knees. It was cold enough to numb my feet. I wished that it could numb the rest of me.

Marjorie Baird was a fiercely competent no-nonsense English woman of breeding and kindness. Matronly and grey, like a storybook headmistress.

'Oh dear, you have been bashed about a bit, haven't you? Did they catch the blighter who did this? You are much better off without him. Tell her, Freddie.'

Freddie didn't have to tell me. She wanted to know how I had ended up homeless without any possessions. 'But what about your family? You must have somebody?'

I squirmed with embarrassment. It was shameful to have nobody.

Freddie nudged his wife. 'Don't hassle the poor girl. She's still traumatized.'

'And your face? Is it any worse?' Marjorie was nothing if not direct.

Freddie, it turns out, was no more diplomatic than his wife. 'Her face is no worse than when I painted it. It is perfect for my requirements. That combination of beauty and pain and damage.'

Damage.

'Oh, my dear, Freddie has barely spent a day in the office

since he met you. Our conservatory is covered in paintings and photographs of *you*.' She said it without any hint of bitterness.

I was surprised. I thought he'd painted me that one time as a kind of experiment. I was alarmed. I did not like to think of paintings of me being scrutinized. I feared that as Freddie clearly moved in the same social circle as Hannah and Isabelle, he would find out the truth about me, about what I had done to my son. I would lose his sympathy for sure.

'Well, I think I've found my muse,' he said. 'And Marjorie is absolutely delighted that you're not . . .' He caught himself in time. Maybe he was going to say pretty, or beautiful, or utterly gorgeous, or any of those words that people once used to describe me. He didn't finish the sentence.

They left shortly afterwards, to check into their own room on the penthouse floor.

The next day, a nurse came to check me over and advised rest and recuperation for another week. Freddie and Marjorie insisted that was not a problem. They invited me downstairs to lunch with them. Marjorie lent me a diaphanous outfit. She was a large woman, but she gave me a scarf to tie around my waist. The look was . . . unusual.

I told them the truth about my unemployment, my violent boyfriend and how we had been evicted from our home and my belongings dumped, and that my friends were not in a position to help me.

'Well, darling, I'm afraid you can't stay here for ever, but I'm going off to do some shopping now. I'm guessing you're a size 8 or 10? You'll need a basic wardrobe, and Freddie has a . . . a proposition to make to you. As far as I'm concerned, it's ludicrous, but I have never yet been able to dissuade my husband from one of his schemes and I am not going to start now.'

Having checked my shoe size and bra size, and taken note of my factor-50 lotion requirements, Marjorie went shopping and left me alone with Freddie.

He was almost gleeful. 'I knew there was something about you,' he said. 'I bloody knew it. Don't you remember? I said you were either trouble or *in* trouble. I'm so glad it was the latter. Not for you, obviously, but it makes it so much easier to help you. I have a plan for you, but you need to tell me the truth. You need to be honest with me or this won't work at all.'

'What won't work?'

'Never mind that now. Why can't you go home to Hampstead?' He leaned on the word *Hampstead* with a weary irony.

'I'm not from Hampstead.'

'Well, blow me down! Tell me something I don't know, Cordelia.'

My name, I thought.

'I was married.'

'Yes?'

'The fire that caused this' – I put my hand under my face – 'it was my fault.'

'You killed your husband! Where was this?'

'I didn't! He divorced me . . . after the fire in our home, in London.'

'Because of your face?'

'No, well, maybe . . .' I hadn't thought of that before, but Peter used to talk so much about my beauty, perhaps that *was* why he'd found it so easy to walk away.

'Why then?'

'It was because . . .' I couldn't tell him. I just couldn't tell him about James. Nobody understands a mother who doesn't want her child, who deliberately doesn't think about him or worry about him.

'Why?' Freddie was insistent.

'I used to drink . . . a lot.'

Freddie sat back, looking into the glass of whisky he'd ordered from the bar after lunch.

'But you don't drink now.'

'Not since that night. Eight years ago.'

'Are you in Alcoholics Anonymous?'

'No. I gave up on my own. I don't need them. I will not drink again.'

'You don't think you need anybody, do you?'

I laughed grimly. 'I'm here at your mercy. If it wasn't for you, I'd be on the streets.'

'That's a different kind of need,' he said quietly.

I didn't understand what he meant.

'Was it your drinking that alienated you from your family? Surely they would accept you back now, if they knew you were sober.'

It was easier to let him believe that than to tell the truth about my family, or any of the people who ever thought they were my family.

'It's too late.'

He stared at me, right into my soul, and I kept my gaze steady, afraid to blink in case he realized the truth. I saw his decision to trust me.

'We are buying an apartment in Monaco, on the Rock. Three bedrooms. We won't be using it that often, but it's a tax thing. It overlooks the harbour. We could pay an agency to maintain it in the months when we're not there, but perhaps you could be our . . . caretaker?'

'What?'

'You may live there rent-free, but you would have to keep it clean and secure, water the plants, alert us if anything needs fixing, that kind of thing. It needs to be lived in, you see. No parties, no alcohol, no smoking indoors, no unsuitable boyfriends, you understand? In order to have residency there, one must live in Monaco for a certain amount of time, use the electricity, the phone, be able to prove a presence there. The authorities check up on these things. I could hire an agent to go in and out for me, but I think you could do everything required in exchange for accommodation? I need to stay for the first three months, but in reality I'd only expect to be there for maybe a month or two a year. The rest of the time it would be yours, if you want it. You will have to get a job, I am not going to support you financially, but I think this arrangement might suit us?'

'Yes! Yes, of course, I'll stay there. Thank you!' I knew that this was the appropriate time to jump up and hug him, but I was in too much pain, and I didn't think either of us were the hugging type.

'There is one condition. You must allow me to paint you.'

'But you have already —'

'You have unlocked something within me. I don't know what it is. For years I have tried to paint, but I never found anything that interested me sufficiently.'

'The rotting seagull.'

'What?'

'In Cornwall, you were fascinated by a dead seagull that day, on the cliff.'

'Was I?'

'Yes, that is what you see in me. The damage. Why does it interest you so much?'

He deflected the question. He was clearly uncomfortable with it. 'Does it bother you?'

I sighed. 'Not if it puts a roof over my head.'

'I don't mean to insult you.'

'Are you very rich?'

'Filthy,' he agreed. 'I have designed oil and gas platforms and deep-sea rigs for the biggest energy companies in the world.'

'So you don't need to sell the paintings, or display them?'

He pulled his head back, suspicious again.

'No. Why? Are you in hiding?'

'Not at all. But you remember how I used to look? I am ashamed.'

Days later, when I was ready to leave the hotel, I called Élise at the museum to tell her I was moving to Monaco. She told me Christian had been shot dead in Marseilles a week after he assaulted me. She relished telling me all of the sordid details of the story. His body had been discovered in a dumpster. There were signs of torture. So that was why Christian didn't come back for me: he was dead. Murdered. He had always blamed me for his violence. I cannot take responsibility for other people's actions.

'You had a lucky escape. You could have been with him,' Élise said. 'How come you are going to Monaco? It's not cheap there. Who's paying for you?'

I didn't want to tell her anything. I realized I had been foolish to think of her as a friend. I lied and said I was staying with a friend until I had recovered enough to go home to Hampstead. I made no attempt to contact her again.

I managed to get another bank card from the bank, as I had listed the theft of my wallet in the police report about the attack and I had my passport for identification. My maintenance payments were mine again. I was starting over, and this time it should have been easy. My life should have been charmed. But I still wanted my face back.

29

The Monaco apartment had the most wonderful sea views. It had three bedrooms on the first floor – two large and one boxroom – and a grand salon on the second with a balcony that overlooked the harbour. I wondered why they had bought such a lavish place when they had no intention of using it much. Freddie explained that it showed a commitment to Monaco, that his residency there was less likely to be questioned if he had invested heavily in the place. It was not illegal, but it was what they had been advised to do by their tax lawyer.

Freddie wanted to paint me while my bruises from the beating were still vivid. I exposed my thighs, my back, one breast, wherever the flesh was spoiled. He was most interested in my hands, which had suffered the most damage.

'May I?' he would say, and I would sit and pose for him on the balcony. 'Sit in the way that is most comfortable for you,' he said, and most times I faced the sea, and he would paint me in profile. I was allowed to smoke out there.

Marjorie pottered in and out, muttering occasionally to herself. I was always flustered when she came into the salon while he was painting, because it seemed as if she was interrupting something intimate. 'Oh, my dear,' she said, noticing me clutching my robe to my chin one day, 'I used to be an artist's model myself when I was up at Cambridge, for pocket money. I've seen it all.'

I looked at her in surprise.

'I was never a great beauty like you were,' she said, 'but I was two stone lighter than I am now, and a natural brunette. I turned heads in my day too. Even if the fire had never happened, your beauty would have paled. I expect it was just a shock to have it disappear overnight.'

I could not imagine her as a young woman. Freddie showed me photos. They were a handsome couple, in their day. Now, she was doughy and faded, and he was balding and wrinkled, though there was still something attractively aristocratic about them.

Freddie was already well known in Monégasque high society. There were often invitations to the palace or to yacht parties or lunches, regattas and festivals, which they went to for the first few weeks, until Marjorie declared she wasn't going to any more 'small-talk torture chambers'. Freddie invited me to come with him instead, but I declined. Despite their kindness, my confidence was at an all-time low. Marjorie tried to bolster me by taking me shopping. She spared no expense, and flattered my still-slim figure and my tiny waist. I liked her very much.

Marjorie stayed for just two months until June and then declared that she couldn't take the heat and was going back to their summer home in Sussex. Freddie had properties all over the world. He had to stay until July to avail of this tax loophole, and to be seen about the place. After the first year, he said, it wouldn't matter so much.

Until my fingers healed, he prepared the food he bought at the market himself, taking over from Marjorie. Charcuterie, olives, cheese, bread, melon, fresh lobster and langoustines. When my poor swollen fingers could not hold the fork or crack the shells, he fed me himself, and all the time he watched me. Where Marjorie had encouraged me to do as much as I could, Freddie liked me to be dependent. I would catch him looking intently at the deformed corner of my mouth, my elbow, the curve of my calf. Once, when I caught him looking at my stomach, I drew in my breath, to flatten it. 'Don't,' he said, 'please don't do that.' He talked of art and artists and the light, and the sea, and oil platforms and deep-sea rigs. I didn't always follow the train of his conversation, but his enthusiasm for his subjects was clear, and even if sometimes he bored me a little, I felt nothing but gratitude for his care and consideration. Sometimes he would stray into the area of the personal.

'Where *are* you from? The accent is English, of course, but there is . . . something?'

I did not respond.

'Why not go home, to London? I'm sure you could find a job, a flat? You could start over. It's a big place. What age are you, twenty-seven, twenty-eight?'

'Thirty-four.'

He nodded, relieved, I think, to hear some truth from me.

'I couldn't stay in London.'

'Are you wanted by the police?'

'No, I am wanted by nobody. Besides, I want to be near the sea.'

He looked into my face, searching for something more than I could give him.

Eventually, he leaned back in his chair. 'Many months ago, when I met you in that gift shop, you interested me, and then I painted you and you inspired me. Your air of mystery, there is something attractive and yet dangerous about it. I have no reason to trust you, but then, you have no reason to trust me.'

I turned the good side of my face to him and winked.

'This . . . coquettishness,' he said, 'it doesn't suit you.' There were moments like that when, despite everything, I hated him. And he commented so much and so often on the scarring, the 'damage', the 'mutilation' of my face, that it was impossible to forget it for a second. These little stabs of hatred excited me though, and I began to feel more alive.

I accompanied Freddie to a dinner party at a friend's house in Eze. Freddie introduced me to people there as his 'curator', and implied that I was helping him with an art project. And so I was. Some of them regarded me with suspicion. One couldn't blame them. Freddie told them all that I'd been in a tragic fire and made me show them my scars, and their furtive glances turned sympathetic. I contained my humiliation and my shame.

There were many other social functions too. I met all kinds of people: an Italian milliner who lived around the corner; Prince Albert's aide-de-camp; a retired British billionaire and his wife, who had Rolls-Royce dealerships all over the world. When they asked me questions about myself, I said simply that I had been in Nice for many years but was from London originally. They tried to connect me to the Russells they knew, but I said my people were from Somerset originally.

I met Freddie's business partner, who looked me up and down with disdain and quizzed me until Freddie rescued me from my discomfort. Freddie's old school friend, Harold Cross, and his beautiful Persian wife Rania, were much kinder. They lived in Monaco full-time and often invited me to lunches and galas, even later, when Freddie wasn't there. They told me that I was good for him. They knew Marjorie well and knew that if she trusted me, so should they.

Rania, one time, wrote down the name of her plastic surgeon, and passed it to me quietly. 'I'm sure he could do something for you.'

Afterwards, Freddie asked what we had been talking about. I showed him the card, and he ripped it up furiously. 'No!' he said. 'I need you this way.'

I was taken aback by his vehemence but did not question him.

Before Freddie left at the end of July, I got a job in a bridal store, after weeks of job searching. I answered an ad in the shop window, thinking it was probably futile but I had nothing to lose. The proprietor, Celine, did not comment on my appearance except to ask my size because she would provide a uniform. She was impressed by my address and my accent. I came home jubilant that day, but Freddie soon put a dampener on my high spirits.

'Well, I suppose it makes sense,' he said. 'They will want to be absolutely sure that the bride is the most beautiful girl in the room, no matter what she looks like.'

When he left for London, I was relieved. He took all of his canvases with him, and finally the apartment felt like my own. Every day, I got up at dawn and walked along the ramparts and down the Rampe Major out to the harbour, then all along the coast until the road forced me back inland, before I went to work. I read voraciously about art and artists and sought advice at the Princess Grace Library as to which books were the most informative about the Riviera, to ensure there was nothing I didn't know. I was determined to become the person that Freddie claimed I was to his friends, and I often took train rides up and down the coast, visiting the museums, art galleries and hotels famed for their collections.

I was an independent woman, but not in the usual sense. I felt special, like Daddy always told me I was. I made a few friends, and when they said they hadn't come across my name in artistic circles before, I confided that my 'curation' services were exclusive, and that I deliberately kept a low profile. People did not pry too much into each other's activities in Monaco. Freddie once quoted Somerset Maugham as describing the Riviera as 'a sunny place for shady people'. But in Monaco, they were a better class of shady.

Freddie had left me a small allowance for the upkeep of the apartment, and now that I had a full-time job, and free rent, and maintenance payments from Peter, I began again to save in secret for my cosmetic surgery.

Freddie and Marjorie came back briefly the following May for the Grand Prix, during which time we were obliged to throw open the apartment to about forty of their friends and clients, as it had a perfect vantage point overlooking part of the circuit. They asked me to hire caterers and organize servers and deliveries of champagne. I was treated as a family friend rather than staff. I had grown in confidence by then, and when Freddie began to explain to them what had happened to my face, Harold asked him to stop, saying that nobody had asked for an explanation and there was no need to give one. Freddie nodded at me. Apologetic.

Over the following years, Freddie returned once or twice a year, usually in the autumn or spring, sometimes with Marjorie but mostly on his own. He always brought with him a generous gift – a piece of jewellery, or a beautiful pen. Marjorie chose these gifts, I think. He seemed happy to see me growing in confidence. He was pleased that I had found friends and a job and that I had taken such an interest in art.

On one visit, he took me to a gallery in Nice to select a painting for his daughter, Audrey, who was now marrying a gold-digging tattoo artist in Dallas. He did not approve of the fiancé, and so he was gifting them something neither of them would know the value of.

'Well, at least her fiancé is an artist,' I said, trying to mollify Freddie. 'You know that some people would say that I am a gold-digger too?' I pointed to the gold bracelet he had presented me with on his arrival.

He looked fierce. 'You never asked me for anything. You have graciously accepted the things I have offered you. There is a world of difference.'

The gallery we visited was familiar to me, and it was not long before Monsieur Arnaud appeared out of a back office, bowing and scraping to Freddie. Freddie introduced me as his adviser, but Monsieur Arnaud did not look in my direction.

'Oh, Monsieur Arnaud and I have met before, Freddie,' I said. 'He interviewed me for a job here and suggested that I was too old to work as a whore for a Russian oligarch.'

Arnaud looked at me open-mouthed, and then began to laugh nervously.

'Really?' Freddie was genuinely shocked.

'Oh yes, isn't that right, Monsieur Arnaud?'

'It was . . . merely a joke. Perhaps the English lady . . . does not understand French humour?'

Freddie looked down his nose at Arnaud, whose forehead had begun to sweat. 'Perhaps,' he said, 'you should always assume that you are dealing with class, even if you are unable to recognize it.' He steered me out of the shop. In the street outside, I had to calm him down.

'I'll have him shut down in a month. That oaf!' he said.

I laughed, and we stopped nearby for a coffee. In the afternoon, Freddie drove us to Cap Ferrat and there, in an isolated spot, Freddie painted me standing in the shade of a dying lemon tree. I looked out into the Mediterranean and imagined that I could see my island.

That week, I accompanied Freddie to a yacht party, the first of many over the years. Most of the people were either rich, beautiful or both. Because I was with Freddie, they assumed I was the former. Although some may have had their suspicions about my relationship with him, most people accepted the truth, that I was a friend. Indeed, Freddie and Marjorie both introduced me to eligible bachelors or divorcees, and I had lovers from time to time, but dropped them as soon as they became too keen or too curious.

I was living the life I had always wanted, and then one day I received a letter, forwarded from my bank.

> June 2002
> Dear Mam/Delia,
>
> I know this letter will be a surprise to you, but I hope it's not a bad one. I'm not sure if I should call you Mam or not, because I don't know how you feel about me, but from what Granny tells me the last time you saw me was the day of the fire twelve years ago. Any time that I asked Dad or Granny about you, they made excuses for not giving me your address, and it's only now that I have turned eighteen that Granny told me the full circumstances of the fire. I know this doesn't make me sound like a good person, but I've been through Dad's files (he doesn't know) and I know he was sending payments to you through your bank.
> The thing is, the fire was an accident. I don't remember it, but chip-pan fires are very common and just because you were drunk doesn't make it your fault. I hope you haven't spent the last twelve years feeling guilty about everything. I know that you were burned too. Granny said that one side of your face was damaged. You probably have photos of me as a little kid (or maybe they were all destroyed by the fire?), but I spent a lot of time in hospitals over the years and I know you would never recognize me if I turned up on your doorstep (don't worry, I won't!). The

operations I've had weren't all successful and I don't want
to put you off by sending you a photograph of what I look
like now. I'm not going to be winning any beauty
competitions, that's for sure. My face has been mostly
reconstructed and I have new eyelids and a new nose from
my most recent operation. They took the skin from my
thighs. I won't go into detail but it was all pretty gross. The
fingers on my left hand had to be amputated, but I have
the use of my thumb and you'd be surprised how much I
can do with it. It's lucky that I'm right handed.

Did you know that I moved to Westport to live with
Granny and Grandad, in 1993? Dad came to visit as often as
he could. Grandad died four years ago and shortly after that
Dad moved home to Westport and now I live with him. He
set up a business here, and so far it's going well and he just
got a government contract recently so there was a party to
celebrate in his factory and there was a picture of him on the
front page of the *Mayo News*. I stayed out of the photograph
and I suppose you'll guess why. Dad designs prosthetic
limbs for amputees. It's all done on computers. And then
the designs are manufactured in Taiwan. The fake hand I
used to have was useless, but Dad has spent years working
on this, so the hand I have now is incredibly realistic. If only
my face was amputated and he could make me a new one!

Dad won't talk about you. Uncle Harry says that you
were beautiful (I'm sure you still are and I hope your face
has mended. From what Granny said, your burns weren't
as bad as mine). Uncle Harry also says you are dangerous,
but Dad always says I shouldn't be talking to him because
he's drunk all the time, and I suppose that's true. I still
haven't finished school, because I missed so much being in
hospital. Only one more year to go! There was a kind of
school in hospital for long-term patients where you're

supposed to keep up with your homework, but that's
hard to do when your eyes are bandaged and you're in
a lot of pain. I hope you weren't in a lot of pain from
your burns?

I hate school anyway. I haven't decided what I want to
be yet, or whether I want to go to college. But at least I can
type with my good hand. Dad wants me to come and work
for him and I guess that's the safest thing, because the
people around here are used to the look of me. The
thought of going to a job interview or up to Dublin or
Galway to college is quite scary. Although maybe more for
other people than for me. Ha ha!

There's so much I don't know about you, about where
you are from, and if you and Dad met in London? I know
you are Irish but either nobody knows or nobody wants to
tell me anything about you. It's really annoying.

If you sent me Christmas cards or birthday presents, I
want you to know that I never received them.

Anyway, I just wanted to say hello and see if you wanted
to write back to me? I'm not putting in a photo of me with
this letter because if you do want to find out about me, I
think it's better that we get to know each other like this
first. And we don't have to do it through your bank so I
hope you can email me at jmmyrssll@outlook.ie.

Look, maybe you don't want to be in touch, but I just
don't want you to feel guilty any more. Accidents happen. I
remember things about you. I remember you taking me to
the zoo and to the cinema and I remember you singing me
nursery rhymes and teaching me the alphabet. I know that
you're not a bad person.

Love from your son,
Jimmy

The letter was a shock. This 'Jimmy', writing in such a familiar way, was my child. I had caused his terrible injuries and yet he was writing to forgive me. It was clear that he remembered Chiara rather than me, because I didn't take him on excursions or sing to him. The trauma of the fire must have wiped the memory of his early years. Harry and Peter were still estranged and, no doubt, blamed me.

Should I reply? What could I say? What if he wanted to visit me? I would not be able to hide a disfigured boy in Monaco. And how could I explain myself, to him or to others?

I have never met anyone who wasn't sentimental about their children, but I simply didn't feel that way about him. I never had a connection to my son. Even when he was a cute little boy and strangers would smile at him on the street, I always felt a pang of jealousy. Peter had done his best to make a family of us. What Peter had never understood is that I did not want one. I did not want to bond, with James, or him, or anyone.

I knew this wasn't normal. I knew that I wasn't normal. I have never needed people, just the comforts they could offer me.

I had not spent years yearning for my son and missing him. And I did not like the obvious neediness in his letter. If I wrote back, there would be another letter and I would be obliged to respond again and he would come to think of me as his mother. I was not heartless enough to write and tell him that I didn't want anything to do with him. Instead, I did nothing.

30

Later in 2002, I became an unofficial art adviser to Harold and some other of Freddie's friends. I would never be an expert, I did not have the education, but I knew what was current. I moved from working in the bridal store to a small art gallery tucked away on Rue de la Turbie. Monsieur Arnaud's business mysteriously came my way, and most of our clientele were art investors rather than art appreciators, so it rarely mattered to them what the painting or sculpture or drawing actually looked like.

My old friend Élise turned up one day in 2003, looking for a job. 'I heard you had fallen on your feet,' she said, hugging me as if we were intimate friends. I had not seen her in the five years since I desperately needed a place to stay. I was polite, but distant. I advised my employer against hiring her and ripped her business card into shreds.

Some years passed: long, almost happy years in the Mediterranean sunlight, beside the sea. I found my community in Monaco. One met so few people that were actually born there. We were mostly ex-pats. We did not refer to ourselves as immigrants. The friendships were all on the surface and we knew it. I think a lot of people there had things to hide – offshore accounts, stolen art, all manner of white-collar crime – and so we lived in the moment and did not pry into each other's backgrounds, although we googled each other furiously to discover the gossip. Harold, I discovered, was named in some financial scandal to do with Gibraltar Savings Association in the late eighties. He had transferred millions into Rania's accounts.

I was relieved to find that Cordelia Russell did not exist in the online world, apart from some passing mentions as a 'loyal friend to Freddie and Marjorie Baird' or, inaccurately, 'art historian Cordelia Russell' in local Monaco society notices. Delia Russell existed in newspaper archives in articles relating to the fire, but nobody here knew me as Delia. Freddie must have known I was Delia because I'd had to give him my passport to register as a resident in Monaco, but he never asked me about it.

My son, however, knew my name.

September 2003
Dear Mam/ Delia,

I don't know whether you got it but I sent you a letter over a year ago, to explain that I am your son James. I was hoping that you'd reply, but then I guessed that maybe you are not allowed to write to me for some legal reason, or maybe you didn't receive the letter, forwarded from your bank in France. I guess you live there, in Nice?

I told Uncle Harry that I'd written to you last year, and he made me promise never to write to you again, but I guess I'm very disobedient because, well, here I am.

Dad and Uncle Harry have never spoken much to each other, and it's only last week that I found out why. Uncle Harry was drunk when he told me, and Dad has tried to stop me seeing Harry now, but in a town this size it's impossible, and anyway, I'm a man now and I can do what I want. I just want to know if it's true what Harry says? That you got pregnant with me, by my dad, while you were going out with Harry? Granny sort of confirmed it by not denying it. I always thought people were whispering about me because of my burned head and not because my mother was, well, I don't know a polite word for it, but I'm sure you know what I mean. Uncle Harry says you broke his heart. I am pissed off (excuse the language) with everyone, because even if you did break Harry's heart twenty years ago, he should have got over it, and Dad and Granny should have told me the truth, and you should have written back to me, because I'm pretty sure you did get that letter I sent, and what harm would there be in writing back to me? Even if it's just to say hello. I don't care if it's a legal thing. You have my email address, jmmyrssll@outlook.ie, and nobody has to know except you and me. I know email is hard for some old people, so if you don't know how to use it I'm sure someone will show you how in an Internet café. If you live in some part of France that doesn't have Internet, you can write to me at Dad's factory, Seafort Digital, where I work now, in Westport, Co Mayo. I did well in my exams and I'm being trained in-house. I'm working on eyeballs at the moment. Most of my friends went away to college and it's a bit lonely here now. Where did you go to school? I'm fed up that I don't know anything about you, and no one will tell me. Please, please write back to me.

I'm sorry for sounding so cross but my head is wrecked with it all (on the inside as well as the outside now).

Love from your son,
Jimmy

I shouldn't have read the letters but curiosity got the better of me, and besides, I was glad to hear that the boy had a job and that Peter was looking out for him. James was right about some things. Harry should have moved on. It was ridiculous that he had seemingly continued this feud with his brother. I had been terribly dishonest with both of them, so they had a lot in common. I thought it was best that I was written out of Westport history. It was good for them all that I was not mentioned there. It was good for me. I did not reply.

July 2004
Dear Mam,

I'm not calling you Delia any more, because you are my mam. I have been in touch personally with your bank and they assure me that the letters I sent over the last few years were delivered to your home address. They will not give me your address though, even though I am your next of kin. As far as I have ever been able to find out, I am your only blood relative.

I've had a lot more surgery since I last wrote, but the bad news is that no further operations can be done. All of the available skin on my body has already been used for grafting purposes. The damage was so severe that I am not a candidate for any of the pioneering leaps in technical surgery and I must live with the body I have. Some of the surgery that was done in the early days might have been a mistake, it seems. There are very few mirrors in our house. I look like I'm wearing a terrifying Halloween mask, according to a girl I used to fancy. Luckily for her, she never saw the rest of my body.

I've never been to France. In fact, I have never left Ireland. You know why? Because I'm afraid that people will be revolted when they see me. I rarely leave Westport. I went to Dublin with some friends last month, but some assholes in a pub there started to wind me up, trying to take sneaky photos on those small digital cameras. But I saw them, so I laid into one of them and broke his nose.

They'll be able to fix his nose, unfortunately. Anyway, I got arrested and Dad had to come to Dublin to bail me out. The guards felt sorry for me apparently, and Dad paid off the wanker with the broken nose. My name was finally on the front page of the *Mayo News*, but thank God they didn't use a photo. Granny said she was ashamed of me.

You're obviously ashamed of me too, or you would have been in touch by now, but I don't know why. I never did anything bad to you. How could I? I was only six the last time I saw you.

I found a photograph of you on the Internet, from your school days. Delia Walsh, that's what Harry said your name was. You went to the girls' school next door to the school I went to, and half this town must have known you, and yet still, twenty years later, nobody wants to talk about you. You are very pretty in the photograph, despite that seventies hairstyle, but I suppose you aren't now, because of the fire. At least you were good-looking when you were old enough to know it. There are photos of me as a toddler on Granny's piano, but I don't recognize myself because there is nothing of that kid left in what I look like now.

Harry says you lived with your aunt and uncle. He showed me the house, but someone else lives there now. Your uncle died and your aunt moved away, but nobody can tell me where. You're probably still in touch with her, aren't you?

Maybe you can tell that I'm a bit drunk writing this letter and I'm annoyed too because for like the tenth time a girl I liked told me today that she just wanted to be my friend, even though we've been hanging out for the last few weeks and I've been buying her and her friend drinks. I've never had a girlfriend. I'm twenty years old and nobody has ever kissed me. You won't know how that feels. I used to think it was unfair that everyone blamed you for what happened to me. I mean, accidents do happen, right? But maybe you shouldn't have been drunk when you were supposed to be looking after me?

I haven't told you this before because I was afraid it would hurt your feelings, but since you won't answer my letters I can see that you don't care about mine. Dad got married again seven years ago to a lady called Caroline who works in the factory with him. I have two half-sisters called Chloe (five) and Abigail (six). They are both extremely pretty and everyone makes a fuss of them everywhere they go. Caroline is nice too, I suppose. It took me a while to get used to her. The girls are brilliant though and when they were born it made everything OK. Even when they were babies, they would stare into my eyes and reach out and touch my face. They don't think I'm a freak. It's a lovely feeling and they are cute and sweet. They are probably the best thing in my life.

I probably shouldn't have told you that. When I told Dad that I'd written to you before, he told me I was wasting my time and that I was not to tell you anything about our lives, but you are my mother, like it or not (probably not), so I think you have a right to know.

I just read back over this letter and realized how self-pitying it is. It's probably the drink talking, but these are things I need to say so I'm going to post it now before I regret it.

Please, please write back. Just a short note, or even a postcard will do.

Love from your son,
Jimmy

So Peter had moved on. I had no strong feelings about that. Perhaps he might set an example to Harry. And Alan was dead. I blame Alan for a lot of things that went wrong in my life. He thought he was doing the right thing, I suppose. But if I'd been able to have that abortion, things would have been so different and I wouldn't be getting unwanted letters from my son.

Thanks to Freddie's status and the approval of a certain number of his friends, I found myself accepted in most quarters, on some occasions at the palace itself. Prince Albert's fiftieth birthday party in 2008 was such an occasion, and I thought then that Daddy would have been proud of me. *My little queen.*

Freddie had changed his painting technique several times since I'd known him, and a couple of years ago had started to experiment with layering oils. 'I'm using black as the base layer for your scarring and then building up the layers to get the texture right. There is something dark there and I can't seem to capture it, no matter how hard I try.'

His obsession with me remained undimmed. At the same time, his relationship with his daughter, Audrey, was terrible. They were no longer on speaking terms. She was reckless with his money and I persuaded him not to cut her off financially. Marjorie was grateful to me for that and maintained contact with her, but Freddie would not have her name mentioned. One time, when Marjorie referred to her in my presence, Freddie snapped at her, 'Cordelia is more of a daughter than Audrey is!'

I knew Freddie's attachment to me was causing friction with Marjorie. She told me that entire rooms of their London home were stacked high with sketches and canvases containing only my image. She was irritated by it, and when

I suggested to Freddie that Marjorie might prefer that I got a place of my own, Freddie wouldn't hear of it. I couldn't help myself – I played one against the other, expressing doubt to Freddie that Marjorie may not like me and implying to Marjorie that Freddie was becoming too clingy. As he got older, his visits did indeed become a little more frequent, and more often, Marjorie stayed at home.

When Freddie came, we would often drive away up to Beaulieu or Villefranche or across the Italian border to Ventimiglia and find a quiet grove, an orchard or some other stunning view, and Freddie would retrieve his easel and paints from the car boot. He had no desire for the fashionable flashy sports cars of his friends. He always hired something functional and well designed. He would arrange me in some pose, always ensuring that I was comfortable, and he would paint me.

It disturbed Freddie that I did not like to study his paintings too deeply. 'Have I got it wrong?' he would say, his face creased from squinting and self-doubt. He did not get it wrong at all. He captured everything. You could see the lies in the nape of my neck and the inside of my wrist.

I would laugh at him and say, 'I'm not a narcissist, you know!' and he would look at me with that puzzled expression on his face.

'One day,' he'd say, 'I'm going to paint you so well that you are going to fall in love with yourself.'

'Why, Freddie, why are you so obsessed by the scarring? What is the big mystery?' I finally asked.

He paused and sighed before he answered and kept his eyes on the canvas as he explained.

'I was a boy during the war. We lived in a large house outside a village in Gloucestershire. My father died shortly after I was born and my mother turned the house into a convalescent home for returning soldiers.'

Freddie was now in his mid seventies. I tried to imagine him as a boy.

'I was home-schooled, so these soldiers became my friends and my playmates. I saw them long after their surgeries, and although some of them were dealing with enormous emotional trauma, their wounds were healing and they were always eager to see me. Mother used me like a therapy dog, I suppose.'

'What do you mean?'

'I was small and innocent and knew nothing of their experiences, and I just accepted without question that these broken men lived with us, and that they were part of my family. I was too young to know that their wounds and scars were indicators of pain.'

I drew my hand to my face again.

'I used to touch their scars and stumps, and I put my small fingers in the places where their eyes had been and traced them. I know it sounds strange, but I was fascinated by their difference, and they were grateful, I think, that someone was not afraid of their impairment.'

'But why have you never told me this before?'

'Doesn't it make me sound like the most dreadful creep? Even Marjorie was horrified when I told her. I'm ashamed. That's why I haven't spoken about it.'

'I understand, Freddie.' I really did understand. I knew what it was like to be thought of as different.

'Do you? You see, their damage was a sign of their nobility and their sacrifice. That is what I am trying to capture in you. What sacrifice did you make for those scars, Cordelia?'

'I did not make any sacrifice. I didn't go to war.'

He said nothing for a moment and then: 'There is something there. I know it. I just have to find it.' Freddie was relieved that he no longer had to carry this secret shame.

Afterwards, he would often tell me the stories of these men and their graphic wounds. I was repulsed and fascinated at the same time, but I never let Freddie see my revulsion.

And so he kept trying, over and over and over, to capture the noble me he thought I was. But she didn't exist and I was happy to forget about her. Meanwhile, I researched dermatology clinics. I found the right one in Paris. I had spent years saving money. Since I'd met the Bairds I'd saved half of Peter's payments every month.

May 2009
Dear Mam,

Today is my twenty-fifth birthday. Happy birthday to me. Thanks for all the cards and gifts you sent over the years. Not. Dad says that sarcasm is the lowest form of wit, but it turns out that I'm pretty good at it.

It's been a few years since I last wrote and still got no reply. I could pretend that I don't care, but we both know that's not true because I'm still writing to you.

I've found out a lot more about you now, and it turns out we are alike. I tracked down Moira Walsh to a nursing home in Ballinasloe. She's very old and feeble but her mind is sharp. Surprisingly, she was glad to see me, though when I say 'see', I am misleading you because she's almost totally blind so she didn't suffer much having to meet me. She told me that your birth family died in a fire on Inishcrann. The irony of that doesn't escape me, and maybe that is why you never wanted to get in touch with me.

Have you thought about getting psychological help to deal with your past? I'm not suggesting you're mental but, well, I've been seeing a counsellor for a while now and I think it might be helping. He says that I need to forgive you and let you go, and that's probably good advice, but it's hard for me to 'let go' of something that I never had, not that I remember anyway. Dad says it was some nanny that brought me to the zoo, and that the memories I have are of her. I don't remember you at all.

The counsellor (Mark) was court-appointed and I'm seeing him in order to stay out of jail. I had to agree to six months of counselling to deal with my 'anger' issues and I had to pay €500 in fines to a girl that I assaulted. It wasn't a sexual assault, I'm not a pervert. Mark says I need to accept responsibility and I'm not saying it wasn't my fault, but I need to explain the circumstances. Firstly, I was drunk (I wonder where I got that from?) and also, the girl was obnoxious. I shouldn't have punched her, but I guess I'm just sick to death of all these girls who just want to be my friend. I was actually dating her properly for six weeks. Nothing much had happened between us, but I guess I got my hopes up. You'd think I'd have learned after all this time. We were in a pub in town and some younger lads from a rugby tour down from Dublin thought it would be great fun to pull my hat off and run down the street with it (I wear a hat all the time, winter and summer, to protect me from UVA and UVB light, and so as not to frighten children). I got thick about it and my supposed girlfriend starts laughing and tells me to calm down. She was laughing AT me, so I told her to go away in less polite terms than that, and then other lads started getting heavy with me, telling me to leave her alone. I think she liked the attention that she was getting from the guys, but then she started acting like she was afraid of me, like I was going to beat her up.

I was angry so I took off to another pub thinking I'd have a few whiskeys to calm me down, but the more I drank the angrier I got. When I was kicked out of there at closing time, I went up to the Castle Court nightclub where I knew everyone was going to be. And I waited in the shadows until she came out. I followed her home and then, when we got near her house, I called out to her and asked her why she was acting like she was scared of me and why she'd been laughing at me. She was as drunk as I was and she just started screaming, so I hit her just once, to shut her up. I didn't even hit her hard. There wasn't even a bruise, but she was hysterical and there were witnesses and the guards were called.

Half the town don't speak to me now. Granny said, 'You're a troublemaker, just like your mother.' So that's what I've inherited from you: drinking and troublemaking. Thanks a lot.

The worst part is that Dad's wife, Caroline, was freaked out and doesn't want me around my little sisters any more. It breaks my heart because those girls knew me from when they were born and they never treated me like I was weird – they were used to me and I love them. And now I'm living in a flat on my own away from them. I suppose I should have moved out of home years ago, but there was never any reason to before. Dad was on my case about the drinking, trying to get me to join AA and all that shite. He hasn't fired me yet. I still work in his factory, but it's only a matter of time before I get thrown out of there too.

Granny died yesterday. She once said that she felt sorry for you, and that you must have been emotionally scarred by your childhood, and then when she'd said it, she felt bad for using the word 'scarred' in front of me. But I think she must have liked you at one time.

She adored me, up until the last few years when I disgraced the family name. My grandfather would be 'turning in his grave' apparently. I went to see her in hospital last week and her last words to me were 'Live your life, stop being afraid.' What do you think she meant by that?

Anyway, that's all the news from Westport. I must go now and polish my shoes for tomorrow's funeral.

You won't write back, but I'm sending this anyway because I want you to know about me. Just in case, it's still jmmyrssll@outlook.ie.

Love from Jimmy

Why was he so persistent? I had never replied to him, so why did he insist on inflicting these miserable letters on me? I was sorry to hear about Elizabeth's death, despite her labelling me as a troublemaker. She had tried to be kind after James was born. But I guess her time was up. I had lost contact with Moira years previously. Keeping up a correspondence with her had been futile.

My son has anger issues. I guessed he might have inherited those from my father, because as far as I knew, Peter's family weren't the violent type. I hoped for his sake and those around him that his counselling sessions worked. I didn't know why he thought that I might need psychological help. My past is in the past and that is where it belongs.

31

In 2009, Freddie did not come to Monaco at all. Marjorie telephoned and said he was unwell. In January 2010, he emailed to say there were shadows on his lungs and that he was coming in March to paint me 'before time runs out'. He arrived, looking skeletal. Ashen. Clearly, the 'shadows' were malignant. Marjorie turned up the day after, furious because he hadn't told her he was travelling. She begged him to come home and start treatment, but he refused, insisting that he had to finish his 'life's work' and that he did not want an extension to his life that would be spent in hospital.

I pleaded Marjorie's case too. I looked it up on the Internet. His type of cancer was not always fatal and chemotherapy treatment had developed so much in previous years that he had a middling chance of survival, or at least a few extra years. He painted me in the apartment, with trembling hands, stopping for coughing fits from time to time. Marjorie was dreadfully upset. Freddie told her he didn't want her there, fussing over him. She couldn't bear it and flew back to London. She warned me to look after him and call if he took any sudden turns for the worse. She begged me to persuade him to take the treatment.

But nursing a sick man was not in my plan. All those years, I had been making my own plans, and now I had saved enough money for the operation to restore my face. Over the previous months, I had been making preparations. I had travelled to Paris twice already and consulted with the best surgeon money could buy. Ten years of savings. The surgeon was even going to slightly lift the good side of my face to raise my eyebrows and smooth out some fine lines that had appeared around my eyes and mouth. Botox on one side of my face would only make things worse, she said. 'Best to do the whole thing in one go.' That month, my operation was scheduled. I did not want to tell Freddie, it was none of his business, but I did not want to leave him alone either. He was not strong enough to cook for himself. Marjorie had been helping him to shower and dress. I could not bear the thought of more intimate tasks as he became sicker.

Two weeks later, as I posed on the balcony yet again, I begged him to go home and have the chemotherapy.

'I have had an extraordinarily good life, Cordelia. I have been lucky. I know the odds. With the treatment, I could go on for another few years, but the chances of the tumours returning are high. I do not want to spend my final months incarcerated in hospitals or hospices. I have access to the best of doctors and as much morphine as I need to keep the pain at bay. I will die here. With you.'

I was startled.

'With me? But surely you want Marjorie, and Audrey?'

He sat up straight and I felt nervous.

'Don't you see? Are you that blind, Cordelia? I need to capture *you* before I go. There is no afterlife. There is only now. You have eluded me all this time, but I need you more than ever. I need to get it right.' He stopped, as a coughing fit convulsed him. I did not move to help or comfort him. When it subsided, he continued, breathlessly, 'The painting. Even unveiled, you are hidden from me. I have been trying to find your soul and to put it on these wretched canvases. I need to find you. You, *you* are my muse. Marjorie is my wife, but it is you that I need.'

I thought back to the early days of our friendship, and Matisse and the nun. He thought that I could be like her. I had never seen him so needy, so desperate, and it disturbed me. I decided to ignore it.

'Freddie, I have to go away, on Monday, to see a friend in Paris. I've already booked my time off from the gallery. I'll be gone for a month or two at most.'

'A friend? In Paris?' He was jealous. I could see it in his eyes.

'Not a boyfriend. Sylvie Morat, an art historian. It's work-related.'

'And you cannot postpone? I would refund the cost of your travel.'

'I'm sorry, I can't. You should go home, Freddie. At least let Marjorie take care of you?'

'She fusses,' he said irritably, 'and I have already made my last journey, to you.'

Another coughing fit ensued, and this time spots of blood appeared at the corners of his mouth. He reached for the box of tissues behind him, but could not grab them. I rose to help him. A spill of crimson pooled down his chin and dripped on to his lap. His body relaxed again, and he looked down at the splotches on his pale trousers. I reached behind his chair for the towel on the shelf behind him. He lifted his head again and his eyes followed me. As I hovered over him in the darkest corner of the room, his face lit up. He tried to spring up from his seat.

'Don't move,' he said, 'stay exactly where you are. It's perfect. I've been painting you in the sunshine, but you belong in the shadows. Do not move.'

I passed him the towel, and he impatiently wiped his chin and neck and dabbed futilely at his trousers. I watched Freddie rifling through his box of pencils, and ripping the canvas off the easel with a vigour that had been missing since his return.

'Stop. Please, Freddie. You have sketched and painted me in every conceivable light, you have marked out my scars in vivid relief and colour – it's time to stop. Give it up.'

His face darkened with anger. 'How dare you tell me to stop? How dare you tell me what to do? I own you.'

We barely spoke for the rest of the day. I maintained my pose and he sketched until the light faded, and then I prepared a simple rice dish that he could easily swallow. He ate half of it, but continued to work on the sketch. When he was too exhausted, he allowed me to take him by the arm to his bedroom. I left him for a while and then, when he had undressed, I took his discarded stained clothes and carried them to the washing machine. I brought him a glass of water and left his medicine beside the bed.

I rang Marjorie and left a voicemail and then emailed her to say that I had to be out of Monaco for a month, and that I thought Freddie would need her.

I got a reply later that night. She would take the next flight and arrive early the next morning. 'I am glad,' she wrote, 'that you have decided to give us this time alone. I cannot bear to watch him die, but it is worse to think that he might die without me. I know it is silly of me to be jealous of you, but sometimes it has seemed that he preferred your company to mine.' She thought my planned absence was altruism.

Freddie was not unhappy to see her the next day but strongly objected to me leaving. He turned nasty. I had never seen him this way before. He behaved as if he were a spurned lover. 'You're an ungrateful, selfish brat.'

Marjorie later apologized. 'It must be the pain. I am so sorry.'

'It's OK,' I said. 'I know he's not like this.'

I caught the bus to Nice and then the train to Paris and put thoughts of Freddie out of my mind. My life was about to start over again. A new face. My old face. Restored.

32

Everybody in the clinic was extremely pleasant and efficient. I don't think they had too many patients who were paying without health insurance, in cash. My surgeon, Madame Chernaux, put me at my ease and showed me several before and after photographs of recent operations. The results were excellent. I fasted that night, and slept fitfully until a kind nurse gave me a sedative which took the edge off my jangling nerves.

When I woke after the surgery, my face was swathed in bandages and all I could feel was my face burning. It felt as intense as the pain I had felt after the fire. The nurses came to increase my intravenous pain meds, and a doctor was quickly summoned to assure me that what I was feeling was normal. 'You should be more comfortable now, and as the week goes on and your face begins to heal, we will monitor the meds to make sure you feel easier.' The bandages were changed every two days and I was given extra painkillers an hour before they did that. Afterwards, even with the high level of pain relief, it still hurt intensely. I could not open my right eye. I panicked that it meant the operation had been botched, but Madame Chernaux came every day to convince me that everything was going to plan. I tried to read books during those days with my good eye, romance novels from the hospital bookshelf in French and English, but I could not identify with these heroines and their passion. I found a stack of *New Scientist* magazines and read those cover to cover instead. When I eventually turned my phone on, there were voicemails and texts from Freddie, increasingly angry, demanding to know where I was and when I was going to return. Messages also from a tearful Marjorie, to tell me that Freddie's condition had deteriorated. He was refusing to go to hospital. She begged me to come back, as Freddie was agitated without me. I did not reply.

Eight days after the operation, the bandages were removed and I was presented with a mirror for the first time. Madame Chernaux and her team warned me first that there would still be a few weeks before it began to look normal, but she promised that I would be happy with the result. The skin was raw and swollen on the right-hand side, and bloodied, but it looked smooth. My brow-line on both sides was lifted and my right eyelid was perfectly in line with my left one. The right-hand side of my mouth matched its opposite. Despite the swelling, I could see that the work they had done was miraculous. My tears and silence alarmed them until I was able to speak. 'Thank you,' I whispered, 'thank you so much.' A little cheer went up among the team, and the surgeon produced from somewhere a small bottle of champagne, which she popped and poured into the water glass on my bedside locker. I did not hesitate for a moment to drink it. I had something to celebrate. It was just one drink.

I moved into a cheap hotel near the clinic for the next three weeks. I didn't want to be too far away in case anything went wrong while there was still a high risk of infection. But the swelling subsided and the raw look began to fade, and I started to see the girl I used to be. Even the good side of my face looked younger. I could not stop looking at myself in the mirror, fascinated to see my familiar face.

On the 30th of April, I was ready to go home to Monaco. Only if you looked closely under my chin and on the right-hand side of my forehead would you notice anything; the skin tone matched perfectly, and only the closest scrutiny would reveal the slight difference in texture of my skin from one side to the other. Make-up would hide all of these minor discrepancies. I went to a salon and had my hair dyed blonde. Let the transformation be total. I still would have to stay out of direct sunlight and wear maximum sun protection lotions for the rest of my life, but it was a tiny price to pay and worth the long years of saving half of my maintenance payments from Peter, accepting Marjorie's cast-off clothes and modifying them to fit me, being beholden to Freddie and ignoring his condescending comments on my ugliness.

I entered the apartment building by the street door, walked up the stairs to the apartment and let myself in the door. A young woman I recognized instantly from photographs stood in the hall. I startled her.

'Who the hell are you?' she said. 'How did you get in here?'

'Hello, I'm Cordelia. Sorry for scaring you.'

She blocked the width of the hallway with her arms outstretched. 'No, you're not. Who are you?'

Marjorie came out to see what the commotion was. 'Oh my God, Cordelia! Your face. Your hair!'

Audrey looked at her mother. *'That's* Cordelia? But . . . she looks *normal.'*

'Oh my, you look *beautiful*! You must have . . . This is why you haven't been in contact?'

'It was something I needed to do. In private.'

'I understand, but couldn't you have waited? There is so little time.'

The Bairds were ultimately selfish. Their needs always came first. Audrey glared at me, folding her arms defensively.

I heard a long low groan from upstairs. Marjorie's eyes

flicked upwards. 'Please go to him. He asks about you every day. He has been angry with me. He thinks I deliberately kept you away.' Her voice broke and I did not want to comfort her. 'Please,' she said again, 'just go to him.'

The change in Freddie was as drastic as the change in me. His bed had been moved into the salon, a drip stand beside it, an oxygen tank on the other side. Thin plastic tubes fed oxygen into his nose. Although he was older than me, I had never considered him *old* before. Now, he was a bed-ridden shrivelled ancient man. The cancer that had clearly spread to his liver cast a sickly yellow pallor over his face, and the sparse hair that covered his bony scalp was lank and white. I called his name gently: 'Freddie, I'm back.'

His eyes flickered open, and he turned his head on the pillow to face me. I smiled my even smile with my matching lips. His eyes widened and, with my help, he sat up.

'What have you done?' he said, labouring each word.

'I got fixed up, Freddie. I am so happy, I would never have been able to do this without –'

He gripped my arm so hard, I almost squealed. Tears sprang to his eyes.

'How dare you?' His anger was fiery.

How dare *I*? As sick as he was, as close to death as he was, I felt my own rage rise within me. He did not own me, despite what he thought. Did he think that talking endlessly about my ugliness and damage was easy for me to hear? I had lived twenty years in the shadows. Did he think I wanted to look like that? That's what *he* wanted. If he actually cared about me, he could have paid for this operation twice over and spared me eleven years of shame and humiliation, but I worked and saved for it. This was my face, this was my life.

'Fuck you!' I snarled.

He let go of his grip on my arm, taken aback by my fury.

Behind me, I heard a movement and turned to see Audrey and Marjorie staring at me.

'What?' I said, belligerent. 'It suited you to keep me ugly, didn't it, Marjorie?'

Audrey went to her father's side. 'It's OK, Dad. Relax, it's OK.'

'He doesn't care about either of you. He only cares about himself. You should hear how he talks about you . . .' I was on a roll now and the venom within me began to spew out.

'Leave,' said Marjorie quietly. 'Pack your bags and get out.'

I turned to Freddie. He had turned away to face the canvas that was standing against the wall adjacent to the bed. A pencil sketch of my face was there, swabbed in a sepia-toned acrylic wash. The loose shape and shadow of my image had been picked out, ready for the oils to be layered on top, to define each ridge and furrow of my scars. Beside the easel, I noticed a long bamboo stick had been firmly taped to a thin paintbrush. The tubes of flesh- and blood-toned oil paints were lined up, waiting for use.

'Freddie,' I said, 'you're no Matisse.'

He did not turn to face me, just said in a low growl 'Get out' and pulled the sheet up over his own head as if he were already a corpse.

Audrey followed me, watching my every move as I packed everything I owned into two suitcases and a box. She talked as I moved around the apartment, calling to her mother occasionally, 'Mum? Does she own that laptop? . . . Does she own the blue pottery mugs?'

She spoke to me in a sing-song voice with an American twang.

'At first, I was sure Dad was having an affair. And then I went home to London one time and saw you in the paintings. That's why I didn't recognize you. I knew he wouldn't lower himself to sleep with someone who looked like *that*, but still, I understood why he let you live here, why he was so obsessed with you. Mum didn't mind. She said you were just one of Dad's waifs and strays. Did you know about them? When I was small, Dad had all these pets that he got from the animal shelter, dogs with one eye, cats with three legs or a misshapen head. The more deformed the better. They never lasted long. They were always sick and dying. But he used to draw them with my crayons or coloured pencils. That's all you were to him, you know. Another deformed creature.'

I stopped listening. When my suitcases were full, I went to see Marjorie. She was on the phone to a doctor outside the door of the salon. 'Yes, please, come now.' She hung up and turned to me, ice in her eyes. 'Why? In the name of God, why did you have to be so cruel to him now? After everything he did for you? I had heard the stories, of course, about how you were so quick to abandon your own child, but Freddie believed in you.'

'What?'

'We've known all along who you are, *Delia*. But you hid your cruelty well.'

I should have apologized but I didn't. I never said any further goodbye to Freddie. I went down the ramparts struggling with my suitcases, until I got to a bar overlooking the harbour. I ordered a glass of wine and lit a cigarette. Within half an hour, I had been joined by two men, 'on casino business' they said. I allowed them to pay for the rest of the wine that night and ended up in a room in the Hôtel de Paris with one of them. I was drunk. I don't remember his name. When I woke up the next morning, he was gone and there was a fifty-euro note on the bedside table. Cheap. I was forty-four. Despite my surgery, my age was against me.

Marjorie

She must have been beautiful before the fire. If you caught her in profile, just the left side of her face, she was breathtaking. Freddie met her when she looked like that originally, though he never mentioned it at the time. When he came home from that party in Cornwall twenty-five years ago, all he could talk about was this broken seagull and how he should have brought his camera. After that, he brought his camera everywhere and took photographs of every rotting thing that came across his path. I'm sure the man who developed our photographs in Boots thought we were most peculiar. Freddie has always been eccentric, but I expect that if one has a brilliant mind, one must have some oddity that goes with it.

He was so excited when he saw Cordelia that day in Nice with her scarred face and neck. She tried to hide behind her hair. The scarring was visible, though not unsightly. 'She's just the ticket,' he said, and he invited her to the villa in Vence and then returned home with hundreds of photographs. I couldn't avoid her in my own home. He wanted to go back and find her. He wanted to collect her like an item from a lost and found department and install her in our home. I managed to persuade him that if he were to suggest such a thing, the girl would think he was an old pervert. I am ten years younger than Freddie, but she is more than thirty years his junior.

And then, she came to us for help, and Freddie felt she was a gift dropped into his lap – that phone call from the hospital in Nice was more than he'd hoped for. She genuinely had nowhere to go and the timing was right.

I warned Freddie that she could be anyone. His wealth has made him a target for conmen and gold-diggers and he has always been cynical, but she cast a spell on him. He declared that he had finally found his muse. I was naturally suspicious and protective. I discreetly asked around the people who had been at Jory Lattimer's party. I learned that, despite her accent, she was Irish and her real name was Delia. Nobody in London had ever known her as Cordelia. Still, she was Cordelia to us. She had been married to an embezzler who had set up in business with that lovely boy, Daniel Wilkes. I heard that she had lost her child tragically in a fire, caused by her own drunkenness. Most people in London had heard that she had died a few years later, in Ireland. I did not contradict them.

By the time I discovered all of this and told Freddie, he told me that she'd already told him everything, except about her son. Freddie insisted it was her business and that we had no right to interfere with her private grieving.

A few years later, I met Daniel Wilkes's mother at a funeral and she told me the real story. Cordelia's child had actually survived the fire but suffered terrible mutilation. The rumours of her death had been put about by her husband. I never told Freddie about the disfigured son because I was afraid he would get fixated on the boy and insist on finding him and painting him too. It disturbed me, though, that a mother would never mention her child or appear to acknowledge he existed. I kept my concerns to myself because Cordelia continued to inspire my husband. I think he liked to be frustrated by her. That elusive quality she had. Even though I knew more of the truth than Freddie, I was always aware that there was something more, something darker at her core, that soul that Freddie tried to find in tubes of oil paint.

I don't blame her at all for trying to fix her face, though God knows where she got the money for cosmetic surgery. But her cruelty to Freddie in his final days is something I will never forgive or understand. My husband died in so much pain, and most of it was not physical.

33

Freddie died just a few days later. I did not see Marjorie again, but she sold up the apartment very quickly. I heard that Audrey went back to America to finalize her divorce from the tattoo artist before he could make a claim on her inheritance, and Marjorie went home to London. I don't know what she told people, but despite my new face I realized quickly that certain doors were closed to me. Everyone commented on my transformation, but then they looked away, embarrassed, as if I had disappointed them in some way. 'But this is how I used to be, before the fire!' I would exclaim, and they would look, in wonder, but it made them uncomfortable.

Freddie's allies saw me as a traitor. The people I had been advising on their art collections withdrew their custom and went elsewhere. The gallery director apologized but said she would no longer be able to employ me because of cutbacks. There was a global recession, she said. It was not news to me, but to my knowledge these ups and downs in the market had never affected Monaco. People came and went. Some stayed on the Riviera, bought sports cars, gambled on the wrong stocks and were never seen again, but they were always replaced quickly by a new crop of middle-aged men, their eyes widened by the size of the yachts in the harbour. In Monaco, there was always someone richer than you.

I rented a small flat in Port de Fontvieille, where the servants and nannies that serviced the rich were accommodated, and began to make jewellery from beads imported from

Taiwan. I tried to sell them to my friends in the gift shops but few of them bought from me. I heard through the grapevine that it was rumoured that I had tried to get Freddie to change his will as he was dying, that I had used his money to pay for my cosmetic surgery. I tried to get the friends who knew me well, like Harold and Rania, to speak for me, to tell the truth, but somehow they were never available to take my calls and if I did meet them on a social occasion they diverted the conversation to superficial matters. The invitations dried up. I was told that I was humiliating myself with my drunkenness.

August 2010
Dear Mam,

Remember me? Probably not. But here is one of your irregular reminders that I exist. I feel like I have to remind you because if I don't, who else will?

Uncle Harry told me a funny story the other day. Not so funny. I think Uncle Harry hates you more than Dad, and that's saying a lot because Dad is pissed off that he has to keep paying you money. Actually, I'd say it's his wife Caroline who's pissed off about it and getting on Dad's case about maybe cutting off your payment. He says he's legally obliged to pay you, but she reckons that I could sue you because of what you did to me. So I've been thinking about suing you and maybe you should prepare for getting less money. I think it's only fair to tell you because you should know, and also because I want to hurt you.

You see, I'm all about justice these days. I was up in court for assaulting a woman again the other day, and this time, despite Dad's expensive lawyers and his position as a pillar of the community, I didn't escape a prison sentence, so I'm serving four months now in Mountjoy (what a great name for a prison), though everyone says I'll get out in two. I have had it with bitches stringing me along, using me, dumping me, so I started going with prostitutes. One of them threw up at the sight of my body when I got undressed, so I hit her. Yeah, I know, you'll be shocked, but remember, you did this to me. You put me in a fire so bad that the only people who will sleep with me have to be paid for it. Whores, hookers, slappers. How fucked up is that?

Not as fucked up as the funny story Uncle Harry told me. He said that before I was even born you wanted to abort me. Dad says that I am not to pay any attention to any of Harry's stories, but I have never known Harry to lie to me. I'm just amazed it took him this long to tell me. Anyway, I spend more time with him than anyone else. He understands me, I think. Sometimes, when we're both floothered, he'll say that you were the only woman he ever loved. He's lucky. I hate you all. Whores, hookers, slappers. Harry and I live together now in Granny's old house. She'd be mortified if she saw it now. We're not great at the old DIY and there's a hole in the roof of my bedroom. I've a bucket underneath it to catch the drips. I hope Harry remembers to empty that bucket while I'm inside.

Prison is fine. I look so terrifying that the lads leave me alone and the ready supply of heroin passes the time and numbs the pain, but not even the shot to the arm can quell the rage I have inside me, especially for you.

There's a chaplain here who has taken a great interest in me. He says he used to go out to Inishcrann in the summers when he was stationed in Galway, many years ago. He had heard about the fire that killed your family. He says I should go visit the island. What do you think of that? Do you think I should go and terrorize your old homeland? Maybe I will. Or maybe one day I'll just turn up on your doorstep to teach you a lesson. Maybe I'll come and burn your house down.

No point in pretending any more that I love you. But my email is here, just in case you ever want to defend yourself. jmmyrssll@outlook.ie.

I had been right not to get involved with my son. He was obviously a very damaged individual, full of hatred and anger, but now I was worried about two things: that my maintenance payments from Peter might cease, but worse, that my son would track me down and harm me. I considered contacting Harry, but after what the Corsicans did to him, I don't think he would have wanted to intervene with James on my behalf. I was incredibly anxious about this, but when I received no further letters, I began to relax again.

A year after Freddie died, it was time for me to leave Monaco. I decided that anyone who thought I had betrayed the Bairds by repairing my face was not worth my company. I was better than all of them, and more beautiful. Daddy was right all along.

I still had some money saved, in case further surgery was required, but my face had settled well, my follow-up appointments found no signs of tissue rejection and I was free to spend the money. I still had Peter's payments coming monthly, despite James's threats. I spoke fluent French, I was beautiful, I was forty-five years old but would pass for ten years younger. I could start again, on my own terms.

I moved all the way around the coast to the small town of Argelès-sur-Mer near the Catalonian border and found a flat. I rented a small shop two hundred yards back from the beach and imported leather goods from China and India. My experience in the gift shops of Nice stood to me, but now with the Internet it was so much easier. I could buy items that would pass easily as designer labels, though I was always at pains to point out the differences to customers. This time there would be no fraud. Well, not much. I sold two expensive briefcases to older, distinguished-looking men on my first day. One of them invited me for a drink.

It felt like the old days again. I was in demand; people sought out my company. I went on dates, had boyfriends, drank cocktails and enjoyed all of the things I should have done as a teenager. The men were courteous and generous mostly, and I obliged, by sleeping with them. Why not give them what they want? It meant nothing to me.

By the end of the summer season, though, there was no trade and I relinquished the lease on the shop.

I thought perhaps that I could become a mistress to a rich man. I was divorced and single. All I wanted was somebody to support me, put me up in a nice apartment somewhere. I was not looking to be an entirely kept woman. I was determined to work but I needed somebody of means, and those men did not holiday in Argelès. I moved back to Antibes and took a job as a receptionist in a dental surgery under my Cordelia Russell name, but the job did not last because although the dentist liked to have sex with me in his lunch hour, he did not like the smell of cigarettes and alcohol on my breath or the shake in my hands first thing in the morning.

The following year I went to Juan-les-Pins and hung out in the Belles Rives, but their clientele was older. There were no business customers, no unattached men looking for more than a one-night stand.

I went back to Nice, got a job in an antiques store and rented a flat one street from the promenade. I did not run into any of the old crowd, and even if I had, they would not have recognized me. I stayed there for five years, moving from lover to lover, and job to job, but I never seemed to have enough money for wine.

Age caught up with me and I could no longer defy gravity. Even though I ate less than ever, my flat stomach pooled at my belly and my breasts needed more upholstery than before. I couldn't bear it. I got fired from a few jobs, for being late, disorganized, intoxicated. I had to go to the social welfare office. I did not declare my maintenance payments. How else could I pay for the wine?

By 2017 I was living in a tiny bedsit with no air-conditioning and I didn't bother walking the mile to the sea every day any more. And that made me sicker.

One day, at the end of the tourist season, I was sitting in a café on the promenade, nursing a glass of cheap rosé, when I heard my name being called.

'Delia! Delia Russell?'

I turned and recognized her immediately. Isabelle. Older, grey hair cut short, pearl earrings, perfectly groomed in a silk dress and Chanel jacket, far from the tie-dyed kaftans of her youth. I hadn't seen her since London, since . . .

'My God, we thought you were dead! Everyone said you'd died, back in Ireland!'

I let my eyes glaze over to a look of incomprehension and affected a French accent. *'Excusez-moi?* My English is no good. Perhaps you mistake me for somebody else?'

She looked at me, aghast. 'Delia, it's me, Isabelle, for God's sake . . . ?'

I continued to stare at her, refusing to acknowledge my recollection of her. She must have known about the fire. Had Peter told everyone that I'd died? Maybe it was better for him to say that in London than to admit he had divorced me when I was at my lowest.

'*Non*,' I said now.

'Delia, come on! You don't have to pretend. I'm not friends with Hannah now, we haven't spoken in years. How is James?'

I did not respond. I watched the doubt creep into her eyes.

'Perhaps . . . I have the wrong person,' she faltered now. '*Vous regarde comme un ami qui est morte*,' she said in badly accented French.

'*Je suis désolée. Je ne suis pas morte.*' I smiled at her and turned back to my lunch.

'The resemblance is so striking. Photograph?' she said, taking out her phone.

'*Non*.' I rose quickly, threw some money on the table, nodded to Jean-René, the proprietor, and left.

'I'm sorry!' she called after me. 'You look so like her, a blonde version. I could have sworn you were her!'

I was rattled. I went to a supermarket and bought two bottles of vodka to stop myself remembering.

In the morning, I was woken by my buzzer. I rarely had visitors, unless they were certain gentlemen callers with whom I had made an arrangement, and they usually came in their lunch hour or directly after work. I looked at my phone. It was 11.30. My mouth was dry and my make-up was caked around my eyes. I still wore the dress I'd put on yesterday morning. My hair was a mess. I stumbled to the kitchen tap and filled a tumbler with water. I got back into bed and pulled the duvet over my head. Still the buzzer rang out, and I knew my neighbours would be irritated. I ignored it and, mercifully, sleep took me again. Half an hour later, the buzzer sounded once more, waking me for a second time. It was incessant. The caller must have been leaning on the button. I heard doors open on the corridor outside and people shouting. I could not imagine who wanted to see me so urgently.

The next noise was a hammering at my door. Somebody downstairs must have let them in. I heard a voice, a thick West of Ireland accented voice calling, 'Delia? Delia! Open the door. I know you're in there!'

Delia! Nobody here knew me as Delia. Harry? Could it be Harry? I barely had time to think how he could have found me again, but I remembered that he once loved me, and even though I never understood it, I knew by now that love was something I needed.

'Just a minute,' I said, as I ran to splash water on my face, scrape a brush through my hair and tear off yesterday's dress and throw on a robe. In my hungover state, I must have thought that I could seduce him. I threw open the door and was greeted by . . . a monster.

Tall, and as broad as my father, most of his head was smothered by a hood but what I could see of his lower face was shocking and revolting. I leaped backwards, and his head shot up, dislodging the hood and revealing the full horror of his injuries. I tried to close the door on him, but he stopped it with his foot.

'Delia, you don't know me, but we're family. I followed you yesterday.' He entered and shut the door quietly behind him. James, my son who had sent me those desperate and hate-filled letters. My son who wanted to hurt me so badly. He lurched forward and I opened my mouth to scream, but he put his hand over my mouth. 'Please don't scream.'

I bit down on his hand and he let go. He stumbled and grabbed at my throat. He was going to choke me. I leaped out of his way and grabbed the vodka bottle, smashed it on the table and, without thinking, plunged it into his neck.

'Why?' I'm pretty sure that's what he tried to say. He gurgled as he collapsed on the floor, crumpled like an old newspaper. His arms flailed uselessly, as the blood spilled from his neck. He was trying to speak, but his tongue lolled in his mouth, and all the while I stood over him, frozen with fright and fear, watching him die.

When it was over I went to lie on my bed and shut my eyes tightly, determined that this was one of those nightmares I could shake off. But I couldn't relax, couldn't stop the image of my hand on the broken bottle, the glass slicing into his warped neck. I got up again, remembering that there was another bottle of vodka. I drank until I could actually look at the corpse on my floor. I put a towel over his hideous head and heaved him towards the corner of the room, trailing darkening blood as I went. His clothes were cheap and smelled of sweat; his shoes were trainers. I stayed in the room with him and drank until I passed out.

PART III

34

The booze and cocaine hangover was bad enough, but I felt ill with horror and fear. I couldn't see a way out. And I was too crippled with anxiety to run. Besides, where would I run? I had no options. There was only me and my dead son and I would go to prison and I would not survive prison. Of that, I was sure.

I opened a window and wrapped a tea towel around my nose and mouth. I looked at the covered body in the corner of my room. How could a dead thing attract such activity, flies feasting on the corpse? Why could I not have stayed sober enough to raid the cloakroom at that party last night? There must have been so many bags and jackets containing wallets. It would have been easy. I looked at the buzzing heap again. I approached gingerly, lifted one heavy arm aside and slid my hand into the chest pocket of the cheap canvas jacket. A wallet, a phone, a passport and a letter addressed to 'Mam'. In the other pocket, a hotel room key-card with its magnetized strip on one side. No marking, so I could not tell which hotel it was.

I opened the wallet and saw banknotes. There must have been six or seven fifties, enough to get me on a flight out of Nice. I hurriedly threw his things together in a bag – to delay identification for as long as possible – along with my basic toiletries, my passport and a few items of my best clothing. Within twenty minutes, I had locked the door of the flat behind me and walked down to the Place Masséna to catch the bus to the airport. As I sat on the bus, I did not look at the sea. Instead, I nervously flipped the envelope marked 'Mam' in my lap. I opened the Irish passport and looked at the grotesque face. It was like a long, melted candle that spilled on to his shoulder, the eye sockets dragging downwards, tiny flaps where there should have been ears. And then I saw the name on the passport.

Conor O'Flaherty.

I turned the passport over again and looked for a different name, looked for James Russell, but there was only one name, Conor O'Flaherty. I was totally confused. Then I looked at the place of birth: *Ireland.* James had been born in London. Why would he have changed his name and birthplace? To torment me? The passport was newly issued. It was only when I saw the date of birth that the truth began to dawn.

12 Feb 1973.

James was born in 1984. I couldn't help a little scream of shock.

Conor O'Flaherty, with that date of birth, was my brother, not my son. But Conor was long dead. Hadn't he died in the fire that killed the rest of my family? Who had I stabbed?

The bus lurched into the airport and I noticed the other passengers looking at me. Tears were streaming down my face.

'*D'accord?*' said a pleasant young man, his hand on my shoulder.

I shrugged him off. I could not speak. I walked into the airport and made my way towards the bar, but swerved at the last minute. I had to keep my head together. I looked at the row of ticket desks at the front wall of the terminal. I could fly directly to almost any city in Europe, but I knew that only the budget airlines were within my reach. I tried to concentrate on the destination I needed, but all I could think of was the dead man in my flat. It must have been James surely, but then I recalled that in one of the letters James had said that he had no fingers on one hand. Which hand? When the man reached out to choke me, I saw his two hands and all fingers were intact. Was one of the hands prosthetic? Peter had made prosthetic fingers for James, hadn't he? I couldn't remember. The hand I bit certainly felt real. Why did he have Conor's passport? Conor was dead. I felt like my head might explode.

I went into the toilets and locked myself into a cubicle. I took the letter out of my bag. 'Mam'. I had to rip it open with my teeth because my hands were shaking so much.

October 2017
Dear Mam,

I'm not giving you any warning because I like to imagine you getting the surprise of your life. I'm sending this letter with your brother, Conor. I only found out he existed a month ago. He is a miracle worker. Listen to his story, but I'll tell you mine too.

I am an addict. First alcohol, and then heroin. I've spent most of the last ten years out of my head. I started on heroin in prison about seven years ago. And then when I got out, I started dealing. Because of my reputation for violence, I was quite successful for a while. But because of all my scarring, I was easily identifiable and a sitting duck for the guards. Dad paid for me to go to various rehab places, but of course the other 'patients' would freak out when they saw my face, so group sessions were just humiliating, and gave me another reason to walk out the door and back to a needle full of smack.

Inevitably, last year, I ended up back in prison, where I served eight months – a drugs charge this time. That's where I met this chaplain who had told me about Inishcrann the first time I was there. I'd been curious about your island for a while. Everyone has always said that half the people of Inishcrann are inbred and the other half are just peculiar, and you were proof of that obviously, because if you're not one, you're the other. And maybe I inherited some of that peculiarity from you?

When I got out of Mountjoy three months ago, I decided to pay a visit. Mostly to go cold turkey and try and change my ways. I didn't like myself, but I liked the sound of a half-abandoned wild place where the people are crazy. Maybe that's where I belong.

I told nobody except Uncle Harry where I was going. He's the only person in town who'll give me the time of day now, and even his patience has worn thin. I packed a bag with a cheap tent and a few tins of food. I planned on staying, firstly to get over the worst of withdrawal, and then maybe to make a life for myself away from bad influences.

It turns out that there is no regular ferry service any more. I had to pay some fellas to take me over on a fishing trawler. They were naturally suspicious and didn't like the look of me (who does?). They said it would be a detour for them, but I paid them well enough. I injected for the last time on the boat on the way over and then I threw the syringe, the smack and the works into the sea. The lads dropped me off and carried on out into the Atlantic.

The island was almost deserted. When I got off at the harbour, there was nobody in sight, and only a few houses are standing. I could see that just one or two were occupied. I realized as soon as I landed that I'd freeze to death if I tried camping, but some of the houses were open, and one on the very edge of the village still had an old bed and a mattress in it. An indoor toilet too that flushed, and running water. I don't think it had been empty for that long, maybe a year. I didn't need much else. So, for four days, I stayed inside that cottage, shivering and sweating with the horror and pain of it. It felt like I turned my body and soul inside out, and yes, I remember the pain of some of those operations I had but it was nothing like the pain of releasing that poison from my system. It didn't want to go. It clung on to every cell of my body like a parasitic worm. But I refused to give in and eventually the sickness left me and I was left in a pool of my own filth.

On the fifth day, I left the cottage and walked the length of the island. God, it's a stunning place. You were lucky to have a childhood there, even though it didn't end well. Barren on one side and wild on the other and I've never felt cold like it, but the beauty of it would take the eye out of your head. I took off my clothes and got into the sea and I thought that the cold would take me then, or that I could just go under the surf and not come back. I thought about drowning myself, but the waves kept tossing me back on to the shore. I gave up, got dressed and sat on a freezing rock and cried. And then I headed back towards the pier. I saw just one or two people, who stared at me like I was an alien, but sure, I'm used to that.

When I got back to the harbour, an old woman stopped me and asked what was my business on the island and why my head was scorched. I told her that my mother, Delia Walsh, was from Inishcrann, and that her people had died in a fire in 1975. She stared at me then as if she was seeing a ghost. She asked me where you were, and I told her you'd been in France for nearly thirty years and that I had no contact with you. Then she told me to follow her and led me to this broken-down old place that used to be a bar, I think. On the way, she said there were only twelve people left on the island, and that one of them was like me. I didn't know what she meant, because there was no one like me, or so I thought. But then I met Conor O'Flaherty. When he walked through from a back room, it was a shock. I'd never met anyone with injuries worse than mine. It was like meeting a brother, instantly. Neither of us knew then that he was my uncle, but we soon pieced it together. He told me the most interesting story about his background.

He told me his family were burned in a fire in 1975. His mother, father and two brothers all perished. He escaped with, as you can see now, severe facial damage. He thinks his mother or father pushed him out of the tiny window to spare him from the flames but the rest of them wouldn't fit through the window, or else the two older boys wouldn't leave their parents. I would love to know why you weren't on the island that night.

A neighbour hid him from the authorities with the collusion of all the islanders. He would have been thrown into an orphanage in Galway with no chance of adoption because of his injuries otherwise. And the school was threatened with closure if the numbers dwindled. So he went to primary school there until he was eleven. He was the last student there, when it shut for good.

Of course, that meant that he never got proper treatment for his burns. They used old island potions and lotions. His face was just allowed to heal in the open wind. But the neighbour, Tom, raised Conor as his own son. The schoolmaster on the island was in on it too. Imagine that? They say it takes a village to raise a child, but in Conor's case it was a whole island.

Conor was supposed to go to the mainland for his secondary education, but Tom kept him on the island and home-schooled him. It all came out in the end when a census taker arrived. Tom was in serious trouble and it backfired badly on the islanders. The county council got involved and there was a new census done and the council used it to say that the island was lawless and needed to be controlled. They set up a 'task force' to assess the viability of the island.

It was only ten years ago that he discovered he had a sister who had survived the fire. He had heard that you'd married a Westport lad in London, but even though he eventually found your adoptive mother Moira, like I did, and looked for you on the Internet when he was on the mainland (no broadband on the island), he couldn't find any trace of you, though he knew that you and Dad had split up. Dad refused to meet him, apparently.

Conor didn't know anything about me at all. I let him tell the story, and then I told him what I knew. That his sister must be my mother. We laughed and we cried. Conor is forty-four and the youngest person on the island by two decades.

Conor had the exact same fear as I did about leaving somewhere familiar. The similarities between his experiences and mine are not surprising, because we are both freaks. But Conor dealt with everything a lot better than me. He has no bitterness whatsoever towards the man who denied him treatment and the people who kept him hidden. 'They love me,' he said, 'isn't that something?' He did venture off the island when he was older. He spent some time living in Galway city, scrounging a living as a painter, and he made friends there and had a community around him. He even had girlfriends, because he wasn't a bitter old shite like me. But the lure of the wild sea brought him back to the island, he said.

Anyway, I might finally believe in humanity because your brother is pure decent. We talked long into the night and all the next day, and I swear, it's as if I have known him all my life. I was able to tell him about all of the trouble I have been in and the drugs and violence and prison. He never judged me for any of it. I don't know how to describe it, but I felt like he was a priest hearing my first confession and that all my sins were forgiven. He is teaching me compassion. He made me see that perhaps you are as scared as I am of the world and its judgement.

When I told him that I'd been writing to you, he was very excited. He thinks that you never responded because of the guilt you feel about me. He is absolutely determined to meet you, and at first we thought we'd make this trip together, but I just need a little more time. I am now as clean as a whistle and haven't even smoked a cigarette since the night I met my uncle, but he is braver than me, so he's going to find you on his own.

I'm sorry for how angry I have been with you in the past. I forgive you for everything and I hope you'll forgive me. Since our first meeting, Conor and I were able to track down where your bank is and Conor hopes to be able to find you through that. I'm not sure how he's going to do it, but he has the courage of a lion and I hope you reunite and that Conor will be able to persuade you to come home. This could be a fresh start for all of us.

Love from your son,
Jimmy
jmmyrssll@outlook.ie or oo 353 82 2413481 if you feel like talking.

I threw up into the toilet bowl until there was nothing left in my stomach. I had killed my own brother. Was that worse or better than killing the son I thought had come to attack me? When he put his hand over my mouth, what was I supposed to think? When he reached towards me, was he trying to *embrace* me?

It was a terrible mistake. Anyone would have done the same when faced with such a monster. He was so frightening.

I should go home. James had forgiven me. I would make him understand.

I threw Conor's passport, phone and the room key and wallet into the sanitary bin and pocketed the cash.

I went to the Ryanair ticket desk and paid one hundred and fifteen euros for a one-way ticket to Dublin. The next flight didn't leave for another two hours. I ordered a sandwich and nibbled at the corners of it, but I needed something else. Wine. I hadn't eaten since the American's steak dinner, but was that only yesterday? Time was expanding and contracting like the bellows of a concertina in play.

I had killed Conor only twenty-four hours ago. How could I explain what I had done since then? When would he be discovered?

I drank steadily until I was ready to make the phone call. I took the phone outside and dialled my son's number.

'Hello?'

'Hi, it's . . .'

'Mam . . . Delia!'

'Yes.'

I started to cry.

'Hey, I know this is weird, but . . .' There was emotion in his voice too. 'I guess Conor found you?'

'Yes.'

'It must have been a shock.' A pause. 'I can't believe I'm actually talking to you, after all these years!'

'I'm coming home.'

'Are you? To Ireland? That's . . . that's great. When?'

'Now. I'm in the airport.'

'Wow, Mam, I mean, is it OK if I call you Mam? I don't know what to say. Did Conor tell you our plans? You can stay too. We'll be a family again . . . if you want . . . Is he there with you?'

'Yes . . . no . . . I . . . he's decided to stay on, for a holiday.' A pause.

'Really? I've been trying to call him, but it goes straight to message. Mam, I'm so glad you're coming. I've been clean for twelve weeks now. I feel strong, and healthy. I'm sorry, for everything.'

'You have nothing to be sorry for.'

'Are you going straight to Westport?'

'Inishcrann. I'm coming home. I'm the one who's sorry.' I broke down in sobs again.

'Mam, it's OK . . . there's nothing . . . But I'm not sure about the island. I'll meet you at Cregannagh village, all right? Tomorrow at six? Will you hire –'

I couldn't speak any more, so I cut him off.

35

Sitting in the boarding area, I was conscious that people were looking at me but I could not keep my emotions in check. When I got to the gate, an old woman came over to me with a tissue and said sympathetically, 'Are you going home for a funeral?' She took my hand and held it. She offered to get me a cup of tea.

'Could I have red wine?' I asked.

'Of course,' she said.

The Irish, famed for their hospitality, generosity and gullibility.

I drank more on the plane. When we landed in Dublin, I got a bus to the city centre and stayed in a bed and breakfast on Gardiner Street. There was an off-licence nearby. I ignored the first text messages from my son:

See you tomorrow, I can't wait. It's going to be emotional. I hope you don't get too much of a shock when you see me. I look weird. I know that you do too but it will be fine.

I can't reach Conor on his phone. Do you know where he was staying?

Are you OK?

I've looked it up. I don't know if you're hiring a car? If not, you can take an 8am bus from Busaras to Swinford, then the 2pm bus from there to Castlebar, and then 5pm bus to Belmullet. The Cregannagh stop is the last one before Belmullet. I'll be there at six. Please come.

To the last one, I replied, 'Yes.' I was too drunk to talk or to text more than the word.

I passed out and woke parched at 7 a.m. The nightmare was still present. The body had now been there for nearly forty-eight hours. I had taken a human life. If I was caught, surely I could claim it was manslaughter. How would I explain that to a jury? The neighbours in my building would soon smell the corpse. I checked my phone. It was 25 degrees today in Nice. His body would decay quickly in that heat. Nobody would know who he was. I couldn't remember if I'd left the window open.

Because social welfare was paying my rent, and I had to register using my passport, the name on the lease was Delia Russell. But everyone knew me as Cordelia. Would they be able to trace me? I had no friends in Nice, just acquaintances, *clients*. Nobody knew anything about me. That was the advantage of having changed identity so many times, and appearance.

I showered and dressed and made sure I had my naggin of vodka to keep me company on the trip. I fantasized about living a solitary life on Inishcrann with my son. I had to look to the future. I had to put my brother out of my head.

I bought my ticket at the bus station and prepared for the long journey. I bought headache tablets and fruit, and a magazine to distract myself, and boarded the bus.

When I was on the second bus, I got more texts from James.

> Did you hear from Conor?? I'm worried about him. He was really nervous about travelling.

> Did you ever use the name Cordelia?

How did he know that? The same number came up when my phone rang, but I didn't answer it. Then another text.

Can you ring me? There's something happening.

And another one, this time with a blurred photograph of me taken from a CCTV image in Nice Airport.

This isn't you, right? You have scars, don't you? French police are looking for you. But I think they have you confused with somebody else. You NEED to ring me.

I changed on to the last bus to Cregannagh village. They had discovered the body already. My name was out there. How had everything happened so fast?

That photo is all over Facebook and Twitter. Whoever she is, she took a flight to Dublin. They think it's you. I'm on my way to Cregannagh. We have to go to the police and clear this up.

I'm calling Tom Farrelly. He lives in Cregannagh now. He's the one who adopted Conor. He'll meet us there.

I think Conor is dead. FUCK!!! What is going on? Why won't you answer the phone? You better have answers for me.

Tom Farrelly. Tom the Crow. My father's best friend, who had told me to get off the island when I turned up there pregnant with James all those years ago. I got up from my seat, moved unsteadily up the gangway and asked the driver to let me out of the bus.

'But you're in the middle of nowhere here, only five minutes to Cregannagh!'

'Please.'

'Are you all right, missus?'

I didn't realize I was crying again. Fear. Horror. Shame. Guilt.

'Please, just let me out!'

He slowed the bus to a stop.

'If you don't mind me saying so, missus, you don't look well.'

I climbed down the stairwell and was relieved when I heard him release the air-brakes and move off again.

I looked around at the road and I was nine years old again. The same stone wall where I'd lain down for a rest while I was waiting for Daddy to catch up with me. Maybe if I waited there, maybe if I lay down for a little bit and closed my eyes, Daddy would come.

A screech of brakes alerted me to reality, and I saw my son for the first time in twenty-seven years. It couldn't have been anyone else.

'Mam. Get into the car.'

His voice was harsh, the forgiveness he had expressed in the letter was gone.

'James, I . . .'

'It's Jimmy,' he said, looking me up and down. 'When did you have the surgery?'

'Seven years ago.'

'Right.'

I went to open the front passenger door, but he said, 'No, get in the back and lie down. The guards are looking for you.' I did as I was told. I had thought he was going to take me directly to the police station, but no, he was going to protect me.

'Jimmy, I didn't know who Conor was! Honestly, I thought he was going to attack me . . .' My words were slurred.

'Shut up. Don't say anything until we get to Tom's.'

We drove for about ten minutes in silence while I lay down on the back seat. The car weaved its way around narrow country roads and finally took a sharp left down what sounded like a gravel path. We must have driven through the village of Cregannagh. When the car stopped, he told me to get out.

I could see we were parked in front of an isolated modern bungalow, and behind it I could see the sea. I staggered a little, and James caught me by the arm and steered me towards the house.

'I need to see the sea,' I said.

'Later.'

The door of the house opened and Tom the Crow stood in its frame. Daddy's best friend. White-haired and slightly stooped, but still wiry with strength.

'Tom!'

He stood back and let me enter into a large kitchen with a pine table and chairs in the centre. It was sparsely decorated, as if he had just moved in. But my eyes were attracted to photographs on the wall. One of them was an old photo of Daddy with his arm around Tom. Two beautiful, strong young men. I stood in front of it and traced the outline of Daddy's face with my finger, the way I used to do when he was alive. The photograph was black and white and I had never seen it before. I had not seen that face in over forty years.

'Sit down,' said Tom.

Tom the Crow

I loved the bones of Martin O'Flaherty. I loved the madness in him and the jut of his collarbone where I rested my head over long nights at sea. I loved his voice and his walk and his eyes. He was tall and broad and strong, with a face carved by the wind as if he had been conceived by the rocks themselves.

We had to hide that part of ourselves, because, well . . . when I was a child, a ram caught mounting another one was shot dead, and his owner, Peadar Carroll, was mocked and called Peadar Pansy for the rest of his life. They say it drove him insane, but Inishcrann drove everyone insane in different ways. I knew Martin to be ferocious in his temper and I knew his humours to be wild, but I loved him still. I didn't know for sure that he loved me until after he was dead.

I never came first with Martin. The island did. He was possessed by Inishcrann, obsessed with it. Our passion for each other was kept hidden. But Martin hated himself for it, and not even because what we were doing was against God, but because what we were doing would never produce a child. Martin felt responsible for the island. He had a notion he was descended from the high kings that once ruled in forgotten centuries. He was always hounding the women on the island to know if they were pregnant, and if not, why not. By 1964, there was a handful of male babies and toddlers on the island and every woman was already married off.

I felt sorry for Loretta. It was my fault, though she fell for him as hard as me in the beginning. Martin and I both knew we'd have to try to marry and produce children eventually. Martin was so handsome, he could have his pick of the tourists, but he was so stubborn, he wanted an Irish girl, if he had to have one. He was approaching thirty-five, and he still hadn't been able to form a friendship, never mind an attachment, to any woman. And then along comes this pretty little American girl doing some project to do with plants, a botany student, she said. She photographed them. She took that photo of Martin and me, the one I still treasure. I thought she was a child, but the way she looked at Martin told a different story. She was nineteen years old, she said. She was staying in Mary Scurvy's guest house, but her gang used to come to my mother's bar every night after their dinner, looking for chat and company. It was rare to see a woman in a bar in those days. But she got away with it because she was a foreigner. I talked to her and heard a little bit about her life in America and her parents. She asked me coyly about Martin, if he was single and where he lived. Women were never interested in me, not that that bothered me in the slightest. I knew Martin wouldn't be interested in a Yank, but one night she told me that she was half Cheyenne, and I thought maybe he might like her after all.

Three times a year, Guts O'Neill from Lisdoonvarna would tour the islands with a projector and a few reels of film. Whoever had the whitest sheet would bring it to the schoolhouse, where it would be pinned to the wall and became our screen. We loved those old cowboy films the best. Martin always took the side of the Indians though, declaring that the cowboys were stealing their land. He said the Indians were a native people who lived by their own traditions and should never have been persecuted and run off their own land. He said that Mayo County Council would try to do the same to us.

When I told Martin about Loretta's roots, he began to take an interest. Privately, he said to me that maybe Indian and Celtic blood would be a good mix, bringing together two ancient civilizations. It was selfish of me, though, not to point out that she was too young to make a decision like that, to throw up her life.

I always knew I was going to have to share Martin with a woman at some stage, and although we both knew that she was being used to populate the island, she was willing. He had his own house then in the village, his family were dead and long gone, and though he was thought peculiar even in those days, he still had the respect of the islanders. I liked Loretta too. We had something in common, after all – we both loved Martin.

Loretta's friends and tutors told her she was crazy to stay on the island at the end of that summer. Her mother objected to the marriage in the strongest of terms and insisted that Loretta go home to Minnesota immediately. But Loretta was as stubborn as her husband-to-be and she married him regardless. She had settled well into the community in the four months she'd been there. In fact, it was Loretta who finally made Nora and Mary come to the bar for the first time. I thought Mam would throw a fit to see island women in the bar, but she looked at it practically. There was an extra few bob in it and, regardless of what Father Devlin said, she could find no mention of women in bars in her Bible. Nora Duggan was Loretta's maid of honour. Loretta's mam wouldn't come. Martin was disappointed not to meet his Native American mother-in-law. Loretta asked me to give her away at their wedding. Afterwards, I watched my lover walk down the lane arm in arm with his new wife. It should have provoked some strong emotion in me, but I had always known it must happen. I was dreading my turn, if the truth be told.

Starting a family was always the objective and Martin wasted no time. I have never seen such joy in a man as I did the night that Delia was born. 'A girl!' he said. 'My daughter will be queen! Don't you see? She can marry one of the island lads and keep us all going. And my next daughter can do the same, and the one after that!'

Martin did not hide his disappointment that his three subsequent children were all boys. He ranted and raved at Loretta – 'What good are boys to us? We need girls!' – as if she had any way of directing the seed he planted in her to grow one way or the other. Martin's affection for Loretta dwindled to nothing over the years. After Conor

362

was born, he told me he couldn't sleep with Loretta again. He couldn't risk having another boy when he could hardly afford the children he had. In the summers, Loretta could lead tour groups or work in my mam's bar, but in the winters there was nothing to be done and no money to be made. We didn't earn much from our small trawler, so I took less of the takings so that Martin could feed his family.

From an early age, Delia stirred trouble in that family. I saw it with my own eyes. Martin doted on her and she knew it. When she was only four years old, she tripped on the harbour wall but she told Martin that Loretta had pushed her. I saw the incident and Loretta was ten yards behind her. It was the next day, when I saw Loretta's bruised eye, that I discovered that Martin had punished Loretta for hurting Delia. He admitted as much to me, saying 'that bitch deserved it', and his anger was so volatile then that I was afraid to tell him the truth. Delia sat in her father's lap while she told the story. 'Mammy was bold and Daddy smacked her and then she was crying,' she said, only a toddler, but with a sly smile on her beautiful face.

Years later, she would take things belonging to her brothers and if they protested she would hurl herself on to the ground and start screaming blue murder. Some of this I witnessed myself and some of Delia's behaviour was described to me by Loretta. She never let an opportunity go by to get her mother or brothers into trouble with Martin.

Martin got more and more obsessed with his daughter and ranted about how she, and she alone, represented the future of the island. I tried to get him to be realistic. 'Sure, she might not come back from the mainland after secondary school. She won't necessarily stay on the island – most of them leave.'

'She's my girl, and she knows where her home is. No matter how far she roams, she'll always come back.'

He began to investigate how he could home-school her. He used to make up wild stories for her about the island's ancient people. At least, I think he made them up. He was determined that she would stay on the island. It's ironic that he was the one to send her away in the end, and that I was the one who wouldn't allow her back.

When Delia caused trouble in the school and Martin moved his family out to the west point of the island, he and I grew closer still. It was easier to be together, when people couldn't see you coming or going. On the nights we weren't fishing, we could moor the trawler in a sheltered harbour and hold each other. He was unhappy. He was impatient with Loretta and the children, and they all lived in fear of him, except for Delia. She had no fear of anyone. He said the only time he got any rest was in my arms.

The night when Loretta kissed me, I knew it was out of desperation. She had no real love for me. I was surprised by it, by the softness of her lips. But I pulled away. Loretta was embarrassed afterwards and I told her to forget it, that we should pretend it hadn't happened.

But Delia had seen the kiss and used it to destroy us all.

I saw the smoke rising as I wandered out towards the western side of the island late that night. I was curious, because in the bar Anthony told me that Martin had put Delia on the ferry to Cregannagh on her own earlier that day, and I had an inkling that something was wrong. I ran when I saw the smoke, but when I got there the cottage was a smouldering mess and it was clear a metal rod had been placed across the door to prevent escape. I heard hysterical screaming and found the little fella, Conor, a blackened mess under the window. It was broken, as if he had been pushed out of it. I took my coat off and wrapped it around him as tightly as I could. My shock turned to horror when at the back of the cottage, I found Martin's body, his head barely attached by some sinew and the shotgun by his side. I still have the note I found pinned to Martin's chest. He must have known I would be the person to find him, and them.

Dear Tom

I never expected her to stay faithful to me, and you know, because I was the fool that told you, she's been talking about taking Delia and the boys to America. I never thought you would betray me too. That you would abandon me and go with her and take my girl with you. You, who I have loved my whole life, would leave me with nothing. Delia heard you talking and saw you making love to my wife. She told me everything.

You knew I had to get married. You pushed Loretta on me and I am not too proud to admit that I was hurt by how easily you accepted her, but I thought that was for my sake and the sake of Inishcrann. But it turns out you wanted her for yourself.

You can blame yourself for what has happened here. Loretta and the boys can go to America in their coffins if they want.

I'm going to hell and I'll wait for you there.

If you ever cared for me at all, please make sure I'm buried here on the island. I have nothing to leave Delia but the island. When she comes back, you must keep her, and mind her.

God forgive me.

M

With a stone, I pushed the iron rod away from the door. It collapsed and all I could see behind it was the charred thatch covering a molten lump, and I could just make out the bodies of Loretta and Aidan and Brian.

I hid the note and took the screaming boy to my mother. He clasped his small hands tightly around my neck as I ran the width of the island, and I clung to him too because he was the only thing I had left of Martin O'Flaherty.

It was Mam's idea to throw Martin's body on to the others and start the fire again. She called a meeting in the dead of night, and though we were all in a state of shock it was decided by everyone that we'd make it look like an accident. The council would use it

365

anyway to poke their noses in, but if there was a hint of murder, the investigations would never end and we could all find ourselves booted back to the mainland. The baby was given whiskey to knock him out and his charred head was wrapped in wool grease and bandages.

I told Mam I wanted to keep the baby and all agreed that we couldn't let him be taken off the island, but Nora and the others said it was a woman's job to raise a child and she'd do it, until Mam spoke up for me. 'Nora Duggan,' she said, 'you have your man and your boys, but there is no wife for my Tom and he needs someone.' I'll never know for sure if she knew. Nora was a wonderful help to me all through the years, but Conor was mine.

Owen came back in the morning with the story that Delia was on the mainland, crying for Martin. We told Owen the truth and then sent him back to the mainland with the lie we had all agreed upon.

Thank God for the storm that blew up then, because it gave us three days to fix everything so that by the time the guards and the doctor arrived, the charred remains of Martin, Loretta, Aidan and Brian were so fused and fragmented that nobody could tell that Conor was missing.

There was always something wrong and twisted about that girl. She killed every single member of her family, including my lover and the man I thought of as my son.

36

James sat opposite me, his head in his hands. His scarring was not as bad as he had led me to believe and nowhere near as bad as my brother's. I noticed the contraption strapped to his arm that gave him the appearance of fingers on his left hand, but I could see the red line of seams around his mouth, across his neck, on one wrist. His bushy hair was brushed forward, I assume covering the absence of ears. Not much flesh was exposed, but what I could see was patchwork, like a scarecrow.

Tom asked me, 'What did you do to Conor?'

I reached into my bag to take out the dribble of vodka that was left in the bottle, but he snatched it from my hands. I wondered why he hadn't called the guards. And then I realized. There has always been justice, and then island justice.

Tom took another photo off the wall and put it in front of me. In this photo, Tom was older and he had his arm around Conor, hideous-looking Conor, his head warped, but his eyes warm and dancing with a smile that the hole in his face could not manage. I couldn't look at the photo without feeling repulsed.

'That's your brother,' he roared at me.

'My uncle,' said James. 'What happened? What did you do to him?'

I told them that I'd stabbed him in the neck because I'd been terrified. I said I thought he wanted to kill me. I started talking and couldn't stop. It poured out of me.

I told them about my entire life: my childhood, my love

for my daddy, my exile from the island, my days in the orphanage, my adoption in Westport, my romance with Harry, my pregnancy with Peter, my shotgun wedding in London, the drinking, the fire, my sobriety, France, my violent boyfriend, Freddie my saviour, my operation that left me isolated and friendless all over again. My attempts to make everything work and how nothing had.

As I recounted the story, they stared at me. Before I got to the end, Tom put his head down and began to sob. It was strange to see a big man like him, shuddering and wailing.

'Can you even hear yourself?' he hissed. 'You are the devil, there's no other word for it. I knew it when you were a girl. You never cared about your mother, or any of your brothers. You lied to your father about me. You killed them all.'

'But I didn't know –'

'Oh, you knew all right. Every child knows right from wrong, but you were tied to wrong, wedded to it. You only ever cared about yourself.'

'Daddy loved –'

'You stupid fucking bitch!' Tom was roaring again now. 'Your father loved the island, and he loved me. You were the only girl on the island. You were the brood mare. That's why he made a pet of you. Do you think he'd have cared if you'd been a boy? He didn't love you, he loved your potential to be a mother.'

I didn't want to hear what he was saying.

'Conor was the only connection I had to your father. I loved him as much as if he were my own son.'

James lifted his head and spoke to Tom. 'She wouldn't understand that. She doesn't love her own son. She tried to abort me. And then she walked away from me and –'

He turned back to face me. 'Wait, why would you think that Conor would hurt you?' His eyes darkened as the truth dawned on him. 'Oh my God, you thought Conor was me, didn't you?'

Anger took over. 'Yes!' I shrieked it at the top of my lungs.

I bolted towards the door, but they picked me up and dragged me into a small utility room and I heard the lock turn behind them. I was trapped. I heard them talking but could not make out their words. I had no food, but I drank water from the taps in a large sink beside a washing machine. I didn't bang on the door. What would have been the point? Nobody knew I was here, and who would want to rescue me? I found some rough, paint-spattered blankets and tried unsuccessfully to sleep. Their voices disappeared and doors slammed and I wondered if they had gone out or gone to bed. I could not think how they were going to punish me, but I knew that I would have been wiser to have gone straight to the police.

When the great silence eventually descended, I was able to hear the sea and it was the kind of noise I remembered from my childhood and I was momentarily comforted. Hours later, I heard birdsong and knew it must be dawn. Shortly afterwards, I heard their footsteps. The door was pulled open. I cried and apologized again. James told me to sit at the table. He made me a strong cup of tea and some buttered toast. Tom said nothing.

'What are you going to do with me?' I asked.

'We're taking you home.'

'What?'

'To Inishcrann.'

I felt an overwhelming sense of relief. Even if there were few people left on the island now, they would not let James and Tom do me any real harm. James's letters had said there were just old people there now. They would remember me. Yes, my people had a reputation for insanity, even cruelty, but these were not medieval times. They would not burn me at the stake.

We went outside around the back of the house. I could feel the salt stinging my face. At the end of the garden, we climbed down some rocks to a small cove. There on the sand, tied to an iron stake, was an inflatable boat, a rib, of the kind that used to take us from the harbour out to yacht parties in Monaco. The two men lifted it into the water, and gestured to me to get in. I climbed aboard and they pushed it out and jumped in themselves. Tom started the engine and diesel fumes plumed into the grey sky above us. We tore out of the cove into open sea.

I was freezing, but exhilarated. My son faced me. He wore a black woollen hat and a hood tied up around his head. His face was wet with sea spray, I thought, but I noticed his shoulders shudder and I realized he was crying. I held out my hand to him, and he paused for a moment before taking it with his good hand. He squeezed it, and I felt my first ever rush of affection towards him. There was no point in conversation because of the noise of the engine and the howling wind. I tried to communicate my feelings to him through my eyes and the touch of my hand, but he would not meet my gaze and looked away towards the Atlantic.

Soon, my island came into view. I felt the temperature drop and could see the lighthouse and the long stone visible at the top of the hill and knew that I'd soon be home. As the rib slowed into the harbour, I noticed there were no other boats, not even old wooden rowing boats. A metal grille blocked the old stone steps up to the pier. Tom steered the rib around the outside of it and aligned it with some rocks.

'Get out,' he said. I had no boots and knew my feet would be soaked, but I didn't argue. I climbed out over the rocks and up on to the pier. The two men watched me from the rib.

'You're home!' called James, and I could see his shoulders shuddering again. He used an oar to turn the rib around and soon the engine noise filled the air and they took off, out of the harbour. I wondered where they were going. To find a spot to tie up the rib? As they disappeared from view, I saw Tom reach out to put a consoling hand on my son's shoulder.

I walked up the pier to the village and noticed something strange about the houses. As I got closer, I could see that every single one of them was boarded up, with large metal plates where their windows and doors should have been. The roofs were caved in. There was no sign of life. I went across the harbour to where old Biddy's bar had been, but there was just a pile of rubble there, a broken bar stool sticking out of the detritus. I went up to the old schoolhouse to find that boarded up too. I started to feel panic.

Back in the harbour, I tried to force my way into one of the houses, but the iron shutters were welded into place and I had no tools to shift them.

I saw a tattered notice, covered in broken plastic, tied to a pole. It had FORMAL EVACUATION NOTICE printed on it, and a signature of a Mayo county councillor and the year 2017. It was only recent. When did James say he'd been here – three months ago?

I ran to all of the houses, along the roads I used to know like the lines of my own palm. The sound of the sea roared in my ears, but no dog barked, no sheep bleated, no generator churned. There was nobody here. I knew James and Tom would not come back for me. I walked the length and breadth of the island. There was nothing left of my old home at the west point, no sign that there had been a cottage, or a family or a sweet daddy who loved me above all else.

I howled into the wind and tried to shelter from it, but my

clothing was no defence against its cruel blade. I knew where I had to go. I walked up the desolate hill to the abandoned lighthouse and to where, beside it, the long stone known as Dervaleen's Bed stood proud. I lay down behind it and felt protection from the wind. And I felt Daddy's strong arm reach up from beneath the sodden earth and hold me close.

Acknowledgements

My agent Marianne Gunn O'Connor has been in my corner from the start, and no writer could wish for a better warrior and cheerleader. Vicki Satlow does the same internationally. Pat Lynch assists them calmly and quietly with great good humour.

Huge thanks to the Penguin team. In Dublin, my superb editor Patricia Deevy compels me to refine, improve and structure my work using her critical eye and her straight-talking, and God knows I need that. Cliona Lewis and Patricia McVeigh are publicity ninjas, their assistant Aimée Johnston is endlessly kind, and the super sales team Carrie Anderson and Brian Walker make sure my books are in your shops. MD Michael McLoughlin is supportive in every way.

At Penguin in London, my thanks especially to MD Joanna Prior, to Amelia Fairney, Cat Mitchell and Rose Poole of the communications team, to Sam Fanaken and all of her colleagues on the sales team, and to Ellie Smith and Cat Hillerton, who make sure the book gets produced (literally).

Thanks to eagle-eyed copy-editor Caroline Pretty, who manages to make me look literate.

Most of my research for this novel was place-specific, so in chronological order of location appearance I must thank Paul Soye for checking and verifying all Westport information, Jennifer Davidson for her knowledge of Ballina, and Judith Gantley and Katherine Garnier for their expertise on the Côte d'Azur. I am deeply indebted to Patrick J. Murphy's wonderful book *An Art Lover's Guide to the French Riviera*.

Lucy Nugent assisted in all matters medical. Aisling Roche generously helped me with information pertaining to goat breeding, and painter Josephine Geaney advised me on painting technique and vocabulary.

Once again, Eileen Conway offered her assistance on all matters relating to adoption, and State Pathologist Dr Marie Cassidy answered my gruesome questions about corpses. Fellow writer Margaret Scott advised me on stock markets, investments and insider trading.

Massimilliano Roveri helped me to write as an Italian in broken English, and Niamh Ní Charra told me of some forgotten Irish funeral traditions.

Many thanks to the Ireland Funds of Monaco and the Princess Grace Irish Library in Monaco for awarding me a residency there in September 2016, and particularly to Judith Gantley, who took me under her wing and made me feel at home.

Thanks always to the Tyrone Guthrie Centre at Annghmakerrig for providing space, time, food, comfort and stimulating company in beautiful surroundings.

I am blessed to have so many brilliant women in my personal and professional life who have encouraged me every step of the way. Our coven grows but we use our collective power for good. You know who you are.

Thanks also to Conor Creamer, who I expect will outsell me any day now, to Madeleine O'Connell, who is one of my favourite readers, and to Sophie and Robert Nugent, who are wonderful niblings and great company at the theatre.

Thank you to readers, reviewers, fellow writers, booksellers, librarians, hard-working bloggers and publishers everywhere. Big thanks to the Dead Good team for all the work they do supporting us crime writers.

My family and in-laws mean everything to me and their support is undimmed. I love them all, as I do my husband, Richard McCullough, who has finally come around to the idea that writers don't have to get dressed *every* day.